CONQUEST

Elizabeth lay naked before this man, as the cord he had tied around her wrists bit into her straining flesh.

She felt his gaze moving over her body. Then with startling gentleness his hand closed over her breast.

For perhaps a minute she stayed rigid, resisting the odd little thrills that seemed to travel from her breast to somewhere deep within. Then all the stiffness went out of her. Something was happening, something she had never experienced before, a sense of warm, liquid swelling. His hand left her breast, moved skillfully downward. Dimly she was aware that her hips were moving, as if her body had a will of its own . . .

Later, as she lay there, spent, she tried to protest, "It was only my body."

But even as Elizabeth spoke, she knew that no part of her now was safe from this masterful man's fiery passion. . . .

NEVER CALL IT LOVE

Big Bestsellers from SIGNET

☐ **LOVE ME TOMORROW** by Robert H. Rimmer.
(#E8385—$2.50)*

☐ **BLACK DAWN** by Christopher Nicole.
(#E8342—$2.25)*

☐ **CARIBEE** by Christopher Nicole.
(#J7945—$1.95)

☐ **THE DEVIL'S OWN** by Christopher Nicole.
(#J7256—$1.95)

☐ **THE WICKED GUARDIAN** by Vanessa Gray.
(#E8390—$1.75)*

☐ **SONG OF SOLOMON** by Toni Morrison.
(#E8340—$2.50)*

☐ **RAPTURE'S MISTRESS** by Gimone Hall.
(#E8422—$2.25)*

☐ **PRESIDENTIAL EMERGENCY** by Walter Stovall.
(#E8371—$2.25)*

☐ **GIFTS OF LOVE** by Charlotte Vale Allen.
(#J8388—$1.95)*

☐ **BELLADONNA** by Erica Lindley.
(#J8387—$1.95)*

☐ **THE BRACKENROYD INHERITANCE** by Erica Lindley.
(#W6795—$1.50)

☐ **THE DEVIL IN CRYSTAL** by Erica Lindley.
(#E7643—$1.75)

☐ **THE GODFATHER** by Mario Puzo.
(#E8508—$2.50)*

☐ **KRAMER VERSUS KRAMER** by Avery Corman.
(#E8282—$2.50)

☐ **VISION OF THE EAGLE** by Kay McDonald.
(#J8284—$1.95)*

*Price slightly higher in Canada

**If you wish to order these titles,
please see the coupon in the
back of this book.**

NEVER
CALL
IT
LOVE

by
Veronica Jason

A SIGNET BOOK
NEW AMERICAN LIBRARY
TIMES MIRROR

SIGNET TRADEMARK REG. U.S. PAT. OFF. AND FOREIGN COUNTRIES
REGISTERED TRADEMARK——MARCA REGISTRADA
HECHO EN CHICAGO, U.S.A.

SIGNET, SIGNET CLASSICS, MENTOR, PLUME AND MERIDIAN BOOKS
are published by The New American Library, Inc.,
1301 Avenue of the Americas, New York, New York 10019

FIRST SIGNET PRINTING, DECEMBER, 1978

1 2 3 4 5 6 7 8 9

PRINTED IN THE UNITED STATES OF AMERICA

1

There were five of them cloaked and eye-masked, crouching below sidewalk level in the pitch-black areaway. Moments earlier, when one of them had seen the approaching figure, they had exchanged a few excited whispers. Now they waited in tense silence. They knew nothing about the woman moving along the sidewalk except that her footsteps were light and young, and that she was alone. But that was enough to know. It made her exactly the sort of prey they had hoped to find that night.

To seventeen-year-old Anne Reardon, the London street seemed utterly deserted. She saw no movement, and heard no sound except that of a fitful November wind, rattling the leafless ivy vines that clung to the tall house fronts and making the widely spaced oil streetlamps gutter despite their protective glass lanterns.

She quickened her steps. With a mittened hand she drew closer around her the hooded cloak that hid her reddish-blond hair and framed her small face. It was a somewhat plain face, thin and slightly freckled, but appealing in its youth and gentleness. There was no reason for her to be afraid, she told herself, even though long stretches of blackness lay between the dim patches of moving light cast by the streetlamps. This was a fine neighborhood. Only the rich and respectable lived in these tall stone houses, with their fanlighted doors that here and there spilled warm light onto front steps and areaway railings. Too, in only a few minutes she would reach her guardian's lodgings in Darnley Square. Nevertheless, she found herself wishing that she had stayed back there with Auntie Maude in the disabled carriage.

The accident had occurred without warning. A barrel-laden cart, drawn by a scrawny horse, had rounded the corner from a side street and locked its left wheel with the right-hand rear wheel of their hired carriage. Sitting beside her plump chaperon, Anne had listened to the carriage driver and the carter exchange invectives so violent that she expected the men at any moment to come to blows. Finally, though, they had settled down to trying to disentangle their vehicles.

It had proved to be a difficult task. Minutes passed, while the grunting, swearing men struggled with the locked wheels. Anne had felt a growing anxiety. It was now not more than a quarter of an hour to seven o'clock, the hour appointed for the signing of the marriage contract. They would all be waiting: Thomas Cobbin, the shy twenty-year-old she scarcely knew, but who nevertheless, in a few months' time, would be her husband; his middle-class, highly respectable parents; and Anne's Anglo-Irish guardian, Sir Patrick Stanford, fourth baronet.

It would not do to arrive late on such an important occasion, especially since her prospective parents-in-law, a London ironmonger and his wife, had not seemed over-eager to have their son marry an Irish girl, even a baronet's ward. Only the generous dowry offered by Sir Patrick had brought them to the point of signing the contract.

The carriage tilted slightly. From the suddenly relieved voices of the two straining men, she had known that the locked wheels were almost free of each other. Then the carriage horse, frightened by a scrap of paper blowing along the street, had backed up in the shafts. With a sound of rending wood, the wheels locked again.

Desperately Anne had turned to her relative. "You stay

here, Auntie," she had said, through the fluent curses of the two men in the street. "I'm going to walk the rest of the way. It's not far."

Auntie Maude's round face was appalled. "At night? Through this wicked town?"

Never before out of Ireland, Maude Reardon feared and hated London. The noisy traffic along the Strand. The dirty, ragged urchins who, if you stepped into St. James's Park to rest your eyes on a bit of green, would surround you, beg for coppers, and then reward your generosity by twisting a button from your best mantle or filching your handkerchief from your pocket. She hated the smart Oxford Street shops where the clerks sneered at her Irish accent. And she had been terrified one evening when a hired carriage, unable to get through a street where two houses were on fire, had taken her on a detour through Covent Garden. With horror she had stared at the painted bawds of all ages sauntering along the sidewalks, or calling, bare-breasted, from upper windows. She had seen gin-soaked men and women reeling across the cobblestones, and heard young boys hawking tickets for elevated seats from which to view the next day's double attraction at Newgate—the hanging of a fifteen-year-old girl pickpocket, and the drawing and quartering of a famous highwayman.

Ireland was poor, true enough, and not unacquainted with violence. But no part of that isle, Maude Reardon felt sure, held anything to match the filth and danger and debauchery of London under the reign of His Gracious Majesty George III.

Anne had said, "I must, Auntie. I can't be late. And this is a respectable street. As soon as the carriage is freed, you can join us."

"I forbid you!" Maude Reardon's pleasant face did its best to look stern. "You know I cannot keep up with you, not with my asthma. And you can't go through the streets alone at night. What would Sir Patrick say?"

"Please, Auntie! It's because of him I must hurry. I cannot bear to have him worried or . . . or annoyed with me." She had slipped out of the carriage, and ignoring the anxious cry her aunt sent after her, hurried away down the street.

It was true that what distressed her most was the thought of displeasing, not the Cobbins, but Patrick. Always she had shrunk from the idea of doing anything to bring disapproval to his face, that rough-hewn face that some might consider cold and proud, but which for her had never held anything but kindness. And he had gone to such effort to secure her future. A month ago he had brought her and Auntie Maude over from Ireland and settled them in lodgings near Grosvenor Square. Twice he had summoned them to his own Darnley Square lodgings to meet the Cobbins and their son, once for morning coffee, and once for supper. Behind the scenes, he had worked out the marriage settlement with the elder Cobbin.

As always at the thought of her guardian, Anne felt a twist of hopeless longing. Only in her wildest daydreams had she pictured herself as Patrick Stanford's bride. At thirty-two he was almost twice her age. And obviously his emotion for her, compassionate and paternal, had not changed since she, an orphaned ten-year-old, had been brought to Stanford Hall as his ward. Besides, when he chose to marry, he would select a fine lady, either from the Anglo-Irish aristocracy or from among the English beauties he mingled with for a few weeks each year during the London season.

But at least she had sometimes hoped that she would be allowed to live out her life at Stanford Hall, where she could see him almost every day. See him dismount from the rangy bay hunter in the cobblestoned courtyard after a run through the misty countryside. See him in his study, dark face frowning over the account books his half-brother, Colin, had spread before him. See him at the long, candlelit table in the drafty old dining hall, sometimes abstracted and silent, sometimes good-natured and teasing. Yes, it would have been wonderful if she could have stayed there always, silently loving him, and someday helping care for the children another woman would give him.

But it was foolish and ungrateful of her to want that. As Patrick plainly realized, it was better for her to marry some quiet, decent man and have children of her own.

It was apparent now that the distance between the disabled carriage and Darnley Square was greater than she had thought. Nor had she expected the street to be this deserted. Perhaps five minutes ago an old-fashioned sedan chair, its white-wigged occupant dimly visible through the glass, had moved past her along the street, with a torch-carrying linkboy running ahead of the bearers. But the sedan chair had soon disappeared around a curve. Since then there had been no street traffic and no other pedestrians. Only darkness, broken at long intervals by wavering yellow pools of light cast by the streetlamps. Only the cold wind tearing at her cloak and rattling the ivy branches. Only this vague feeling that had crept over her within the last minute or two, this presentiment that some terrible danger lurked nearby.

A wild, inhuman scream from somewhere at her right. Heart lurching, she stopped short. A lean cat, white or light gray, shot between two pickets of an areaway railing and scurried across the street. Anne clutched the railing until her heartbeats began to slow. Then, smiling a little in her relief, she hurried onward. It could not be much farther now. A few yards ahead, the street curved. And beyond that curve, surely, she would see Darnley Square. She passed another areaway.

Behind her, there below street level, one of the masked figures gestured silently. He led them softly up the stone steps. Then, sure that surprise and terror would render her voiceless for the necessary few seconds, they all rushed after her.

At the sound of running feet, she whirled around. Two of them seized her arms. As she opened her mouth to scream, one of them who had moved behind her slipped a cloth gag between her jaws. Too paralyzed with terror to struggle, she felt herself lifted in someone's arms.

A voice said, "Christopher! You've lost your hat." It was a male voice, and young.

The man who held her said in a low, angry tone, "Then pick it up, you damn fool. And don't use my name like that."

He had carried her down the areaway steps now. "Open the door," he said impatiently, "and strike some lights."

She had begun to struggle. The arms holding her tightened their grip, pinioning her own arms to her sides. She heard a door creak open, and then, after she was carried into deeper blackness, close behind her.

A sound of a scraping flint, and then candlelight, falling on a bare wooden table, on a huge fireplace hung with cooking pots, and on the dark, masked figures jostling around her. Two of them held candlesticks aloft to light the way as she was carried up steps, along a short corridor, into a formal entrance hall. Eyes bulging with fear, tongue trying to free itself from the painful gag, she gained a jumbled impression of a floor marbled in black and white squares, and of gilded nymphs holding candelabra aloft at the foot of a wide stair.

She was borne up those stairs, along a corridor, and into a room. Evidently it had been unused for some time, because the air smelled musty. Her darting, terrified eyes showed her it was a bedroom, furnished in the massive style of the previous century. Across the room, near the bed canopied in dark red velvet, a huge gilt-framed mirror hung. In it she could see a dim reflection of hovering, dark-cloaked figures, and of her imprisoned self, mouth stretched into a grotesque grimace by the gag.

Gathering all her strength, she turned and twisted. She got one arm free, and raised her hand to claw the face of the man who held her. Her curving fingers caught his eye mask, and the string that held it in place gave way. Then he again imprisoned her thrashing arm.

She looked up into the face of a very young man, a face so beautiful it almost might have been a girl's. Very pale yellow hair hung to his shoulders in ringlets. His cleft chin, sensually full mouth, and straight nose were like those of a young Greek god. And his large eyes were the deep blue of the ocean on a cloudless day.

The very beauty of that face heightened the impression it gave, an impression of overwhelming evil. She could see that evil—cold, inhuman, obeying nothing but its own appetites—looking down at her from behind those blue eyes.

Annoyance had crossed his face when she pulled down the eye mask. But now he smiled and set her on her feet. He stepped back from her, as if waiting with amused curiosity to see what she would do.

She stood swaying. Her eyes flew to the doorway. Three of them, grinning below their masks, stood there beside a small table upon which the lighted candles had been placed. But across the room, beside that huge mirror, she had seen another door.

Because she had no other hope, she ran to the door, tried vainly to turn the knob, pushed with all her frail strength against the panels. They stood as solid as the wall itself.

She turned then, with the blood surging in her ears like the pound of distant surf, and stared at those nightmarish figures. When the blond youth began to move leisurely toward her, she pressed her back against the door, as if in some insane hope that her body would melt into it.

He stopped before her, and while she stood paralyzed, undid the button that held her cloak closed at the neck. His hand reached down inside her bodice until he grasped, not only her gown, but the top of her shift, too. Stepping backward, he ripped both garments to their hems. Then he stepped even farther back, the torn lengths of material trailing from his hand. As if again curious to see what she would do, he looked at her, smiling faintly, head tilted to one side.

Her torn clothing dropped from his hand. Someone— not he—gave a low, excited laugh. And then, like a pack of animals, the blond youth and all the others closed in upon her.

2

In the lamplit room on an upper floor of the Darnley Square house, a tension filled the air, almost as palpable as the ticking of the ornate gilt clock on the marble mantelpiece or the snapping of flames in the grate. Sir Patrick, replacing in its stand the poker with which he had just prodded the logs, broke a silence of several minutes. "I cannot understand what is delaying Anne and her aunt."

Seated in an armchair beside the fire, fat stomach stretching his fawn-colored trousers and embroidered waistcoat, red face frowning beneath his glossy brown peruke, Jeremiah Cobbin said, "Nor can I." His wife, sitting tight-lipped beside him, sharp features shadowed by her richly plumed hat, gave an audible sniff.

Thank God, Patrick Stanford thought, that a domestic crisis—a small fire in the scullery of their house near the Strand—had caused the Cobbins themselves to be almost half an hour late. Otherwise, dowry or no dowry, they might long since have taken their offended selves and their son down the stairs.

Patrick glanced at Thomas Cobbin, who sat stiffly on a straight chair a little apart from his parents. He was an ordinary-looking young man, short of stature, dark-haired, and sallow-complexioned. In Patrick's estimate, he lacked the shrewdness and energy of his successful father. But on the other hand, Patrick had detected in him none of the cruelty that sometimes lurks beneath the surface of seemingly meek men. He had no reputation for debauchery. And most important of all, he would someday inherit the Cobbin ironmongery. Yes, it would be a remarkably fine match for an Irish fisherman's orphaned daughter.

It never occurred to Patrick to wonder if the two young people would ever come to love each other. Marriage for love was a luxury reserved to the poor. For the middle and upper classes, marriage was a practical business, a means of advancing one's family status, socially or financially or both. True, Patrick had known a few fortunate couples who had found love within marriage. But usually love was something a man felt for a mistress, or that a woman felt for a lover, admitted by some trusted servant to her house and to her bed during her husband's absence.

"Anne's aunt sometimes gets things muddled," he said. "Perhaps she lost the message I sent this morning, and then recollected the appointed hour as eight o'clock, rather than seven."

"Perhaps," Jeremiah Cobbin said shortly. He looked at

the mantel clock. Its hands pointed to ten minutes of eight. "Very well. We will wait until the hour strikes."

Patrick felt a growing uneasiness. Could Anne and Maude Reardon have met with an accident? The thought made him realize how fond he had become of the reddish-haired girl who had been in his charge these past seven years. He recalled the night she had arrived at Stanford Hall, a thin child, motherless since two days after her own birth, her small face set in a mask of grief that made her look almost old. He had felt compassion for her then, and a sense of deep responsibility, because it was at his orders that Tim Reardon had gone to his death. In Patrick's opinion, it had been a hero's death, but his small daughter did not know that. Only Patrick and his half-brother, Colin, and a few others would ever know why Tim's fishing boat had caught fire and sunk in the Irish channel one moonless night.

Now he realized that over the years he had come to value the fisherman's quiet daughter for her own sake, so much so that he would miss her when he returned to Stanford Hall, so much so that now the thought of her having met with some accident brought him sharp anxiety. But no, Maude Reardon, like many of the Irish, had a dreamy, feckless streak. She must have laid his message aside, been unable to find it, and then decided that the appointment was for an hour later than he had stipulated. After all, when he had entertained the Cobbins and his ward and her aunt at supper the previous week, he had asked them for eight o'clock.

With a murmured apology for turning his back, he moved to the front window, a tall, lean man in black velvet coat and breeches. He looked down. Here in Darnley Square, one of the fine residential areas developed during the last few years as London spread west and north, the streetlamps were more closely spaced, affording the rich householders added protection against night prowlers. He realized that he was fortunate to have lodgings—a bedroom and sitting room—in this fine house, with meals cooked and served by a manservant and his wife in permanent employment here. The house's owners, a socially ambitious merchant and his wife, now on a long tour of the continent, were glad to charge a baronet only a nominal sum for lodgings during the London season. And that was fortunate, because Sir Patrick had other uses for his money. He needed it for buying fine clothes in which to appear in London ballrooms. He needed it for nights at the gaming tables with profligate Englishmen he despised, and with Anglo-Irish landlords, absent most of the year from their estates, whom he despised even more.

Directly below him, the Cobbins' carriage stood at the curb, with its driver huddled in his cloak against the night's chill. Directly opposite, a sedan chair and two carriages stood before Lord and Lady Armitage's house. Evidently they had bidden friends to a small gathering, probably a whist party. One night the previous week he had gone to a well-attended ball in that house, and the season before, to an even larger one.

As sometimes happened, a memory from that night nearly a year ago crossed his mind. Elizabeth Montlow, that young woman with the glossy chesnut hair and direct, intelligent gray eyes. It was not just her beauty that had caught his attention, although she was indeed beautiful, with classic features, and a slender-waisted, high-breasted body molded by a satin gown the same shade of gray as her eyes. What also had impressed him was the fact that she appeared to have reached twenty-one or -two, a somewhat advanced age in London society for a young woman, especially such a lovely one, to be still unmarried. He also noticed that her face, in a roomful of beauties with white complexions made even more so by powder, had a light golden tinge. When they met in the figures of the dance, he had said, "I notice that you do not affect the London pallor."

She smiled, showing a fugitive dimple, and widened her eyes in mock astonishment. "How perceptive you are, sir."

Later, during the interval between a schottische and a gavotte, they had chatted for a few moments over glasses of punch. "Tell me," he had persisted, "why it is that you are not like the other ladies, shunning sunlight as the devil shuns holy water?"

"I live in the country most of the time. I love to walk, and to ride. Should I go about swathed in veils ten months of the year, just so that I can present a fashionable London paleness the other two?"

He looked down at her, sensing in her a rare forthrightness and independence of mind. How was it that she, part of a world in which drawling, languid artificiality was the rule for both sexes, could have developed such qualities?

And then he'd had a sudden vision of himself and this young woman, riding side by side across his own green fields and hills through the misty Irish sunlight, toward where the land dropped away to a rocky beach and the Irish channel. He sensed that a man, married to her, might be one of those rare husbands in love with his own wife.

And she? Was it because she hoped to marry a man she could love that she was still a spinster?

The orchestra, seated on a platform at one end of the mirror-hung ballroom, had begun to play again, and Elizabeth's partner for that dance had come to claim her. But the next evening at Harry's Coffee House Patrick had made inquiries about her. A fat young marquis, far gone in his cups, had been especially informative.

The Montlows, he said, were of an old but untitled family, with a country estate, called the Hedges, about fifteen miles north of London. They also had a town house, only a few hundred yards off Darnley Square, on King-man Street. The family consisted of the widowed Mrs. Montlow and her daughter and son, a youth still at Oxford.

"The house and the country estate are entailed to the son," the marquis said. "But there's twenty thousand pounds held in trust for the daughter. It's to be paid to her when she is twenty-five, or before that, if she marries." He added sourly, "But she'll probably die an old maid, since she's so proud. Although why she should be proud, I don't know. Twenty thousand is no great fortune."

"She's had suitors?"

"Aplenty, but she's turned them all down." Patrick suspected that the marquis had been one of those turned down. "They say she may marry a neighbor's son, a fellow who never gets to town. Plans to be a parson, once the living his uncle controls falls vacant."

The marquis looked up at him with drunken slyness. "Thinking of trying your luck there? I'll admit she's an appetizing wench. But twenty thousand pounds isn't much. A baronet, even an Irish baronet, ought to be able to do better than that."

Patrick chose to ignore the slur upon his Irishness. The fellow was drunk. Besides, even before the reign of Charles II, when Patrick's great-grandfather had been awarded an estate confiscated from an Irish rebel, the Stanfords had been landed English gentry for several generations.

And the fellow was right about twenty thousand pounds' being no great fortune. Patrick hoped to acquire a wife with more than that, much more. Besides, if Elizabeth Montlow's taste ran to parsons, she would scarcely fancy an agnostic such as himself. He had abandoned the idea of calling upon the Montlows in their town house on Kingman Street. Since then he had given only an occasional rueful thought to the girl with the gray eyes and golden skin.

Now, still looking down in the square, he reflected that perhaps after all, when he returned to Ireland, he should marry Moira. A widow of twenty-seven, Moira—Lady Moira Ashley—received rents from more than two hundred tenant farmers working the land of the three estates she had inherited from her husband and from her own family, the Rawlings. And lord only knew she was good-looking enough. Over the generations, the Rawlings, like the Stanfords, had intermarried with the native Irish. Moira's beauty was entirely Irish. Glossy hair so dark that, like a blackbird's wing, it showed blue highlights. Eyes of such a dark blue that by candlelight they looked black. Skin the shade of rich country cream. And there was a boldness about her full-lipped face, and in the way her curving, almost buxom body moved, that made any man want to take her to bed. According to rumor, at least a few had, including the steward who managed her estates.

For a minute or so one day the previous summer Patrick had thought that he was about to take her to bed. After attending an auction of thoroughbred horses, they had returned to Wetherly, the vast house of gray stone left to her by her husband. In the salon, after a footman had brought sherry and Irish whiskey and then left the room, Patrick had drawn her into his arms. As he kissed her yielding mouth, her body had pressed close against his. But when his lips had sought her swelling breasts, left almost naked by her low-cut gown, she had broken free of him. "No, Patrick."

"Why not?" Plainly she wanted him. Desire had expanded her pupils until her eyes were almost black, and had brought a faint flush not only to her face, but to her throat and bosom.

She said, "You will have to marry me first."

Thwarted and angry, he had said in a cold voice, "You do me too great an honor, madam," and turned toward the door. When he reached it, though, he turned back.

"Moira, I'm sorry I said that. We have been friends and good neighbors for a long time. I hope we always will be. But marriage is something that deserves long and serious consideration."

"Besides, you hope to marry some rich virgin, so that you will be reasonably sure that your children are your own."

He was silent. It had indeed occurred to him that with Lady Moira a man would never be quite certain on that point.

"But if you think you would have to worry about that with me," she said, "you're wrong, Patrick. Married to you, I would be faithful."

He had moved to her then, kissed her lightly, and said, "We will talk of it another time. I must go now. Colin and I have some estate business to attend to."

Now, behind Patrick, Jeremiah Cobbin cleared his throat. Patrick turned and looked at the mantel clock. Its hands pointed to three minutes of eight. "Perhaps I had better send someone to see . . ."

Breaking off, he turned back to the window. "They are here," he said with relief. Another carriage had stopped directly behind the Cobbins' vehicle. The driver got down from the box, opened the carriage door, and let down the steps.

Only Maude Reardon descended. And it was obvious from the agitated manner in which she spoke to the driver, and from the way she climbed the steps with unwonted haste, that something was very wrong.

"Please excuse me," he said to the Cobbins, and hurried out of the room and down the stairs. He had the door open before the knocker sounded twice.

Maude Reardon, bonnet awry, face deathly white,

cried, "Oh, Sir Patrick!" Then, with a whimper: "Oh, dear holy Mary, mother of God."

He grasped the plump shoulders. "Maude! What is it?"

"It's Anne, sir. She's been taken to Guy's Hospital."

"She's been hurt? How?" His voice sharpened. "Answer me!"

"I don't rightly know, sir. She was found in the areaway of a house back there on Kingman Street. They say she fell from an upstairs window, or was pushed. And, oh, sir! The poor child had been stripped naked."

She began to weep. Shock held him numb and silent for several seconds. Then he gave her shoulders a shake and said, "Maude! Try to tell me what you know."

Sobbing, at times incoherent, she told him. The cart that had locked wheels with the hired carriage. Anne's decision to go on by foot. The two drivers' long struggle with their entangled vehicles, while other carriages waited behind them.

Finally other drivers had joined in the task, and after a while the carriage's wheel had been lifted free—only to slide sidewise on its axle and break beneath the vehicle's weight.

Left stranded, Maude had promised a street urchin a copper if he would find another public carriage for her. He had darted away down a cross street. Perhaps twenty minutes had passed before he returned, perched on the driver's step of a carriage. Maude had handed the boy his copper, and given the driver Sir Patrick's address.

Farther along Kingman Street, the carriage had slowed, then halted. Maude had poked her head out of the window.

"There was a carriage in front of the house up ahead, and a small crowd on the sidewalk. Two men was carrying someone into the carriage, someone wrapped in a blanket. Then I saw her red hair and I knew—oh, my God, sir—I knew it was our little Anne."

Maude had gotten out of the hired carriage just as the vehicle holding Anne had driven away. Moving as fast as her asthma would allow, she joined the sidewalk crowd.

"There was one of Sir John Fielding's bailiffs there, the ones they call Bow Street Runners. I guess someone had gone to fetch him after it . . . happened."

"Did he talk to you?" Patrick forced the words through a throat that had grown hard with pain and gathering fury.

"Yes, sir. After I told him who I was, he took my name and address and told me what he knew."

It was a maid in the house opposite, the Bow Street Runner told her, who had been a witness, probably the only witness. Retiring to her garret room after fourteen hours of hard work, she had looked down from her window, to see something odd going on in front of the area-way across the street. A group of men, five or six of them, were there on the sidewalk. "The Runner told me the maid said they was young gentlemen, to judge by the look of them." One of them was carrying something or somebody.

Too curious now to sleep, the housemaid had kept watch. She had seen a faint glow for a minute or so through the front door's fanlight. After that, darkness and silence. She had been about to go to bed when again she saw faint light, this time beyond a long window in the upper story. Then had come the sound of shattering glass, and a drawn-out, despairing scream, and the sight of a thin white body hurtling down through the night.

The housemaid had hurried down to tell her employers, who were still at supper. It was they who told the Bow Street Runner their housemaid's story, and who volunteered their carriage to take the girl to the hospital.

"He said she seemed to be in a bad way, sir." Maude wept. "She may be dying."

"Go on upstairs. Wait for me."

He turned around. They were standing on the stairs, faces shocked and outraged, the respectable couple who would never be Anne's parents-in-law, the nondescript young man who would never be her husband.

With cold rage swelling his heart, he said, "You must excuse me." He went down the steps and into the carriage Maude Reardon had left waiting.

3

Young gentlemen, he thought, as the carriage moved forward. He knew of them, those groups of wellborn youths who prowled London by night.

They were aping the Hellfire Club, of course, that group of aristocratic debauchees who met for their orgies well outside London, in the ancient ruins of St. Mary's Abbey at Medmenham. There such profligates as Lord Sandwich and Sir Peter Dashwood, robed and cowled and chanting obscene parodies of Christian liturgy, celebrated the Black Mass and tried to summon up the devil. To a religious skeptic like Patrick Stanford, their blasphemous antics would have seemed merely absurd—except that part of their ritual required the raping of virgins on the ancient altar. In the countryside around Medmenham, the wretched and powerless poor whispered of torchlight flickering at night through the abbey's ruins, and of chanting mingled with terrified screams, and of girls, some as young as twelve, wandering dazed and bleeding along the roadsides in the early morning.

Already vicious, but too young to be welcomed by the

Hellfire Club, a number of aristocratic youths had formed into gangs. They gave themselves the names of American Indian tribes—the Mohawks, the Algonquians, the Saginaws. And at night they moved through the ill-lit London streets, robbing the well-dressed, assaulting the penniless, and raping any girl found alone and unprotected in the darkness.

Patrick Stanford was sure that it was such a group who had seized his ward.

Up ahead, a small sidewalk crowd still lingered before one of a solid row of houses. Despite his anxiety to get to Anne, he rapped with his stick on the cab's trapdoor, signaling the driver to stop. A bulky man with the authoritative air of a Bow Street Runner turned around. As if sensing that the carriage's passenger belonged to the gentry, he moved briskly forward and raised a crooked forefinger to his tricorne hat. "Good evening, sir."

"My name is Sir Patrick Stanford. I already know something of what occurred here. Do you have any idea who they were, the men who carried the girl into this house?"

"No, sir, except it appears they was housebreakers. There's a broken window into the scullery, and the door is locked, so I guess that's how they got in, through the window."

"And the girl has been taken to Guy's Hospital?"

"Yes, sir, in St. Thomas Street."

"One more thing. Whose house is this?"

"It belongs to a family named Montlow. The people across the way told me the place has been empty since last winter. The ladies, Mrs. Montlow and her daughter, are in the country, and the young gentleman, Mr. Montlow, is away at Oxford."

Patrick again looked at the house, recognizing it now. It was the house where once, before he had decided against it, he had thought of calling on the girl with the chestnut hair, sun-warmed complexion, and clear gray eyes.

"Thank you," he said.

Again the Bow Street Runner touched his hat. Patrick rapped on the trapdoor for the driver to proceed. As the carriage rattled forward over the cobblestones, he wondered how she would feel, that girl with the sensitive, intelligent face, when she learned of the brutal violence that had taken place in her house.

The brother, "the young gentleman away at Oxford." Could it be that he was one of . . . ? But no. Surely he would have no need to break into his own house.

Unless the shattered window was a trick, designed to mislead the authorities. . . .

He hoped Elizabeth Montlow's brother was not one of those degenerates. But if he were, he would pay for it. If the Prince of Wales himself were among those who had taken Anne into that house, he would pay for it.

Thirty minutes later, he moved beside a doctor through a series of lofty-ceilinged, dimly lighted hospital wards. Occasionally a groan or a strangled snoring came from one of the beds set in cubicles against the walls. Otherwise there was no sound except the hollow tread of their footsteps. Now and then the doctor raised his walking stick and sniffed at something, undoubtedly perfume, carried inside its knob. Patrick did not have to wonder about the reason. With the windows tightly closed against the "infectious" night air, the series of rooms was redolent of sweat, excrement, and bitter medicines. Patrick, though, was too filled with anxiety and rage to be more than dimly aware of the foul air.

The doctor, plump in his floor-length gown and flat velvet cap, conducted him through another doorway. "This is the ward. I fear, Sir Patrick, that there is little hope. We have not bled her. Bleeding is of no efficacy against multiple fractures of the bones. No doubt, too, the spleen has been ruptured, releasing foul humors throughout the body. . . ."

Pompous ass, Patrick thought, and stopped listening. A few seconds later they stopped beside one of the cubicles.

Except for the reddish-blond curls, she was unrecognizable. One light-blue eye was open, the other swollen shut in her puffed and lacerated face. Her right arm, miraculously undamaged, lay outside the coarse sheet. With despair he saw that already her arm had taken on the waxy look of death.

He bent over her. "Anne. Anne, my dear child."

A spark of expression lit that one open eye. "Patrick!" It was a bare whisper, little more than a stirring of her swollen lips. But there was an urgency in that one blue eye that made him bend closer.

". . . can say it . . . now. I love you."

He felt as if a metal band had tightened around his throat. There was no mistaking her meaning. To him, she had been at most like a young sister, and he had believed her feeling for him to be of the same order. Now, for the first time, he realized what impossible longings had swelled her young heart, perhaps even as she said, "It is kind of you, Patrick, to speak of me to fine people like the Cobbins," and, "Yes, Patrick, I think Thomas Cobbin is a very seemly young man."

Again the swollen lips stirred. "I . . . did wrong. But I did not want to shame you before the Cobbins by being late. That is why . . ."

The whispering voice ceased. The blue eye turned vacant. He reached a hand to the thin wrist. No beat of life against his fingertips. He put his hand down under the sheet and rested it just below the small left breast. No sign of breathing or of heartbeat.

The doctor said stiffly, "Perhaps it would be better that I, a physician, ascertain . . ."

Not answering, Patrick turned away from the cubicle

and stared at the floor. After a moment the doctor said, "This young woman is dead." Patrick was aware of the man's movements as he drew the sheet up over Anne's face.

"You say, Sir Patrick, that she was your ward?"

"Yes."

"Then you intend to make arrangements . . ."

"I will pay for the coffin. Her aunt will accompany the body to Ireland for burial."

He himself would not be standing in the churchyard in her native village when Anne's body was lowered into the ground. Now he had urgent business here. He strode back through the wards. You won't go unavenged, Anne, he promised silently. Someone will pay for your death.

In the hospital courtyard he entered the waiting carriage. "Where is the nearest place to hire a mount?"

"That would be Gorman's, sir, just off the Strand."

"Take me to my lodgings first." He would have to tell Maude Reardon the news. "Then take me to Gorman's."

It would mean riding half the night. But by morning he would know the first thing he had to find out—whether or not young Montlow was still at Oxford.

4

The small side parlor at the Hedges was warm and peaceful, its silence broken only by small domestic sounds—the snapping of the fire in the grate, a faint rustle as Elizabeth Montlow turned the pages of her book, and now and then, whenever the embroidery thread knotted, an annoyed exclamation from Mrs. Montlow.

Now and then Elizabeth glanced up from the page to enjoy the dim reflection of firelight and candle flame in the long glass doors opposite. Beyond them she could see, bathed in the blue light of early evening, the brick terrace with its rose trellis. The espaliered rose vine was bare now, but no matter. Just as she enjoyed the other seasons here in the country, she enjoyed the winter months. In leafless winter you could see the basic shape of things, the low rock walls hemming in brown fields, and the inverted-heart shape of beeches against the sky, and the meandering branches of that rose vine out there.

Sighing, Mrs. Montlow laid her embroidery hoop on the rosewood stand beside her wing chair. She was a slender, pretty woman of forty-odd, with graying blond hair, blue eyes, and almost doll-like features. "Three more weeks," she said.

Even if her mother's gaze had not gone to the portrait above the fireplace, Elizabeth would have known what she meant. Three more weeks until Christopher came home for the Christmas holidays.

Elizabeth too looked up at the portrait. Christopher had been eleven when John Montlow, as one of his last extravagant acts, had commissioned Sir Joshua Reynolds to paint his son. In the portrait, Christopher, wearing a red velvet suit, stood with one hand resting on the head of a half-grown mastiff. His other hand held his plumed red hat. His seraphically handsome face, framed in pale shoulder-length curls, looked at the viewer with a smile that would have melted the stoniest heart, let alone the proudly fond ones of his mother and sister.

"I'm afraid last Christmas was dull for him," Mrs. Montlow said. "This year we must bid our neighbors to a party." She added discontentedly, "Those few who are here, anyway."

Recognizing one of her mother's almost daily complaints over the fact that they had not gone into town for the season, Elizabeth said nothing.

"We'll hang greenery in the large parlor, and hire a small orchestra."

"Not an orchestra, Mother. Perhaps we could hire Mrs. Wells to play the spinet for dancing." Mrs. Wells, an impoverished gentlewoman, lived in the nearby village of Parnley, and supported herself by giving lessons in music and drawing.

"There you go, Elizabeth! I realize we must economize. But sometimes it seems to me you are actually tight-fisted."

Elizabeth kept silent. It was best, Dr. Farnsworth had warned her, to allow her mother these occasional explosions of discontent. Opposition might bring on one of those terrifying times when Mrs. Montlow, lips turning blue, gasped for breath.

"Things were so different when your father was alive. We kept two carriages then, and four horses. Every time I see the carriage house standing empty out there, I feel like weeping."

Elizabeth ventured mildly, "Father left debts. They had to be paid." It was only after his death that they had learned it was borrowed money that had supported his family's style of living. Even now a small indebtedness remained. From quarterly interest earned by the twenty thousand pounds left in trust for her, Elizabeth had gradually reduced that debt.

At least her father had never borrowed against that twenty thousand pounds. Sometimes Elizabeth wondered about that. Had he foreseen that someday his daughter would be responsible for making sure that his widow lived in modest comfort, and that his son received an education?

Perhaps, too, that was why he had provided her with

more than the usual female education. From her tenth year until her seventeenth, when her father had died, private tutors had taught her history and mathematics.

Mrs. Montlow sighed. "Yes, the debts. I've never understood how that happened. But then, I'm not clever like you."

If she was "clever," Elizabeth thought somewhat grimly, perhaps it was because she'd had to be.

With one of lightninglike changes of mood, Mrs. Montlow said, "And, Liza, I'm grateful that you're clever. What would Christopher and I do if you were not? And I do understand about not going into town this winter. Christopher's college expenses come first. Who would have dreamed they would be so high?"

They were high indeed. By almost every other post, he requested money. Always the reason he gave seemed legitimate. A spark from the grate in his room had set a small fire, which, before it was extinguished, had destroyed not only expensive books but also his best greatcoat, left drying before the hearth. Someone—he suspected a charwoman—had stolen his last allowance. His good friend, Lord Stanley's son Geoffrey, leader of the "smartest set" in Christopher's college, had suggested that each of his friends contribute a pound toward a party at an inn in Oxford village. He was sorry to ask for money so soon again, but he knew that darling Mama and dearest Liza appreciated how much the friendship of people like Lord Stanley's son might mean to his future. . . .

Mrs. Montlow never doubted her son's letter. Elizabeth sometimes did. True, she adored the brother, almost six years younger than she. From his infancy onward, no one in the household had been able to resist his beauty, his winsome smile, his way of clambering on laps to demand kisses. But there were other things she could remember, like that kitten, when Christopher was eight. . . .

It had been a shock to fourteen-year-old Elizabeth to come into her small brother's empty room and see the golden kitten dangling from a table by a length of cord. She had removed the looped end of the cord from around a paperweight and taken the kitten's still-warm body onto her lap. She had just finished untying the other end of the cord from around the tiny animal's neck when she looked up, to see Christopher standing in the doorway.

He had rushed toward her, tears welling in the great blue eyes, and asked what had happened to Marigold. When told his kitten was dead, he buried his face on Elizabeth's lap, his pale curls mingling with his pet's golden fur, and sobbed out that he'd been trying to teach Marigold to walk on a leash. After he left the room, the kitten must have gotten up on the table and then jumped off, with the loop in the cord catching around that paperweight.

He had raised his tear-wet face. "You won't tell Father or Mama, will you, Liza? I don't want them to know what a bad, careless boy I was. Promise me, darling Liza. We'll just say we don't know how Marigold died."

She had promised.

Now she brushed the thought of the kitten aside. There was no point in dwelling upon that, or on the other things, such as the print of an engraving she had found, crumpled up on the floor of his clothespress after his last visit home. It had been a print of a naked woman cowering on a floor with a man standing over her, cat-o'-nine-tails in hand. As she crumpled the print and carried it downstairs to toss it on the side-parlor fire, Elizabeth had tried to tell herself that perhaps many young men passed such pictures around among themselves.

Mrs. Montlow was again complaining of their lost season in town. "It is just that the country in winter is so dull for me."

Elizabeth realized that. Her mother did not ride, took

little pleasure in reading, and regarded with puzzled dismay her daughter's habit of taking walks over the muddy countryside in all but the worst weather. Little wonder that she wished herself in London, whirling from "morning coffees" to afternoon whist parties to evening balls, where, even though her weak heart no longer permitted her to dance, she could enjoy the music and the sight of richly dressed people moving gracefully beneath blazing crystal chandeliers.

Elizabeth did not miss at all the morning coffees, exclusively feminine gatherings where the talk was of clothes, approaching marriages, and rumored adulteries of those not present. Because she often won, she found the whist parties less unpalatable. But she disliked seeing the feverish look on the face of some player trying to recoup a heavy loss. And sometimes there were repellent episodes, such as that of one afternoon last season, when she had suddenly realized that a dowager duchess at her table had been cheating. Elizabeth had said nothing. The duchess was almost three times her age, as well as the party's hostess. But apparently the duchess had seen knowledge of her cheating in those clear gray eyes, because, to Elizabeth's relief, she received no more invitations to whist parties at that particular house.

Elizabeth did enjoy the balls, though, because she loved dancing. No matter that she found most of her partners, from callow youths to grandfathers, laughably artificial with their languid airs, their drawled compliments, their often rouged faces. There was still the joy of moving through the figures of the dance.

Once in a while at those London balls she had met a man that attracted her. Notably, there had been that tall, dark-haired man, Sir Patrick Stanford, whom she had met at Lord and Lady Armitage's house last season. He had not been handsome in the conventional sense. His dark face, with its high cheekbones, strong nose, and square jaw, had been too rugged for that. Nor had their brief conversation over glasses of punch been anything of consequence. He had commented on her complexion, if she remembered rightly. But she had liked the way he had moved, not with the languid saunter now fashionable in London, but with an outdoorsman's easy grace. She had liked his coat and breeches of dark green velvet—rich enough, but less flamboyant than the pink and blue and silver brocades worn by the other men. And she had liked an impression she had somehow gained, a sense of some sort of depth and seriousness in him.

There had been something else, too. As they chatted, his dark gaze had traveled from her face to the curve of her breasts, revealed by her square-necked ball gown. She was used to such glances. A woman who followed the current mode in dress of course expected that men would look at her almost bare bosom. But she was not used to the odd thrill his gaze sent along her nerves.

Even though she had already given her affections elsewhere, she had hoped for almost three days that he would call at their Kingman Street house. Then, over a whist table, she learned something she had not known before. He was an Irish baronet, with lands on the southeast coast near Cork. After that, convinced she had been wrong in her impression of him, she no longer wanted him to call. She had heard how the titled Anglo-Irish obtained the money with which they tried to outdo their English counterparts each London season, buying rich clothes and throwing away vast sums at the gaming tables. More avaricious than English landlords, they kept subdividing their lands into smaller and smaller strips, so as to obtain rents from more and more tenants. Left with little land to cultivate, the average Irish peasant and his family lived off the potatoes he grew. All other crops had to be sold to meet the rent.

Picking up her embroidery, Mrs. Montlow said with a

sigh, "I suppose I should be thankful that you too don't find the country dull. Perhaps if you could not see Donald almost every day, you would find it so."

Elizabeth smiled, and picked up her book, a copy of Fielding's *Tom Jones*. Donald had given it to her two days ago, just before he left to visit his uncle in Bath. "Perhaps you're right, Mother."

She could not remember a time when Donald Weymouth had not been an important part of her life. The Weymouths, whose land adjoined that of the Montlows, were not an "old" family. Of yeoman stock, they had only in the past two generations been considered gentry. (But then, as Donald had once said to her with his winning smile, "It's odd that we should speak of old families. If every human being is descended from Adam and Eve, then all families are equally old.")

Like the Montlows, the Weymouths were far from rich. But Donald, two years older than Elizabeth, and educated for the church, had an assured future. A well-to-do and childless brother of Mrs. Weymouth's controlled the living in the local parish. As soon as the present vicar retired, the post would be Donald's.

Unlike many of England's hard-drinking, fox-hunting parsons, Donald was prepared to take his vocation seriously. Perhaps a little too seriously. He read, and discussed with Elizabeth the works of Calvin and other Dissenters. But then, as he once said to her, probably he was just sowing his "intellectual wild oats." In time he would find no difficulty in abiding by the tenets of the Church of England.

As soon as he became vicar, they would announce their engagement. Not long afterward, his church salary would be supplemented by Elizabeth's inheritance and one from Donald's uncle. There would be more than enough money to keep themselves and their children and Elizabeth's mother in comfort. As for Christopher's future, no one need worry about that. He would have not only this country estate and the house in town. With his looks and charm and ancient though untitled name, with the influential friendships he was making at Oxford, he could go about as far in the world as he liked, either by means of some high political appointment or by marriage to some great heiress.

She realized that both she and Donald, too, might be able to make more "advantageous" marriages elsewhere. But to them their union would offer every advantage worth having—shared tastes for books and riding and country life in general, and a warm, serene love with roots in their childhoods.

Mrs. Montlow said, "Are you sure we couldn't have at least a small orchestra for Christopher's Christmas party? A violin and a flute, as well as the spinet?"

Elizabeth laughed. "All right. I'll see if it can be managed."

Several seconds passed in silence. Then Mary Hawkins, the cook who had come to the Hedges as an upstairs maid the year before Elizabeth's birth, spoke from the doorway. "Could I see you in the kitchen for a moment, miss?"

Elizabeth felt a stab of anxiety. The woman's face was pale, and her voice held scarcely controlled tension. "Of course," Elizabeth said quickly.

Neither of them spoke until they had gone down the hall to the large and very clean kitchen, with its rows of copper pans gleaming in the light of the tallow lamp, and supper's chicken browning on the fireplace spit.

"What is it, Hawkins?"

"Mr. Tabor was just here. He brought Sunday's joint." Henry Tabor was the village butcher.

"And?"

"There's a story in the village that the house in town

was broke into last night by . . . by some young persons."

"Our house?" Hawkins nodded. "Was much stolen?"

"As to that, I don't know, miss. But, oh, miss! There was a woman, a young girl."

"Girl? What girl?"

"I don't know. But she's dead, miss. She jumped out a window, or they pushed her. She was found in the areaway, dead and naked."

5

Shocked and sickened, Elizabeth said, "My mother must not learn of this, not until I've decided how to break the news to her."

Mary Hawkins' broad, lined face looked reproachful. "Can you believe I would say anything to upset the dear lady?"

"I know you wouldn't. After supper I'll tell her myself."

She moved back along the hall. Thank God there were no longer young housemaids to whisper excitedly among themselves and thus betray to Mrs. Montlow that something was being kept from her. These days, household tasks other than cooking were performed by Elizabeth herself, with the help of a charwoman from the village twice a week.

Mrs. Montlow looked up as Elizabeth appeared in the sitting-room doorway. "What is it? Black beetles again?"

"No. Hawkins was afraid the butcher had overcharged

for Sunday's joint of mutton. But I put it on the kitchen scale, and it weighs exactly what he'd told her." Lest her mother have time to realize that Mary Hawkins herself could have weighed the joint, Elizabeth added swiftly, "I think I will take a short walk. I feel the need of exercise." Always she found that she could think better out-of-doors.

"But it will be dark soon! And it may rain. I'm sure I heard thunder a few minutes ago."

"I won't stay out long."

She went upstairs to the big corner room at the rear of the house that had been hers ever since she outgrew the nursery. As she took down her warmest cloak from the clothespress, she glanced out the window. Between the tall ilex hedges that gave the house its name, a gravel path meandered among flowerbeds back to the carriage house. The flowerbeds were empty now except for bare rose bushes and withered stalks of last summer's marigolds and flox and daisies. In the old days those dead plants would long since have been cleared away. But there was no gardener now, only Elizabeth herself to tend the flowerbeds. Busy indoors, she often neglected the garden.

I must at least dig up the dahlia roots, Elizabeth thought, and then realized that she was trying to postpone consideration of something far more unpleasant than a neglected garden.

Leaving the house by the front door, she went along a brick walk between rows of dwarf boxwood that needed pruning, through a white wooden gate in the front hedge, and then down a short path. When she reached the narrow road that led, over rising ground, toward the village, she turned to her left.

Her mother had been right about the coming rain. In the west, black clouds were massed below the gray overcast. Now and then lightning flickered, followed by a growl of thunder. Above the empty brown fields, rooks hovered, cawing in that excited way that always presages a storm. Knowing that she could not stay out long, Elizabeth climbed the slope at a quickened pace.

A girl. A girl naked and dead, or at least dying, in the areaway of the Montlow town house. Why had she, the moment she heard of the girl, thought of Christopher?

She hated herself for it. It was monstrous that she should think, even for a moment, that her little brother . . . And it was illogical, too. Christopher was at Oxford, watched over by dons and proctors and by the porter in the gate lodge of his particular college. And even if by some strange circumstance he had been in London last night, he and the "young persons" would not have had to break into the house. As befitted someone approaching man's estate, he had been supplied with keys to both the Hedges and the London house before he enrolled at Oxford.

And yet she kept thinking of the hanged kitten and of the engraving she had found on the floor of her brother's clothespress.

She had reached level ground now. She walked on, past fields that were part of Montlow lands, dimly aware that the last of the dull light was going and that the thunder had grown louder. Just why did she feel this shrinking reluctance to tell her mother? True, the news would be a shock. But when a bailiff arrived to notify them officially of the break-in, Mrs. Montlow need not even see him. Elizabeth would take care of that, and also, if necessary, go to London to assay whatever damage had been done to the house and its furnishings.

Would she also be asked to try to identify the girl, or had someone already done that? She fervently hoped someone had.

The girl. Christopher and the kitten.

Only half an hour ago she had been thinking of how

she and Donald, in a violent world made up of the ruthless rich and the hopeless, often criminal poor, would live out their lives somewhere in between, in a little oasis of warmth and peace. Now she had a sense of some cruel force gathering itself to shatter that modest dream. . . .

The first large drops of rain struck the hood of her cloak. With a start, she realized that it was almost completely dark. What was more, she had walked farther than she had intended to. Turning, she hurried back toward the Hedges in its cup of low hills.

Before she had gone more than a few yards, the storm was upon her, blotting out what remained of the light, drenching her with rain. Lightning flashed, giving her an eerie glimpse of the rain-darkened road and the empty fields stretching away beyond their low stone walls. The bolt had grounded somewhere nearby, because only a split second later she heard the deafening thunderclap. Despite the mud now weighting her shoes and the hem of her cloak, she broke into a half-run.

Another flash, lighting up the trunk and leafless branches of an oak a few yards ahead at the roadside. When the almost simultaneous roll of thunder died away, she heard another sound, a muffled clop of hooves. Somewhere in the darkness behind her, a horse and rider were approaching at a gallop.

Probably it was just some farmer, hurrying on one errand or another to the village a few miles the other side of the Hedges. But in these perilous times, with hundreds of highwaymen roaming about to rob stagecoaches and lone travelers, hoofbeats by night were an ominous sound even on country roads such as this one. Heart hammering, she moved even faster. She must be close to that oak tree now. Yes, she could see it, a deeper dark against the darkness. She moved to its far side and stood motionless against the thick trunk. Mount and rider were so close now that she could hear not only hooves but also the jingle of a bridle.

Perhaps the horse caught her scent. She heard a frightened whinny. Then lightning flashed. She had a glimpse of a rearing gray horse and a dark-clothed rider bathed in blue-white radiance. For a frightened instant she thought the rider must surely see her. But apparently he was too absorbed in trying to control his mount to even glance at the roadside.

Darkness swallowed up horse and rider. She heard the horse whinny again, and the man say, "Stop it, you bloody fool." Then he rode past. His face, shadowed by his tricorne hat, had been invisible to her. But there had been something familiar about the set of the broad shoulders beneath the enveloping cloak, and something familiar about his voice. She waited until she could no longer hear the beat of hooves. Then she moved out into the road.

The storm proved to be as brief as it had been violent. Before she had gone more than a few yards, the rain dwindled. Finally it ceased. A full moon, still thinly veiled, sent a diffused radiance over the muddy road and the drenched fields. She looked back and saw, in the now cloudless strip of sky above the western horizon, the planet Venus shining like a miniature second moon.

She had gone through the gate in the tall hedge and was hurrying up the walk when Mrs. Montlow opened the front door. "Drenched to the skin! Elizabeth, I will never understand you. How is it that a clever girl can behave like a backward child?"

"I'm sorry," Elizabeth said, moving past her mother into the house. "I know it's almost time for supper. I'll go right upstairs and change my clothes."

Two hours later the Montlow women again sat in the small side parlor, Mrs. Montlow with her embroidery, Elizabeth pretending to read. She had not wanted to upset her mother at the supper table. But soon now she would have to lay her book aside and break the news.

A tapping against the glass doors that led onto the terrace. Elizabeth's head jerked up. Mrs. Montlow said, half-delighted, half-alarmed, "Why, it's Christopher!"

For a moment Elizabeth sat rigid, staring at the slender cloaked figure, the troubled, angelically handsome face in its frame of pale hair. Too late, she thought. Too late now to prepare her mother—although to prepare her for what, Elizabeth could not have said. Aware that her mother was getting to her feet, she too stood up, crossed the room, and unlatched the glass doors.

"Liza!" Then: "Please, Mama! Please sit down again."

Obediently, Mrs. Montlow sank back into her chair. Christopher's tricorne hat dropped from his hand to the floor. Then he crossed to his mother, fell to his knees, and buried his head in her lap. "Oh, Mama! Forgive me!"

Still with that look of pleasure mingled with bewilderment and alarm, Mrs. Montlow touched his hair. "Forgive you for what, my son? What has happened, my darling?"

"I was sent down."

"Sent down? From Oxford?"

"Three days ago. They said that some of my friends and I made old Quigley fall down the stairs."

"Quigley? Who is—"

"He lays the fires in our rooms. And he stole my ring. I know he did. We were trying to make him admit it when he somehow lost his balance and fell down the stairs."

Christopher was proud of that bit of invention. Sooner or later he would have had to explain the ring's absence from his finger. Best to blame old Quigley.

"Your grandfather's ruby ring? Oh, how dreadful! Didn't you tell the dons he'd stolen it?"

"They wouldn't have believed me. I had no proof. And Quigley's been there about a hundred years. They would all have been on his side. And I was afraid that if I tried to argue they would *never* let me back into Oxford. I know how much that would grieve you, Mama. I knew you'd feel my education was more important than any ring."

"Of course, my darling."

"Then you won't say anything to the dons about the ring?"

"But, Christopher! A ring that valuable—"

"It would just make things worse for me, Mama. I'd never get back in."

As he waited for her answer, he thought angrily of old Quigley. Everything had been his fault, really. If he hadn't kept jabbering about how that part of the college was haunted—by a student who was killed in a duel nearly two hundred years ago—they wouldn't have known he was afraid of ghosts. They would never have thought of dressing up in sheets and jumping out at him there on the dark landing. As he'd backed away from them, white as a ghost himself, Christopher had been unable to resist making a lunge toward the old idiot. Quigley had shied backward, teetered on the top steps for an instant, and then slid headfirst down the stairs.

Everything still might have been all right if they'd had a chance to scatter to their rooms and strip off the sheets. But at that moment, on the floor below, a don had poked his head out of a doorway and seen them up there at the top of the stairs.

Mrs. Montlow said, "Then of course I won't make a fuss about the ring, my darling."

His sister had said nothing since he came into the room. He turned his head so that he could see her, standing motionless beside the fireplace. Her face was rigid. God's blood! Could she already have heard about the girl?

His mother said, "But if you were sent down three days ago, where have you been since then?"

"Geoffrey was sent down with me. Lord Stanley's son, you know. His parents are in Rome, so there was no one but a manservant in his London house. I spent the first two nights there." That much, at least, was true.

"And last night?"

"Oh, Mama! That is what I am too ashamed to tell you."

Elizabeth's heart set up a frightened pounding. She knew she must say something, do something, to protect her mother from what he was about to reveal, but a kind of paralysis held her motionless and silent.

Mrs. Montlow said sternly, "No matter how ashamed you are, you must tell me, my son."

"I spent the night with Mrs. Frazier-Fitzsimmons. I went to her house for tea yesterday afternoon, and I . . . I didn't leave there until early this morning."

In her relief, Elizabeth felt an impulse to burst into hysterical laughter. Here she had pictured her young brother involved in some unspeakable crime the night before. And all he had done was to share the bed of the smartest and most expensive bawd in London.

Mrs. Montlow, though, was horrified. At many of the morning coffees she had attended in London during past seasons, Mrs. Frazier-Fitzsimmons had been avidly discussed. The ladies had speculated about the cost of the house bought for her by a certain duke, and had disputed as to which of her other lovers had given her a carriage and pair, and the diamond tiara she wore when attending the theater at Covent Garden.

"Son! How is it you even know a woman like that?"

He explained—and again, so much was true—that Geoffrey had introduced them during last summer's "long vacation." He and his friend had been strolling one afternoon in Hyde Park. "Mrs. Frazier-Fitzsimmons' carriage stopped beside us, and Geoffrey presented me, and she made it clear that . . . that she liked me very much,

Mama, liked me enough that if I called on her I wouldn't be expected to give her . . . any sort of present."

Mrs. Montlow looked down at her son, feeling disapproval mingled with a tender, faintly amused pride. Her little boy had grown into a man now, a man so attractive that a woman like Mrs. Frazier-Fitzsimmons would grant him her expensive favors for nothing.

"That was wrong of you, my son. You should have nothing to do with such women."

She realized the futility of her own words. As she herself had said, she was not "clever," but she was clever enough to know that forbidding a boy of his generation to stay away from such women was like forbidding a young eagle to fly.

"I know." Still kneeling, he raised his head and looked up at her. "There is more I have to tell you. None of it is my fault, but it will . . . distress you, Mama."

Again Elizabeth's nerves tensed. Her mother said, "Tell me, Christopher. Don't be afraid."

"I . . . I was still asleep this morning when Peggy—I mean, Mrs. Frazier-Fitzsimmons—came back upstairs. She said her maid told her that she'd heard that the Kingman Street house had been broken into early the evening before."

"*Our* house?"

"Yes. It was a group of young men, and they had some girl with them, and there was some sort of accident. She fell through a window or something. Anyway, Peggy said there were bailiffs—Bow Street Runners—looking for me to arrest me."

"Bailiffs! Arrest you! But why . . . ?

"I don't know. I suppose it was just because it was my house." Aware of his sister standing rigid and silent, gray eyes fastened on his face, he began to speak very rapidly. "Anyway, I was frightened. I wanted to get to you and Liza before the bailiffs found me. Peggy took me in her carriage as far as Highgate, and I . . . I walked all the way from there, Mama. When I got near home—it was early this afternoon then—I realized how hard it would be to tell you all this. And so I slipped through the garden's back gate and into the carriage house. I . . . I've been hiding out there for five or six hours, trying to get my courage. . . ." His voice faltered.

Elizabeth stared at the slender, kneeling figure with the face of a Botticelli angel. How much of his story was true? Had he really spent all last night with that woman, and then left London this morning? Or had he fled the city last evening, soon after a girl had fallen to her death, and then walked fifteen miles through the darkness to the carriage house? Perhaps he had been hiding out there since not long after the previous midnight, rather than just since early this afternoon.

Her mother said, "You have told us, my son, and now there is no reason to be afraid. You cannot be arrested for something you didn't do. Isn't that right, Elizabeth?"

"If a bailiff comes here with a warrant for Christopher's arrest," Elizabeth said, "he will have to execute that warrant." She saw her brother's large blue eyes throw her a swift, wary glance.

"But Elizabeth! When the house was broken into, Christopher was with that woman." Fleetingly Mrs. Montlow wondered if the house had been damaged and if the "accident" involving the girl her son had mentioned had been a serious one. But all of that was a minor consideration compared to Christopher's welfare. "All Christopher has to do is to tell the bailiff he was with that woman last night. She will confirm his story. Why not? She has no reputation to lose."

Christopher got to his feet. "Liza is right, Mama. If a bailiff comes here with a warrant, he'll have to arrest me, no matter what anybody says. And it won't matter what

Peggy tells the authorities, now or later. The word of a woman like that won't carry any weight.

"And that is why," he rushed on, "that you and Liza have got to say I came home yesterday afternoon, and had supper with you, and slept last night in my room. Hawkins has to say it, too. If you all three say that, and keep saying it, I may not even have to stand trial. And even if I do, I'll be freed."

"Stand trial?" Mrs. Montlow's face was still bewildered. "I don't understand any of this. Even if you had done it, which you did not, how could they make you stand trial for breaking into your own house?"

"The girl, Mama. Remember I said they had a girl with them? What if she was badly hurt? What if she is . . . dead?"

His mother's face went white. She whispered, "Oh, Christopher!"

"Don't look like that, Mama! It will be all right if you and Liza stand by me. All you have to say is that I have been with you since yesterday afternoon."

"Oh, my son! Of course we will. Won't we, Elizabeth?"

Elizabeth said, after a long moment, "He is asking us to commit perjury."

Outraged color dyed Mrs. Montlow's face. Seeing it, Elizabeth felt that at least it was less frightening than her pallor of a moment before. "Perjury!" Mrs. Montlow said. "Here your brother may be put on trial for . . ." She could not say the word. "And you stand there using silly words like 'perjury.' "

She got to her feet. "Christopher, are you hungry?"

"Yes. Very hungry."

"Go upstairs to your room. I want to talk to your sister alone. Then I'll bring some food up to you."

"Thank you, Mama." He bent, kissed her cheek.

He had to pass close to Elizabeth as he left the room. He gave her one sad, appealing glance, and then, head

bent, went out into the hall. The two women heard him
climbing the stairs.

"Now!" Mrs. Montlow began firmly.

"Mother, if we're going to talk, please sit down."

"Very well." Mrs. Montlow sank into her chair. Elizabeth crossed the room to a small cabinet, took a vial of
smelling salts from its upper drawer, and then came to
her mother's side. "Breathe this."

After an apprehensive glance at her daughter's face,
Mrs. Montlow took the vial from her hand and inhaled
deeply. Then she said, "What is it? Do you have something more to tell me?"

"That girl in our house last night. She did die."

Mrs. Montlow lost color. Holding the vial to her nostrils, she again breathed deeply. Then she said, almost
calmly, "How is it you know this?"

"Hawkins told me, just before I went out for a walk
this afternoon. The butcher had heard the story in the village, and he told her about it when he brought the joint
of mutton. I was about to tell you when Christopher
tapped on the terrace door."

"I see. Then you must realize what you must do. If a
bailiff comes in the morning, you must tell him that Christopher has been with us since yesterday afternoon."

"I am sure a bailiff will be here in the morning. But I
won't see him. I intend to stay in my room, indisposed."
She had made up her mind to that within the last few
minutes. "You and Hawkins can tell the bailiff whatever
you like. If he has a warrant, it will make no difference."

Thin-lipped, her mother looked at her. "And later on,
if your brother has to stand trial? What will you do
then?"

"It depends upon what Mrs. Frazier-Fitzsimmons tells
me tomorrow. I shall walk to the village in the morning
and take the stagecoach to London."

She paused, half-expecting her mother to protest that

no respectable woman could dream of entering Mrs. Frazier-Fitzsimmons' house. But evidently right now her mother had no room for concern about anything except her son.

Elizabeth went on, "If that woman confirms Christopher's story, I'll be willing to swear that he has been here with us since yesterday afternoon. Because he's quite right about her, you know. No jury would believe the testimony of a bawd, even one who has been kept by a duke."

Mrs. Montlow flinched slightly at the word "bawd," but all she said was, "And if she tells you that Christopher was not with her last night?"

"I don't know what I will do then."

"You would accept that woman's word against your own brother's?"

"I don't *know*. I just know that a girl is dead. I just know that I have to learn more about this before I can bring myself to . . . to stand up in court and swear before God that Christopher could have had nothing to do with her death."

Mrs. Montlow got to her feet. "You have been a fine daughter to me, Elizabeth, and I love you. But I must tell you that sometimes you lack human feeling."

Elizabeth made no reply to that. "Shall I get a tray of food for Christopher and take it up to him?"

"I think he would prefer that I brought it to him. Hawkins will help me prepare a tray. I must wake her up and talk to her, anyway."

She left the room. After a few minutes, staring into the fire, Elizabeth knew that her mother must have aroused the cook from her slumbers in the room off the kitchen, because she could hear the distant, agitated sound of their voices. Elizabeth had no doubt that Hawkins would swear to anything Christopher wanted her to. Like Mrs. Montlow, like Elizabeth herself—at least, until a few hours ago—Mary Hawkins had been his adoring slave ever since he was an infant.

From the back of the chair her mother had occupied she picked up a knitted red shawl and wrapped it around her. Quietly she went down the hall and out the front door. Through cold moonlight so bright that she could have read large print by it, she went down the brick walk, still damp from the early-evening rainstorm. At the gate she turned and started back toward the house.

From somewhere not far away came the whinny of a horse.

Instantly she thought of the dark-cloaked rider, revealed by a lightning flash as he fought to control his mount. Had he been a bailiff? Was he still somewhere nearby? Her eyes swept the hillside to the west of the house. Nothing but a copse of leafless oaks and maples, rising from dead brown grass bleached almost white by the moonlight.

After a moment she realized that the man could not have been a bailiff. The bailiff, when he arrived, would be in a coach, so that he could take his prisoner away with him.

Probably that whinny had come from farther away, in the fields beyond the hill's crest. And probably it was one of the Weymouth horses she had heard. Often Weymouth animals strayed onto Montlow land.

To comfort herself, she pictured Donald Weymouth. His light brown hair, his thin, sensitive face with its steady hazel eyes and warm smile. No matter what happened, Donald's loyalty and love would not waver. It was impossible to think of a circumstance that could deprive her of that love.

And then suddenly she shivered. Something colder than the chill air had touched her. It was a return of that dark presentiment that had assailed her earlier, a presentiment of herself alone and helpless under the onslaught of some sort of violence.

The moment passed. Clutching the shawl close around her, she hurried the rest of the way up the walk and into the house.

6

It had been a good meal. Cold chicken, bread, plum tart, and tea scalding hot, the way he liked it. Christopher laid the chicken bone on the tray, resting on the stand beside his bed, and then snuggled deeper under the eider-down.

He was home. He was safe. Even if the girl was dead by now—and he felt sure she must be—he was safe. The worst that could happen to him would be a few months' imprisonment until the next General Sessions at Old Bailey. There was not a more respected name in the kingdom than the Montlows', and not a more irreproachable matron than his mother. What jury would fail to take her word, backed up by Liza's and Hawkins', especially since all that was involved was the death of a servant girl?

Certainly they had thought she was a servant girl when they saw her hurrying along the sidewalk. Who but a harlot or a servant girl, sent on some errand by her employers, would be out alone on the London streets after dark? And no harlot would show herself in that respectable neighborhood.

Certainly, too, she had appeared to be a servant girl when they got her into the house and had a good look at

her. An Irish servant girl, with the carroty hair many of
the Irish have, and light blue eyes. And she had sounded
like a servant girl. "Oh, please, sirs!" she kept saying, as
they held her down on the bed's dusty counterpane. And
every once in a while she would call upon the Blessed
Virgin, the way the Papists do, and Blessed St. Anne.
From the way she kept calling upon St. Anne, Christopher felt that must be her name saint.

They had not meant for her to die. They had meant to
take her afterward to the mews behind the house, pay her
enough money to buy her silence and to compensate her
for damages to her clothing, and then send her on her
way. There would have been little risk in that. Few servant girls would accuse young men of their class with
rape. They could always say that she had solicited them,
and gone willingly with them into the house.

But unfortunately, while they still had her upstairs in
that long-unused back bedroom, it had occurred to him
that it would be fun to let her think for a moment that
she could get away from them. They had all stepped back
from her, and she, after lying there for a moment like a
rabbit surrounded by hounds, had gotten up and dashed
out of the room. With two of them carrying the candles,
they had run after her. But she hadn't turned toward the
rear staircase, as he had expected. Instead the silly wench
had turned in the other direction. With them pounding after her, she had raced toward the long front window at
the end of the hall. His outstretched hands had almost
grasped her, when she plunged through the glass and fell,
screaming, through the darkness.

But at least he'd kept his nerve, and his head. He'd
told the others to wait inside the rear entrance to the
house. He'd gone back to that bedroom for his hat. Then
he'd gone down two flights of stairs to the kitchen and out
into the areaway.

The girl had been lying there on the flagstones, a still

white shape in the darkness. Quickly he had averted his eyes from her. Wadding his cloak around his fist, he had struck the kitchen's windowpane several times, and heard the glass tinkle to the floor inside. When he was sure the opening was wide enough to admit a supposed housebreaker, he had slipped back inside the kitchen, and locked the door with the same key with which he had unlocked it earlier that night. Then, as rapidly as he could manage, he made his way through the darkness back to where his friends waited, huddled in an anxious knot just inside the house's rear entrance. He had told them to scatter as quickly as possible, and to of course say nothing to anyone. With another key he had unlocked the back door, followed his friends out, and relocked the door.

Yes, he had managed everything quite nicely. Still, because that silly girl had thrown herself out of the window, there would be an investigation. That was why he needed to have his mother and Liza and Hawkins testify that he had been here at the Hedges, fifteen miles from London, when a person or persons unknown had broken into the house on Kingman Street.

One recurring thought made him uneasy. What if the girl had not been a servant? Her clothes had struck him as being of rather good quality. What if she had someone of importance to be concerned about her, someone other than an illiterate parent or two steeping themselves in gin in a London slum or scratching a living out of the soil somewhere miles away in the country?

Who, for instance, was Patrick? Just before she had plunged through that window, she had not called upon the Blessed Virgin, or one of those popish saints. Instead she called out, in a strangled voice, "Patrick! Oh, Patrick!"

He shoved the worry aside. Patrick was probably some fellow servant, some stableboy she had fancied.

Light footsteps passed the closed door of his room. His

sister, on her way to bed. His sister, with those eyes that tonight had seemed to look right through him. Thank God he had foreseen that Elizabeth might be a problem. That was why he had resisted the impulse last night to get out of London as fast as he could. Instead he had first paid a brief visit to Peggy Frazier-Fitzsimmons.

Before she would agree to perjure herself, Liza would go to Peggy. He had seen that resolution forming in his sister's face tonight, down there in the side parlor. Well, let her go to old Peggy. God, the woman must be almost thirty-five!

Regretfully he rubbed his right thumb over his ringless second finger. Well, better a ring missing from his hand than a rope tightening around his neck.

In her room, Elizabeth undressed and put on her night-shift. Then, too tense to go to bed just yet, she moved to the window. Even with a three-branched candelabrum burning on the dressing table behind her, the moonlight appeared to her extraordinarily brilliant. Striking some of the glossy ilex leaves at just the right angle, it made the hedge appear to be hung with tiny silver-blue lights.

She must stop asking herself questions she could not answer, such as who was the girl, and had Christopher been in any way responsible for her death. She would have the answer to both questions by this time tomorrow night.

And if she were forced to conclude that Christopher was responsible? Would she still swear to a lie, in order to save him? She thought of her mother, that frail woman who probably would not live—would not even want to live—if her son was carried, hands bound behind him, in a jolting cart to the gallows at Newgate, and there, before an excited, jeering crowd . . .

Stop thinking, she told herself. Try to get some sleep.

She turned, blew out the candelabrum's flames, and moved to her bed.

Standing there in the hillside copse beside his tethered gray horse, Patrick Stanford went on looking at that upstairs window. It was dark now, but only a moment ago Elizabeth Montlow had been standing there, chestnut hair like a cloak around her shoulders, slim body dimly visible through the thin stuff of her shift.

He knew that her brother also was in the house. Two hours earlier he had seen a male figure, hat in hand, pale hair gleaming in the moonlight, leave the carriage house and move swiftly to that side terrace. Patrick was resolved to make sure that Montlow did not leave the house until a bailiff arrived in the morning to take him away.

He knew that a bailiff would arrive. In fact, in the past sixteen hours he had learned quite a lot about Christopher Montlow's recent past, and about what Patrick grimly hoped would be the youth's short, inescapable future. Arriving at the gatehouse of young Montlow's college before daybreak, he had interviewed first the porter and then two of the dons. Patrick had learned that Montlow had been the ringleader in a prank played upon an aged college servant, an episode that had caused Montlow and four other students to be sent down.

Because by then both he and his hired mount needed rest, Patrick had gone to an inn for three hours' sleep, and then returned to London. At Sir John Fielding's office in Bow Street, he learned that a warrant was out for young Montlow's arrest. It had been issued because of additional evidence, furnished only that morning, by an eyewitness across the street from the Montlows' town house. Since then Bow Street Runners had been searching London for the young man. If he was not found in the city, a bailiff would be dispatched early tomorrow morning to the Montlow country house near the village of Parnley.

Pausing only long enough to hire a fresh mount, Patrick had ridden to Parnley and asked the way to the Montlow house. Through a brief but violent rainstorm, he had ridden to this hillside copse, with its excellent view of the house.

Young Montlow was a ringleader, those Oxford dons had said. And everything, including the fact that she had been carried into the Montlow house, indicated that he had been the ringleader in the assault upon Anne.

That sister of Montlow's. In the past, Patrick had thought of her, not just with desire, but with something he could only call respect. How could she have such a vicious degenerate as a brother? But it happened sometimes. In almost any family a moral monster could appear, outwardly normal, even brilliant and charming, but with an essential quality missing from his nature, that quality called conscience.

For not the first time during the past two hours, he had to fight down an impulse to stride into that house and choke the truth out of Christopher Montlow. But no, he must not take the law into his own hands. He must not draw unfavorable official attention to himself, lest he jeopardize his purpose, a purpose even more important to him than avenging Anne's death. Let the law see that Christopher Montlow paid for that, dangling from a rope at Newgate.

But if, by one means or another, he escaped the gallows? In that case, no matter where he went, Patrick would track him down and take his life in payment for Anne Reardon's.

He sat down, leaned his back against a tree trunk, and prepared to wait until daylight.

7

Around ten the next morning, standing at the front window of the upstairs hall, Elizabeth watched Christopher and two bailiffs go down the path toward a waiting carriage. Christopher carried a small leather portmanteau, which she knew must contain shirts and underclothing. She waited until the carriage had driven away through the misty sunlight. Then she went downstairs.

Mrs. Montlow was standing in the lower hall. With relief, Elizabeth saw that her mother, despite the aggrieved look on her fine-featured face, seemed fairly calm.

"Well, miss! So you have decided to make your appearance, now that they have taken your poor brother away."

"What did you tell them?"

"That he had been here with us since Wednesday, day before yesterday, of course! Hawkins told them that, too. But it did no good."

"Christopher and I both told you that if bailiffs came with a warrant—"

"I know, I know. Well, Elizabeth, what do you plan to do now?"

"Have breakfast, walk to the village, take the stagecoach to London."

"To see that Mrs. Frazier-Fitzsimmons?"

"Yes."

"Elizabeth, I will never understand you. You won't take Christopher's word for where he spent the night before last, but you seem ready to take the word of that

51

. . . strumpet. Why on earth, if it wasn't true, would the boy have confessed to us that he was at her house?"

To keep us from thinking he had been doing something much worse, Elizabeth wanted to say. But she could see that her mother was in no mood for logic, and so she kept silent.

"If you insist upon going into London, will you take some money from the safe for Christopher, and make sure that he gets it? He'll need a few small comforts in that place." She meant his room at Newgate Prison. "It may be days before they admit they have made a mistake and let him go. In the meantime he'll need writing paper, and candles, and decent food sent in. He'll have to send his shirts and underlinen to a laundress. . . ."

"Of course I'll see that he gets some money." She would also see their family solicitor, Mr. Fairchild, in his rooms at the Inns of Court, to arrange for her brother's defense. But there was no point now in trying to make her mother realize that in all probability Christopher would have to stand trial. Obviously Mrs. Montlow chose to believe that in a few days he would be released.

"And you'll wear a veil? Someone who knows you might see you going into that dreadful creature's house."

"I'll wear a veil. I had better have breakfast now, Mother, so that I can walk to the village in plenty of time."

"There is no need to hurry. Hawkins went to the village early this morning, and told the stage master there that you would pay extra if the stage called for you at our house."

She went on, with dignity, "There are some things, Elizabeth, that I cannot save you from. I cannot prevent your doubting your own brother's word. I cannot keep you from going to that notorious woman's house. But at least I can save you from appearing in London with muddy slippers."

Peggy Frazier-Fitzsimmons was at the window of her private upstairs sitting-room when she saw the carriage stop in front of her house. For the last ten minutes she had been admiring her newly acquired ruby ring, turning it this way and that so that the sunlight awoke fire in the gem's depths. Now she crossed hastily to her dressing table, dropped the ring into her jewel box, and returned to the window. A heavily veiled woman, slender and obviously young, was descending from the carriage.

Kit Montlow's sister? She must be.

Again Peggy flew to her dressing table, and inspected her face in its frame of blond ringlets. It was quite an attractive face, despite fine lines bracketing her mouth, and even finer ones radiating from the corners of her brown eyes. From downstairs came the sound of the front door's knocker.

She adjusted one of the ringlets on her forehead. A touch of rouge? No, better not.

Her maid-of-all-work, Lucia, appeared in the doorway. Like her husband, Peggy's coachman, Lucia was of southern Italian descent. She said, olive-complexioned face impassive, "A Miss Montlow to see you."

"Tell her I will be down immediately."

When Peggy entered the salon only moments later, her visitor, now with veil flung back, rose from a French-style settee of fruitwood upholstered in pale yellow satin. Like the whole house, the salon was small, but comfortably, even luxuriously appointed.

"Miss Montlow?" Tactfully, Peggy did not offer her hand.

"Yes."

"I am Mrs. Frazier-Fitzsimmons."

There had never been a Mr. Frazier-Fitzsimmons. Peggy had assumed the name when, at the age of eighteen, she had realized that she did not have to continue through life as Bertha Crouch.

"How do you do?" Elizabeth said.

What a beauty, Peggy thought. That lustrous brown hair, those gray eyes, that figure, with a waist so slender that the high breasts beneath her dark brown velvet gown looked fuller than they actually were. Of late years, Peggy had sometimes, at a price, introduced lovers weary of her own charms to certain young women. Wistfully she thought of the price she could obtain for this one.

"Please sit down, Miss Montlow." Peggy moved to the bell rope hanging beside the marble-manteled fireplace. "May I offer you refreshment? Tea, perhaps?"

"No, thank you," Elizabeth said swiftly. Then, aware that she might have sounded ungracious: "I cannot stay long. I have much to do before I leave London at four o'clock."

"I understand." Peggy sat down in a yellow satin arm-chair, facing her visitor.

"I have come here about my brother. Did Christopher come here for tea last Wednesday afternoon? And did he ... stay here until the next morning?"

Peggy cast her eyes modestly downward. "Did he tell you that?"

"Yes."

Peggy thought of how Christopher Montlow had visited her the previous Wednesday, but not until many hours after teatime. In fact, Lucia and Giuseppe had already retired to their quarters above the carriage house, and Peggy herself, in her upstairs bedroom, had begun to feel sleepy, when she heard a handful of gravel patter against the windowpane. She had gone to the window and looked down. Kit Montlow had stood down there in the garden, pale hair shining in the rectangle of light cast by her window.

She had felt glad to see him. Since she had first met him in Hyde Park the previous summer, they had been to bed seven or eight times. She had found his youth a stimulating novelty. And he had proved to be a potent lover, although a somewhat selfish and impatient one. She descended quickly to the lower hall, where a tallow night lamp burned on a table near the rear door, and let him into the house.

"Kit, you young scamp! Why didn't you go to the front door?" Then she saw from the look on his face that this was no ordinary visit. "What is the matter? Are you in trouble?"

"I may be."

"With the law?"

"Perhaps."

"Then get out of here! Immediately! I cannot afford any trouble with the law."

"You won't have any. I'm not asking you to say anything whatever to anyone connected with the law."

"Then what are you asking?"

"Probably my sister will be here in a day or two. I want you to tell her that I came here at teatime this afternoon—*came here for the first time,* do you understand? And that I spent all of tonight with you, and then left early in the morning."

She looked at him shrewdly. "Is that what you are going to tell her?"

"Yes, and my mother, too."

"Then you must have been up to something really bad tonight, if you would rather have them believe you were here! Now, what has happened?"

"My house on Kingman Street was broken into, that's all."

"By you?"

"Why would I break into my own house?"

"I don't know why. I just know that you might do anything. Now, what happened?"

"There was a girl with whoever broke into the house. She's . . . hurt."

Peggy took a step backward. "I don't want to hear anything more about it!"

"You don't have to. All you have to do is tell my sister what I ask you to."

She studied him. "Are you sure you are not hoping I will furnish an alibi for you to the bailiffs?"

"Don't be a fool, Peg. Of what use would be an alibi furnished by you? Who would believe a woman everyone knows to be a whore?"

She took the insult with narrowed eyes, but calmly. "You're very foxy for a lad of eighteen, aren't you?"

"If you convince my sister I spent all of tonight with you, she and my mother will furnish me with an alibi, one that *will* be believed."

She considered, no longer afraid that he planned to involve her with bailiffs or the law courts. Clever young devil that he was, he had realized, even before she herself did, that such help from her could only harm him. She said, "And in return, what will you do for me?"

He stripped a ring from his finger and handed it to her. Even though she had seen it before, she held the ring close to the lamp and looked appreciatively at the glowing ruby. It was worth a hundred pounds, possibly more.

"Just what do you want me to tell your sister?"

They talked for several minutes. Then he moved toward the door. She asked, "What are you going to do now?"

"Walk fifteen miles to the Hedges. I should get there well before morning. I don't dare hire a horse. The stable owner would remember me."

"And when you reach the Hedges?"

"I'll hide in the carriage house until dark tomorrow night, just in case there might be someone watching the place, and then slip into the house."

He had said good night to Peggy then, and gone out the back door.

Now, eyes still cast down, Peggy said to Elizabeth Montlow, "If he himself told you that he spent the night with me . . ."

"He did."

Before she turned to more lucrative endeavors, Peggy had appeared on the London stage. Her theatrical training served her well now. The eyes she lifted to her visitor were filled with timid shame.

"It's true, Miss Montlow. He appeared on my doorstep last Wednesday afternoon about four o'clock, and reminded me of the time last summer when a young friend of his had introduced us. I gave him tea. And then he began to talk wildly of how he had been unable to get me out of his mind all these past months . . ."

Her low voice faltered for a moment. Then she went on, "I know it must seem incomprehensible to a young lady like you. But I let him stay the night. In the morning I left him, still asleep, and went downstairs. Lucia, my maid, had just returned from the market. She told me there was some rumor about your house on Kingman Street, and about a girl, and about Bow Street Runners looking for Christopher.

"When I went upstairs to my room and told him, he was terribly distressed and frightened. In an instant, he reverted to a little child. All he could think of was getting as fast as possible to his mother and to Liza, as he called you."

Elizabeth, taking a deep breath, felt as if a terrible weight had been lifted from her.

"I know it must seem depraved," Peggy went on, "my allowing a young boy to make love to me. But perhaps his very youth was the reason. I could not help having this . . . this motherly feeling for him. You see, Mr. Frazier-Fitzsimmons and I—we had been married only a year when he died—he and I never had a child. . . . But then, you don't want to hear about that."

She was correct. Elizabeth did not want to hear about the sort of maternal feelings that could lead a woman to bed down with a boy half her age. All she wanted, now that she had learned the truth, was to leave this house.

She got to her feet. "I must go now. Thank you, Mrs. Frazier-Fitzsimmons. I am very grateful to you."

"Grateful?" Peggy looked puzzled. "For telling you that your brother and I . . . ? Oh!" Shock widened her brown eyes. "You can't mean because of that girl found in front of your house here in town. Surely you never believed that Christopher had anything to do with that!"

Although she colored slightly, Elizabeth's voice remained even. "I had to make certain."

"Is Christopher all right? Surely your coming here does not mean that he had been . . . arrested?" For the past hour, ever since her coachman had brought back the latest news from a Covent Garden grog shop, Peggy had known that Christopher was in custody.

"Yes, he has been arrested. But I know now that everything will be set to rights eventually. Thank you again, Mrs. Frazier-Fitzsimmons. And good-bye."

She went down the steps to the hired carriage and asked the driver to take her to the Bow Street house of Sir John Fielding. A younger half-brother of the novelist Henry Fielding, Sir John had been knighted for having founded his Bow Street Runners, London's first organized defense against crime.

As the horses drew the vehicle swiftly over the cobblestones, Elizabeth felt almost lighthearted, so much so that she could enjoy the sight of smart private carriages moving along the street, and well-dressed men and women strolling along the sidewalks. Now that she knew that her brother had been guilty last Wednesday night of nothing except consorting with a notorious whore, she felt not the slightest scruple about lying to save him. True, such a lie, told under oath on the witness stand, still would constitute perjury. But she would not be perjuring herself to obstruct justice. She would be doing so to prevent a possible miscarriage of justice, one that might leave Christopher hanging dead from a noose, and her mother dead also, or wishing she were.

When she reached the Bow Street house, she gave her name to a cheerful-looking youth who guarded the door. He returned in a few minutes to lead her through a room where ragged miscreants sat dejectedly on benches under the watchful gaze of a pair of burly Runners. Then he stood aside for her to enter a smaller room.

A man with a massive head and a leonine mane of gray hair stood up from behind his desk. "Good afternoon, Miss Montlow." Even though she had heard that he had been blinded by an accident at the age of nineteen, the sight of the closed eyelids in his broad face was a shock.

"Please sit down." She took the straight chair on the opposite side of the desk. "May I say that I regret the circumstance that I am sure brings you here?"

"Not so much as I do, Sir John. My brother is being held for no reason. On the night in question, he was fifteen miles from London. He was with my mother and me, in our house near the village of Parnley."

He said, "You will be willing to swear to that in court?"

Something in his tone made her nerves tighten. She had heard eerie tales of this blind man's powers. It was said that he could recognize more than three thousand London criminals just by their voices. Had he also developed a sixth sense that told him when someone was lying?

"Certainly I will so testify. But why should his case come to court? I see no reason why he should have been arrested at all. Surely your bailiffs told you that both my mother and our servant stated that my brother had been with us Wednesday night."

His voice was perfectly neutral. "They told me. But he

cannot be released. He has already been remanded to Newgate Prison to be held for trial at the next General Sessions."

"May I ask upon what evidence? Surely not just because the . . . the crime was committed in our empty house!"

"Upon additional evidence submitted the morning after the crime by an eyewitness, a maid employed by a family across the street. She did not tell immediately everything she had seen. Perhaps in her excitement she forgot it. Perhaps she hesitated to accuse a neighbor of her own employers. But the next morning she did tell them, and her employers brought her here to give her evidence to me."

Elizabeth's pulse was beating hard in the hollow of her throat. "What had she seen?"

"Your brother has very distinctive hair, has he not? Yellow hair so pale it is almost silvery, the sort of hair that is usually observed only in young children."

"Yes."

"When the youths were carrying the girl into the house, one of them lost his hat. Because of his hair, the housemaid recognized him as Christopher Montlow."

"Just by his *hair*? There must be thousands of young men in London with hair that shade."

"Not thousands. Scores, perhaps."

"I don't care if there is only one other! The man she saw could not possibly have been my brother. And I shall so testify." It did not matter, she told herself, that this blind man did not seem to believe her. He would not be the judge at Christopher's trial, nor a member of the jury.

"That is your privilege, Miss Montlow." After a moment he added, "You might be interested to know that we have questioned the four youths who were sent down from Oxford along with your brother. Oh, yes," he said, almost as if he could see the start she gave, "we know the circumstances of their having been sent down."

She sat there in silence, heart pounding. Could one of those boys, out of some sort of malice, have tried to implicate Christopher?

He went on, "All of them, including Lord Stanley's son, say that they have spent every night since being sent down at Lord Stanley's house here in London. A manservant confirms their story."

From his tone, she could not tell whether he himself believed it.

"Each of them says that at no time were they near the Montlow house on Kingman Street. But they also say that your brother, although he stayed with them for the first two nights after they left Oxford, was not with them Wednesday night."

"Of course he was not! He was at our house in the country."

"So you have told me."

A silence lengthened. Then Elizabeth said. "The girl. Has she been identified?"

"Yes. She was an Irish girl, Anne Reardon. She was seventeen. Her guardian had brought her to London to arrange her marriage to an ironmonger's son."

Pity swelled Elizabeth's heart. Only seventeen. And a respectable girl, apparently. Whoever they were, those youths who had savaged her until she went screaming to her death—they deserved hanging.

"Was it her betrothed who identified her?"

"No, her guardian."

"Who is he?"

"An Irish baronet, with lands near County Cork. His name is Sir Patrick Stanford."

She stiffened. Patrick Stanford, that tall, graceful man who, in a ballroom filled with clashing perfumes, had somehow made her think of green fields, and cool fresh air, and waves pounding on a rocky coast. That rugged-faced man whose touch as they moved through the figures of the dance, and whose dark gaze, moving from her face to rest on her almost bare bosom, had stirred her senses.

Would he, like John Fielding, not believe the testimony she was determined to give?

She said, eager to end the interview, "May I take some money to my brother?"

"I am afraid you cannot see him today. Certain formalities, necessary whenever a new prisoner is admitted, will not have been completed as yet."

She reached into her reticule and drew out a small chamois bag. "Then you will see to it that he gets these five sovereigns?"

"Certainly. I will send for a clerk and have him make you out a receipt."

Five minutes later, as the carriage moved down the Strand toward the Inns of Court, Elizabeth no longer felt lighthearted. She was troubled by the thought that the housemaid's evidence, although obviously mistaken, might count against Christopher. Too, now that she knew more about that young girl, she felt doubly oppressed by the thought of her cruel death. And in her mind's eye she kept seeing Patrick Stanford's dark face. It had worn a smile at their first meeting. She did not like to imagine how his face would look the next time she saw it.

But at least her interview with the family solicitor, when she reached his gloomy office in the Inns of Court, was more comforting than that with the blind man. No look of skepticism crossed Mr. Fairchild's thin old face when Elizabeth explained why Christopher could not possibly be guilty.

"Dear, dear!" he said. "What a shocking ordeal for you and your dear mother. But don't worry, my child. No jury will convict him after you and Mrs. Montlow testify that he was with you that night."

"Nevertheless, I want him to have the best defense possible."

"Of course. I was about to suggest Sir Archibald Wade, a most able barrister for this sort of case. True, we could engage someone whose fees are lower . . ."

"No." This was no time to economize. "Please get in touch with Sir Archibald." She rose. "I must leave now, Mr. Fairchild, if I'm to catch the four-o'clock stage."

It was not until well after dark that she walked up the brick path between the untrimmed boxwood bushes. Just before she reached the front door, her mother opened it, her face taut with anxiety.

In the hallway Mrs. Montlow said, in a low, rapid voice, "Donald Weymouth is here, in the side parlor."

"But he wasn't to return from Bath until several days from now!"

"Nevertheless, he is here. He has been waiting for you for over an hour." she paused. "Well? Did you see her?"

"Yes. He was with her from Wednesday afternoon until early Thursday morning."

Mrs. Montlow's face went slack with relief. "Thank God! Then you will—"

"Of course I will testify that he was with us that night." Joyful tears sprang to Mrs. Montlow's eyes. Elizabeth said, with contrition, "Mother, forgive me for not having believed him right from the first."

"Of course I forgive you. And I was wrong this morning to call you unfeeling. I know it is because you have strength of character that you had to . . . make sure. And I realize that sometimes in the past the boy has been . . . rather strange." Some memory shadowed her eyes.

Elizabeth had never told her mother about the kitten dangling from its noose, nor the crumpled print in Christopher's clothespress. Had there been other such things of which her mother had been aware, but had preferred to keep secret?

Mrs. Montlow said, "Did you see Christopher?"

"I was not allowed to. But I left the money for him, with Sir John Fielding. And I saw Mr. Fairchild. He thinks Christopher is in no danger whatsoever."

"But he will have to stand trail?"

"Yes, Mother. Now, about Donald. What did you tell him?"

"Just that Christopher had been arrested, and why, and that he could not possibly be guilty, because he was with us that night."

"What reason did you give him for my being in London?"

"I said you had gone to take Christopher some money and to consult with Mr. Fairchild."

"Good. I had best go to him now. May I ask him to supper?"

"Of course, my darling."

Elizabeth went down the hall. Evidently Donald had heard her footsteps, because when she entered the parlor, he was already on his feet, a thin young man in a dark gray coat and breeches. He crossed the room to meet her and to take her outstretched hands. "Elizabeth!"

He kissed both her hands, and then her lips. "Your mother has told me all about Christopher." His gaze went over her face. "I imagine you don't want to talk about it. You look tired, my dearest."

"I don't mind talking about it. But first I would like to know why you came back from Bath so early."

His thin, intelligent face broke into a warm smile. "Because I couldn't wait any longer to tell you my news. Come over here."

They sat down on a small red plush settee facing the fire. He said, "We can be married sooner than we planned. The vicar has written my uncle that he will retire in June. After that, the living will be mine."

"Oh, Donald! I'm so glad."

He drew close to her and kissed her, his lips far more ardent than ever in the past. Once, he had told her that for the last five years, ever since he was twenty, he had wanted to marry her. Five years was a long time for a man to wait.

He released her. "We can be married in June, can't we? Surely by then this trouble of Christopher's will be well in the past."

She nodded. "His case will come up in February."

He hesitated. "Surely you won't stay at the Kingman Street house. . . ."

"During the trial?" She shuddered slightly. "No, I'm sure we can stay with Aunt Sara. Her house is very near Old Bailey." Sara Finchley, Mrs. Montlow's older sister, was also a widow. Although badly crippled by rheumatism, she always welcomed visits from the Montlows.

"Good." He got to his feet. "I must go now."

She said, dismayed, "But won't you take supper with us?"

"I must not. I must see my parents. They may have heard by now that I arrived on the stagecoach this afternoon." He laughed. "I was so eager to see you that I walked right past my own house to get to yours."

They moved to the parlor doorway. There he said. "You are not worried about Christopher's trial, are you?"

"No, not really."

"It will be all right. From now on everything will be all right for you. I feel there is no evil that I could not guard you against."

He kissed her, more gently this time. "I will see myself out. You stay by the fire, and rest."

She listened to his footsteps go down the hall. Then she moved to the fire and held out her hands to its warmth. There was no evil he could not guard her against, he had said. Surely that was true. As long as they both lived, his love would be like a warm, shielding cloak around her.

Then why, even as she held her hands to the fire's warmth, did she feel cold, almost as if she stood stripped and shivering in the blast of some black tempest?

8

On this, the last day of Christopher's trial, an icy February wind swept the streets outside Old Bailey, so that pedestrians hurried along with bent heads, and horses scrambled for footing on the freezing cobblestones. But here inside the courtroom, with every bench packed with excited spectators, and with oil wall lamps blazing in their brackets to augment the feeble daylight that fell through the windows, the air seemed suffocatingly warm. Or perhaps, Elizabeth reflected, as she sat on the bench directly behind tall, portly Sir Archibald, it was sheer anxiety that had brought the perspiration out on her forehead.

For her the trial had been a series of disjointed, nightmarish vignettes. The coroner on the stand, describing in technical but still far too vivid detail the state of Anne Reardon's violated, broken body. Patrick Stanford, his face a dark, controlled mask, telling of how he had brought his ward to London to be married. Sir John Fielding, a striking figure on the stand with his massive head and tightly closed eyelids, telling of Christopher's arrest.

After that there had been a don from Christopher's college at Oxford, recounting the episode that had caused Christopher to be sent down, and stating that "young Montlow was always a troublesome young man, a troublesome young man indeed." And there had been that housemaid from Kingman Street, describing the dark figures on the sidewalk, the dislodged hat, and then, later on, the white body hurtling down through the night.

Elizabeth had been heartened by the way Sir Archibald had deflated the prosecution witnesses. He had forced the Oxford don to admit that Christopher's college pranks had never been actually criminal in nature. He had made him concede, also, that he had dealt with many "troublesome" students in his long career, some of whom had gone on to become members of Parliament, respected churchmen, and even ministers of the crown.

As for the housemaid, one Dorcas Small, his questions soon reduced her to frightened incoherence. How was it that by night, and from a window four floors above the street, she could identify an individual just by his hair? Was she sure it had even been hair—"Remember you are under oath, my girl!"—and not a wig? At last, apparently having learned that her eyesight was not of the keenest, he had asked her to describe the clothing and features of a woman spectator at the rear of the room. "Come, come, Dorcas, if you could recognize that man in the street at night, surely in this well-lighted place, and at no greater distance, you can see and describe that lady."

"She's wearing something blue, sir, but whether it's a coat or a cloak, I can't say," Dorcas finally answered, and then burst into tears. With a lordly wave, Sir Archibald dismissed her from the stand.

But if the prosecution witnesses had seemed to Elizabeth inept, those for the defense had seemed even more so. She felt sure that Mary Hawkins' testimony had been sheer disaster. Graying head topped by a black bonnet, she had spoken in wooden tones, sometimes breaking off abruptly, and then repeating her last phrase before she was able to go on. The effect was that of a witness thoroughly rehearsed, as indeed she had been, by Sir Archibald.

But at least the lawyer for the crown, a little man whose wizened face framed by his long wig reminded Elizabeth of a monkey, had been unable to budge Mary Hawkins from her memorized answers. The best he could do was to establish that she had spent her entire adult life with the Montlows, and otherwise was completely alone in the world, with no living relatives. "In that case," he said, "would it be fair to assume that you are devoted to the Montlows?"

"That I am, sir," she blurted. "It's as if they was my own flesh and blood."

Before dismissing her, he turned to the jury with a raised eyebrow and a slight smile, as if to say, "Do you see? This woman would testify to anything to help her employers."

As for Mrs. Montlow, she had succeeded in irritating everyone—the fat judge in his scarlet robe, Sir Archibald, the wizened lawyer for the crown, and, Elizabeth feared, even the jury. She had not been content to testify as to the essential point, Christopher's presence in her home that night the girl died. Instead she had interwoven her answers to Sir Archibald's questions with garrulous praises of her son. "He never gave me a moment's worry from the time he was in his cradle," and, "Everyone said they had never seen such a sensitive, tenderhearted boy."

Those irrelevancies had given the crown attorney a chance to cast doubt upon her truthfulness. "Are you asking this court to believe, Mrs. Montlow, that your son never misbehaved? There was not even the usual childish naughtiness?"

"Never!"

"Then how is it that he became so naughty after he went to Oxford?"

She glared at him for a long moment and then said feebly, "Any boy is apt to fall in with bad companions."

Elizabeth was to be the last witness called by Christopher's attorney. Now, while on the bench in front of her Sir Archibald and his clerk conferred in low tones, Elizabeth realized with frightened dismay that her brother's life might depend upon her own behavior during the next few minutes. She sat with her eyes fastened on her clasped hands. In her anxiety, she could not even look at Christopher, pale from his months in prison, there in the dock.

And she knew she must not, lest she go to pieces completely, look at Patrick Stanford, there on a bench across the aisle and a few rows back. For the last few days she had avoided even glancing at him, because she knew she might see him looking at Christopher, looking with a deadly hatred in his dark eyes. No one seeing that look could doubt that Sir Patrick Stanford longed to watch her brother strangling at the end of a rope.

And if Christopher escaped the rope? That look on Sir Patrick's face seemed to say plainly that he would not escape some other form of death. It was to thwart that cold resolve in the Irishman's face that, several days ago, Elizabeth had made certain arrangements . . .

Sir Archibald was standing up, was saying something. It took Elizabeth several seconds to realize that the time had come for her to testify. Trying to look calm despite her pounding heartbeats, she moved to the stand. She threw one glance at her brother's pale, anxious face. Then her eyes sought Donald. He had stayed in London ever since the trial began, occupying rented rooms next door to the house owned by Sara Finchley, Elizabeth's aunt. Each day, he had escorted Elizabeth and Mrs. Montlow to and from Old Bailey. Now, seated halfway back in the courtroom, he gave her an encouraging smile.

With deft questions, Sir Archibald led her through the account that she herself had given him as soon as he had agreed to defend Christopher. She told of her brother's arrival at the Hedges near teatime that Wednesday afternoon, his confession that he had been sent down, the supper of roast chicken he had shared with her and their mother. With growing confidence, she felt that she was telling the necessary lies very well, in a voice that sounded calm and convincing.

And then she saw that Mrs. Frazier-Fitzsimmons, gowned and bonneted in demure gray, sat among the spectators.

Sir Archibald asked, "And after supper?"

"My brother was tired, and so he soon went upstairs to his room."

"Did you see him again that night?"

"Yes, I feared he might be coming down with a chill, and so I took a posset up to his room."

Again she looked at Mrs. Frazier-Fitzsimmons—and stiffened with shock. Inwardly, the woman was convulsed with merriment. Laughter was plain in the brown eyes beneath the blond ringlets, and in the twitching lips.

Why was she laughing, as if in contemplation of some sort of fool? The woman had seemed well-disposed at their first meeting, even friendly in a tentative sort of way.

And then, like a blow, the possible explanation struck Elizabeth. Perhaps the woman *had* made a fool of her. Perhaps Christopher had not been with Mrs. Frazier-Fitzsimmons that Wednesday evening. And if that were the case, then almost certainly she herself had been telling these lies, not in defense of an innocent man, but of . . .

She tore her gaze from the woman's face, only to find herself looking at Patrick Stanford. He looked back at her with scorn and fury. "Liar," that dark gaze said. "Liar and perjurer."

Unable to look away from him, she began to tremble. Suddenly it seemed to her that everyone in the courtroom must realize that she had been lying. She knew that Sir

Archibald was speaking to her, but somehow, perhaps because of her heart's pounding, she could not distinguish the words.

At last she was able to look away from that accusing dark face. "I am sorry. Will you please repeat your question, Sir Archibald? I did not quite hear."

His tone was soothing. "Of course. And don't be sorry. We all realize what an ordeal this trial has been for a sheltered, delicately bred young woman. What I asked you was the hour at which you took the posset up to your brother's room."

The lawyer's little speech had given her time to regain self-control. "It was just before ten. I heard the clock strike as I carried the empty glass down the stairs."

"And so at no time on the date in question, from three in the afternoon until ten o'clock at night, was your brother out of your sight long enough to go to your neighboring village and back, let alone to London.

"I have no further questions," he added, and made a courteous little bow to the lawyer for the crown.

With an apprehension she tried to hide, Elizabeth watched the wizened man approach. He looked at her sourly for a moment, and then up at the scarlet-robed justice. "I have no questions for this witness, your Lordship. The crown rests its case."

Sir Archibald shot to his feet and said jubilantly, "The defense also rests."

She became aware that the jury had risen and was filing out, and that his Lordship, banging a gavel, had dismissed the court. Dazedly she realized that the trial was over. Now there was nothing to do but to wait for the verdict.

Sir Archibald, extending a plump hand to take her cold, trembling one, helped her down from the stand. She said, beneath the babble of voices around them, "I did very badly."

"You did splendidly."

"Splendidly! Why, when I saw that . . . that girl's guardian staring at me, I completely lost control."

"That is what was so splendid. I know he was glaring at you. I turned and saw him. The jury must have seen it, too. Those jurymen are all good Londoners, my dear, brewers and wool merchants and clothmakers and such. They hate the landed gentry, and they hate the Irish, and Sir Patrick is both. When he looked at you in that murderous fashion, and you began to tremble, you became beauty in distress, *English* beauty in distress."

"I pray you are right." She paused and then asked, "Why didn't the lawyer for the crown question me?"

"Because he had seen that he had lost the case. He also knows London juries."

By this time Elizabeth was quite in command of herself. Why had she leaped to the conclusion that Mrs. Frazier-Fitzsimmons had deceived her? There was a simpler explanation for the woman's amusement. Perhaps, recalling her young bedmate of that Wednesday night, she had been convulsed by Elizabeth's account of him as a penitent schoolboy lying chastely in his own bed and accepting a posset from his sister's hand.

Sir Archibald said, "Here come your mother and Mr. Weymouth. Now, go to your aunt's house, and don't worry. As soon as the jury returns, I will send a boy to summon you back to court. And I'll wager that won't be more than half an hour from now."

9

Sir Archibald's guess was uncannily near the mark. The Montlow women and Donald had been in Aunt Sara Finchley's parlor less than forty minutes, discussing the cruel weather, and British reversals in the war with the rebellious American colonies, and anything and everything except the trial, when a boy sent by Sir Archibald knocked on the door. The jury, he told them, had reached its verdict.

Afraid to trust her rheumatic legs to the icy sidewalks, Aunt Sara remained behind. Mary Hawkins, though, chose to accompany her employers and Donald the few hundred yards through the blustery cold to Old Bailey. Just before they reached the courtroom, Elizabeth managed to whisper to Donald, "Is the carriage . . . ?"

"It's waiting, there in the alley. I slipped out long enough this morning to make sure."

The courtroom was even more crowded than it had been for that morning's session. Space, however, had been reserved for the prisoner's family on the bench directly behind Sir Archibald. As she took her place, Elizabeth sent a swift glance toward a door at the right of the jury box, the door through which Christopher had been led in and out of the courtroom each day. Yes, the bailiff to whom she had given a gold sovereign yesterday, a tall man with a saturnine face, was waiting beside the door.

The jury filed in. The foreman, a stout man with the flushed face of someone overly fond of port wine, looked at the prisoner, and then, with a smile, at Elizabeth. Overwhelming relief swelled her heart. She did not need to hear the words "We find the prisoner not guilty" to know that they had won.

The verdict was greeted by a few cheers and a few angry murmurs, both gaveled into silence. Even before Christopher had stepped down from the dock, Elizabeth was on her feet. Trailed by her mother and Hawkins and Donald, she moved toward her brother, who was already the center of a small crowd.

She gave him time to embrace and kiss his mother, and then threw her own arms around his neck. "There is a carriage waiting in the alley," she whispered. "It will take you to Southampton." Reaching into the pocket of her cloak, she took out a small pouch of soft leather and put it in his hand. "Here is money. Take the first ship out. Write to us. I will tell you when it is safe for you to come back to England."

His blue eyes, looking down into hers, held no questions, only a vast relief. He too had read the death sentence in the Irishman's face.

The bribed bailiff had opened the door. "Go!" she whispered fiercely. Without a word Christopher turned and went through the door. The bailiff closed it, and then stood with his back to the panels.

Mrs. Montlow said, bewildered, "Where has Christopher gone? Isn't he free to come with us?"

"Of course he's free, Mother. It's just that there are a few formalities to be gone through." She added hurriedly, "Sir Archibald is coming toward us. We must thank him."

As she spoke, she glanced swiftly to her left. Patrick Stanford stood halfway back in the rapidly emptying room, his grim gaze fixed on the small crowd near the prisoner's dock. Obviously he had not yet realized that Christopher was no longer a part of the crowd.

Sir Archibald bowed an acknowledgment of Mrs.

Montlow's tearful thanks. "My son will thank you too, as soon as he comes back."

"Comes back?"

Elizabeth said swiftly, "He went through that door there. He said there were some matters he had to attend to."

Sir Archibald looked at the door where the bailiff stood, barring the way. When his gaze returned to Elizabeth, it held admiring comprehension. "Ah, yes. Certain matters. Perhaps a warden is here, with personal property Christopher had with him in prison."

Again Elizabeth turned her head and looked at the tall Irishman. His gaze still searched the crowd, but there was the dawn of understanding in his face now. For an instant his cold, furious gaze swung to Elizabeth. Then he turned and strode rapidly toward the courtroom's front entrance.

Elizabeth, drawing a sharp breath, looked at Donald. Without a word he too strode toward the entrance. Mrs. Montlow said, "Now, where is Donald—"

"It is all right, Mother. He will join us at Aunt Sara's. So will Christopher. You will tell him we have gone on, won't you, Sir Archibald?"

"Of course."

After a few protests, Mrs. Montlow accompanied Elizabeth and Mary Hawkins from the courtroom, across Old Bailey's forecourt, and into the windy street. They had almost reached Sara Finchley's house when Elizabeth heard rapid footsteps behind them. With a stab of fear she halted and turned.

To her relief, she saw it was Donald. He gave her a slight nod and a smile.

So Christopher's carriage had gotten away in time. Now there was only one task left to her, one she dreaded. She had to tell her mother that it might be some time before she saw her adored son again.

In Sara Finchley's parlor, with a fire snapping in the

grate, the two sisters wept joyfully in each other's arms. Then Aunt Sara's maid-of-all-work, a thin and not very bright girl of seventeen, brought in the tea cart. Mary Hawkins moved beside her, carrying small glasses and a bottle of sherry on a tray.

Fully a quarter of an hour passed before Mrs. Montlow said, "What on earth can be keeping Christopher?"

She might as well know now, Elizabeth realized. She crossed to her mother, removed the teacup and saucer from her hand, and placed them on the cart. Then she sat down on a footstool beside her mother's chair.

"Christopher won't be here today."

"Won't be here!"

Elizabeth took her mother's hands in her own. "Don't look like that. He's all right, Mother. But he must stay out of England for a while."

"Stay out of England! Elizabeth, have you lost your—?"

"Listen to me. That girl's guardian. In spite of everything, he believes Christopher is guilty. I saw it in his face."

Mrs. Montlow had turned pale. "Yes, I saw him looking at Christopher in that . . . dreadful way. You mean, he intends to . . . harm my boy? . . ."

"If he can. Donald and I have tried to make sure that he cannot. Christopher is on his way to Southampton now. I told him to take the first ship leaving port."

Mrs. Montlow said, in an anguished whisper, "But where . . . ?"

"We won't know where he has gone until he writes to me. Perhaps he will have time to send us a message from Southampton before he boards a ship. Perhaps not. Anyway, he has enough money to last him several months. By that time, surely Stanford will have gone back to Ireland."

Surely by that time, too, he would have abandoned the murderous resolve she had seen in his face. Not even an

Irishman's vengefulness could stay at white-hot heat indefinitely.

Mrs. Montlow shuddered and buried her face in her hands. "That man! That dreadful man." Then she lowered her hands and asked, "Couldn't we have him arrested?"

"Upon what charge, Mother? He has done nothing so far. He hasn't even said anything. You cannot have a man arrested because of an expression on his face."

"You ought to be able to!" Mrs. Montlow cried. She was silent for a moment or two, and then said feverishly, "We must go to the Hedges at once!"

"Very well, Mother."

"We must be there. Christopher may send a message." She stood up. Then she swayed, and would have fallen if Donald had not stepped forward and caught her in his arms.

He carried her to the sofa. Taking a vial of smelling salts from her reticule, Elizabeth knelt beside the sofa and held the vial to her mother's nostrils. With terror she looked at the closed eyes, the white face, the bluish lips. She heard her aunt cry distractedly to the little maid, "Run, Agnes! Fetch the doctor."

After a moment Agnes said, "What doctor, mum?"

"My doctor, of course. Dr. Quill. You know where he lives. You fetched him only last week."

"I don't know as I rightly remember, mum."

"He is across the street and four houses to the left. Now, hurry!"

For what seemed like half an hour, but was probably only ten minutes, Elizabeth stayed there beside her mother, watching the uneven rise and fall of her breathing. Then the front door opened and closed, and footsteps sounded along the hall. Dr. Quill came in, a thin, middle-aged man who, Elizabeth noted fleetingly, lacked the pompous air of most of his colleagues. He looked down at

Mrs. Montlow and then said quietly, "Will you please leave me alone with the patient?"

Twenty minutes later Elizabeth and Aunt Sara and Donald were sitting in the dining room, with Agnes and Mary Hawkins hovering anxiously beside the doorway, when Dr. Quill joined them. "The lady needs rest and quiet," he said. "If possible, she should remain right here for at least a week or ten days."

"Of course it is possible!" Sara Finchley said. "All of you can stay here."

"Not all, I am afraid." He looked at Elizabeth. "Your mother wants you to return to your home. She became quite agitated in her insistence. Apparently she is hoping her son will send some sort of message."

Appalled, Elizabeth thought of leaving her mother here, with no one but rheumatism-crippled Aunt Sara and dim-witted Agnes to care for her.

Mary Hawkins stepped forward. "Please, Miss Elizabeth. Let me stay here. I know it will be lonely for you in the country, but your mother needs me."

"*Let* you, Hawkins! Why, I will be more grateful than I can say."

Dr. Quill gazed with approval at the tall, competent-looking woman with the graying hair and concerned face. "A splendid arrangement." He turned to Donald Weymouth. "And now, sir, if you will help me take the patient upstairs . . ."

It was four o'clock by the time Elizabeth said good-bye in an upstairs bedroom to Mrs. Montlow, still weak of voice, but now with a little color in her face. Thus, darkness had fallen when the carriage Donald had hired for Elizabeth and himself passed the last of London's straggling outskirts and then moved north through a silence broken only by the clop of hooves over the frozen road, the barking of a dog in some isolated farmhouse, and the occasional sound of their own voices. Most of the time they rode with hands clasped, not speaking.

They were within a mile or so of the Hedges when Donald said, "I received a letter from my uncle yesterday. My parents had sent it on to me. He wants me to come down to Bath again."

"When will you leave?"

"I don't intend to go at all. He says that he has more matters concerning his estate to discuss with me. But I feel that all he really wants is to argue more about philosophy. The old man has been reading Bishop Berkeley, you know, and he keeps demanding that I refute that silly argument that no one can prove the existence of anything except his own mind."

"Still, if he wants you to come . . ."

"But I want to see you every day. You will be lonely enough as it is."

"Nonsense. I have been there alone before. Twice when Mother and Hawkins went into London for the season, I stayed behind for a few days to cover the furniture with dust sheets and tidy up the garden. Besides, my dearest, your uncle is an old man, and you are his heir. Thanks to him, we will have many years of comfort and happiness together. Surely you can spare a few days in which to argue with him about Bishop Berkeley."

Donald was silent for a moment. Then he smiled, drew her to him, and kissed her. "That's my Elizabeth. Warm of heart, clear of head. All right, I will leave tomorrow and stay in Bath for a week. The sooner I go, the sooner I can return."

When they reached the Hedges, they left the carriage waiting and walked up the path to the house. He took the heavy key she gave him, unlocked the door, and then, inside the hall, struck a flint and lighted the tallow lamp on its narrow table.

They smiled at each other through the upward-striking

light, aware of the silence around them. She did not ask him to linger, nor did he indicate he wanted such an invitation. They were both aware that for a betrothed couple very much in love, an evening in a house empty of everyone but themselves might constitute too strong a temptation.

He kissed her gently. "Good night, dearest. I will write to you as soon as I reach my uncle's."

When he had closed the door behind him, she not only turned the key in the lock but also shoved the bar into place. She lit the candle standing in its holder beside the lamp, carried it into the side parlor, and kindled a fire in the grate. Then, with a second candle in her hand, she went to the kitchen, assembled bread and cold meat and fruit preserves on a tray, and carried the tray back to a small table in front of the parlor fire.

Despite her brave words to Donald, she was aware as she ate her supper that she did feel lonely. She thought of her mother, lying ill in a bedroom fifteen miles away. She thought of her young brother—a fugitive now, not from the law, but one man's murderous intent—riding through the darkness toward Southampton. How could it be that within a few short months the lives of the Montlows had changed so disastrously?

She realized that her thoughts were veering toward self-pity, and that would not do her or anyone else any good. In the morning she would be in better spirits. If the weather moderated, she would work outside in the garden. There was no chance of digging those dahlia roots, not with the ground frozen hard. But perhaps she could pull up some of those long-withered flower stalks. And certainly she could trim that neglected boxwood.

How silent the world was when you were alone in winter. No insects bumping against the terrace doors, no nightingale singing, and tonight, no breath of wind whispering through bare-branched trees. Even the fire burning in grate no longer snapped, but made only soft, hissing sounds.

She stood up, lifted the tray, and started to turn toward the door into the hall.

From the corner of her eye she saw movement, over there beyond the glass doors to the terrace.

She stood motionless for an instant, heart thudding painfully, and then turned her head. Weak with relief, she realized that what she had seen was her own moving reflection in the glass panes.

She carried the tray back to the kitchen. What was she so afraid of, her in this house, this peaceful countryside, where she had lived without fear all twenty-three years of her existence? Patrick Stanford? He would not be here. Perhaps he was pacing up and down his lodgings somewhere in the city. Perhaps he was in some tavern, trying to drown his frustrated rage. Far more likely, he was galloping along a road leading out of London, hoping to overtake Christopher. But he would not be seeking his quarry on the road to Southampton. He would have of course concluded that Christopher would flee to the nearest port, Dover. It was for precisely that reason that she had arranged for her brother to be taken to much-more-distant Southampton. No, whatever else he might do, Patrick Stanford would not waste his time coming here.

Nevertheless, before she went to bed she made sure that all the downstairs doors to the outside were locked, and all the ground-floor windows latched.

10

The next day dawned cloudy but much milder. Giant icicles hanging from the eaves began to drip, and then crashed to the ground. On the hillsides, rapidly spreading patches of winter-brown grass appeared in the thin snow cover. Early in the afternoon, beside a cedar tree at the foot of the garden, Elizabeth found a harbinger of early spring, a cluster of snowdrops.

Just as she had known she would, she began to enjoy her solitude. It was pleasant to work in the garden with no sense of her mother watching from the house, her face reflecting her discontent that her daughter should be performing tasks proper only to servants. It was pleasant to take meals whenever she chose, and to go to bed as early or as late as she felt sleepy.

On the third morning after her return from London, she still had received no message from Christopher. In a way, that was a good sign. It probably meant that he had gone aboard some ship immediately before sailing, with no time to write and post a letter.

There were letters, though, from both her mother and Donald. Mrs. Montlow was feeling much stronger, she wrote. Dr. Quill had said that she could go home in another week. But in the meantime, she was frantic to learn if there had been any word from Christopher.

Donald's letter included an account of his running argument with his uncle over Berkeley's theory. "The old gentleman still challenges me to refute his argument that I cannot prove the existence of anything outside my own mind. I think he is hoping that I, like Hume, will howl, 'Thus I refute it!' and kick a large stone. But since I know that I would accomplish nothing except to acquire a sore toe, I shall not oblige my uncle.

"I long to see you, and will do so within three or four days after you receive this letter."

Elizabeth wrote her replies, and walked to the village to post them. Because she knew that she had only a few days more in which to enjoy the freedom of utter solitude, she loitered on the way back, stopping to watch white clouds move slowly across the pale blue sky, or to look at swelling buds on a roadside maple tree. When she reached the house, she went into the small library opposite the side parlor and took down *Tristam Shandy* from among her father's books. Glad that she did not have to answer her mother's questions as to whether the book was a suitable one for a young woman, she carried it outside to a sun-warmed bench against the rear wall of the house, and sat reading until almost dusk. After supper she read several more chapters, and then, pleasantly tired, went to bed.

Afterward she never knew at what hour of the night her ordeal began. She only knew that she came awake in the darkness, rigid with the knowledge that she was no longer alone in the room.

The drain, she thought numbly. Someone had climbed up the heavy drainpipe that ran past her window to the gutter along the roof's edge.

Heart hammering now, she called out, "Who's there?"

For several seconds there was silence. Then: "You had best strike a light, Miss Montlow." The voice, cold and deep, was one she had last heard speaking from the witness stand at Old Bailey.

Her icy hands groped on the bedside stand for the flint

box. After several fumbling attempts, she managed to light the candle in its holder. The small flame showed her that he stood, wearing a dark coat and breeches, a few feet inside the open window. If he'd had a cloak and hat, he must have left them on the ground before he began his climb. The candlelight gleamed dully on the leveled pistol in his hand. But the weapon frightened her far less than the cold resolution in his dark face.

She asked, from a dry throat, "What do you want?"

"Christopher Montlow, of course. Where is he?"

"Get out of here! If you don't, I will scream. There is a pistol downstairs. My servant—"

"What servant? You are alone here. I have watched this house for hours today, and seen no one but you."

Watched. He must have been up in that hillside copse, gaze fixed upon her as she sat reading in the afternoon sunlight.

"Now, where is your brother?"

"I don't know."

He ignored that. "In Southampton yesterday morning I learned that seven ships had sailed in the last few days, two merchantmen for Calais, another merchantman for Brussels, and one for the West Indies, and a troopship and two supply ships for the American colonies. On which of those ships did you arrange passage for your brother?"

So he had not reached Southampton until yesterday. That must mean that, as she had hoped, he had gone to Dover first, and vainly searched the docks and inns and grog shops for people who remembered a youth of Christopher's description. But in her fear she could take no satisfaction in the success of her stratagem.

"Which ship did that unspeakable degenerate take, Miss Montlow?"

"I don't know."

"You must have arranged for the carriage in which he

sneaked away. I cannot imagine your mother doing it, or your servant. Or was it Weymouth's doing?"

Donald! This man was quite capable of killing him. But surely he would not kill her, a woman. She said swiftly and truthfully, "I hired the carriage. But I have no idea what ship my brother took."

The dark eyes studied her. "If you are lying, you had best reconsider and tell me where I must go to look for him. Someone is going to pay for murdering my ward. Better that it be him than you."

Her mind tried to tell her that he would not carry out such a threat. But her body, under the thin nightshift, seemed to shrink in upon itself, as if sure that soon a pistol ball would smash through flesh and nerve and bone.

Perhaps, she thought desperately, if she could get out of bed and stand facing him, she would feel less terrified, less at an overwhelming disadvantage. She said, "Please, Sir Patrick. Would you mind turning your back for a few moments?"

"Turn my back, when perhaps you have a pistol or a knife in the drawer of that nightstand? You see, Miss Montlow, I have learned not to underestimate you."

"Then . . . then will you toss my robe to me? It is there on the chair back."

He moved to the chair near the foot of the bed, gathered up the blue woolen robe with his left hand, and threw it to her. Aware that he watched her every movement, she thrust her arms into the robe's sleeves, got out of bed, and knotted the sash around her waist. On legs that trembled, but with a gaze she tried to make direct and calm, she stood facing him.

"I know, Sir Patrick, how you must feel. . . ."

"Do you? Do you know what I felt when I looked down at Anne Reardon in a stinking hospital ward and watched her die? Do you know what I felt as I heard you tell your lies on the witness stand?"

"They were not lies!"

"Stop that!" he said harshly. "It was plain in your face that you lied. It was plain, too, that you realized I knew you were lying. Your brother was nowhere near this house that Wednesday. It was Thursday evening when I saw him sneaking up to a side door from the carriage house, where he'd been hiding. . . . For how long, Miss Montlow? How many hours did it take your brother, after Anne Reardon landed in that areaway, to reach your carriage house?"

Guilt and terror were clouding her mind. Several seconds passed before she thought to say, "If you were watching this place, if you did see Christopher come out of the carriage house, why didn't you tell the court about it?"

"Because even though I am sure it was your brother I saw, I had no proof to offer. Besides, I was sure he would be convicted. It did not occur to me that those mutton-headed jurymen would fail to see that all three of you women were lying. Now, admit that you lied."

Perhaps it was a trick of the candlelight, but it seemed to her that his forefinger had tightened on the trigger. Best to admit she had lied. Perhaps the confession would appease at least some of his fury.

"Very well. Christopher was not here that Wednesday night. But neither was . . . was he at our house in town. He spent that night with a Mrs. Frazier-Fitzsimmons."

"Peggy Frazier-Fitzsimmons? He told you that?"

"She herself did, also."

"I wonder how much he paid her to say it. You see, I know Peggy."

Before she could check herself, she said, "No doubt."

He smiled. "There is one thing I admire about you. Your spirit." His smile vanished. "But if you chose to take that harlot's word, it was only as a sop to your conscience. You knew it was not true."

She remembered the terrible moment on the witness stand when she had become convinced that she had been tricked, and that her brother, standing pale and tense in the dock, had caused an innocent young girl's death. The memory must have shown in her face, because Patrick Stanford said, in a flat voice, "Yes, you know he is guilty. And you know that in shielding him from the death he deserves, you become guilty of that poor girl's murder, too. Now, which ship did he take? And don't tell me again that you don't know."

She stood silent, mind working furiously. If there was some way she could distract his attention, grapple with him for the pistol . . . She could not hope to wrest it from him. But perhaps she could cause it to discharge harmlessly into the floor. And then she would have at least a chance to flee down the hall to the room that had been her father's and lock herself in. There was a brace of pistols hanging on the wall in that room, and powder and shot in a cabinet drawer. . . .

He said, "Which ship, Miss Montlow?"

Giving a slight start, she looked past his shoulder to the window, her eyes widening in an expression of surprised joy.

He turned swiftly to follow the direction of her gaze. Instantly she launched herself at him, and with both hands grasped his right wrist.

For a moment the pistol pointed floorward. Then, seemingly without effort, he tore his wrist from her grasp. Before she could step back from him, his left arm encircled her body and arms and pulled her close against him, fingers biting into her upper arm. Sick with disappointment and heightened fear, she looked up into his face.

He said, "You are full of tricks, aren't you?"

Then, with the pulse beating like a caged wild thing in the hollow of her throat, she saw his face change. He looked down at her for several seconds more before his mouth came down on hers, savage and bruising. His other arm went around her, slanting down across her hips, pressing the entire length of her body tightly to his. She struggled, dimly aware that her movements only excited him the more, and yet frantic to break free.

He released her, so abruptly that she staggered, and stepped back from her. With the pistol leveled at her body, he said in a thickened voice, "Take off that robe and shift."

She stood motionless.

He said, "You will be getting off lightly. At least you will be still alive, not like Anne Reardon."

Still she did not move.

"I can knock you onto the bed, you know, and rip those garments off you. But in that case, I might not be content just to rape you. I might choose to have you found as Anne was found, at the foot of a long drop from a window."

The words "Death before dishonor" flitted grotesquely through Elizabeth's mind. Whoever wrote those words had not been a woman, seeing both death and dishonor looking at her from a man's face, a face flushed with murderous anger as well as lust.

With numb fingers she undid the sash of her robe, then drew the garment from her shoulders and let it fall to the floor. Despite the pounding of her blood in her ears, she tried to think clearly. Best not to add more fuel to his rage. Best to submit completely. That way, it would be over sooner. And that way she might live to see daylight.

She loosened the drawstring at the neck of her night-shift and let the garment slide off her shoulder to the floor. Head drooping, she stood there, feeling his gaze move over her body.

He stepped past her and with one sweep of his arm flung the upper sheet and the eiderdown quilts to the foot of the bed. "Lie down."

Not looking at him, she obeyed. Eyes closed, arms at her sides, she had a sense of waking nightmare. She heard a metallic click, and knew that he had placed the pistol on the bureau. After that, rustling sounds told her that he was undressing.

The mattress gave slightly under his weight. He was sitting on the bed's edge. Don't fight him, she warned herself, don't fight him. Still with her eyes tightly closed, she felt his fingers seize a handful of her hair outspread on the pillow. Not moving, she endured the bruising pressure of his mouth upon hers. But when she felt his naked weight on her breast, felt his legs trying to thrust her legs apart, her body forgot her mind's command to submit. She fought, trying to free her arms to strike him, trying to turn her head so as to sink her teeth into his bare shoulder.

His open hand struck her left cheek, rocking her head on the pillow, making dots of light dance before her eyes.

She stopped struggling. She felt a painful pressure, and then the sharper, rending pain of his brutal thrust inside her body. She gave an anguished cry, and opening her eyes, looked into the dark face close above her own. Then her eyelids closed. Grimly, helplessly, she endured the hard thrust and withdrawal, thrust and withdrawal, until the final one left him lying spent and motionless upon her.

After a few seconds he rolled away, to lie beside her. Blindly she reached down, caught one corner of the upper sheet, and drew it over her.

Silence in the room, except for a sputtering sound as a current of air from the open window bent the candle flame. She opened her eyes. He lay with his brooding face resting on an elbow-propped hand. She closed her eyes and said, before she could stop herself, "Someday I will kill you for this."

"Why? Because, as the saying goes, you are now ruined, unmarriageable?" His tone was mocking. "I am willing to marry you."

A shudder ran down her body.

"After all," he went on, "I could use your twenty thousand pounds."

So he even knew, this Irish devil, the amount of her inheritance. She said dully, "Will you go now? Or do you still believe I know where you can find my brother?"

After a long moment he said, "No, I don't think you are lying about that. Perhaps I am wrong, but I think that if you'd known what ship he had taken, you would have told me, in the hope of preserving . . . What is the phrase for it? Woman's dearest treasure?"

She detected a forced note in his mockery, as if he were trying to hold some emotion, perhaps guilt, at bay. But what good could his guilt do now, she thought bitterly, what good could anything do? She turned over and buried her face in the pillow.

She heard him get out of bed, heard the subdued rustling sounds of his dressing. At last he said, "Is the key in the back door's lock?"

She said, her voice muffled in the pillow, "Yes."

"Then I will go out that way."

She did not speak.

He moved down the dark stairs and along the lower hall to the back door. His hand found the key in the lock, turned it. He closed the door behind him, and under a moonless sky brilliant with stars, walked over to the bench and picked up the hat and cloak he had left there. As yet there was no glow of dawn in the east. When he reached the copse where he had left a roan mare tethered, he looked down at the house in the hollow. Feeble candlelight still shone from the window of her room.

He rode down the country lane to the sleeping village, and then took the wider highroad that led toward London. That thin fellow, Weymouth, who had accompanied

her and her mother to the trial each day. Almost surely
he was the future parson that, according to the drunken
marquis in Harry's Coffee House, Elizabeth Montlow intended to marry.

Well, perhaps they would still marry. She would not be
the first nonvirgin bride in history. And a parson could
use twenty thousand pounds as well as any man.

Anyway, she had deserved what had happened to her,
the lying bitch. She had deserved more than that, after
helping that young monster escape. He tried to keep
thinking of Anne Reardon's unrecognizable face as she
lay dying. He tried to think of Christopher Montlow stepping down from the dock, freed by a jury of Irish-hating
Englishmen.

But another memory kept obtruding itself. A girl with
faintly golden skin and clear gray eyes, smiling up at him
as she said, "I live in the country most of the time. I love
to walk, and to ride. . . ."

Pale light showed along the eastern horizon now. He
urged the mare to a faster trot. To hell with Elizabeth
Montlow. And to hell, at least for the present, with trying
to find her brother. Eventually he would deal with Christopher Montlow. At the moment, all he wanted to do was
to get out of England and cross to that beautiful, tormented island that was his homeland.

Elizabeth had waited several minutes after she heard
the back door downstairs open and close. Then she rose
from the bed and stared numbly down at the sheet,
stained with her own blood. Finally she stripped the sheet
from the bed, dropped it in a heap on the floor, and
moved to the washstand. With cold water from the
pitcher and a sponge, she bathed herself as best she
could. There was a tin-lined bathtub in one corner of her
bedroom. She wished that she could fill it with steaming
water as hot as her body could stand, and then immerse

herself in it. But she had neither the will nor the strength to kindle a fire downstairs, and heat water, and carry it back to this room.

Besides, hot water could not bring her purification, or even the illusion of it. Nothing could.

She looked at her reflection in the mirror above the washstand. Despite the dimness of the candlelight, she could see that her cheek was still reddened from the blow he had given her. Would it look bruised in a few hours? If it did, pray God the bruise would fade before her mother saw her, or Donald.

Donald! Her heart twisted with hopeless grief at the thought of the sensitive, humorous man she loved. She could not marry him now, not without telling him what had happened to her. And she dared not tell him. With that implacable fury that gentle people, once aroused, can display, he would track Patrick Stanford down and kill him.

And that must not happen. Donald, at least, must be saved from the tempest of violence that had battered the Montlows, leaving her brother a fugitive, her mother anxious and ill in London, and herself, no longer virgin, staring at her own shock-widened eyes in the mirror. Donald must live out his life in this peaceful countryside, preaching each Sunday from the pulpit in the village church, and ministering to parishioners who would honor and love him.

Her thoughts veered. That kitten, dangling from its noose. Her father was still alive then. If she had told him about the kitten, would he have dealt with Christopher in a way to keep him from becoming what he had become? Perhaps. Perhaps not.

Suddenly she realized the significance of her thoughts. She no longer had the slightest doubt of Christopher's guilt.

But she would not think of that tonight, or of anything

else. She must try, if she could, to find a few hours' oblivion in sleep. But not in that bed, not even in this room.

She picked up her nightshift and slipped it over her head. Carrying the candle, now burning low in its holder, she went down the hall to her mother's empty room.

11

The next day was ironically bright and springlike. As if in the grip of a bad dream from which she could not awaken, she moved about the garden and the silent house, clearing dead leaves away from around the pale green shoots of early daffodils, removing ashes from fireplace grates, polishing furniture that already shone. With dull thankfulness she had seen that her cheek was not badly bruised. Surely her face would appear quite normal when next she saw her mother and Donald.

Donald. What would become of her and Donald? For the first time she realized what people meant when they spoke of one's thoughts going around like a squirrel in a cage. Her thoughts of Donald were like that. She could not marry him without telling him what had happened to her, and, for his own sake, she dared not tell him that. Therefore, she would not marry him. But what reason could she give him—except the one she dared not tell— for breaking their bethrothal?

Late in the afternoon she found one small bit of comfort. She went into her father's library, with its hundreds of volumes relating to everything from astronomy to zoology. From a top shelf she took down a book, a medical treatise, in a badly worn leather binding, and carried it over to the window. The book had been written early in the last century. The print was fine, the style crabbed, and the involved sentences sprinkled with Latin phrases. Nevertheless, she finally found the sort of passage she was looking for: "Protolinus to the contrary, it be seldom, albeit not unknown, that impregnation results from *coitus primus* of a virgin."

It be seldom. At least there was one thing she would be spared—Protolinus to the contrary. Fleetingly, as she placed the book back on the shelf, she wondered who Protolinus had been.

There was no letter from Christopher that day, or the next, or the next. That must mean that he had not taken a ship bound for some nearby port across the English channel. Instead, he must have sailed on one of the other ships Patrick Stanford had mentioned, a vessel bound for the West Indies or for North America. Sometimes she gave a thought to her brother, picturing him on a storm-tossed vessel in mid-Atlantic, and wondering if he still had some of the money she had given him, or had lost it to thieves, or on a toss of the dice. But most of the time her thoughts had no room except for her own dilemma.

On the fourth night after Patrick Stanford's devastating visit, she sat huddled before the fire in the side parlor, and forced herself to face the fact that there simply was no way out. If her problem was to be solved before the day in late June set for her wedding, someone or something outside herself would do the solving. In the meantime, she would be like a shipwreck survivor on a raft, drifting nearer and nearer jagged rocks, and hoping that some miraculous reversal of the current would save her.

The next morning there was a letter from Donald. His uncle was to celebrate his seventy-fifth birthday in two weeks, and wanted him to stay on until then. She had never dreamed that a time would come when she could

welcome Donald's continued absence. But now his letter
seemed to her like a temporary reprieve.

Early in the afternoon several days later, a carriage
stopped out in the narrow road. With mingled gladness
and anxiety, Elizabeth watched Mary Hawkins get out,
and receive the two portmanteaus the driver handed down
from the box. Then Mrs. Montlow got out of the carriage,
and both women moved toward the house. Afraid of what
her mother might read in her face, she stretched her lips
into a bright smile before she opened the door.

She need not have worried. Mrs. Montlow was too
taken up with thoughts of her son to search her daughter's face. As soon as she was inside the door, she asked,
"Has there been word from Christopher?"

"Not yet."

"Where *is* the child?" With distracted fingers she untied
the ribbon bow beneath her chin and handed her bonnet
to Hawkins. "He's dead. I know he's dead!"

"Mother! Unless he went to France or the Netherlands,
it is far too early for us to hear from him. It would take
him weeks to get to America or the West Indies, and
weeks more for his letter to reach us."

After a moment Mrs. Montlow said, "I suppose that is
true. And I suppose," she went on broodingly, "that the
poor child has tried to get as far away as possible from
that black-hearted devil."

Elizabeth said in a strained voice, "Do you want to go
upstairs, Mother? Or would you like me to bring you
some tea in the side parlor? No, no, Hawkins. I can attend to it. The water is already on the boil."

As the spring advanced, sunlight alternated with gentle
showers. The daffodil shoots surrounding a maple's huge
trunk in the garden unfurled their first blooms, and on the
tree itself fat buds along the branches waved like strings
of coral beads against the tender blue sky. Elizabeth tried

to find some of her usual delight in greening grass, and drift of cloud across a spring sky, and song spilling down from larks that circled above newly planted fields. But she found taking joy in the earth's renewal difficult. And before long it became impossible, because a new fear haunted all her waking hours.

She tried to tell herself the fear was absurd. The strain of the past few months had been enough to upset any woman, not only in mind and spirit, but in bodily functions. Besides, there was the reassuring phrase in that tattered old book. . . .

On a Saturday afternoon, unable to find more household or garden tasks to occupy her, she began to walk along the road to the village. She was about a third of the way there when she saw, with joy and terror, that Donald was walking toward her. He called her name, and quickened his pace. When they reached each other, his smiling gaze went over her face. Then he took her in his arms. "Oh, my dearest, how I have missed you!"

"And I have missed you," Elizabeth said, and then, to her dismay, burst into tears.

His arms tightened around her. "Elizabeth, Elizabeth. I should not have stayed away so long."

She said, between sobs, "It's just . . . just that everything . . . has been so . . ."

"I know. Even though you were my brave girl all during the trial, I know it must have been a terrible strain for you."

With his handkerchief he dried the tears from her face, and then kissed the lips that were trying to smile. Hands clasped, they moved back down the road toward the Hedges.

"Have you heard from Christopher?"

"Not yet."

"Then no wonder you are so distressed! But try not to worry, my darling. Wherever he is, he is all right."

"Yes," Elizabeth said.

12

Misty Paris sunlight, filtering through the lace curtains at the long windows of the Left Bank house, struck highlights from Madame Yvette Cordot's auburn hair. She sat at the dressing table in her boudoir, wearing a yellow silk peignoir, and smoothing powder on a face that had the relaxed, dreamy look of a woman newly risen from a bed shared with a lover.

Half-reclining on a gold brocade chaise longue, Christopher watched her from narrowed eyes. He would have to come to some new arrangement with her, and right away. His money was running low.

With a favoring wind, the ship he had boarded at Southampton more than a month ago had crossed the channel in about twelve hours. In Calais the next morning he had taken the post chaise to Paris, and found cheap lodgings on one of the narrow streets east of the Grand-Châtelet prison.

He had met Yvette his second day in Paris. After crossing the Seine to a theater on the city's Left Bank, he had bought a ticket for an afternoon performance of Moliére's *Tartuffe*. He already knew the play, and he had thought that his knowledge of French, acquired from a tutor even before he went to Oxford, would be adequate. But all the actors delivered their lines rapidly, and some of them spoke in a patois unintelligible to him. He was about to leave in disgust when he noticed the woman seated across the aisle, with a vacant seat beside her.

She was richly dressed in a dark blue velvet gown and plumed, matching hat. She was not too young—thirty or a bit past. And she looked lonely. Christopher settled back in his seat.

At the end of the performance, watching her from the corner of his eye, he managed to move out in the aisle just in time to collide with her. He caught her arm as if to steady her.

"Oh, madame! Are you hurt? Forgive my clumsiness."

She looked up into a face so handsome it was almost beautiful. "It is all right, monsieur."

"But I am sure I trod on your foot."

"A little. It does not hurt."

He looked earnestly down into her face. Although her nose was a trifle too long, it was a reasonably attractive face, set with large and vulnerable-looking brown eyes. He said, "But you must allow me to make amends. Allow me to at least see you to your carriage."

She allowed him. In the bronze-colored light of late afternoon they waited until her carriage, one of a dozen or so moving along the edges of a cobblestoned square, stopped in front of them. A footman as well as a coachman, both in scarlet livery, sat on the box. Before the footman could descend, Christopher opened the carriage door for her.

She said from the carriage window, "Thank you, monsieur."

He smiled. "The pleasure and the privilege were mine—all too briefly enjoyed, I might add."

She looked at the melancholy ardor in the deep blue eyes. "Can I take you to your destination, monsieur?"

"Oh, madame! My lodgings are on the other side of the river. I could not dream of imposing, of taking up your time. . . ."

"Nonsense. Get in. For a widow, having one's time taken up is never an imposition."

As they crossed a bridge over the Seine, where Notre-Dame on its isle rode the sunset-streaked water like a giant ship, they exchanged names, and she began to tell him a little about herself. Her late husband, a man many years her senior, had left his business to her. "It is a store, Monsieur Montlow, near St.-Germain-des-Prés. I do not think you have stores like that in London. It is not just one shop, but many shops, all under one ownership, and under one roof. Some departments sell hats, others dress materials, others household articles, and so on."

A store. He had already guessed that she belonged to the French middle class rather than the aristocracy. Well, so much the better.

"And you, Monsieur Montlow? How is it that you, an Englishman and so young, are alone in Paris?"

"Madame Cordot, I do not want to weary you with my troubles."

"Please! Tell me."

"Very well. My mother is dead. My father recently remarried. My stepmother does not like me, and in some way I cannot understand, has poisoned my father's mind against me. He told me that he could no longer pay my expenses at Oxford. He gave me a small sum of money and told me that before it was gone I would have to find some means of supporting myself until I am twenty-one. An inheritance from my grandmother will be turned over to me then.

"I suppose I should have gone to London, rather than spending money on passage to France. But I was so desperately unhappy that I wanted to get out of England for a while."

"Of course you did!" She was silent for a few moments as the carriage rolled along a narrow, winding street. "Tell me, is your stepmother younger than your father?"

"Yes, about half his age."

So! Her guess had been right. Surely it was not the

stepmother, but the father himself who had decided that the poor boy must be turned out. What man, newly married to a woman half his age, would want his superlatively handsome son around?

As the carriage moved through the warren of streets near the Grand-Châtelet prison, Christopher said, "Please tell the coachman to stop just beyond that lamp."

The carriage halted at the foot of an alley, scarcely five feet wide, which sloped upward between two rows of moldering houses. Lines of laundry fluttered between the houses, and ragged children played on doorsteps.

She said, shocked, "You live here?"

"In a room on the top story of the third house." He smiled. "I am poor, madame, but not so poor that I cannot buy you coffee tomorrow, if you will permit me to."

The next afternoon he bought her coffee at a small Left Bank Café and then accompanied her to her store, Cordot's Emporium. Impressed, he looked at the customers crowding the aisle between counters laden with silks from the Orient, fine porcelain from Limoges, English silver, and laces from Brussels. Later she took him to her three-story house near the Sorbonne for what she called tea "á l'anglaise."

However love-starved, Yvette was basically a conventional woman. He was a guest in her house two more times before he managed to maneuver her past her scruples and into her bedroom. Since then they had spent hours together each day. She had paid for their restaurant meals and their visits to the theater. But she had not offered to pay for his room in that slum, let alone for better lodgings. And his money was disappearing rapidly. Soon he would have scarcely enough for his return passage to England.

And he did not want to return to England, not just yet, not even if he learned he could return in safety. The chances were excellent that Oxford, after the notoriety of his trial, would refuse to readmit him. Geoffrey and his other friends who had been with him in the Kingman Street house that night would avoid him. Aware that they themselves might have stood in the dock at Old Bailey, they would shrink from the companionship of someone who actually had.

And besides, even if that Irishman with murder in his eyes had gone back to his miserable island by now, there was no reason why he could not return to England. Better to keep well out of his way for at least a year. By then even an Irish lust for vengeance might subside.

No, Yvette must be more generous. Otherwise he could not go on wasting his time with her.

He rose and crossed to the dressing table. He put his arms around her, cupped her breasts beneath the thin yellow silk in his hands, and rested his chin on the crown of her auburn hair. They smiled at each other in the mirror.

Then he said, his smile dying, "Yvette, when I think of having to get along without you . . ."

"Without me!" Breaking his embrace, she turned around on the brocaded stool. "What are you talking about?"

"A letter from my father came today. He has relented. I can go home. I did not want to tell you . . . earlier. I wanted us to have this one last time together. . . ."

"But, Christopher! You do not want to leave me. Tell me you do not!"

"Of course I want to stay here in Paris with you. But how can I? My money is almost gone. And where in France can an Englishman find employment? What can I do but go home?"

She was silent for a long moment. Infatuated as she was, she still realized that she would become a laughing-stock if she married him. But perhaps something short of that . . .

She said, "You can live here." Never mind that her

friends would still laugh. In the case of some of them, there would be envy behind the laughter.

"Live here? With you, in this house? Oh, Yvette, my darling Yvette!" He caught her hand and held it to his cheek.

"And you need not worry about employment, my darling boy. I will speak to Monsieur Durand." Marcel Durand managed Cordot's Emporium for her. "He will give you employment."

That was the middle class for you, Christopher thought coldly. She would not allow him just to live here. She wanted to put him to work.

"What sort of employment?"

She laughed. "Don't look like that, my dear one. Did you think I planned to have you stand behind a counter? Monsieur Durand will make you his assistant. Didn't you say that you did excellently in mathematics at Oxford? Well, I will tell him that you are to handle the accounts."

The accounts. With his two hands he tilted her face upward and kissed her on the lips.

13

At the Hedges, the maple tree unfurled its first tender green leaves. The daffodils planted at its base gave way to scarlet tulips and deep blue dwarf iris. Swallows returned, soaring and diving through the bright sunlight, and began to build a nest under the carriage-house eaves.

Elizabeth moved, busy and silent, through the glorious spring, now dreading Donald's almost daily visits. At first he made anxious inquiries about the circles under her eyes, and her abstracted air. She was all right, she would protest. It was just that she was not sleeping too well. Perhaps she was still feeling the aftereffects of the trial. Finally he stopped questioning her. But often she was aware of a look in his hazel eyes—puzzled, worried, a little hurt—that sent an almost physical pain through her heart.

One morning in early April she descended the stairs, feather duster in hand, and started back along the hall to the kitchen. Her mother hailed her joyfully from the side parlor. "Elizabeth! We have a letter from Christopher!"

When Elizabeth came into the room and stretched out her hand, Mrs. Montlow said, "No, no! Sit down. I'll read it to you.

"It is from Paris," she went on. He starts out, 'Dearest Mama and Liza,' and then he says, 'Forgive me for my silence. I did not want to write until I had good news for you.' "

Mrs. Montlow looked up from the page, beaming. "You see? The poor foolish boy didn't realize that we would be less worried by bad news than by no news at all." She resumed her reading:

I have employment, Mama, really excellent employment. It happened like this. I was wandering along the Seine one day, missing you and Liza dreadfully, and yet afraid to come home, and so wondering what I should do next. As I was looking at a river barge, a middle-aged couple, a Mr. and Mrs. Yves Cordot, stopped beside me, and we fell into conversation. They asked me to have an ice with them at a café near Luxembourg Palace. There Mr. Cordot told me that he owned Cordot's Emporium, of which you maybe have heard.

He seemed to like me, Mama. Anyway, I called

upon him the next day at the emporium, as he had asked me to do, and he offered me employment. I help with the accounts, and soon may be in full charge of them.

Now, I can just hear you, Mama. What a disgrace, you are saying. A Montlow, in trade! But perhaps, dearest Mama, people of our class take a false view of life. There is nothing wrong with honest employment. I think Liza will agree with me. Think of how hard she works in the garden and in the house. And think of how proud we are of her, and how grateful to her!

As for my education, I can continue it myself, in the evening hours. True, books are expensive, but not so expensive as attending Oxford!

For a few months I must repay Mr. Cordot's kindness with as much diligence as possible. But after that, if you and Liza think it is safe, I would like to pay you a visit.

I remain,

                    Your affectionate son and brother,

                                        Christopher.

Mrs. Montlow looked up, blue eyes shining. "How earnest he sounds, how mature! Perhaps the terrible ordeal he suffered has been good for him, after all. And just think of the proud, loving things he says about you!"

"Yes, that was kind of him. And it is wonderful to know he is all right. Will you excuse me now, Mother? I still have things to do."

She went back to the kitchen, where Mary Hawkins was shelling green peas, and hung the feather duster on its hook on the wall. Then she went out the back door, picked up a rectangle of old carpeting from the bench against the house's rear wall, and carried it down to the maple tree. Kneeling on the carpet, she began to pull up the small weeds sprouting among the iris and tulips.

She had heard of Cordot's Emporium. Probably her brother had been given employment there. But Elizabeth doubted the sex of his benefactor. Christopher's ways, however winning, were not such as to recommend him as an employee to a hardheaded merchant.

The flowerbed looked clean now. She stood up.

Nausea in the pit of her stomach. A gray mist closing in on her, turning black, engulfing her.

She opened her eyes, to find herself lying on the ground. Mary Hawkins was beside her, cradling her shoulder and head with one arm, holding a glass of water in her other hand.

Elizabeth said, "I fainted?"

"Yes, miss. I saw you from the kitchen window. Drink this."

Elizabeth took a sip of water. So she had fainted. She had been fifteen when she found one of the housemaids, Ellen, crumpled in a faint on the scullery floor. Weeks later the girl had been sent home in disgrace to her family's tumbledown farmhouse a few miles the other side of Parnley. Sometimes Elizabeth had caught a glimpse of Ellen, scrubbing the front steps of some village householder or carrying water from the farmhouse well with her bastard child, a girl, walking beside her.

Hawkins said, "Best to get in the house before your mother sees you. Do you think you can walk?"

"Yes."

As she moved toward the kitchen door with Hawkins' hand supporting her elbow, the older woman said, "You have been overburdened, Miss Elizabeth. All that trouble over Mr. Christopher. And now, planning for your marriage. It is to be in late June, isn't it?"

"Yes."

"If you will forgive my saying so, miss, I wish it were

sooner. I don't believe in long betrothals. They are a strain on everyone concerned."

Elizabeth darted a side glance at the woman. Did she suspect? It was impossible to tell from her face. But if she did suspect, plainly she thought that the child was Donald Weymouth's, conceived when she and Donald, sometime during Mrs. Montlow's stay at Aunt Sara's house, had succumbed to temptation.

Would that we had, Elizabeth thought bitterly. Would that the child she carried was Donald's. But as it was . . . Again she had a vision of how Donald would look if he ever learned how Patrick Stanford had treated her. All the gentleness and humor draining from that beloved face, and in its stead a cold, implacable fury.

In the kitchen, Elizabeth said, "I had best go upstairs and lie down."

Hawkins nodded. "You do that, miss."

Elizabeth moved down the hall toward the open door of the side parlor and the closed door of the library opposite. "It be seldom, albeit not unknown . . ." that old book of her father's had said. Why had she taken so much comfort from the first phrase that she had ignored the second?

Her mother, absorbed in perhaps the fifth rereading of her son's letter, did not look up as Elizabeth passed the doorway. She went on up the stairs to her room, closed the door, and then stood at the south window, staring blindly at a green hill now dotted with golden dandelions.

There were at least two alternatives open to her. In the back streets of London, she had heard, there were women who, for a fee, would end an unwanted pregnancy. The thought of seeking out such a woman sent a shudder through Elizabeth. It was not just moral scruples, nor the fact that women so aborted sometimes died. Even in her misery and terror, she felt a certain responsibility toward the new life within her. However conceived, the child was *her* child.

She could cross the channel upon some pretext or another—to visit Christopher?—and prolong her stay in Amsterdam or Brussels or some other city until her child was born. Then she could promise some woman a quarterly sum to raise the child as her own. But what excuse could she give her frail mother, already deprived of a son, for her own absence of many months? How could she prevent Donald from following her and learning the truth?

And how would she feel in the years ahead, making excuses to cross the channel for furtive visits to her child, and in the long stretches between visits, wondering how the child fared?

She grew very still. Perhaps there was a third alternative.

Patrick Stanford, lying beside her on that bed over there, and saying, "I am willing to marry you. After all, I could use your twenty thousand pounds."

Had he just been mocking her? Undoubtedly. But still, if she wrote to him . . .

Because of what had happened in this room, she could never feel anything for him but loathing. And yet, justice compelled her to acknowledge that he had not been without provocation. Nor was he an entirely evil man. There had been real grief behind the savagery in his voice when he spoke of his ward dying before his eyes. A truly heartless man would not have felt that grief.

And even if her own plight struck no compassionate chord within him, there was still her twenty thousand pounds. The thought was matter-of-fact. In her extremity, irony was an emotional luxury she could not afford.

Surely she had another two months before her condition became apparent to everyone. Her letter would take about a week to reach him, and his answer another week

to reach her. If she received a negative reply, or none at
all, she would still have time to decide between the crone
in the London back street and the lonely months posing
as a pregnant young widow in Brussels or Amsterdam.

What was his address? She recalled him on the witness
stand, his face a cold mask as he said, "I am Sir Patrick
Stanford, baronet, of Stanford Hall, near Cork, Ireland."

She crossed to the small mahogany desk in one corner,
sat down, and took letter paper from the desk drawer.
With the quill pen in her hand she sat, motionless, sickened and terrified by a memory. His body, weighing her
down there on that bed across the room.

But that had been an act of revenge and hatred rather
than desire. Surely a man like Patrick Stanford had no
lack of willing bed partners. Perhaps all she had to do
was to make it clear . . .

She drew the sheet of paper toward her and began to
write.

14

As long as Patrick Stanford could remember, the servants at Stanford Hall had displayed a cheerful non-
chalance toward black beetles in the scullery, lamps in
need of trimming, and dust on chandeliers of Waterford
glass. Patrick was quite used to it. As he sat in the big library, Elizabeth Montlow's letter in his hand, he was not
aware that books leaned every which way on the shelves,
that the ashes of a fire kindled ten days earlier still lay in
the grate, and that there were smears on the windowpane

through which he gazed somberly at a distant line of green hills.

He looked down at the letter and began to reread it. It was as stark and forthright as any business communication, holding none of the terror and desperation that must have caused her to appeal to him, her despoiler. She had written:

My dear Sir Patrick,

I find I am with child.

At our last meeting, you described yourself as willing to marry me. Even though I realize that you did not mean it at the time, I am writing now in the hope that you would be willing to contract such a relationship.

As you apparently know, my inheritance consists of approximately twenty thousand pounds. It would of course pass to your control upon our marriage, although I hope you would make some small provision for my mother.

I am sure you realize that what I propose would be a marriage of form, not fact. Accordingly, I would make no objection to any other relationship you might choose to enjoy.

It was only in the last two sentences that she had given him a glimpse of her desperation:

If we do not marry, I must very soon decide upon some other course of action. Therefore I would appreciate an early reply.

She had signed herself, "Your obedient servant, Elizabeth Montlow."

He found his breathing restricted, as if a band had tightened around his chest. A child. His child.

Whenever a twinge of regret had struck him these past weeks, he had conjured up justifying memories. Little Anne's dying face. Elizabeth Montlow, telling her lies on the witness stand. Christopher Montlow, stepping down from the dock. That carriage, the one his sister had arranged for, rattling away down the alley behind Old Bailey, with a vicious and unpunished young murderer inside it.

Such defenses failed him now. All his mind's eye could see was Elizabeth. Elizabeth standing stripped before him, head drooping like that of a stricken doe. Elizabeth when he had left her, her face hidden in the pillow.

Somehow, more poignant than either of those memories was one of a year earlier. Elizabeth at that ball in London. An Elizabeth who had impressed him as charming but not coy, self-assured but not vain, looking up at him as she said, "Should I go about swathed in veils ten months of the year . . . ?"

Would she ever be like that again, or had that Elizabeth died forever that night in her bedroom?

He crossed to the massive table in the center of the big room, and after a certain amount of rummaging, found a leather box of letter paper engraved with the Stanford crest. He drew up a chair, and then sat motionless for a while. How to frame his answer?

In such a relationship as theirs, begun in hatred and violence, there could never be mutual goodwill, let alone warmth. The best that could be hoped for would be formal courtesy. Undoubtedly it was that realization that had caused her to write in such stiff, businesslike terms. It would be best if his answer was couched in the same manner. He wrote:

My dear Miss Montlow,
 I am in receipt of your letter.
 Tomorrow I shall book the earliest possible pas-

sage for England. In the meantime, I hereby ask you
to do me the honor of becoming my wife.

Since it would be best for us to marry as soon as
possible, perhaps you will make preliminary arrangements as to posting of the banns, et cetera. Your letter did not mention the possibility of religious
barriers, and so perhaps I should tell you that there
are none. My father, although born a Catholic,
renounced his faith and became a member of the
Church of England, in order to avoid the disabilities
which English law decrees for Catholics in Ireland.

As for your mother, I shall accede to your wishes
that proper provision be made for her.

I remain,

Your obedient servant,
Patrick Stanford

After further rummaging, he found sealing wax and a
stamp incised with the Stanford crest. He folded the letter
and addressed and sealed it. For a few moments he sat
motionless. Then he shoved back his chair and went out
into the vast, shadowy hall. Twin staircases of oak, built
in massive Tudor style, curved upward to a balcony that
ran along three sides of the hall. He walked back beyond
the left-hand staircase to an open doorway.

Inside the room, a much smaller one than the library,
his illegitimate half-brother, Colin, looked up smilingly
from a ledger outspread on a desk. At thirty-five, Colin
was three years older than Patrick, and yet his dark-eyed
face looked younger than his brother's.

Perhaps it was because he had always lived more quietly. He had never been to London, nor did he have any
desire to go there. The management of his brother's estate
and of his own much smaller one ten miles away filled
most of his life.

Colin's smile wavered and then died. "What is it?"

Patrick walked over to a casement window, open on this fine day, and looked out at the rear courtyard and the line of stables beyond. A stableboy of about fourteen was leading two rangy black Irish hunters across the cobblestones, lest their muscles stiffen after their brisk morning exercise.

Patrick turned back into the room. "I am to be married."

Colin had turned around from his desk. He said, once more smiling, "So she finally caught you."

"If you are thinking of Moira Ashley, you are mistaken. It is not Moira that I intend to marry."

"Who, then?"

"Her name is Elizabeth Montlow."

After a long moment Colin said incredulously, "Montlow! The sister of that Christopher Montlow, who—"

"Yes."

Fine dark eyes fixed on his brother's face, Colin said nothing. Patrick began to pace up and down. "I went to the Montlows' country house to try to find where that scurvy young monster had gone. So much I told you. What I did not tell you was that his sister was alone there. Apparently Mrs. Montlow and the servant had remained in London. Anyway, Elizabeth Montlow is now carrying a child, my child."

Colin stared at him, stunned. "You mean that she, knowing how you hated her brother, nevertheless . . ." He broke off, and then added, "Patrick, I must say this. With a woman like that, how can you be sure the child is yours?"

Patrick stopped his pacing. "Because she is not like that! It did not happen like that! I was angry," he went on, almost incoherently. "She had lied under oath. She had tricked me, spirited her brother away from me before I knew what was happening. And that night, she was up to more tricks. She distracted my attention, tried to get hold of the pistol . . ." He stopped speaking, his face flushed.

Colin said into the silence, "I begin to see. You took your revenge. You forced her. And now she is to have a child."

Patrick blazed, "I'll have none of your damned preaching!"

"I don't intend to preach. I merely want you to know that I understand what happened."

"All that needs understanding is that I am sailing for England, tomorrow if possible, and that I will be back in about three weeks with a wife." He paused. "Forgive me, Colin. I did not mean to rail at you."

"There is no reason to ask my pardon. I can imagine how upsetting it must be for a bachelor to learn, at ten o'clock on a sunshiny morning . . . Besides, there is Moira. She will be disturbed indeed. These past weeks I have been sure you intended to marry her. Perhaps the has been sure, too."

"I know, I know," Patrick said distractedly. He gave a strained smile. "Why don't you marry her?"

"You think she would have me, with nothing but Edgewood to offer her?" Edgewood was the small estate that their father, the third baronet, had left to Colin. "Besides, it has always been you she fancied, not me."

He closed the ledger and crossed the room to place it among a number of similar volumes on a shelf. It became apparent then that there was another reason why Lady Moira, a woman fond of riding and dancing, had never "fancied" Colin. He walked with a distinct limp.

Patrick was used to his brother's limp. But this morning, already none too pleased with himself, he felt a stab of guilt at sight of that uneven gait, almost as if Colin's accident had happened yesterday. In fact, it had happened when Patrick was eleven and his brother fourteen. Proud that he was the better horseman, even though Colin was older and at that time taller, he had challenged his brother to put his mount over a four-foot-high stone wall. Patrick's horse had taken the jump cleanly, but Colin's had balked. Thrown from the saddle, Colin had suffered multiple breaks in his right leg. The bone, knitting improperly, had left him with one leg two inches shorter than the other.

Patrick said, "I hope you will not let my marriage make any difference to you. Don't go to Edgewood. Let your steward go on running it. I need you here."

"I know you do." Away much of the time, and even when at home taken up with other matters—matters that Colin was sure would bring disaster someday—Patrick left most of the details of estate management to his brother.

"Besides," Colin went on, "I have always known that sooner or later you would bring a bride here. I never had any intention of leaving when that time came."

Patrick smiled. "Not even to take a bride of your own to Edgewood?"

"You and I have been over that several times. I am quite content with Catherine." Catherine Ryan, a schoolmaster's widow, with two almost grown sons, lived in the coastal village of Haleworth, eight miles away. For the past nine years, Colin had been a regular visitor to her neat cottage. By now their relationship was as placid and comfortable as that of any long-married couple.

Limping over to a liquor cabinet, he brought out a bottle of brandy and two glasses. "I think we should drink a toast to the child," he said, handing a filled glass to Patrick.

Patrick said, "To the child," and drank.

"To the child," Colin echoed. "May he be a fine son."

15

As she descended the stairs, Elizabeth could feel the smoothness of the folded piece of notepaper she had thrust down the bosom of her dress. Since Hawkins had brought the letter up to her half an hour before, she had been standing at the window of her room rehearsing what she must say to her mother.

The door to the large, seldom-used main parlor was open. Mrs. Montlow stood inside, lips pursed as she sat looking at a pair of blue brocade window hangings. Elizabeth said from the doorway, "May I speak to you for a moment in the side parlor?"

Mrs. Montlow looked annoyed. "I am busy, Elizabeth. Can't you talk to me here?"

"Please, Mother." Elizabeth felt it would be easier to tell her in the familiar side parlor than in this stiffly formal room.

"Oh, very well." She moved past Elizabeth and led the way down the hall. When she had sat down in the armchair she usually occupied, she looked up at her daughter, standing before her. "Now, what is it?"

"I am to be married."

"Of course you are to be married! Why do you think I was inspecting the parlor hangings? They must be replaced before the wedding party, Elizabeth. We can make new ones ourselves, if you insist. There is still plenty of time between now and June."

"I shall be married as soon as possible, not in June.

And not to Donald. I am going to marry Sir Patrick Stanford."

Her mother stared at her blankly. "It is not like you to make a jest about an important matter," she said finally, "especially a jest in such bad taste. But then, you have not been yourself lately."

"Mother, it is not a jest. This morning I received a letter from Sir Patrick, asking me to marry him. By now he must be on his way here. I . . . I am asking you to arrange for the first reading of the banns at tomorrow morning's church service."

After a long moment, Mrs. Montlow said slowly, "What you have told me makes no sense whatever. That man, out of all the men in the world. I cannot believe he has even written you such a letter, let alone that you would accept his proposal. Why, you have never even exchanged a word with him."

"But I have. I met him at a ball at Lord and Lady Armitage's, winter before last. You weren't feeling well enough to attend, remember? And then after . . . after the trial, he came here."

Mrs. Montlow clutched the arms of her chair. "Here? To the Hedges? Why?"

"He wanted to know what ship Christopher had taken. I told him I didn't know."

"He was here with you while you were alone in the house?"

"Yes."

Mrs. Montlow's eyes, wide with alarm now, swept her daughter's slim figure. "Elizabeth! Could it be that you have done something . . . dishonorable?"

Yes, Elizabeth wanted to say, I perjured myself. Instead she said, "Mother, are you sure you want to know what happened in this house while you were in London?"

They looked at each other. After a moment, Elizabeth saw the dawn of horrified comprehension in her mother's eyes. Mrs. Montlow's lips moved. "That devil. That black-hearted devil. No!" she cried. "I don't want you to tell me about it."

She leaned back in her chair, her breathing ragged. Swiftly Elizabeth turned toward the cabinet that held the smelling salts. "No, I am all right," Mrs. Montlow managed to say. At least, she was thinking, the man was willing to marry Elizabeth. And Christopher would be safe. Surely not even that Irish devil would hunt down his own brother-in-law.

Elizabeth said, "Then you will see to the posting of the banns?"

"Yes," Mrs. Montlow whispered. "Yes, my darling girl."

"And will you do one thing more for me, a . . . a very difficult thing? Donald will be here very shortly. I cannot, I simply cannot . . ." Her voice broke. She waited a moment, and then went on, "Will you tell him that Sir Patrick has proposed to me, and that I have decided to accept? Just that, nothing more. Once you have told him that, I will come down and say good . . . I will come down and speak to him."

"Yes, I will tell him." She, who had always looked younger than her age, now looked years older. "Elizabeth, perhaps I have not been a good mother to you. Always I have been too much taken up with Christopher."

"Nothing that has happened has been your fault, Mother."

Mrs. Montlow went on, as if Elizabeth had not spoken, "But my son seemed to need more of my attention than my strong, sensible daughter. It never meant I loved you less." Even as she spoke, she realized, guiltily and helplessly, that that was not true. Always it was her handsome, wayward son who had held first place in her heart.

Elizabeth glanced at the mantel clock. "Please, Mother,

please don't cry. I know you love me. But right now I must get upstairs. I am afraid that Donald . . ."

"I know." Mrs. Montlow took a handkerchief from inside the lacy cuff of her dress and dried her eyes. She said, shoulders straightening, "Go on upstairs. I will tell him."

About ten minues later, standing rigidly at the window of her room, Elizabeth heard the front-door knocker strike, and then Donald's footsteps going along the lower hall. Not more than another ten minutes passed, although it seemed to Elizabeth an eternity, before Mary Hawkins said from the open doorway, "Miss Liza."

Hawkins had stopped calling her that when she was fourteen. Elizabeth turned around. The older woman's face, filled with pity and sorrow, told her that her mother had already broken the news to Hawkins.

"Mr. Weymouth is alone in the side parlor now, miss."

"Thank you, Hawkins."

On legs that felt wooden, she moved down the stairs and back along the hallway to the side parlor. Donald stood in front of the unlighted fireplace. His face was as white as if he had bled from some actual although invisible wound. But at least such a wound would not kill him, Elizabeth told herself desperately. Donald would live, and assume the spiritual leadership of this parish, and eventually marry some gentle, loving woman.

He said, "Your mother tells me that while I was in Bath, you formed . . . formed another attachment. . . ."

"Yes."

Something died out of his eyes, perhaps a faint hope that Mrs. Montlow had been mistaken. "I suppose that is why you have been so strange ever since I returned. You were afraid to tell me."

"Yes."

"It is impossible for me to comprehend, of course. I

could not imagine my own affections . . . But I know such things happen."

He stopped. Throat closed, Elizabeth found herself unable to speak.

"Sir Patrick is a handsome man," he went on, "and a baronet." His lips stretched into a parody of a smile. "Compared to him, a country parson is scarcely a dashing figure."

She cried, "Don't say things like that."

"I don't say it to reproach you. It is just that I am trying very hard to understand."

Pray God, Elizabeth thought, that you never do.

He said, "You will go to Ireland to live, I suppose."

"I suppose."

In the ensuing silence, the ticking of the mantel clock sounded very loud. At last he said, "Then there is nothing left to say, except to wish you . . ." Apparently he could not even say that, because he broke off and walked past her, not touching her, to the doorway. There he turned.

"Elizabeth, if you ever need me / at any time, and for any reason whatsoever . . ."

She dared not look at him, lest her self-control break entirely and she run sobbing into his arms. Back turned to him, she said, "I know."

Standing, motionless, she listened, for what she knew was the last time, to his footsteps moving away down the hall.

16

The Stanford carriage, drawn by two perfectly matched grays, moved briskly along Ireland's southeastern coast. Sometimes, when the road dipped into a valley, the blue waters of the Irish channel, breaking into foam on a pebbly beach, were very close. Other times, the sea was far below, its waves invisible. Now and then, as the curving road approached a headland, Elizabeth caught a glimpse of heavy seas foaming high against a cliff.

The carriage and its driver, Michael, a stocky, cheerful man of forty-odd, had been waiting when the ship docked at Waterford. He had said, "Welcome to Ireland, Lady Stanford, and may you find every happiness." Then, to Elizabeth's astonishment, he had added with a wink, "And congratulations to you, Sir Patrick," and clapped his employer on the shoulder.

The channel crossing had been rough. Elizabeth had not minded. In fact, having to fight down nausea had distracted her somewhat from memories of the recent past, especially the memory of Donald's white, set face when she and Patrick had turned away from the altar in the crowded village church. Donald had joined the line of those congratulating the newly married pair as they stood at the church door. But apparently he had been unable to bring himself to attend the reception at the Hedges afterward.

That ghastly reception. Mrs. Montlow had moved among her guests with her head held high, trying to look

120

as if her daughter's choice of a husband was a fulfillment
of her own most cherished dreams. The guests themselves, lifelong friends and neighbors, gathered in subdued
little groups, exchanging the conventional pleasantries,
but with faces that reflected their puzzled wonder. They
all knew that Christopher Montlow had fled within
minutes after his acquittal, and that it must have been because he feared the tall Irishman who now moved about
this room, looking coolly self-assured in his wedding fin-
ery of bottle-green velvet. How could it be that Elizabeth
Montlow had jilted Donald Weymouth, a man they all
loved and honored, in order to marry a man the
Montlows had every reason to fear and dislike?

Much as it pained her to leave the home that had been
hers all her life, Elizabeth was actually glad when it was
time to go upstairs, and with Hawkins' help, change from
her white satin wedding gown to a traveling costume of
brown rep.

The road turned inland, past fields where men and
women and even small children weeded on hands and
knees between rows of blossoming potatoes. Stone walls
marked the divisions between the fields. Sometimes, Elizabeth noted, the widths of the fields were scarcely a
hundred yards. A few of the people working between the
potato rows looked up with sullen faces as the coach
passed. A man of about thirty, leading a scrawny cow
along the road, looked equally sullen as he drew the animal aside to make way for the coach. So did a woman,
hanging out clothes in the grassless yard of a tumbledown
thatched cottage.

For the first time in perhaps half an hour, Elizabeth
spoke. "These people look so thin."

"A not unnatural consequence," Patrick said, "of not
having enough to eat."

She threw him a startled look. She had expected that
he, a landowner, would react defensively to her remark.

Was he so hardened to the wretched state of the Irish peasantry that he felt no need of a defense? She asked, "Are these your lands?"

"No, not yet."

The fields gave way to uncultivated land. Perhaps the numerous gray boulders thrusting up through the long wild grass explained why the earth had not been plowed. Soon after they had passed a lake—small and intensely blue, with a wooded islet in its center—clouds blotted out the sun, and gentle rain pattered on the coach roof. The shower was brief. When it had passed, Elizabeth saw the jaggedly broken towers of a ruined castle on a hilltop. Above it in the now clear sky hung an iridescent fragment of a rainbow.

Patrick said, his gaze following hers, "The Normans built that castle. Essex occupied it when Queen Elizabeth sent him over here to subdue Ireland. It fell into ruins after that, but Cromwell used it as an arsenal when he was here." He spoke as if Ireland's invaders, most of them centuries dead, were men he had known. Were many of his countrymen like that, so steeped in Irish history that this island's long and bloody past seemed like something that had happened yesterday?

The carriage rolled on past another lake, with floating white swans mirrored in its surface, past a small stone church with the cross of Rome atop its steeple, and daisies starring the unclipped grass of its churchyard. For a while they moved through a narrow glen, filled with the chatter of a noisy little stream. Leaning out of the carriage to look up through the fern-smelling dimness, Elizabeth saw a ruined watchtower, built by some ancient Irish king or some invader, rising from the steep hillside.

Despite the sullen poverty of those tenant farmers, and despite her anxiety as to what sort of life awaited her in Patrick Stanford's house, Elizabeth felt a stir of response to this land, with its wild loveliness so different from that of the tidy English countryside.

They left the glen and traveled along a level stretch toward a line of distant blue hills, shadowed by clouds, that held promise of another shower. Here the stone walls dividing fields of potatoes and grain were much farther apart. The cottages they passed seem in better repair, and the cows grazing in occasional stretches of meadowland well-fed. To Elizabeth's relief, the few people she saw seemed less hostile. A man guiding a hand plow between rows of potato plants raised a battered black hat from his head and waved it. Three towheaded, laughing little boys slid down from a stone wall and ran alongside the carriage for a few yards, shouting something up at Michael in a language she knew must be Gaelic.

She asked, "Whose lands are these?"

"Mine."

"The fields are larger here."

"That is because I have not as yet been in need of obtaining more rents."

As yet. Perhaps her twenty thousand, Elizabeth reflected somewhat wryly, would make it possible for his tenants to work decent-sized holdings for some time to come.

They had reached another stretch of meadowland, dotted with grazing cattle. Up ahead and to the left, a magnificent black horse, with a woman perched on the saddle, soared over a stone fence and cantered toward them. Unbidden, Michael halted the carriage. With admiration Elizabeth looked at the rider, noting how easily she sat in the sidesaddle, one knee beneath her long dark blue velvet skirt hooked over the horn, her back very straight, her head with its matching velvet hat held high.

When she was a few yards away, she checked her mount and slid gracefully to the ground. Leading the horse, she approached the carriage window. Elizabeth saw that she was beautiful indeed, a tall brunette with classic features and wide-set eyes of a deep indigo blue. An ivory-colored plume swept around the brim of her hat, to touch a smooth cheek of almost the same shade.

She said, "Welcome home, Patrick." Her gaze went quickly from his face to Elizabeth's and then back again. Despite the proud carriage of the woman's head and her bright smile, Elizabeth caught an impression of anger and hurt, even pain.

Patrick said, "Thank you, Moira. May I present my wife? Elizabeth, this is our neighbor, Lady Moira Ashley."

"Welcome to Ireland, Lady Stanford. Everyone in the neighborhood is waiting eagerly to meet you."

"Thank you, Lady Moira."

"Do you ride?"

"Whenever I have the opportunity."

Moira laughed. "You will have no lack of opportunity here. Perhaps someday you and I can ride together. And you must allow me very soon to give a party for you and your husband."

"That would be very kind of you."

Lady Moira said, starting to turn away, "I must not keep you. I am sure that after your long journey . . ."

"Permit me." Patrick opened the carriage door and stepped to the ground. Long hands almost spanning her waist, he lifted Lady Moira into the saddle. For a moment she looked down at him, smiling slightly, but with anger and pain plain in her eyes now. Although Elizabeth could not see Patrick's face, she observed tension in his shoulders and the back of his neck as he looked up at the woman.

Moira's hand tightened around the handle of her riding crop. For a startled moment Elizabeth thought that the woman was going to lash Patrick's face. Instead she raised the crop in a farewell gesture, wheeled her mount, and sent him cantering back across the meadow.

Moments later, as the carriage moved down the road, Elizabeth asked, "Is Lady Moira your mistress?"

She felt rather than saw the startled look he threw her. "That is a very forthright question, madam."

"I see no reason why you and I should not be forthright about such matters."

"Ah, yes. What was that phrase in your letter? Something about making no objection to any other relationship I might choose to enjoy?"

Elizabeth made no reply. He said, "Perhaps I should take this opportunity to make it clear that I do not accord the same privilege to you. No matter what our marital relations, or lack of them, I have no intention of sporting horns before my neighbors."

Elizabeth said in a dry voice, "Surely you can have no immediate anxieties on that score. For some time to come, I shall be too taken up with other matters to start thinking of a lover."

"I merely wanted there to be no misunderstanding about that point." After a moment he added, "No, Moira Ashley is not my mistress, nor has she been."

Perhaps that was true, Elizabeth reflected. Nevertheless, they were anything but indifferent to each other. "Does she know about the child or . . . the other circumstances of our marriage?"

He said shortly, "Of course not." Then he added, "Only Colin knows that."

"Colin?"

"My brother. You will meet him soon."

A few minutes later the carriage left the main road for a narrower one that led through a stand of oaks and alders Sunlight, now tinged with late-afternoon bronze, slanted through breeze-stirred leaves, to cast moving splotches of light on the road, the carriage, and the sleek hides of the matched grays. When they emerged from the woods, Patrick said, "There is Stanford Hall."

17

Leaning a little way out of the carriage, she looked across a wide sweep of meadow grass at the house where she would bear her child and, perhaps, live out her life. Of reddish stone, it rose three stories behind its wall of similar stone. Dozens of mullioned windows blazed with sunset light. Round towers set at the north and south ends of the broad facade gave it a fortresslike aspect.

"It is an imposing house," Elizabeth said. She did not add that she much preferred the modest beauty of that house fifteen miles north of London.

"My great-grandfather built it after he received his grant of Irish land from Charles II. Except for the round towers, it is a duplicate of the house the Stanfords had built in England."

The carriage moved through open wrought-iron gates into the courtyard. Leaping down from the box, Michael opened the carriage door. As she and Patrick mounted stone steps, the massive oak doors of the house also swept open.

She found herself in a vast hall filled with reddish sunset light. From the shadowy reaches above hung a huge and perhaps almost priceless crystal chandelier. To judge by the dullness with which it reflected that reddish light, it long since should have been taken down and washed. Ahead of her, in the space between the twin staircases, stood the servants in two ranks, the women on the right,

126

the men on the left. Appalled, she realized that there must be about twenty of them.

A plump gray-haired woman in a black dress and white linen mobcap stepped forward. Patrick said, "This is Mrs. Corcoran, our housekeeper."

The little woman curtsied. "Welcome, milady. And may you and Sir Patrick find every happiness." The beaming smile on her rosy, blue-eyed face made it clear that she meant it.

Patrick conducted Elizabeth down the double line of servants. Gertrude, the cook, a red-haired woman almost as tall as Patrick. Another Gertrude, one of two scullery maids. Matthew, chief footman. After that, as she smiled at housemaids and pot boys and kennelmen, Elizabeth stopped trying to remember their names. In time she would sort them out. She noticed a housemaid's torn cap, and badly tarnished buttons on the men's liveries. But if their buttons lacked luster, their smiles, touched with that faint ribaldry that always greets a newly married pair, were bright enough.

"And these are Padric and young Joseph, stableboys." He need not have named their occupation. A faint aroma, mingling with that of the lye soap with which they had scrubbed themselves, had already told her.

"Padric and young Joseph are the sons of Joseph, our head stableman. You will meet him later. Now he is seeing to the carriage horses."

Was that why Stanford Hall, until now a bachelor establishment, had so large a staff? Were servants' offspring automatically given employment here?

A man was moving toward them from the shadows beyond the left-hand staircase, a tall, dark-haired man who walked with a limp. Patrick said, "So there you are!" Then: "Elizabeth, this is my brother, Colin Stanford. Colin, this is my wife."

She looked up into a face that resembled Patrick's but

was softer-looking, with the planes of cheekbone and jaw less well-defined. For a moment she saw a startled look in his dark eyes. Then he bent above the hand she offered and kissed it. "Welcome, Lady Stanford."

"Thank you."

"I shall see you at supper. But if you will excuse me now, I have some work I must finish. Besides, I know you must be wanting to rest." He turned and limped away down the hall.

Menservants were carrying trunks and portmanteaus up the stairs now, with Mrs. Corcoran toiling behind them. As Elizabeth and Patrick turned to follow, she asked, "How much younger is your brother?"

"He is three years older."

"Older! Then how is it that you, rather than he, are the fourth baronet?"

"You might as well know now. Colin is a half-brother, and illegitimate. After two years of marriage to my mother, my father began to fear he would have no legitimate children, and so he brought Colin here. The next year, I was born."

"I see. Who was Colin's mother?"

"A former governess, employed by Dublin friends of the Stanfords."

"She did not come here with her son, I suppose."

"Of course not. She stayed on in lodgings my father had provided for her in Dublin."

What had Colin's mother felt, deprived of her two-year-old son? And what had the last Lady Stanford felt, finding her husband's byblow added to her household? Probably no one except the two women involved had thought the questions important enough for consideration.

They had reached the balcony now, which, with its oaken balustrade, ran around three sides of the big entrance hall. As they moved past dim old portraits hung on the paneled wall, Patrick frowned down at the dark red carpet. It was almost threadbare in spots, and here was an actual hole. He had never noticed it before. How long had it been there?

Where the balcony turned, an open doorway afforded a glimpse of a flight of stairs. They must lead down, Elizabeth realized, to the kitchen and the servants' quarters. As they moved past the doorway, Patrick said, "If you want to have any of the household's furnishings repaired or replaced, please do so. In fact, I think you should."

She inclined her head in acknowledgment. So that was to be the destiny of part of those twenty thousand pounds.

The menservants had disappeared by then, but Mrs. Corcoran waited, smiling, beside an open door up ahead. When Patrick and Elizabeth had moved through the doorway, he turned back to the housekeeper. "Would you mind leaving us alone for a moment, Mrs. Corcoran?"

Her smile broadened. "Of course not, sir." Her brogue made the final word sound like "sor." She backed into the hall and closed the door.

Standing beside the trunk the menservants had left, Elizabeth asked, "Is this my room?"

"Yes. Do you find it satisfactory?"

Elizabeth looked around her. A worn but still beautiful Aubusson carpet. Massive oaken chests and bureaus of Tudor design. A small Queen Anne desk of rosewood. A wide four-poster bed, with an unusual and beautiful headboard. Its six slender columns, carved in a grape-leaf design, echoed the four much larger corner posts. The bed hangings, like those at the mullioned windows open to the sunset light, were of green and gold brocade. And everywhere—on the bureaus and chests, and beside the five-branched candelabrum on the bedside table—stood vases of apple blossoms.

But the brass candelabrum was tarnished, the hem of a window drapery sagged from its broken threads, and across the room, beneath a chest of drawers, Elizabeth could see a roll of furry gray dust at least six inches long.

"It is a very handsome room."

"It was my mother's. After she fell ill, she occupied it until her death, about fifteen years ago."

"I see." She hesitated. "And your room?"

"Beyond that door." As her gaze flew to it, he added, "No, there is no lock. But that does not signify. If I chose to come in, no lock would keep me out."

Elizabeth's only answer was cool silence.

"About your wardrobe," he went on. "You have worn the same traveling costume throughout the journey from England."

She thought of the journey, a wretched one redeemed only by the fact that there had been no question of her sharing sleeping quarters with her husband. In Bristol, their embarkation point, there had been no accommodations for her except in a room already occupied by a woman and her almost grown daughter, and none for him except a room shared with three other male travelers. On the small ship in which they had made the rough channel crossing, there had been one large cabin for the men passengers, and another for the women.

"Naturally I did not change my traveling costume, since it is the only one I have," she said coldly. "I hope you will not find my wardrobe too deficient. Circumstances scarcely gave me time to assemble a larger one."

His tone was equally cold. "That can be remedied. We can have gowns made for you in Dublin."

"Dublin!"

He flushed. "Yes, milady, Dublin. Many of you English are woefully ignorant about that city. Some Dublin neighborhoods are as fine as any in London. And there is a dressmaker there, a Frenchwoman, who is as skilled as any in Paris. Moira Ashley's gowns are made by Madame Leclerc."

So that was it. He had felt this afternoon that she cut a poor figure beside the resplendent Lady Moira. His pride would not allow that, and so—also out of that twenty thousand pounds, no doubt—she would be clothed in velvets and brocades and Brussels lace. Well, at least some of her money was to be spent upon her own person. Many a wife, she knew, had stood helplessly by while her husband threw away her fortune at the gaming tables.

She said, "Just as you wish."

"I am going to Dublin within a few days. I will call on Madame Leclerc and make sure that she has an ample supply of materials." He added, "Supper is at eight. I will send Mrs. Corcoran in now."

He went out. She heard him say something to the housekeeper. Then the little woman stepped through the doorway. "Do you find everything to your liking, milady?"

Mrs. Corcoran had been surprised by Sir Patrick's letter ordering her to prepare this long-unused room for Lady Stanford. Strange that a husband and wife, particularly newlyweds, should occupy separate rooms. But then, perhaps that was the custom among the English gentry.

"It is a beautiful room, and I do thank you for the apple blossoms. But, Mrs. Corcoran, would you not agree that the staff, with only Sir Patrick and his brother to please, have become a bit slipshod about their work?"

Seeing the hurt astonishment in the woman's face, Elizabeth instantly regretted her words. It was apparent now that Mrs. Corcoran and the other servants, spurred by the prospect of Elizabeth's arrival, had achieved what were for them new heights of diligence and efficiency.

Elizabeth said lamely, "It is just that I noticed a dust roll under that chest."

Mrs. Corcoran crouched down and stared at the furry gray cylinder as if contemplating something absolutely new to her experience, such as an infant alligator.

"Why, so there is!" Grunting slightly, she stood up. "You need have no fear, milady! I will give those lazy girls a scolding they will never forget."

Elizabeth smiled. "Don't be too hard on them. In time, you and I together will set everything to rights."

Elizabeth did not know it, but with those four words, "you and I together," she had won Mrs. Corcoran's heart for life. "That we will, milady," the housekeeper said. "And now I will go fetch Rose, and she and I will unpack your trunk."

Later that evening, in the large dining hall, Patrick sat at one end of the long oaken table and Elizabeth at the other, with Colin seated between them. Elizabeth soon found that if the housekeeping at Stanford Hall was inadequate, the cooking was not. Hungry after the long day of traveling, she helped herself generously to the roast lamb, green peas, and boiled potatoes proffered by two red-haired footmen. Patrick, silent and seemingly abstracted, left most of the conversation to Colin and Elizabeth.

She said, smiling at her brother-in-law, "How is it that I have never seen you in London during the season?"

He returned her smile. "Since I do not dance, London balls don't interest me. And I have never cared for gaming. Besides, I have much to occupy me here at the hall and at Edgewood."

"Edgewood?"

"The small estate Patrick's father and mine left to me at his death ten years ago. It is less than two hours' ride from here." He hesitated, and then said, with a glance at Patrick, "I suppose that you know we are half-brothers."

It was Patrick who answered the question, his voice curt. "I have told her the circumstances."

For several moments no one spoke. Then Elizabeth turned to Colin. "Is your mother still in Dublin?"

"No. As soon as I inherited Edgewood, I brought her there to live."

"How wonderful for her!" Elizabeth cried. "She must have been so lonely for you all during those years she spent in Dublin."

Patrick said, as if scenting a criticism of the third baronet, "I would assume she was glad that his father and mine acknowledged Colin and brought him here to raise as his son."

Colin's large dark eyes looked steadily at his brother. "Of course she was glad. But nevertheless, Lady Stanford is right. My mother was lonely in Dublin."

"Please!" Elizabeth said. "Must you call me Lady Stanford? After all, I am your sister-in-law."

He smiled at her. "Very well, Elizabeth."

Abruptly Patrick got to his feet. "If you will excuse me, I will not wait for the last course. I want to go over the ledgers."

After a moment Colin said, "Then I had best go over them with you." He stood up. "Please excuse us both, Elizabeth."

The fact that she ate her plum tart in solitude did not lessen Elizabeth's enjoyment of it one whit. Afterward she went to her room. Mrs. Corcoran and Rose—a stocky girl whose pink-and-white face under a bedraggled cap did indeed somewhat resemble a wild rose—were hanging the last of the trunk's contents in the wardrobe. To judge by the time the task had taken them, they must have examined and discussed each garment. And to judge by the rueful look with which the girl hung up an untrimmed dark cloak, she and Mrs. Corcoran, like Sir Patrick, had found Elizabeth's garments lacking in splendor.

But the smile with which the girl turned to her was both eager and respectful. "Will you be wanting me to help you undress now, milady?"

"Thank you. Thank you both. But I am very tired and would rather do for myself tonight."

A few minutes later she slipped between the linen

sheets on the vast bed and blew out the five candles in their branched candelabrum. She had dreaded this first night in a strange house in an alien land, and not only because she feared that Patrick Stanford, after all, might demand his conjugal rights. She had also anticipated that she would lie awake for hours, tormented by the memory of Donald's white, suffering face.

But she was exhausted by almost fifty miles of travel and a host of new impressions. Within minutes she fell asleep.

When Patrick Stanford finally went to bed on the other side of that heavy oak door, he was not so fortunate. He lay awake in the darkness, brooding gaze fixed on the barely visible bulk of a bureau across the room. What a damnable situation, married to a woman who probably right now was weeping into her pillow over that parson fellow.

And the way she had behaved at table that night, talking so easily to Colin, and smiling at him. She had never smiled at *him* so warmly, no, not even that night when they had first met, at the Armitages' ball. Perhaps she had no taste for anyone except bookish men who would sit around discussing Milton with her.

Or perhaps she had been friendly with Colin in the hope that he, Patrick, would react with irritation. In that case, it would be best in the future not to appear irritated. And as a matter of fact, why should he care how often she smiled at Colin, as long as it went no further than smiling? As he had warned her today, he had no intention of allowing her to make him a cuckold. And that was not just because of considerations of honor. To have standing with other men, a man needed their respect, and he could not command it if he wore horns.

Damn the woman! True, he had wronged her dreadfully, but his provocation had been great. And after he had received her letter, he had tried to behave as well as he could. He had not only married her, but had tacitly agreed to stay out of her bed. He had thought that would not be difficult. After all, the world was full of women, many of them both attractive and willing. He had not expected to lie awake like this, thinking of her on the other side of that door. . . .

He needed to get away from her, as soon as possible, so as to sort out his feeling about her. On the tenth, taking a sum of money with him, he was to meet with some men at a Dublin inn. There was no reason why he should not go up there a few days ahead of time. He would start out at daylight tomorrow.

He sat up, thumped the bolster several times with his fist, and then lay down again.

In his bedroom off the opposite side of the gallery, Colin Stanford also lay awake. His sister-in-law was not at all what he had expected. Somehow he had pictured her as a plump, rather languid blond. Certainly he had not expected a slender girl with glossy brown hair and clear gray eyes. Now that he had met her, he wondered even more at the brutality to which his brother had subjected her.

True, he himself had known Anne Reardon, and been fond of her, and so he could understand Patrick's bitter grief and rage over her fate. But still, to avenge himself as he had . . .

Well, Patrick had made whatever amends he could. Besides, Colin reminded himself, the whole matter was something that should be no concern of his.

Colin long ago had become reconciled to the fact that he was a bastard, and a cripple. On the whole, he considered himself a fortunate man, with a number of blessings: an occupation he enjoyed, plenty of books, and the companionship of the pleasant woman whose bed he often shared. Most of the time, he was content.

He found that tonight he was not.

He groped for his box of flints, found it, and lit the candelabrum on the stand beside his bed. Then he took a copy of Jonathan Swift's *A Modest Proposal* from the low bookcase on the other side of the bed and began to read.

18

A knock on the door, blending with the patter of rain against the windows, brought Elizabeth awake. She sat up in bed. "Come in."

The door opened slightly. Rose backed into the room, nudging the door farther open with her hip, and then turned around. She carried a mahogany lap tray holding a silver teapot and a teacup and saucer of pink china. "Good morning, milady." With another deft nudge of her hip, she sent the door swinging closed. Then she moved to the bed and placed the tray across Elizabeth's lap.

"Thank you, Rose." As she poured the fragrant brew, Elizabeth saw her reflection in the teapot's rounded side. "How beautifully this silver is polished."

Rose beamed. "I did it myself, this morning. And I have something else for you, milady." She plunged a hand into the pocket of her black dress and then laid a folded and sealed sheet of paper on the tray. "From Sir Patrick. Gave it to me himself, he did, just before he left."

"Left?"

"For Dublin. He rode off two hours ago."

"In the rain?"

Rose laughed. "If the Irish let rain keep us home, we would almost never stir out-of-doors."

Hands respectfully folded, she waited at the foot of the bed, hoping that Lady Stanford would open the note. She felt concern as well as curiosity. It was strange that Sir Patrick should ride off like that the morning after he had brought his bride to her new home, and such a lovely bride, too. Had they quarreled last night? Rose hoped not.

"You mustn't wait," Elizabeth said, smiling. "I like to take my time over morning tea."

When the door closed behind the reluctant Rose, Elizabeth broke the seal on the note. With neither salutation nor signature, it said, "I shall be away for about a week. I trust Mrs. Corcoran will do everything possible to make you comfortable."

Elizabeth felt annoyed, and wondered why. True, his message was curt to the point of rudeness. But she ought to welcome the news that tonight she and his pleasant brother would dine alone, with no glowering Patrick at the end of the long table.

Rain fell most of that day, and for nearly a week thereafter. Elizabeth did not mind. She had much to occupy her indoors. With Mrs. Corcoran, she toured the house from attic to scullery, and looked into each of Stanford Hall's forty-odd rooms. Many of them, unused for about a century, were so filled with rotting fabrics and cobwebs that Elizabeth abandoned all thought of having them cleaned. But there was much that she could accomplish. Before the week was out, the huge chandelier in the entrance hall had been taken down by two footmen working from tall ladders, disassembled, washed, and then, when put back together again, hung from its long iron chain. Windows had been washed, fireplaces cleaned, andirons polished. Housemaids' caps had been mended, and footmen appeared with a full complement of buttons, all of them shining. She had been prepared to hear a certain amount of grumbling from a staff used to an easygoing bachelor regime. But there was only a little complaining, even at first. And by the end of the week it became evident that the servants, as she had hoped, had begun to take pride in the new, smart appearance of both the house and themselves.

The evenings were pleasant. At no time during her suppers with Colin did she ask him why her husband had gone to Dublin, nor did he volunteer any information. In fact, they scarcely mentioned Patrick. Instead they talked of farming, books, and of the still-not-suppressed rebellion of the American colonists. After the meal they would go into the library to leaf through the now-dusted books, or to play chess. Although she never won, not even when Colin handicapped himself by removing one of his rooks from the board, she enjoyed those games.

She awoke one morning to see sunlight lying on the lovely old carpet. Delighted, she went to a pair of the mullioned windows and flung them wide. A blue sky, apparently cloudless, arched over a world that was even more brilliantly green than it had been a week earlier.

Rose knocked, and then came in with the tea tray. "A good morning to you, milady."

"A good morning to you, Rose, and a fine one it is." With amusement Elizabeth realized that already her speech had taken on some of the rhythms, if not the accent, of the Irish. "Will you please tell Joseph that I would like to ride this morning? I'll let him select a mount for me."

An hour later, wearing a plain brown habit that was more than five years old, she emerged into the rear courtyard. A pack of about a dozen foxhounds, penned in a kennel against the far wall, set up a chorus of barks. In front of the stable door, Joseph stood holding the bridle of a sleek black mare with one white stocking. A thin man with dark hair, a long face, and prominent front teeth, Joseph himself looked rather like one of the animals in his care.

"Here she is, milady. There's not a more delicate foot or a softer mouth in all of Ireland. And she's spirited, but not too spirited. Her name is Satin."

Elizabeth looked with appreciation at the gleaming flanks, the slender legs. "A good name for her."

Something cold and moist touched the back of her hand. She looked down, to see a dog of wildly mixed breed looking hopefully up at her. The curly black coat and tufted tail suggested poodle. The ears, one erect and the other drooping, hinted at collie. The friendly amber eyes, partially obscured by hair, might have been those of an English sheepdog.

"Away with you!" Joseph waved one arm. "Don't pester her ladyship."

"He's not pestering me." She put her hand on the dog's head. "Is he yours?"

"No, milady. And I should have put him down before this. To tell you the truth, I haven't had the heart."

"Put him down! But why? Why should he be killed?"

"Oh, milady! Two of Sir Patrick's prize bitches will soon be in heat. We can't risk them throwing whelps sired by that one, now, can we?"

"Surely you can prevent that from happening."

He said, after a moment, "We can, if we take care. And if you have taken a fancy to the animal, milady, there will be no question of putting him down."

With interlaced fingers, Joseph made a stirrup of his two hands, and helped Elizabeth swing into the saddle. The dog still looked up at her, waving his tufted tail and making eager noises deep in his throat. Elizabeth asked, "Where did he come from?"

"I think he belonged to a band of Gypsies who were

camped near here until about two weeks ago. Somehow he got left behind. Off chasing a coney, I'll wager, when the caravans moved on."

"Have you given him a name?"

"Certainly not, milady. Give an animal a name, and you find yourself getting fond of him."

"Well, he has a name now." She struck her riding crop lightly against her thigh. "Would you like to come with me, Gypsy?"

Perhaps he understood her tone and gesture rather than the words. In a frenzy of anticipation he chased his tail for perhaps twenty seconds, barking wildly. Then, as Elizabeth and her mount started across the courtyard, he trotted, grinning, at the mare's heels.

Elizabeth struck off toward the southeast, because Colin had told her that the nearest approach to the sea lay in that direction. A few fluffy white clouds, scudding before currents in the upper air, had appeared in the sky, but they only added to the beauty of the day. Their shadows flew across grassy meadows, stone walls, still-blossoming orchards. Elizabeth followed a narrow lane for a while, passing a thatched cottage where a sow and her piglets rooted in the yard, and then took an even narrower path across uncultivated land that sloped upward. When she reached the hill's crest, she halted. From here the land fell away, in gentle green folds, to the still-distant blue of the sea.

She heard a scurrying sound through the long grass and small clumps of gorse. Turning in the saddle, she saw a small brown shape bound down the hill's opposite slope, a steeper one than that the mare had just climbed. With a joyful yelp, Gypsy darted after the rabbit. "Come back!" she called, but already he was at the foot of the slope and racing along a narrow gully, invisible among the grass and bushes except for his tufted tail. Then even the tail disappeared, as suddenly and completely as if the earth had swallowed him up.

Puzzled and a little alarmed, she dismounted. There was no path down the slope. Best to descend it on foot. She tied the mare to a birch sapling and then made a cautious descent, holding her skirt close around her to keep it from the spiny clutch of the gorse bushes.

There seemed to be a path of sorts leading through the gully. She moved along it, calling for Gypsy. After a few yards, having caught neither sight nor sound of him, she halted and stood undecided.

A current of cool air touched her right cheek. At almost the same moment, she heard a faint scratching sound. She turned and looked at a tangle of gorse and tall Scotch broom just coming into flower.

So that was it. Cautious of the gorse spines, and steeling herself to the possibility that furry dark shapes might fly out at her, she parted the vegetation with her gloved hands and moved forward. At the threshold of the irregular opening, about five feet high, in the hillside, she stopped.

She need not have feared bats in this particular cave. If such creatures had ever lived here, they must have abandoned the place to human invaders, because she could see no bat droppings on the hard-packed floor, not on the large wooden cases stacked against one rocky wall. There were four of them, each tightly secured with rope.

What did they hold? Tea from Ceylon? Tobacco from Virginia? Whatever their contents, she was sure no duty had been paid upon them. Smugglers had brought these cases ashore at night, and then, through the darkness, carried them up to this natural hiding place.

Elizabeth felt no impulse to inform the authorities. Like most people, she registered smugglers almost as public benefactors. To finance his Majesty's far-flung wars, the government had raised impost taxes so high that, in En-

gland, many otherwise law-abiding middle-class folk
knowingly bought smuggled goods. And here in impoverished Ireland, surely most of the people would be without
even the comfort of an occasional cup of tea were it not
for the smugglers.

Again that scratching sound. By now her eyes had
grown sufficiently used to the dimness that she could see
the dog at the back of the cave, scratching at some hole
through which the rabbit had disappeared. It must have
been a small opening indeed, because his body hid it
completely from her view.

"Give it up, you idiot," she called. "You'll never get
that rabbit."

Evidently Gypsy had come to the same conclusion, because he backed away, turned, and looking sheepish,
moved toward her. With the dog following, Elizabeth returned to her tethered mount. She led the mare to a small
boulder, and using the rock as a mounting block, swung
into the saddle. When she had ridden a hundred yards or
so along the hill's crest, she saw that the path, turning
left, led down over the gentle folds of green earth to the
sea.

She followed it. After a while she could see a little
cove, with boats lying at its wharf. Farther along the
cove's edge, a church spire rose above trees. It was not
until she reached level ground that she saw that there
were other buildings, about a dozen whitewashed thatched
cottages, strung out along a single village street.

As she moved past the wharf, two men furling the sail
of a boat doffed their hats to her. On the village street
two little boys riding stick horses stopped their play at
sight of her, stared solemnly, and then, when she smiled,
shyly smiled back. A tall blond woman with a basket over
her arm wished Elizabeth a good morning.

The old stone church was at the end of the street, and

set at right angles to it. In the churchyard, sunlight slanted through oaks and maples onto the granite headstones. Attracted by the quiet beauty of the place, Elizabeth slid to the ground and tethered Satin to the hitching post. "And you stay here too, Gypsy." Apparently the dog understood, because he lay down beside the mare and sank his head on his extended paws. Elizabeth went through the gate in the churchyard's white-railed fence.

Plainly only the humble rested here. There were no granite mausoleums or marble angels, only the modest headstones. Those near the fence were the oldest. Some bore dates of more than two hundred years before. Others, probably even older, were so worn that their lettering was indecipherable. As she moved back along the gravel path, she saw newer headstones, including one of granite so unweathered that it might have left the stonecutter's shed only weeks before. She paused beside it. The words engraved upon it struck her like a blow. "Anne Reardon. Died age seventeen and two months, twentieth day of November, 1778."

Footsteps sounded on the gravel. She turned, to see a plump woman, gowned and bonneted in black, with a bouquet of field daisies in one hand. At sight of Elizabeth, she stopped, as if surprised, and then came on, smiling. "A good morning to you, Lady Stanford."

"Good morning. Do I . . . I mean, have we met before?"

"No, milady. But everyone in these parts has heard a description of you by now." She paused. "I am Maude Reardon."

"Reardon! Are you . . .?" Elizabeth was unable to finish the sentence.

"No. I'm not the poor child's mother. She's dead long since. Anne was my niece, my brother Tim's child. Sir Patrick had to stay in London after . . . it happened, so I brought her back here in her coffin."

Stiffly she knelt and placed the flowers on the grave. When she started to rise, Elizabeth bent and put her hand under the woman's elbow. "Let me help you, Mrs. Reardon."

"Thank you, milady." She got to her feet. "Only, it is Miss Reardon. I never married."

"Yes, of course. You said you were Tim Reardon's sister." She looked down at the grave and then asked, almost against her will, "What was she like?"

"Anne? A usual sort of girl, milady, neither plain nor pretty, and perhaps a little quieter than most. Sensible, though. When Sir Patrick decided to arrange that fine marriage for her with an ironmonger's son, Anne never said a word to show how she felt, although I could see it fair broke her heart to leave Stanford Hall, she was that daft about him."

"Daft about . . . I am afraid I don't understand."

"About Sir Patrick, milady. She fair worshiped the ground he walked on."

A sudden thought held Elizabeth motionless. His rage and grief over the girl's death, his grim determination to have revenge. Could it have been because . . .?

Before she could stop herself, she asked, "And was Sir Patrick daft about her?"

"About Anne?" It was Maude Reardon's turn to sound puzzled. Then horror came into her face. "Oh, milady! No one ever thought that of Sir Patrick. Why, she was his *ward.*"

Elizabeth felt color in her cheeks. "I see. It is just that I never knew Anne. And as a matter of fact, I haven't known Sir Patrick very long."

"No, you haven't, have you, milady? And I am not saying he is a saint. He is like other men. But everyone knows he was honor itself where Anne was concerned."

She looked down at the grave and sighed. "It was a sad

business for him, what happened to her. And a sad business for you, having your own brother falsely accused like that."

"Yes." Elizabeth's voice was stilted. She went on, reluctant to ask the question, and yet needing to know the answer, "I suppose it was his acquittal that made you sure my brother had been falsely accused."

"Oh, no, milady. Many a scoundrel has 'scaped the hangman. It was Sir Patrick's marrying you that made me sure your brother wasn't guilty. Sir Patrick would never have asked you if there had been the slightest doubt about that point."

"I see." How reasonable Maude Reardon's assumption was, and how utterly mistaken. Swiftly Elizabeth changed the subject. "Anne's father was a fisherman?"

"From the time he was a young lad until his boat caught fire and sank, eight years ago."

"How is it that his daughter became Sir Patrick's ward?"

"Why, because Tim and Sir Patrick were friends, milady."

Strange, Elizabeth thought. In England, men of such disparate classes might feel mutual respect and goodwill, but they would not consider themselves friends. Well, evidently it was a case of other countries, other customs. She thought of Michael, the coachman, winking at Patrick the day they had landed, and clapping him on the shoulder.

Maude Reardon said, "I had best take myself home. A good day to you, milady, and please remember me to Sir Patrick."

"I will."

Elizabeth lingered beside the grave for several minutes, looking at the headstone with its brief, sad legend. Then she went out to the hitching post and untethered Satin.

She stepped onto a mounting block worn hollow by generations of booted feet, and got into the saddle. With Gypsy following, she set out for Stanford Hall.

19

In the dining room that night, as she and Colin lingered over sweet sherry, Elizabeth asked, "What is your opinion of smugglers?"

He smiled. "They are reprehensible and highly necessary members of society. Why do you ask?"

"I wanted to make sure of your sentiments before I told you. You see, I think I discovered a smugglers' cache today." She told him of the cave and the stacked cases.

"Where was this?"

She described the spot as best she could. "Is that Stanford land?"

"I don't think so. I think it is Moira Ashley's. But smugglers play no favorites. They will use anyone's land." He paused. "Where else did you ride?"

"Down to that little fishing village on the cove." Reluctant to speak of that encounter in the churchyard, she said, "Well, I must go to my room. I want to write a letter to my mother tonight."

"I thought we might play chess."

"Perhaps tomorrow night." If, she amended silently, Patrick was not home by then. She had a feeling that he would resent those chess games and would try to see to it, by one means or another, that they were discontinued.

Up in her room, she took paper from the drawer of the pretty little desk and began to write. She was completing the last sentence of her letter when she heard a voice in that vast hall downstairs, speaking so loudly that it penetrated the thick walls of her room. After a moment she realized that the voice was Patrick's, and that he sounded angry. Angry over what? Had he returned to find that Colin or one of the servants had disobeyed some instruction he had left? Whatever the trouble, it was no concern of hers. She signed and sealed her letter, and then glanced at the clock on the desk, with its gilt frame of cupids and lovers' knots. Only a little after nine. Nevertheless, she felt sleepy, perhaps because of that long morning ride.

She was moving toward her wardrobe when someone knocked. She crossed to the door and opened it. Mrs. Corcoran stood there. "Sir Patrick is home, milady. He wants to see you in the library."

The round face looked frightened. So the master of the house really was in an angry mood. "Very well. Tell him I will be down soon."

"Please, milady! He said to come right away."

Elizabeth said swiftly and soothingly, "Then tell him I will be down in a moment."

The housekeeper hurried off. Elizabeth moved to her dressing table and tucked a stray lock of chestnut hair into place. Then she went along the balcony, down the right-hand staircase, and through the open library doors. Just beyond the threshold, she halted.

Patrick leaned against the massive table, arms crossed over his chest, booted feet crossed at the ankles. His face was black with anger.

"Close the doors!"

She looked at the tray, holding a brandy bottle and an almost empty glass, which rested on the table near him.

Then, with cool deliberation, she turned and pulled the doors closed.

She said, facing him, "What is it?"

"I shall tell you what it is, madam! Before coming home, I stopped to see Maude Reardon in the village. She told me of your conversation with her today. How you implied that I might have taken advantage of my ward. . . . What a mind you must have, madam!" He picked up the brandy glass and drained its contents.

Cheeks aflame, but trying to keep her gaze steady, Elizabeth watched him in silence.

"Is it not enough that the child died as she did? Must you defame the character that nobody questioned while she was alive? And what of me? Did you really think that I made that girl my mistress, and then tried to palm her off on a respectable London family?"

Her own anger had kindled now, speeding her heartbeats. "Did you expect me to regard you as the soul of honor and chivalry in your relations with women? Why, after your treatment of me, I think you should not be surprised if I think you capable of any outrage!"

The blood had rushed to his face. "But you gave me provocation! Anne Reardon did not. She was no liar, no perjurer, intent only upon saving a depraved monster from the gallows."

Elizabeth's voice shook. "Is that all you have to say to me?" She turned toward the door.

"No! I forbid you to go to the village ever again."

She whirled around. "Forbid? I am your legal wife, but not your prisoner. I shall go wherever I please. The only way you can stop me is to lock me up." She opened the doors and, head high, moved out into the hall.

"Perhaps I will lock you up!" he shouted after her. He stood motionless for a moment, and then splashed more brandy in his glass.

Damn the woman. And to think that in Dublin he had

found himself eager to get back to her. Why, he had even bought her that dress. . . .

He had seen it in Madame Leclerc's shop, fitted on some sort of wire contraption in the shape of a woman's body. It was of ruby-colored velvet, with long cuffs of white lace falling below elbow-length sleeves. Instantly he had thought of how that color would bring out the warm tints of Elizabeth's face, and contrast with her gray eyes. Too, it would look well with his mother's ruby necklace and earrings.

Yes, Madame Leclerc told him, the dress was for sale. A Dublin lady had ordered it, and then, when it was completed, had decided the color did not suit her. "But have you the certainty that it will fit Lady Stanford? The lady for whom it was made is of the slender figure."

"So is Lady Stanford. And if necessary, she can have it refitted, when we come to Dublin to order other gowns from you."

At his request, she had wrapped the dress in several layers of stout canvas. All the way from Dublin, he had carried it strapped behind the saddle. Then he had stopped in the village to see poor Maude and to give her the present—a pair of black lace mittens—he had bought for her in Dublin. By the time he had reached Stanford Hall, he was in such a rage that he had told Joseph to unstrap the canvas bundle and throw it in a storeroom somewhere.

He drained his glass, set it down, and started toward the doorway. Then he turned back, and inverted the glass over the bottle. Carrying the bottle by the neck, he went up to his room.

He undressed, put on a dressing gown of dark red brocade, and poured himself more brandy. Seated on the edge of his bed, he stared at the connecting door. He could hear her moving about in the room beyond.

Well, it was true he had grievously wronged her, but he

had tried to right that wrong as best he could. And true, he had realized that he could expect little of a marriage such as theirs. But surely she'd had no right to ask those insinuating, slanderous questions of Maude. Surely she had no right to defy his order to stay away from the village. Perhaps he had not really meant the order, but even so, she had no right to throw it back in his teeth.

He pictured her moving about in there, a smug, triumphant little smile on her lips.

Suddenly he swore, got up from the bed, and lunged at the doorknob.

Elizabeth had been about to put on her nightshift when she heard the door burst open. She whirled around, clutching the thin garment to her. "What are you doing in here? Get out of my room!"

"Your room, madam?" He moved toward her. "*Your* room! Every room in this house, including this one, is my room."

"Don't you come even one step nearer, you brandy-soaked brute!"

He took the step. Clutching her garment closer with her left hand and arm, she reached out with her right hand, fingers curved to rake her nails down his face. His hand shot out and imprisoned her wrist.

For a moment or so they glared at each other silently, like two combatants-to-the-death in a Roman arena. Then his gaze broke with hers. His eyes went over the shawl of bright hair around her bare shoulders, down the thin garment her left forearm clutched to her body.

"So the cat wants to scratch, does she?" He was smiling now. "Well, there is a way to deal with scratching cats."

He seized her left wrist, and despite her resistance, easily brought it together with her right. The nightshift collapsed onto the carpet. With both of her wrists imprisoned in the long fingers of one hand, he drew her—

twisting and struggling and trying to kick at his legs—across the room to the window beside the bed. Careful to keep clear of the kicks from those bare feet, he used his free hand to rip loose a narrow length of brocade that tied the window draperies back into place. Still grasping her wrists, he impelled her backward onto the bed. With her body thrashing beneath his weight, he looped the length of brocade around her wrists, and then, so swiftly that she had no chance to pull a hand free, drew the loop tight.

"You see," he said, tying the ends of the brocade around one of the headboard's slender columns, "I have no intention of allowing you to put my eyes out."

He got to his feet. She looked up at him. Furious and yet thoroughly frightened now, warning herself not to provoke him to even greater violence, she lay motionless except for the quickened rise and fall of her pink-nippled breasts. Then, as he unknotted the belt of his dressing gown, she turned her face away and closed her eyes.

He was beside her now, thumb and forefinger pressing into her cheeks as he turned her face toward him. His mouth came down on hers, roughly at first. Then, to her surprise, his kiss became gentle. Eyes still closed, she felt his lips brush along her cheek to her temple, felt his hands reaching through her hair to cup itself around one side of her head. With his breath warm against her ear he said, "Elizabeth," in a harsh, almost painful-sounding voice.

She was aware that he had raised himself to one elbow. For several seconds she felt his gaze moving over her body. Then his hand closed gently over her right breast. She stiffened.

One of his fingers had begun to brush back and forth across the nipple now. He lay down beside her, and she felt his lips close around the nipple of her other breast, felt his tongue moving against it, just as his finger brushed her other nipple. For perhaps a minute she stayed rigid, resisting the odd little thrills that seemed to travel from her breasts to somewhere deep within her body. Then all the stiffness went out of her, and she lay limp.

Something was happening to her, something she had never experienced before, a sense of a warm, liquid swelling within her. His hand left her breast, moved down to insert itself between thighs that parted at his touch. Then his finger returned to its gentle teasing of her breast. That swelling and tightening within her had become an almost unbearable tension, clamoring for release.

Dimly she was aware that her hips were moving, as if her body had some will of its own. He raised his head. She opened her eyes—drowned-looking eyes now—and looked for a moment into his dark, intent face. Then her eyes closed. She felt the naked weight of his long body, felt his legs moving her legs farther apart.

The first thrust of him inside her was not painful now. Instead, deep within her, it brought her a pleasure she had not dreamed existed, a pleasure so great that suddenly her body seemed boneless, melting. Eagerly she awaited that thrusting, awaited it again and again and again. His body seemed to be carrying her own higher and higher, toward some unknown and yet desperately longed-for climax.

Gradually that pleasure deep within her was becoming so intense that it was a kind of torment, a desperate need for a release that only his thrusting body could bring her. Out of her growing urgency she arched herself, so that she fitted more closely against him. The still-deeper thrusting only intensified that exquisite torment, that almost unbreable delight, that desperate longing for release. Then, just when she felt she could not endure that pleasurable torment one instant longer, release came, as if something within her had opened up, like the petals of a suddenly unfolding flower.

She cried out, and then felt the long, delicious, shuddering fall.

As she lay there, spent, she felt his kiss upon her mouth. Then he was beside her, untying her imprisoned wrists. She brought her hands down, lay for a moment more weighted by an odd languor, and then began to rub her wrists.

Gradually that strange spell he had cast upon her lifted.

What a barbarian he was! Breaking their tacit agreement. Tying her up in that humiliating fashion. And, worst of all, somehow making her behave as she had behaved. . . .

"Elizabeth, open your eyes."

She opened them. They were no longer drowned-looking, but clear and cool.

She said, "It was only my body."

He knew what she meant. Only her body had surrendered, not her spirit. It looked out at him from those gray eyes, as proud and remote as ever.

Well, what had he expected? A few minutes' lovemaking could not erase everything that had happened before. No, not for either of them, he thought, feeling a stir of returning anger. Just as she would never forget a certain night in that house north of London, he would never forget a woman lying under oath on the witness stand, or a carriage rolling away down an alley behind Old Bailey.

His eyes left that cool face and traveled over the rest of her. The small, high breasts, the slightly rounded belly, the glossy brown triangle, the long, straight legs ending in high-arched feet.

He said, smiling, "Only your body. Even so, madam, I should be reasonably content with my lot." He leaned over her and kissed her mouth.

20

The days lengthened. The leaves of maple trees, only a short time before almost as pale as lettuce, took on the rich, dark green of full summer. In the flowerbed cultivated by Joseph beyond the courtyard's south wall, late iris withered and early roses bloomed. In the meadows, wild daisies gave way to yarrow and Queen Anne's lace.

By day, Elizabeth and Patrick moved in separate worlds. She was busy drawing up lists of draperies and carpets to be replaced, conferring with Mrs. Corcoran and Gertrude, the cook, and in general administering the household. He was away for hours at a time, whether visiting his tenant farmer or on other errands, Elizabeth had no idea. When they did meet during the daylight hours, they treated each other with careful correctness, like two guests at a house party who do not know each other very well.

But he continued to visit her room several nights a week. Often at dinner, as they made polite conversation about the weather or the ripening wheat fields or the news in the latest paper sent from Dublin, she would wonder if in two hours or so she would find herself moaning with helpless pleasure in his arms.

Increasingly there were just the two of them at supper. Sometimes she wondered if, despite their formal behavior to each other, Colin had somehow sensed that at night in her room she and Patrick were not only lovers, but wildly

154

abandoned ones. Perhaps that awareness had made him feel like an intruder. In any event, he was often absent from Stanford Hall overnight.

On the first night that Colin did not appear at the supper table, Elizabeth asked about him. "He often goes to Edgewood to see his mother," Patrick said, "and to find out how matters are going at his estate there."

"Does his mother help manage Edgewood for him?"

"No, he has a very capable steward, a Mr. Slattery. Still, Colin needs to confer with him from time to time. And of course he also goes into the village to visit Catherine Ryan, a woman he has there."

"What is she like?"

"Pleasant enough. Tall and yellow-haired, and about thirty-five or a little older."

Elizabeth remembered the tall woman she had seen walking down the village street, a basket over her arm. She made no mention of the woman, though. Since that wild night when Patrick returned from Dublin, neither of them had spoken of her visit to the village, or of Anne Reardon, or of Christopher, or of any of the sources of bitterness between them.

She had received news of Christopher, though. Her mother had written:

Your brother was here yesterday. He made that long trip from Paris just to spend one day with me! Mr. Yves Cordot could not spare him from the emporium for more than a short time.

The poor boy seemed eager for details of your wedding—who had been there, what food was served at the party here afterward, and so on. Then he asked wistfully if I thought it would be all right for him to visit you in Ireland. He said, "Surely Sir Patrick no longer has any idea that I was responsible

for that poor girl's death. Surely Liza has gotten any
such notion out of his head by now."

I told him I still thought it would be best to wait
for a while. Besides, I doubt that Mr. Cordot would
allow it. I gather that by now Mr. Cordot finds him
almost indispensable.

Folding the letter, Elizabeth had reflected grimly that
her mother's advice to Christopher was sound. It would
be best indeed for him to stay away from Patrick Stanford
for a while longer—a good while longer, such as forever.

There were no letters from Donald, of course. And
Mrs. Montlow, perhaps reluctant to cause her daughter
useless pain, made no mention of him in her own letters.
But he often appeared in Elizabeth's dreams, smiling that
gentle, humorous smile she had always loved. And although she tried to avoid thinking of the past, often the
memory of him as she had last seen him there in the
church—very pale, with lips stretched into a parody of
that familiar smile—brought her a stab of almost physical
pain.

Several times during late spring and early summer she
and Patrick went to neighborhood parties, one of them at
the great gray pile, Wetherly, that Lady Moira Ashley
had inherited from her late husband. Smiling, but with
cool reserve in her dark blue eyes, Lady Moira led Elizabeth through lofty rooms hung with tapestries and lighted
by hundreds of perfumed candles, and introduced her to
other guests. If Patrick thought that his wife's gray satin
gown, the one she had worn the night he first saw her,
contrasted poorly with their hostess's gold-colored velvet,
he did not tell Elizabeth so.

But in late June, at his insistence, she and Patrick went
to Dublin, traveling in the same carriage that had brought
them from Waterford to Stanford Hall. Both the inns at
which they stopped were primitive, with no accommoda-

tions for couples. Elizabeth slept with other women travelers in a long sleeping room, and Patrick in the far-more-crowded room provided for men. But in Dublin they obtained a bedroom and sitting room in a comfortable inn, once a private mansion, on one of the city's finest streets.

They had arrived early in the afternoon, with sufficient time to visit Madame Leclerc's establishment. The Frenchwoman, small and dark and businesslike, greeted them pleasantly but with no trace of deference. Obviously she, the most successful modiste in Dublin, knew her own worth. She took down from the shelves the materials she had obtained for Elizabeth's wardrobe—fine lawns for morning gowns, brocades and satins for ball gowns, dark green velvet for a new riding habit. Finally the two women left Patrick at the window, staring out into the street, and retired to a dressing room. Elizabeth stood in her shift and corselet while the Frenchwoman plied a measuring tape.

"Did the gown please Lady Stanford?"

Elizabeth said, puzzled, "What gown?"

"Why, the ruby-colored velvet Sir Patrick bought from me when he was last in Dublin."

After a moment Elizabeth said, "Oh, yes. It was very nice."

So he had brought home a gown for her. What had he done with it? In his rage that night, probably he had told one of the servants to put it away someplace. Then he had forgotten about it.

Then another thought made her stiffen slightly. Perhaps he had not bought the gown for her. Ruby-colored velvet would be the perfect foil for Moira Ashley's dark loveliness.

Madame Leclerc said, "Lady Stanford is *enceinte, non*?"

"Yes, madame."

"Is it permitted to inquire when the child will be born?"

"In late November."

"Then it is best that I do not make the final fitting until after the child's birth. Your gowns will not be completed until then, anyway. There are many of them, and there are other orders that I must complete before I start on yours." She stepped back. "I have finished now."

With Madame Leclerc's aid, Elizabeth put on her gown. Her conversation with the Frenchwoman had made her sharply aware that it was high time that Patrick stayed in his own room every night.

When she and Patrick emerged onto the sidewalk, he said, "I have business back at the inn. Would you prefer to go to your room, or would you like Michael to drive you around the city?"

"I would like to drive."

For several hours the carriage took her around Dublin, halting now and then whenever Michael thought that some stately gray-stone church, some view of the broad Liffey River, might appeal to her. She had no doubt that in other parts of Dublin slatterns sat at windows of moldering tenements, and ragged children dodged carts and wagons in the filthy streets, and men with no jobs and little prospects of any sat at curbstones numbing their misery with gin at a penny a cup. But what she saw was Anglo-Irish Dublin, with broad, tree-lined streets, mansions almost as fine as any in London, and strolling men and women with rich clothing on their bodies and proper Church of England sentiments in their heads.

When she returned to the inn, she found that Patrick was not among those seated in the comfortable common room reading newspapers or writing at desks along one wall. But as she passed the open doorway of the taproom, she saw that he was one of three men seated at a table over pint mugs of ale or stout. One of the men was about forty, with a thin, dark face. His clothing, although of a cut that looked vaguely foreign to Elizabeth, was excellent enough that he did not seem out of place in Dublin's finest inn. But as she climbed the stairs, she wondered briefly about the other man. Stocky and red-faced, he had been dressed in a plain coat and breeches of brown broadcloth, the sort of clothing a moderately prosperous farmer might save for important occasions. Perhaps he *was* some farmer, trying to buy land from Patrick, or to sell some to him.

Upstairs in their sitting room, Elizabeth stood by the window and watched the long day fade into twilight. At eight someone knocked on the door. Elizabeth opened it, to find one of the inn's menservants standing in the hall. Sir Patrick Stanford sent his regards to Lady Stanford, and begged to inform her that he would take supper downstairs. Would Lady Stanford care to have her own supper brought up now?

Lady Stanford would. By nine she had finished an excellent meal of mullet cooked in wine sauce. Still Patrick had not returned. His business with both of those men, whatever it was, must be complicated indeed. Wryly she reflected that if he were buying more land, probably it was her money that enabled him to do so. But he had never offered to discuss financial matters with her, and she had felt too proud to ask questions.

At ten she went to bed. Sometimes during the night she came awake for a few moments, dimly aware that Patrick now lay beside her, and then went back to sleep.

Thus it was not until the next day, as their carriage moved south from Dublin, that she told him what she had resolved upon in Madame Leclerc's fitting room. "When we return to Stanford Hall, you must stop coming to my room. We must think of the child's safety."

"Very well."

He had been expecting her to say that. But why did she

have to say it, the little hypocrite, in that cold, offhand manner, as if their lovemaking had been for her only a disagreeable duty? He knew that was far from the case. And yet, probably in a way, she *was* pleased to have an excuse for shutting him out of her room. She must have found it a constant source of chagrin that, despite the en- mity between them, she could not resist the pleasure she found in his arms. Yes, making that little speech a moment ago must have brought her considerable satisfac- tion.

Well, why should he care? She was far from being the only desirable woman of his acquaintance. He recalled a note from Moira that one of the Wetherly servants had brought him the day before he and Elizabeth had set out for Dublin. It had been a reminder, formal in tone, that soon he must call upon her to discuss the "young en- try"—the preseason fox hunt designed to acquaint the young hounds with hunting procedures. Early in September, huntsmen, horses, and foxhounds would all assemble at Wetherly.

She had written a postscript:

> As I am sure you will perceive, all the above is mere subterfuge. Once I said to you, "You will have to marry me first." Now I cannot impose such a stricture. In short, my dear Patrick, I have decided that half a loaf is better than none.

He gazed at his wife's profile, cool against the side- swept brim of her black velvet hat. As soon as possible, he would reply to Moira's note, in person.

During the next few weeks Patrick not only stayed out of Elizabeth's room. He also often stayed away from the supper table. She did not question him about his ab- sences, nor did he volunteer any explanation. At first she thought he might be trying to annoy her by staying away.

Soon, though, she realized he must have a more compelling reason than that. She thought of Moira Ashley on the sidesaddle, looking down at Patrick with hurt and anger plain in her face. Yes, surely it was Lady Moira who kept Patrick away from Stanford Hall, not only at suppertime, but often at night.

Well, Elizabeth asked herself, what else would one expect of a man like Patrick Stanford? Even if the circumstances of their marriage had been different, even if she had not stated in writing that she would not question his pursuit of "other relationships," no doubt before long he would have been unfaithful. If she felt jealousy at all, she assured herself, it was entirely physical, induced only by memories of his lovemaking.

As before, she busied herself with household matters. But often a strange restlessness drove her out-of-doors. She no longer dared to ride. However, Joseph had produced, from a cobwebby corner of the carriage house, a two-wheeled cart. With a placid old dapple gray named Toby plodding between the shafts, and Gypsy perched on the wooden seat beside her, she sometimes went for drives. Most of the time, though, she preferred to walk through a countryside washed by the full tide of summer. With Gypsy frisking beside or ahead of her, wearing the collar Joseph had placed around his neck, she wandered through meadows where bees settled hungrily on clover blossoms, and past orchards where apple-tree boughs bent under the weight of ripening fruit.

As she turned her reluctant steps homeward, she would wonder if Patrick would sit at the other end of the long table tonight, and then feel angry with her own thoughts. It was not, she assured herself, that she was lonely for the sight of him sitting there. It was just that she felt awkward, seated alone at that long table.

But after a while she seldom took supper alone. From late July onward, Colin spent more and more of his time at Stanford Hall. For a while, he said, long-needed repairs at Edgewood had required his attention, but now matters were so well advanced that there was nothing his steward, Mr. Slattery, could not handle. Elizabeth accepted his explanation but wondered privately if he had guessed that she found it unpleasant to dine alone so often. Whatever the reason for his presence, she was glad of it.

On evenings when Patrick was not present, she and Colin played chess in the library after supper. Often when she made a move and then looked up from the board, she observed what appeared to be sympathy in Colin's dark eyes. Several times she thought he was about to make some comment concerning his brother's absence, but he never did. His silence on that point only strengthened her belief that Wetherly was the place where Patrick spent most of those hours when he was absent from Stanford Hall.

One night, as they were putting the chess pieces away in a tooled-leather box, she said, "Colin, haven't you ever been away from Ireland?"

"Once. I was only nineteen then, and had not yet . . ."

He checked himself. He had been about to say that in those days he had not yet reconciled himself to certain things—his lameness, his illegitimacy.

He said, "I had not yet realized that the life I was best suited for was right here in Ireland. And so I took ship for the West Indies. For a while I stayed with an English family who had a sugar plantation."

"Is it a beautiful part of the world?"

"Beautiful, and sinister."

He spoke of shimmering blue water that became green or turquoise in the warm shallows, and of pink sandy beaches fringed with coconut palms bending in the trade wind. But he also spoke of slave ships, discharging their wretched cargo of men and women and children to labor in the cane fields, or in the mines, where the gentle Carib

Indians, the islands' original and now almost extinct inhabitants, had sickened and died in the foul air and under the overseer's lash. He spoke of voodoo drums in the hills throbbing through the hot darkness, and of the white settlers' constant fear that some night those drums would signal a murderous descent of the blacks upon the plantations, the pretty, European-style little towns. . . .

Elizabeth was so fascinated that, until the tall clock in one corner struck the hour, she did not realize it was midnight.

One afternoon in early September when she returned from a long walk, she found Patrick standing in the library doorway. He said, "May I speak to you for a moment?"

Together they moved into the room. Tomorrow, he told her, the neighborhood hunt would assemble at Wetherly for the young entry. "Although of course you are unable to join the hunt, Moira thought you might care to attend the ball she will give tomorrow night."

Elizabeth said coldly, "Please thank Lady Moira for her kind although extremely belated invitation. Tell her that just as a woman in my condition cannot ride to hounds, she also cannot dance."

Aware that her movements must appear slow and clumsy, she turned and left him.

But even though she could not join the hunt, she saw it the next day. She was walking down a narrow lane with Gypsy, when she heard the sound of the horn, and the hounds giving tongue. Hastily seizing Gypsy's collar, she stopped beside a tree. Not more than a few yards in front of her, the fox streaked across the lane and under the bottom rail of a fence into an uncultivated field. The hounds were next, some not fully grown, scrambling through the rails in clamorous pursuit. Then, as she tightened her grip on the wildly excited Gypsy, the riders began to stream past, the men in pink coats, the women in formal black habits. Patrick was among those in the lead. As he approached the fence, he turned his head for an instant and looked at her beside the tree, trying to control the plunging, barking dog. He leaped the fence, rode on. The rest of the riders streamed past, Moira among them.

Elizabeth waited until the hunt had disappeared around a copse of oaks and maples. Then she turned back toward the hall. How beautiful Moira Ashley had looked as she guided her mount over the fence. And how awkward, even ridiculous, she herself must have looked, swollen body bent, hand gripping the noisy mongrel's collar.

Loneliness swept over her. But soon she would not be lonely, she told herself. Soon there would be the child.

Clarence, the taller of the two red-haired footmen, opened the door for her. "There is a letter for you, milady. Mrs. Corcoran put it in your room."

As she laboriously climbed the stairs, she wondered who the letter was from. Perhaps from her mother. Perhaps from the Dublin midwife, recommended by Mrs. Corcoran, to whom she had written last week, asking her to attend her lying-in.

Moments later, she stared with surprised joy at the letter, addressed in a familiar hand and postmarked Dublin, which lay on her desk. With trembling fingers she unsealed it. Donald! A letter from Donald.

His bishop, he had written, had sent him as an observer to a synod of Anglo-Irish churchmen in Dublin. "I shall be here five more days. After that I would like to call upon you, if that is agreeable to both you and Sir Patrick. I would arrive on the tenth, and stay perhaps three days—but only, again, if that is agreeable to both of you."

He had signed himself formally as "Your obedient servant, Donald Weymouth."

The tenth, a week from now. In a week, she would see Donald. True, Patrick might resent his coming. But surely not even he could deny a woman in an advanced state of pregnancy the comfort of a visit from someone she had known since childhood. She cried for a few minutes, out of sheer joy. Then she sat down at the desk and drew letter paper toward her.

Late that night, after the last of Moira's other guests had left, Patrick lay in the ornately gilded bed in her room. She was astride him, her head, with its waist-length black hair, flung back, her lovely face distorted as she strove for her climax. She reached it and collapsed, still shuddering, upon his chest. After a while she rolled to one side and lay with her head on his shoulder.

Moments passed. Then she nuzzled his lean cheek. "A penny for them."

"I was thinking of how beautiful you are."

He had been thinking something like that. But also he had been thinking of Elizabeth. She had appeared considerably less than beautiful beside that tree, body awkwardly bent, face strained with her efforts to control that grotesque-looking cur. And yet there had been something about her at that moment, something lonely and vulnerable, that had stabbed him to the heart.

Moira asked, "As beautiful as your wife?"

She too had seen the awkward figure beside the tree, and had been freshly aware of her own graceful beauty. And yet she had felt painful anger, too. No matter that the Englishwoman was, and probably would remain, neglected by her husband. She was still the wife of Patrick Stanford, fourth baronet, and might soon be the mother of the fifth. In short, by some inexplicable mischance, she occupied the place that should have been Moira's.

Patrick said, "This is scarcely the time, or the place, for us to be discussing my wife."

"My, how proper we are." She raised herself on one elbow and looked down at him. "An honorable man does not discuss his wife while in bed with his mistress. Is that it?"

Gaze directed past her at the ceiling, he said nothing.

His silence stung her into recklessness. "But I scarcely see how she could be considered sacrosant," she went on. "I have not mentioned it before, but if Lady Stanford is so virtuous, how is it that she, a bride of four months, appears to be at least six months pregnant? I imagine that the whole neighborhood is wondering about that."

"Then let them," he said furiously, "if they have nothing better to do. But you and I are not to discuss it. Do you understand!"

Eyes narrowing, she smiled. Then she leaned down to him, full breasts flattening against his chest, and kissed him on the mouth. "Have a care, Patrick," she said. "I am not some servant girl, to be spoken to any way you please. Someday you will use that tone once too often."

21

It was not until the next night that Elizabeth had a chance to tell her husband of Donald's impending visit. Around ten o'clock she was seated at her dressing table, too keyed up with mingled anticipation and anxiety to even think of sleep, when she heard Patrick's footsteps approaching along the corridor. Quickly she laid down her brush, and with hair hanging loose around her shoulders, crossed the room and stepped out into the hall. Hand on the knob of his own door, Patrick turned to her with a surprised look.

She said, "I have something to tell you. Donald Weymouth is in Dublin. He wrote me, and I replied, inviting him here for a three-day visit. He will arrive on the tenth."

She spoke calmly, and with lifted chin. But Patrick could see in her gray eyes a fear that he would forbid Weymouth to enter his house. Again, as when he had seen her standing beside the tree with her hand on the collar of that lunging cur, he felt a stab of pity and vain regret. "What is Weymouth doing in Dublin?"

"His bishop sent him to a synod as an observer." She paused, and then added, careful to keep all reproach out of her voice, "I would have consulted you before I answered his letter if you had been at home, but you were not."

When he made no reply, she asked, "Well, do I have your consent to receive him?"

"You have." If she could derive any comfort from seeing her milksop parson, let her do so.

"Thank you," she said, and started to turn away.

"Did you say he will arrive on the tenth?"

She turned back. "Yes."

"Then I will make a point of being home for supper that night, so that I too can welcome him."

Her voice trembled. "I would appreciate that very much. Good night." She went into her room.

After a moment, Patrick entered his own room. How was it, he wondered, that he had gotten himself into this quagmire? Here he was, married to a woman who not only loathed him, but somehow had the power to keep him feeling guilty. Just now, even the gratitude in her eyes had made him feel ashamed. He started to take off his coat, and then, with an oath, put it on again. He would not try to sleep. As he passed the library, he had seen Colin replacing a book on a shelf. Best to go down, challenge his brother to a chess game, and try to pretend for an hour or so that he too was still a bachelor.

At her dressing table, Elizabeth resumed brushing her hair. So at least Patrick was prepared to behave decently to Donald. But still she must worry about Donald's first sight of her. In her letter she had told him that she expected a child, but had not said when. The moment he saw her, he would know that she must have become pregnant well before the date of her marriage.

She thought of the night after Christopher's trial ended, when she and Donald had driven alone back to that empty house north of London. He had been careful to come no farther than just inside the front door. What pain he would feel now, believing that soon after that night she had granted wantonly to another man what he had forbidden himself even to ask of her.

But better, far better, to have him believe that than to have him know the truth of how her child had been conceived.

She had a sudden chill sense that she should have told Donald not to come here. But no. She could no more have denied herself the chance to see him than a starving person could refuse a sip of broth. She laid down her hairbrush and moved toward her bed.

On the afternoon of the tenth, she was standing at the window of her room when Donald, on a bay horse, rode through the wrought-iron gate into the cobblestoned courtyard. All that day she had scarcely stirred from that window, lest he arrive without her knowing it at once. Heart beating fast, she left her room and went down the stairs.

Clarence, one of the red-haired footmen, had already opened the massive front doors. She went out onto the terrace, and then paused, looking down. Back turned,

Donald was saying something to Padric, the elder of the stableboys. She moved down the stone steps. "Donald."

He whirled around, joy in his face, and took her outstretched hands. In that first moment she knew with mingled elation and despair that her love for him had lessened not one whit. Nor had his own feelings changed. His love for her was plain in his thin face.

Then his gaze swept down her body. After a moment she saw the surprise in his hazel eyes turn to shocked realization.

She said again, "Donald." This time it was a plea.

Despite the sudden pallor of his face, he managed a smile. "How are you, Elizabeth?"

"I . . . I am well." she withdrew her hands and turned to Padric. "Please take care of Mr. Weymouth's horse. And then have someone bring his saddlebags up to his room."

As she and Donald climbed the front steps she said, "I am sorry that there is no one else to welcome you. My . . . my husband is out just now, and so is his brother. But probably they will both be here for supper." She paused. "Was your journey from Dublin pleasant?"

"Very pleasant."

"I'm glad." She was aware that even as they exchanged these formal courtesies, their eyes were carrying on an entirely different dialogue.

When they reached the vast entrance hall, she said, "Clarence, this is Mr. Weymouth." Then, to Donald: "Clarence will show you to your room. Will you be ready for tea in half an hour?" She gestured toward the library's open doorway. "We will take tea in there."

"Splendid." He was looking at the twin staircases and the shadowy gallery above them. "I trust they don't keep you awake every night."

"They?"

"The ghosts. Surely all the ghosts in the county must flock to such an ideal promenade."

She laughed. Darling Donald! Despite the shock and pain the sight of her swollen body had brought him, he was able to make a small jest. "No ghosts," she said.

When he entered the library half an hour later, she was already seated at the tea table. She poured his tea and added a teaspoonful of sugar. As she handed him the cup, she saw that he too realized what she had done. With no need to ask how he liked his tea, she had added sugar automatically, just as she had done so many times back at the Hedges.

Stirring his tea, he asked abruptly, "When will your child be born?"

She was glad that he had brought himself to ask that question right away, so that they could put it behind them. "Ten or eleven weeks from now."

"I see." Just as she had known he would, he forbore asking more questions or making any comment. Instead he said, "I often see your mother. You will be glad to know that she is well."

"And not too lonely?" She felt a pang as she thought of her mother, deprived of both son and daughter.

"Oh, she's lonely. But in the past few weeks I have managed to interest her in the church mission society, and that seems to help."

"What is it like to be the new vicar?"

He smiled. "Everything is much the same as it was under the old vicar. The sexton still gets drunk and goes to sleep in the graveyard. Old Mrs. Crawley still sings too loud and off-key, and then snores through most of the sermon. And Mrs. Canby is still as alert as a bird dog to see that no Low Church tendencies creep into the liturgy."

Elizabeth smiled. "And Sally Cobbin? Did she marry the butcher's son?"

"She did."

As they went on talking of people in that little English village, she had a sense that everything that had happened in the past ten months had been a bad dream. Once more her brother was a student at Oxford, her mother had nothing worse to worry about than lack of money, and she and Donald were talking over teacups in the side parlor at the Hedges, with their whole lives stretching serenely before them. Then the tall clock in the corner struck five. Reluctantly she rose and pulled the bell rope, so that someone would clear the tea things away.

Patrick not only appeared well before the supper hour to greet the guest. He was also courteous, even pleasant, throughout the meal. As Clarence moved around the table, pouring the sherry that was to accompany the soup, Patrick asked, "Did you buy your horse in Dublin, Mr. Weymouth?"

"Yes. I plan to resell him in Waterford before I sail."

"Take him to Hadley's stables. Hadley is always ready to buy a good saddle horse, and he pays a fair price." He paused. "Does your family keep horses?"

"Yes. Carriage horses, of course, and three hunters. Then, there are the farm horses. We use Clydesdales for heavy hauling."

Patrick nodded. "I too prefer them to Percherons."

With relief Elizabeth saw that the conversation was launched upon a safe topic. It was Colin who, much to her surprise, displayed hostility toward the guest. When a lull in the talk came about midway of the meal, Colin turned to Donald and said, "Tell me, Mr. Weymouth, what are your views on predestination?"

Patrick laughed. "Listen to my brother! Here is a man who doesn't go to church three times a year, and yet he wants to talk about predestination."

Colin's dark eyes shot Patrick an angry look. "But I

read. A man doesn't have to go to church to form religious opinions."

Donald said lightly, "I hope you do not influence others to stay home with their books on Sunday. As it is, we poor parsons find ourselves preaching to rows of empty pews."

Colin said evenly, "Considering the confusion that Calvinist doctrines have brought to the Anglican church, I am not surprised."

Elizabeth looked at Colin with amazement. She recalled now that one night over a chess game he had mentioned Calvin, and she had said that "a friend back in England, the new vicar of our parish church," had for a time been interested in Calvinism. Colin had remembered that bit of information, and was now using it to attack Donald. Why? What had gotten into her usually quiet and even-tempered brother-in-law?

Patrick said, "Colin, you don't give a tinker's dam about Calvin, any more than I do. Now, to get back to horses." He turned to Donald. "If you want to ride one of my hunters tomorrow, please do so."

"Thank you. Perhaps I shall, sometime before I leave."

When the meal ended, Colin announced abruptly that he had work to do, and went back to his office. Elizabeth and the other two men—she with coffee, they with glasses of port—settled down before the library fire. At ten, pleading tiredness after a long day's ride, Donald went upstairs.

Alone with Patrick, Elizabeth said, "Thank you for being so . . . amiable this evening."

He shrugged. "Why shouldn't I be? The man's a guest. And he seems a good sort, for a parson." He looked at her sardonically. "What did you expect the barbaric Patrick Stanford to do? Slip poison into his soup?"

"No, of course not. Nevertheless, I wanted to thank

you." She placed her coffeecup on the small table beside her chair, rose, and said good night.

Apparently Patrick felt he had fulfilled his duties as a host, because when Elizabeth awoke the next morning, she learned from Rose that he and his brother had ridden off right after an early breakfast. Elizabeth did not mind—far from it—and certainly Donald did not seem to. With rain beating against the windows, they browsed through the books in the library and talked endlessly of that village north of London and of people they had known all their lives. After their midday meal, which they ate seated companionably close at one corner of the long table, they returned to the library for more talk of home.

Around three o'clock the rain slackened, then ceased. Elizabeth said reluctantly, "Do you want one of the hunters saddled for you?"

"When you cannot ride with me? Of course not."

She hesitated. "In the past few weeks, I've been driving about in an old farm cart. It is not a stylish vehicle. But then, there would not be many people to see us in the lanes around here. . . ."

"My dear Elizabeth, I wouldn't care if our route lay through Piccadilly Circus."

Half an hour later, with Donald driving the ancient dapple gray, the tall-wheeled cart lumbered down a narrow lane. Gypsy was with them. At first, deprived of his usual place beside Elizabeth on the seat, he made sounds of displeasure deep in his throat. Now, though, he had settled down in the bed of the cart. With the sky clear of clouds, the sun shone as warmly as it had any day in midsummer. But everywhere there were signs of autumn's approach. Leaves of oaks and maples had turned a duller green. Fringed gentians blossomed at roadsides. In the orchards, apples lay thick upon the ground, with bumblebees, half-drunk on fermenting fruit, making languid circles above them.

The cart turned off onto a still narrower track that led across uncultivated, gently rolling land to a bluff above the sea. There they stopped and looked out across sparkling blue water. About half a mile away two square-rigged ships, sails spread to the breeze, moved southward. Elizabeth could see the dark round circles of their gun ports. She asked, "Ours?"

Donald nodded. "They are trying to keep French warships and privateers out of the Irish channel. Poor England!"

Elizabeth knew what he meant. When the American rebels had sent the English reeling back at the Battle of Saratoga, King Louis of France had seen his opportunity. Since then he had been waging sea warfare on the already weakened English wherever he could—off Gibraltar, along the coast of India, and among the Caribbean islands.

Elizabeth asked, "Will he lose the American colonies?"

"I fear so. Edmund Burke is right, you know. If King George and his ministers wanted to retain the colonies, they should have adopted milder policies years ago." After a moment he went on, "But right now I find it hard to be concerned with such matters. Elizabeth, are you happy?"

Afraid to look at him, but keenly aware of his hand loosely holding the reins, and of his thigh only inches from her own on the wooden seat, she said nothing.

"Aren't you going to answer me?"

She forced the words out. "I am reasonably content." Then, swiftly: "You must not ask such questions. You know you must not. Let me . . . let me just enjoy being with you for these few hours. Otherwise I shall be sorry I asked you to come here."

After a while he said quietly, "Very well." For a minute or so they looked at the patrolling warships. On a different tack now, the vessels were veering westward toward the Atlantic. Then he said, "I must leave by ten tomorrow."

"I know. If . . . if it is possible, I would like to accompany you in the cart for a mile or so."

"I hope you can."

He did not ask what might keep her from doing so. Apparently he realized that such a plan would become impossible if Patrick Stanford chose to be present to speed the parting guest.

"We must go back now," Elizabeth said.

He sat motionless for several seconds. Then he backed the cart and turned it toward Stanford Hall.

Patrick was absent from the supper table that night, but Colin was there. Apparently he regretted his strange outburst of hostility the previous evening, because his manner no longer was challenging. The three of them talked easily about Dr. Johnson's dictionary, and Sheridan's play, *The School for Scandal,* a performance of which Donald had seen in Dublin. After the meal they moved into the library for port and coffee and more talk. Elizabeth took an almost feverish pleasure in every moment. And yet, despite her enjoyment, the words "the last time" kept sounding in her mind like a dirge. Probably this was the last time she would see firelight playing over Donald's light brown hair and sensitive face, the last time she would hear his warm voice speaking.

She lay awake for hours that night. Thus she was still asleep when Rose came in with morning tea. Hearing the rattle of the cup in its saucer, Elizabeth came instantly awake. She sat up in bed.

"Has Mr. Weymouth had breakfast?"

Rose settled the tray across Elizabeth's lap. "He is having it now, milady. I took a tray to his room ten minutes ago."

"And Sir Patrick? Did he return last night?"

Elizabeth's question had not specified where her husband might have returned from. But Rose knew that her mistress must realize that probably he was at Wetherly. And a crying shame it was, too, that he should be spending his nights with that highborn trollop. "No, milady. Sir Patrick is not here."

"Will you have someone tell Joseph that I would like to have him hitch up the cart for me?"

Voice expressionless, Rose said, "Yes, milady." Like the other servants, Rose did not enjoy seeing her beautiful ladyship drive around in that old cart like some tenant farmer's wife. But then, everyone knew that women in the family way often took strange notions.

Shortly after ten, with Donald keeping his mount reined to a walk beside her, Elizabeth drove the cart through the courtyard gates, across the field, and along the narrow lane that led through oaks and alders. When they emerged from the grove, they turned onto the road leading to Waterford. Overhead, sullen gray clouds promised rain before long.

They spoke little. Once Elizabeth said, "Be sure to tell my mother you found me well," and Donald answered, "I will." After that, they moved in silence down the road, past isolated cottages, past fields where men and women dug the now ripe potatoes with long-handled forks. When they had gone a hundred yards or so beyond a gap in the low line of hills, Elizabeth drew on the reins and brought the dapple gray to a halt.

"I had best turn back now."

They looked at each other through the gray light. "Elizabeth . . ." he said in a harsh, shaken voice. "Elizabeth."

"Please! Just go." Then, to her horror, she began to cry.

Swiftly he dismounted. He tied his horse's rein to one of the cart's corner posts. Then, reaching up, he aided her clumsy, tear-blinded descent to the road. He took her face in his hands and kissed her lips with desperate hunger.

"Don't go back there. Come with me. There's a fairly large town ten miles ahead. Maybe I can hire a hackney coach for the rest of the way to Waterford."

"Donald, Donald! You know I can't."

After a moment he said in a flat voice, "Yes, I know." She was another man's wife. In less than three months she would bear that man's child. "I know," he repeated. He tried to smile. "But you see, my darling, I love you so very much."

Since the chances were overwhelming that they would never see each other again, she let herself say it. "And I love you. I'll love you until the day I die. Help me back into the cart now. And then go. Don't look back at me. Just go."

Face very white, he kissed her again. Then he helped her onto the high wooden seat. He untied his mount's reins, swung into the saddle. As she had asked, he rode away without looking back.

She watched him until he disappeared around a bend in the road. She backed the cart, turned it. Then her hands, jerking the reins spasmodically, brought Toby to a halt.

On the hillside about a hundred yards ahead, Patrick sat astride his rangy black hunter. His very immobility told her that he had been there for at least several minutes. There was no chance in the world that he had not seen her in Donald's arms. For several seconds she and Patrick stared across the distance that separated them. Then he whirled the hunter and disappeared over the crest of the hill.

She sat there for several more seconds, heart thudding with dread, before she started driving through the gray light toward Stanford Hall and the infuriated man she would find awaiting her there.

22

As she drove through the courtyard gates, young Joseph came hurrying around the corner of the house to take charge of the dapple gray. Then the massive front doors opened, and Clarence came down the steps and helped her to the cobblestones. Heart pounding now with not only dread but also a growing defiance, she went into the house.

As she had expected to, she saw Patrick standing just beyond the library's doorway. Without waiting for him to speak, she swept past him into the room, head held high. He closed the doors and then turned toward her. For several seconds his infuriated gaze locked with her defiant one. Then he said, "Well, madam?"

She didn't answer.

His rage fueled by her silence, he said, "Is this the way you repay trust and generosity? I let you ask that parson fellow here, even though I knew you might be making sheep's eyes at each other. I welcomed him as best I knew how." His voice gathered fury. "And then today I see you making a public spectacle of yourselves—"

"Scarcely a spectacle, since there was no one to see us."

"*I* saw you! And others may have, too. I warned you, Elizabeth. I warned you that I would not let you make a fool of me."

She could no longer keep her bitterness in check.

"Whereas you are free to behave just as you please with Moira Ashley."

His voice turned cold. "You were the one who set forth the terms upon which we were married. You wrote that you would have no objection if—"

"Yes! I wrote that because I was desperate. And I was desperate because you had—"

"Stop that! God knows that whatever I did, I had provocation for it. Besides, that is all in the past."

"Is it?" she said furiously. "Is it? You dare to tell me it is all in the past, when I stand here carrying the child you . . ."

Rage closed her throat. Trembling all over, she moved toward the doors and then spun around to face him again. "But there is one thing you cannot do to me. I love Donald. And the only way you can stop my loving him is to kill me."

Blood rushed to his face, making it even darker. "By God, madam, if you don't watch both your behavior and your tongue, I may take up that challenge."

She wrenched the doors open and at an awkward run moved through the gloomy light toward the stairs. Blinded by tears, she started to climb. Halfway up, her toe caught on the rounded edge of a riser, and she fell heavily forward.

For a moment she just lay there, half-stunned. Then pain seized her like a giant hand. Dimly aware of what was happening, she screamed, not only from the pain but a foreknowledge of loss and sorrow. The giant hand relaxed, then squeezed again.

Patrick was beside her now. She heard him say, "Oh, my God, my God!" Then: "Colin! Tell Padric to ride to the village as fast as he can and bring back the midwife."

He lifted her in his arms and carried her on up the stairs.

23

She came awake, to see afternoon sunlight lying on the beautiful old carpet. What day was it? The same day that she had fallen on the stairs? No, there had been an interval of blazing candlelight. Faces had looked down at her through that light as she lay racked with pain. Patrick's face, and Mrs. Corcoran's, and the face of a middle-aged woman who must have been the village midwife.

Weakly she raised her head and looked down at her body, lying flat beneath the coverlet. So that was how it had ended. That new life, conceived in violence, had been snuffed out in a welter of blood and futile suffering.

"Milady!"

Until Mrs. Corcoran spoke, rising from her chair in one corner, Elizabeth had not known the housekeeper was in the room. The woman hurried over to the bed. Even though she already knew the answer, Elizabeth asked, "Then the child is dead?"

Mrs. Corcoran compressed her lips to stop their trembling. "Yes, milady. There was no chance of it being otherwise. You were well short of your seventh month, you know."

"Was it . . .?"

"You would have borne a son, milady." The housekeeper's face was swollen from recent tears. Elizabeth thought: I wish I could cry.

"Is there anything I can get for you?"

"Not right now, thank you."

Mrs. Corcoran hesitated, and then burst out, "Please try not to grieve, milady. You will have other children." Perhaps this miscarriage would prove a blessing in disguise, the housekeeper was thinking. Perhaps now Sir Patrick would stay closer to home, instead of chasing after that woman who, for all her lands and grand title, had always reminded Mrs. Corcoran of a mare in heat. Certainly he had seemed distressed enough last night, although whether it had been because of his wife's suffering or because of losing the child, it would be hard to say.

"Sir Patrick is downstairs, milady. He told me to tell him as soon as you felt able to see him."

She might as well get it over with, Elizabeth decided. "He can come up now if he likes."

Mrs. Corcoran hurried out. Elizabeth stared at the ceiling. Something she once had read flitted through her mind. Anne Boleyn, and the miscarriage she had suffered after a violent scene with her abominable husband, Henry VIII. His majesty had rushed into the room where she lay weeping with pain and terror, and had shouted at her, "Madam, you have killed my son!"

Would Patrick . . .?

Someone knocked. She called, "Come in."

The door opened. He stood there for a moment, his face well-controlled, and yet holding tired lines that told her he had slept little, if at all, during the last twenty-four hours. He crossed the room and stood beside her bed. "Are you in pain?"

"No. I am merely . . . very tired."

He wondered, looking down at her white, remote face, if she meant that she wanted him to leave her as soon as possible. Probably she did. "Colin set out early this morning for Dublin. He will bring a doctor back with him."

"A doctor?"

"Yes. I must know how you are."

No doubt what he must know, Elizabeth thought, was whether or not Lady Stanford was still capable of providing Sir Patrick Stanford with an heir.

He saw how her mouth had twisted, as if at the taste of something bitter. He said, "Is there anything I can do for you right now?"

"No, thank you. I think I would like to sleep." Bruised-looking in her white face, her eyelids closed.

"Very well. I will be down in the library, in case you need me." When she did not reply, he added in a rapid, almost harsh voice, "I am sorry about the child." He walked out of the room.

As he moved toward the stairs, he reflected that he should have known there would be no living child. What good could come of a marriage such as theirs?

If only there was some way of turning time back, some way that he and Elizabeth could become once more the man and woman they had been at first meeting, smiling at each other over punch in a candlelit London ballroom. But of course they could not, any more than a stream could flow uphill to its source. They were what they had become, and that was that.

In the library he added a small log to the feeble fire in the grate. He would stay at Stanford Hall until he heard the doctor's verdict. After that, it would be high time to set out on the long and crucially important journey he had planned for late September, a journey that would take him as far north as Belfast and as far west as Galway.

Trying to blot out all thought of his wife and dead child, he stood with palms propped against the mantelpiece and stared into the fire.

Three more days passed before Colin returned from Dublin with the doctor. On each of those days Patrick visited Elizabeth in the morning and again in the afternoon. Their brief conversations, concerned with the weather or minor household matters, included no mention of the son they had lost.

The doctor, a stocky, reserved-looking man of about forty, arrived late in the afternoon. When he had completed his examination, he told Elizabeth that her health had suffered no permanent damage. And there was no reason why she should not have half a dozen children. "You are young and strong," he said, as he prepared to leave. "You should be completely recovered within two or three weeks."

After Rose had taken her supper tray away that night, Patrick came into the room. "The doctor gave a good report of you."

"Yes. Is he still here?"

"No, he decided to start back to Dublin tonight." He paused. "I came to tell you that I too am leaving on a journey."

"When?"

"Early tomorrow morning."

As a matter of fact, he intended to leave Stanford Hall within the half-hour, ride over to Wetherly, and in the morning set out from there. He could no longer put off seeing Moira. News of Elizabeth's miscarriage must have traveled to Wetherly within an hour or two after it happened. Ever since then, Moira had been sending messages demanding that he come to see her.

Elizabeth said, in a tone of polite interest, "How long will you be gone?"

"Perhaps a month. You see, I am thinking of leasing additional farmlands and then subleasing them, not only here in the south but in other parts of Ireland."

Was he telling the truth? If so, it was the first time he had revealed any of his financial dealings to her. And if he was not telling the truth . . .

She looked up into his dark face, realizing that she still knew very little about him. What was he really like? And his frequent absences from Stanford Hall. Could visits to Moira and to his tenants account for all of them? Or were there times when he was doing . . . something else? She felt a stir of a new kind of uneasiness, so vague that she could not identify it.

He said, "You look tired. I had best say good night."

She answered, still in that polite voice, "Good night. I wish you a pleasant journey."

As the doctor had predicted, her health mended rapidly. In another two days she was sitting at her desk, writing to her mother about the miscarriage, but going into no details. A little more than a week after that, she was once more consulting with Mrs. Corcoran and Gertrude about menus, and even moving out of her room for brief inspection tours of the rest of the house.

Now that Patrick was away, Colin spent more time at Stanford Hall. He not only took supper with Elizabeth each night. Often he was there all day. With the potato and grain harvests in, he explained, there was no need for him to visit tenant farms, either those of Patrick or his own. Several mornings after Elizabeth was fully recovered, they went for horseback rides, moving with Gypsy past fields where grain had been gathered into shocks, and past apple orchards where the trees stood bare of both fruit and leaves. One such morning, hoarfrost covered the ground. Turning in the saddle, Elizabeth saw the hoofprints her mount and Colin's left on the gray-white rime, prints that disappeared so rapidly that they might have been made by ghosts.

In mid-October she received a letter from Madame Leclerc in Dublin. The Frenchwoman begged to inform Lady Stanford that her gowns were now finished, and could be fitted at any time after Lady Stanford's *accouchement*. Elizabeth folded the letter quickly after reading it. As much as possible she avoided thinking of the child she had lost.

As for the gowns, perhaps when Patrick returned he would suggest that they go to Dublin to get them.

The next night, she was in her room, changing, with Rose's help, before going down to supper, when she heard a clatter of hooves in the forecourt. Quickly she slipped into a robe and then went to the window. By the light streaming through the front doorway she saw Patrick hand his mount's reins to young Joseph and then turn toward the steps. Heartbeat strangely rapid, she turned back to Rose. "Please help me into my gown. Then I won't need you any longer."

She was alone in the room, pulling the stray tendril of hair into place before the mirror, when someone knocked. "Come in."

He entered the room, looking rumpled and with dust on his boots. "Colin tells me you have quite recovered," he said, "but I wanted to see for myself." He looked at her face in its frame of chestnut curls. "Yes, I see that he is right."

Elizabeth felt faint color in her cheeks. "And your journey?"

"It went well enough." He turned toward the door. "I must try to tidy myself before I go down to the supper table."

"Just a moment." Then, as he turned back to her: "Madame Leclerc has written that my gowns are ready. I was wondering if we might go to Dublin within the next few days."

"I am sorry. But I will be busy here for at least a week."

Busy doing what? Having a prolonged reunion with Moira Ashley?

Until now, when she felt a sharp pang of disappointment, she had not realized that she had very much wanted that trip to Dublin with Patrick. She was not sure why. Perhaps over the past weeks she had begun to hope, not for a happy marriage—that was quite impossible—but at least for a certain companionship with her husband.

Or—humiliating thought!—perhaps her treacherous body, now restored to health, had begun to clamor for the lovemaking of this man she had every reason to loathe, and yet could not help desiring. Perhaps without her ever admitting the thought to her consciousness, she had hoped that during the course of a few nights away from both Stanford Hall and Wetherly, she might lure him permanently away from Moira's bed.

He said, "You could take Mrs. Corcoran to Dublin with you. Or if you want to wait awhile, perhaps I could go with you. But not now. In fact, I plan to ride out again right after supper, perhaps to be gone several days."

"In that case," she said coldly, "I will not wait. I will go with Mrs. Corcoran."

24

In Dublin one afternoon less than a week later, Elizabeth stood in the sitting room of her two-room lodgings, the same lodgings she and Patrick had occupied the previous summer. In her hand was a note a manservant had just brought to the door. Frowning, she read it for the second time:

My dear Lady Stanford,
    Since I too am staying at this inn, would you grant

me the great pleasure of serving you tea in my
rooms? They are directly above your own.

I do hope to see you at four this afternoon.

Your obedient servant,
Moira Ashley

Elizabeth's gaze went to the traveling clock she had
placed on a desk in one corner. Almost three-thirty.
Should she go? Even as she asked herself the question,
she knew that she would. Curiosity alone would impel her
to do so.

What did Moira Ashley want? Was her arrival at this
particular inn at this particular time a coincidence? Elizabeth did not think so.

She herself, with Mrs. Corcoran riding beside her in the
Stanford coach, had arrived in Dublin the day before, too
late in the afternoon to visit Madame Leclerc's establishment. It was not until this morning that she had gone to
the Frenchwoman's shop. In a letter written from Stanford Hall, Elizabeth already had informed Madame
Leclerc of the miscarriage. Yesterday the modiste, after
expressing sympathy, had abandoned the topic. Nevertheless, as Elizabeth turned this way and that at the Frenchwoman's direction, she thought of how differently she had
once visualized her second visit to this establishment, with
herself describing to an appreciative Madame Leclerc the
charms of her little son or daughter.

"*Voilà!* This gown will now be of the perfect fit
through the waist. Can you remain in Dublin until late tomorrow afternoon, Lady Stanford? *Bon!* I will have your
gowns ready to put in the trunk of your carriage."

Elizabeth had returned to her rooms at the inn. Only
minutes later, Lady Moira's note had arrived.

How had Moira known that Elizabeth was even in Dublin, let alone at this particular inn? Through Patrick?
Probably, but not necessarily. Servants from both Weth-

erly and Stanford Hall, traveling to and from the village on various errands, regularly exchanged information.

She laid the note on the desk. Briefly she considered ringing for one of the inn servants, so that he could fetch Mrs. Corcoran from her room in the east wing of the building. But no. She did not need the housekeeper to help her change. In fact, she would not change. Here at a public inn, the violet bombazine she wore was quite elaborate enough for tea. Besides, the chances were that Moira Ashley had been watching from her window when the Stanford carriage had returned from the modiste's a few minutes ago. If so, she had seen the bombazine dress. Elizabeth felt that she would be at a disadvantage if Moira could picture her, in response to that note, hurrying to make herself sufficiently grand to take tea with a peeress. Elizabeth would tidy her hair, and leave it at that.

At four o'clock she knocked on the door of a room directly above her own sitting room. She heard light footsteps. Then the door opened. Lady Moira stood there in a silk gown, the color of champagne, that left her shoulders bare. Her dark hair, informally loosened, curled about her face. No matter how long it had taken Moira to achieve it, the effect was one of careless déshabillé. And she had never looked more beautiful.

"How kind of you to come, Lady Stanford!"

Murmuring that it was pleasant to have been asked, Elizabeth stepped into the room. The shades had been drawn at the windows, shutting out the gray light of the October afternoon. Only candleglow fell on the tea table, with its trays of scones and buttered bread and small chocolate cakes, its silver tea service so elaborate that Elizabeth realized her hostess must have brought it with her from Wetherly. Not even the finest inn in Dublin would provide its guests with a teapot that valuable.

When they had settled themselves at the table, Elizabeth asked, "How long have you been in Dublin, Lady Moira?"

"Since last night. And I will leave for Wetherly early tomorrow morning. Milk, Lady Stanford?"

"A little. No sugar, thank you."

Moira handed her guest a teacup, and then said with a laugh, "I am here on what Patrick calls a fool's errand."

At the other woman's easy use of Patrick's name, Elizabeth felt her hackles rise. "What sort of errand?"

"Have you ever heard of the Brazilian Company? No? Well, it has been formed to exploit newly discovered diamond mines in South America. Some shares have earned as much as thirty percent a year! Here in Dublin this morning I arranged with my banker and my lawyer to mortgage Wetherly and my other properties. The money raised will be invested in the Brazilian Company." She gave an excited laugh. "By this time next year, I should be the richest woman in Ireland!"

"But isn't there a risk . . .?"

"There is always risk when one sets out to make a great deal of money. But as I told Patrick, it is not in my nature to take the prudent course." She laughed again. This time the sound was tenderly amused. "He is quite exasperated with me. He advises me in all financial matters, you know, and usually I take his advice. Thus he is doubly annoyed when I do not."

Elizabeth had no doubt that her husband and this highly desirable woman were lovers. But the knowledge that they frequently shared the same bed conveyed to her less of a sense of their intimacy than the thought of him advising Moira in business matters, arguing with her, losing his temper, and telling her she was a fool. To behave like that, a man had to feel more than just desire for a woman. Her welfare had to be important to him.

"Anyway," Moira went on, "when I heard you had

gone to Dublin, I decided to make my visit here at the same time, in the hope we could have a talk."

"Who told you I had gone to Dublin?"

Moira's indigo eyes widened. "Why, Patrick, of course."

Had he? Or had she heard through servants' gossip?

"Now, as for what I felt we should talk about." She leaned forward and placed her teacup on the table. The gesture seemed to say that the polite skirmishing was over, and the real battle was about to be joined. After a moment's hesitation, Elizabeth also placed her cup on the table.

"Yes?" she said.

"How long, Lady Stanford, are you going to prolong a situation that must make you even more unhappy than it makes Patrick and me?"

Elizabeth said, sparring for time, "Unhappy?"

"Come, come, Lady Stanford! You know how little time Patrick spends at his own home. Where do you think he does spend it?"

Anger at the other woman's arrogance speeded Elizabeth's heartbeats. "And what are you proposing I do about it?"

Moira leaned forward. "You could petition for divorce."

"Divorce!"

"Yes! It can be managed. Consanguinity—you know, blood relationship—is the best grounds. A clever lawyer could find some degree of relationship between the Stanfords and the Montlows, even if it was many generations back. Almost anything can serve as a pretext. Why, did you know that a marriage was once dissolved because the husband, years before his marriage, had stood godfather to a baby who was a cousin of his future wife's? All it takes is a clever lawyer and a sufficient amount of money."

"No doubt," Elizabeth said dryly. After a moment she added, "Did Patrick know you were going to discuss with me the possibility of divorce?"

"Why, of course!"

Somehow the tone was a little emphatic, and the dark blue eyes too wide and candid, to carry conviction.

"I see. And after dissolution of the marriage, you would become Patrick's wife. Is that it?"

"Exactly. Patrick and I have always been perfectly suited to one another. Now, I don't know how it is that he married you . . ."

"You don't?" So it was apparent, Elizabeth thought grimly, that the understanding between Patrick and Moira was not as complete as the lady represented it to be.

As if aware she had blundered, Moira said quickly, "Oh, I know in a general way. I know it was because you . . . became pregnant. But my point is this. Patrick and I are right for each other by any standard you can mention—rank, temperament, even nationality."

"Perhaps so. But why should I oblige you and Patrick by consenting to divorce?"

"Because then you would be free to marry that Englishman."

"So you know about Donald Weymouth." Moira nodded, smiling. "Then you must know also that he is a clergyman of the Church of England. As such, he could not possibly marry a divorced woman."

"No law compels him to be a vicar! He could leave the church."

Elizabeth said quietly, "That is something I would strive at all costs to keep him from doing."

"Why must you be such a fool! Why do you want to keep all three of us unhappy? No, four, counting your Englishman. I should think that your miscarriage—or rather, the quarrel leading up to it—would make you re- alize that nothing can turn out well for you and Patrick."

"What do you know of that quarrel?"

"Why . . . why, I know it was because you and the Englishman had left the hall together, he on horseback and you in a cart. Patrick came home, heard about it, and flew into a rage. Not out of any sort of jealousy," she added quickly. "He just felt that you, a woman at least legally his wife, had made a fool of yourself, trailing alongside the departing guest in a farmer's cart."

So, Elizabeth thought, Patrick had not told her of seeing his wife in Donald Weymouth's arms. More than likely, Patrick had told Moira nothing about that quarrel. All she knew was what she had learned from servants.

Elizabeth said, "Lady Moira, if Patrick wants his marriage dissolved, then let him tell me so. And now, since you have been so free with advice, I should like to give you some. Why don't you try to get over your obsession with my husband?"

"Obsession!" Rage, swift and to Elizabeth inexplicable, expanded Moira's pupils until her eyes looked black.

"Yes, obsession. Here you are, beautiful, rich, and still young. Surely you could have your choice of a number of men. And yet nothing will content you short of marrying a man now legally tied to another woman."

"But only legally." Moira was one of those people who smile when most infuriated, and she was smiling now. "I should think that your pride would welcome a chance to be free of such a marriage."

"There are some kinds of pride that one cannot afford. True, my situation now is a humiliating one. It would be much more so if I returned to England alone, penniless, and unable to marry the one man I ever wanted to marry."

"There would be no need for you to return penniless. As you have said, I am rich."

Elizabeth smiled. "I am afraid I do have pride, after all—at least, enough that I could not possibly accept money from you. Nor can I believe that Patrick suggested that you discuss with me the possibility of divorce. Cowardice is not one of his faults. But if by any chance I am mistaken, if he did send you to Dublin to find out whether I would consider such a step, then tell him I will not, unless he himself asks me to."

She rose. "Perhaps I had best go now."

Lady Moira also stood up. "Perhaps you had," she said evenly.

When her guest had gone, Moira crossed to the window and with angry force swept the draperies apart. The last of the daylight came in to mingle with the candles' glow. Face white with rage, she looked down into the street.

Obsession. It was that word which had enraged her even more than Elizabeth's apparent determination to remain Lady Stanford. It was a word she hated, because ever since her earliest childhood she had heard it applied to both her mother and her Aunt Sara.

It was her aunt, the elder of Lord Rawling's daughters, whose behavior had first scandalized his neighbors there in the misty northern countryside near Belfast. At the age of twenty-one she had fallen in love with an artist who had been commissioned to do her portrait. After stealing a large sum from her father's strongbox, Sara had pursued the unfortunate painter to London. Despite his repeated rejections of her, she had followed him from one European capital to another. Finally, in Venice, she had tried to kill him with a knife. When the attempt failed, she had stabbed herself fatally through the heart.

As for Moira's mother, her obsession had taken an even more bizarre turn. When Moira was three, her mother had given birth to a male child who lived less than a week. Moving into the room that had been set aside for the child, the bereaved woman had insisted that all the shades be drawn permanently. By the light of one candle she had sat there day after day, year after year, all during Moira's childhood and girlhood, rocking the empty cradle.

She was dead now, but she had still been alive at the time of Moira's marriage. Both Moira and her father knew why she, a beautiful and spirited viscount's daughter, had not been courted by any of the local young men of sufficiently high birth. All those men were aware that there was an "odd" streak on the maternal side of Moira's family. In the end, Lord Rawling had felt fortunate to be able to marry his daughter to a rich visitor from southern Ireland, even though Sir Kevin Ashley, a widower, was three times her age.

She thought of the afternoon eight years ago when she, a bride of a few weeks, had walked out onto a terrace at Wetherly and found her stooped, graying husband in conversation with a tall young man. Sir Kevin had made the introduction. For a second or two before he bent to kiss her hand, Patrick Stanford's eyes had looked straight into hers. She'd had a strange sensation, as if her heart quite literally had moved within her breast. Oh, she had known it was not love at first sight. Perhaps there was no such thing. But it was recognition that here was a man she could love. And certainly it was desire at first sight. Her husband's ineffectual lovemaking had awakened her sensuality without satisfying it. She knew instinctively that Patrick could satisfy her.

She had no doubt that he too had felt the strong pull of attraction between them. But apparently he was determined not to betray his lifelong friend and neighbor, Sir Kevin. After that first afternoon, he stayed away from Wetherly except for large balls and for meetings of the local hunt.

Other men were not so scrupulous. During the four years that passed before Sir Kevin was found crumpled up on the floor of his dressing room, dead hand still clutching

at his chest, Moira had taken several lovers. But they had
been only substitutes for the man she wanted.

After her husband's death, suitors for her hand had appeared as soon as the official mourning period was over.
But Patrick made no proposal of marriage. He did give
every indication, however, that he wanted to share her
bed, now that Sir Kevin was gone. Angrily, Moira had refused him what she had granted to others. "You'll have to
marry me," she had told him.

Instead, he had married that gray-eyed Englishwoman.
And at last, Moira, after eight years of frustration, had
capitulated and become his mistress. Now she was more
in love with him than ever, more determined than ever
that their union would become permanent and legal.

She felt the pressure of tears behind her eyes. What
had she ever had out of life? A childhood and girlhood
shadowed by her mother's madness. Four years of
marriage to a man old enough to be her grandfather. And
now, when she was more than ever in love with Patrick,
more than ever needing to become his wife, she found her
way barred by a whey-faced creature who did not love
Patrick and who—oh, surely!—was not loved by him.

Damn Elizabeth Stanford! Damn her!

She whirled around, seized the cup from which her
guest had drunk, and hurled it. Leaving a trail of spilled
drops across the pastel floral rug, it shattered against the
door.

Two nights later the Stanford carriage emerged from
the grove of oaks and alders and moved across the
meadow toward Stanford Hall. In one corner Elizabeth
sat with her gaze fixed on the rows of mullioned windows reflecting the light of a three-quarter moon. In the
other corner Mrs. Corcoran slept, her chin sunk on her
chest.

As she had told Moira Ashley, Elizabeth had no inten-

tion of even considering a divorce unless Patrick asked
her to. And yet, all during the journey from Dublin she
had been aware of the irony of those elaborate gowns
back there in the carriage trunk, gowns that in all likeli-
hood she would seldom if ever wear. As their relations
were now, it was unlikely that they would be giving
many parties, or going to them. And she felt sure that if
Patrick went to London for the season, it would be without her.

Was she going to live out her life like this, bound in
marriage to a man who had ceased even to desire her?

She reached over and touched the housekeeper's arm.
"Wake up. We are here."

As Mrs. Corcoran straightened her bonnet, the carriage
clattered through the wrought-iron gates and into the
courtyard. The hall's door swung open, and Clarence
came down the stone stairs to open the carriage door and
let down its steps. Elizabeth asked, "Is Sir Patrick at
home?"

"No, milady. He has not been here since this morning."

Of course not, Elizabeth thought. Leaving Dublin well
before she herself had, Moira must have reached Wetherly last night. Undoubtedly Patrick was there with her
right now.

25

Elizabeth was wrong about Patrick being at Wetherly.
He was a good five miles from there in an upstairs room
of the fishing village's one public house. With a

companion, the same vaguely foreign-looking man Elizabeth once had glimpsed in the taproom of that fashionable Dublin inn, he sat a rough table, drawn up close to the fire on this crisp night. On the table, amid the remains of the meal they had shared, lay a map of Ireland and several sheets of paper, each covered with writing in Patrick's bold hand.

With the tip of a quill pen, Patrick was pointing to some of the score of inked X marks on the map. "Near Londonderry we now have almost a hundred muskets hidden in the vaults of a ruined abbey. Here in an inlet of Sligo Bay, in a cave, are fifteen cannon your people shipped to us a year ago. Near Castlebar . . . But perhaps you would rather read the information. On those sheets of paper are the lists of arms and gunpowder stored at each of the locations marked on the map."

Georges Fontaine nodded and then pulled the map and sheets of paper close to him. He was that rarity, a taciturn Frenchman. Over the years he and Patrick, without becoming friends, had developed respect for each other. It was not a respect that extended to the separate causes for which they worked. To Patrick, France was a country sadly misruled by fat, stupid King Louis and vain and extravagant Marie Antoinette. To Georges, the Irish were a people so feckless, so divided among themselves, that the rebellion Patrick strove for probably would not succeed, any more than had the Irish rebellions of the past.

But they had a common enemy, England. And each man was fully aware of the courage and determination of the other.

Patrick got up, walked over to the fireplace, and stood, as he often did, palms propped against the edge of the mantelpiece, gaze directed at the blazing logs. Then, unable to stand quietly, he began to pace the room. Within a few months, all he had worked for these past ten years would bring the beginning of a glorious triumph, or a bloody shambles of defeat, just one more of the defeats that island had suffered in its six-hundred-year struggle against the English invader.

In one respect he had been reckless. Unlike previous landowners who had led rebellions, he had not counted upon using mercenaries—usually Scots—to do the fighting. Instead, he planned to do something that no rebel leader—whether Irish or Anglo-Irish, Catholic or Protestant—had yet dared to do. He would distribute to desperately poor tenant farmers the arms, smuggled in from France, that he had been stockpiling over these past years.

But if he had been daring in one respect, he had been cautious in others. Always he had maintained the facade of the self-indulgent Anglo-Irish landlord, breeding fine hunters, maintaining a pack of foxhounds, and going to London each winter to attend balls and royal levees and to throw away money at the gaming tables. With a very few exceptions, not even the men who would take leading roles in the uprising knew the identity of its chief planner. During his recent tour of Ireland he had inspected firearms sufficient to supply seventeen thousand men, but he had met face to face with only six. Among them was a young baronet with an estate near Limerick, one of the few men of property willing to risk their lands in an attempt to shake off the English yoke. The other five were all either tenant farmers or owners of only a few acres.

As for the great mass of men who for years had drilled by night in isolated fields, and who would use those hidden arms when the time came, they knew only their local leaders. Most of them, far from knowing that Patrick Stanford was the chief architect of the coming rebellion, had never even heard of him.

Georges Fontaine, studying the map and the handwritten sheets of paper, began to drum his fingernails against the table. The sound reminded Patrick not only of the

Frenchman's presence, but of Henry Owen, the man who had sat with him and Fontaine at a taproom table in that Dublin inn the previous summer.

At one time Owen had been a tenant of Patrick's. Through his own efforts, plus a small loan from Patrick, he had managed to buy a few acres near Waterford. Patrick had felt that if he could trust anyone, he could trust Henry Owen. The man was intelligent and hardworking. He had risen too recently from the tenant class to be callous to their sufferings. Until that meeting in Dublin last June, Patrick had confided in him almost as completely as he had in the French agent, Fontaine.

But in that Dublin taproom Patrick had received an impression of something false and overhearty in Owen's manner. That impression had been reinforced when, only a few days ago, Patrick had visited Owen at his small farm. The next day in Waterford he had seen Owen's wife coming out of a shop, clad in a brown velvet gown and an ostrich-plumed hat. At sight of her, a coachman had scrambled down from the box of a smart new carriage and opened its door for her.

How could a farmer make enough from a few acres of potatoes and wheat to buy velvet and ostrich plumes, and a carriage and pair? Well, perhaps Owen had not. Once he had mentioned to Patrick that his wife's uncle, a Belfast merchant, had "done very well in the tobacco trade." Perhaps Mrs. Owen had inherited money.

Nevertheless, Patrick was glad that he had never turned over to Owen a master list giving the size and location of arms caches all over the island. Always he had told Owen that he would be supplied with such a list "later."

Behind him the Frenchman said, "I see from this list that our recent shipment of eighty muskets reached you."

Patrick turned. "Yes, four days ago. I was waiting in Waterford when they arrived." Transferred by night from a French merchant ship to an Irish fishing boat, the arms had been concealed not only by false deck but by a day's catch of herring.

Fontaine asked, "May I keep this list and the map?"

"Yes. I have duplicates in my strongbox at the hall."

Rising, Fontaine stuffed the papers inside his greatcoat. "I had best leave. Tomorrow afternoon I have an appointment with a wine merchant in Cork." It was in the innocent guise of an agent for a French wine-exporting firm that Fontaine traveled all over Ireland. "I want to ride part of the way yet tonight."

Patrick waited a few minutes after the Frenchman had gone. Then he too left the public house, rode through the sleeping village and up the steep path to the moon-flooded headland and the rolling, uncultivated land beyond it. There he turned, not toward Stanford Hall, but Wetherly.

Nevertheless, he found himself wondering if Elizabeth had returned from Dublin. As always when he thought of her—and he avoided doing so as much as possible—he felt a mixture of anger and guilt. Perhaps that morning last September he should have realized that a quarrel might endanger the unborn child. Perhaps he should have turned there on that hillside and ridden away, and never even let her know he had seen her in Weymouth's arms. But he was not capable of such restarint.

And later on, certainly, he had tried to be gentle with her. Despite the fact that the uprising for which he had risked his property and even his neck all these years was now imminent, he had been willing to go with her on a frivolous errand to Dublin, just as soon as he had the opportunity. But that had not been enough for her. While he waited in Waterford for that arms shipment, she had gone off, not even leaving him a message. He'd had to question the servants to learn the whereabouts of his own wife.

With an effort he turned his thoughts from Elizabeth to the woman he would see in a few minutes. Early that morning a Wetherly servant had brought him a note from Moira, demanding that he come to her as soon as possible. He hoped that she did not plan to bring up again that preposterous idea that he petition for divorce on some trumped-up grounds.

He hoped also that she had gone no further with her plan to invest heavily in that South American diamond company. The little fool! She had no need to gamble recklessly. She was sufficiently rich. But where money was concerned, she was insatiable, just as that ivory-skinned body of hers was insatiable for lovemaking.

That particular thought brought him a pleasant glow. Busy with other matters, he had not been to bed with her for more than a week. He urged his mount to a brisker trot.

When he entered the long-familiar room with its thick Aubusson carpet, its blazing candelabrum on a dressing table covered with scent bottles and little silver pots of rouge, he knew at once that she had not given up hope of seeing him that night. Her hair, falling around shoulders left bare by a diaphanous green nightshift, had been brushed to blue-black luster. Her full mouth was rouged. Smiling, she came into his arms. He kissed her, one hand between her shoulderblades and the other on her hips, pressing the whole length of her full-breasted body against him.

She looked into his dark face, its eyes half-lidded with desire. Should she talk to him about it now, or later? Now, she decided, while his hunger for her would lend force to her arguments.

"I've been to Dublin since I last saw you."

He said, not sounding very interested, "You have?" With one hand he drew the bodice of her nightshift lower and kissed one ivory breast.

She stepped back from him. "I stayed at the same inn as your wife. We had tea together." She saw his face grow rigid, but nevertheless rushed on. "Oh, Patrick! I don't think she will oppose a divorce, not if you tell her you want it."

He said slowly, "Let me understand this. You took it upon yourself to go to Dublin and talk to my wife about—"

"I had to, for both your sake and mine! Otherwise we would have gone on like this year after year, just because you're too softhearted to—"

"Softheartedness has nothing to do with it." His voice was ice-cold now. "I have told you several times that I will never try to divorce my wife. A marriage is a bargain. And an honorable man keeps his bargains."

She smiled at him. "But, my darling, it was such a foolish bargain! I'll never understand why you thought you had to marry her, just because she was weak and silly enough to let you get her with child. In fact, I'll never understand why she let you, a cold-as-a-fish woman like her . . ."

"Moira! I've told you before that I will not discuss that."

She said hurriedly, still with that coaxing smile, "But think how happy we could be, Patrick. It's not just that we love each other. I'm rich, and I'm going to be even richer, and you need money. We could give her money, too, enough that she could live comfortably back in England."

He said, after a long moment, "Did you tell her that? Did you offer to buy her husband from her? Yes, I can see that you did. Moira, you're an imbecile. Do you think that a woman like Elizabeth would take money from . . .?"

He broke off. For several moments she looked at him, her face turning white, her eyes large now and very dark. "What were you going to say? From a wanton? A slut?"

"Of course not. I was going to say 'from my mistress.'"

"But I'm not just that to you! Patrick, Patrick! We love each other."

He said quietly, "Have I ever told you I loved you?"

She stood motionless for a moment. Then her face twisted. "But you do love me, you do!" Tears welled to her eyes and streamed down her cheeks. "It's only because you're so stiff-necked that you won't . . . You've got to love me! You're all I have in the whole—"

"Moira! I had best leave now. We will discuss this when we are both calm." He started to turn away.

"Oh, no, we won't!" Sudden fury blazed in her tear-wet face. She sprang forward and grasped his arm with both her hands. "We'll discuss it now! Are you in love with that scrawny Englishwoman? Maybe you're hoping that someday you will get everything you want in bed from her. In the meantime, I am . . . a convenience."

"Moira! You know you've been more than that to me."

She rushed on, unheeding. "But if you've been making a fool of me, you've been making a fool of yourself, too. She'll never love you. She told me so. Her life with you is miserable. She stays with you because she has no money, and because she can never have the man she wants, that vicar of hers."

Anger replaced the softening he had felt at sight of her tears. He pulled his arm free of her grasp and turned toward the door.

"Patrick! If you leave me now, don't ever come back!"

"Good night, Moira." He opened the door.

Her voice rose to a scream. "You're going to be sorry for tonight! You have no idea how sorry!"

Her last sentence came to him through the door's heavy panels. He descended the broad staircase, walked past a footman, who stared discreetly straight ahead as he held the front door open, and went out into the night.

During the ride of a little more than half an hour to the hall, some of his anger cooled. Would Moira have him turned away at the door if he again went to Wetherly? He doubted it. But beautiful and desirable as she was, he also rather doubted that he would want to see her again. It was not just his distaste for the thought of her following Elizabeth to Dublin and offering her a bribe. Despite those tears that momentarily had touched him, there had been something almost frightening about her tonight. Oh, their tempers had clashed a few times in the past, but never before had he gained the impression of a woman ... not quite sane.

That threat of hers as he went out the door crossed his mind. He shrugged it off. An enraged woman would say anything. And what revenge could she take, aside from excluding him from her bed and taking some other man into it?

A sleepy-eyed Clarence opened the door to him. "Good evening, Sir Patrick. Her ladyship has returned."

"She is in her room?"

"Yes, she retired more than an hour ago."

He looked up at the shadowy gallery above the twin staircases, remembering Moira's words. "She'll never love you. Her life with you is miserable." Had Elizabeth really said that? Surely not, at least not in those words. She was too reticent, too well-bred, to make such confidences, especially to her husband's mistress. Nevertheless, those words probably described what she felt.

And yet, there had been a period of several weeks when she had not seemed too wretched, at least when she lay moaning with pleasure in his arms. But surely the loss of the child had ended all that. Surely all he could expect now, if he went to her bed, was cold acquiescence. And despite that violent episode in the house north of London, he was not by nature a rapist. He could take little pleasure in a woman who merely endured his possession of her body.

He turned toward the library. Glancing to his right, he

saw a thread of light shining beneath the door of Colin's office. He hesitated, and then decided he wanted no company tonight.

In the library he found only one of the oil sconce lamps lit, its feeble glow mingling with that of the dying fire. He lit more lamps and added a log to the embers. Women, he thought. What endless trouble they were. Surely the Almighty, if there was one, could have chosen some more sensible way to perpetuate the species than by creating two sexes.

Resolutely he turned to the strongbox in one corner of the room, opened it, and took out a duplicate of the list he had given to Georges Fontaine that night. He spread the papers out on the heavy table and looked down at them. Only two more shipments, one of cannon and one of muskets, were due to arrive. The cannon would be hidden with others at Sligo Bay. As for the muskets, there was still room in that cave near the fishing village.

And a few weeks from now—on the day before Christmas, to be exact—designated leaders all over this island would pass out arms to the men under their command. English soldiers stationed in Ireland, already drunk on Christmas grog, would respond slowly to simultaneous attacks on their garrisons. Across the channel, England too would be caught up in the annual celebration, with Parliament in recess and the king's ministers scattered to their country houses. By the time the English realized that now theirs was a three-front war, and sent what reinforcements they could muster across the channel, all Ireland would be in Irish hands.

Soon he was deep in thoughts that had nothing to do with the two women, either the one at Wetherly, who walked the floors with angry tears streaming down her face, or the one who, despite her lonely and hopeless thoughts, had finally managed to fall asleep in her four-poster bed here in his own house.

26

Fall slipped into winter, the mild winter of southern Ireland, with only occasional light snow but many days of chill rain or of fog so thick that from her bedroom window Elizabeth could not see the courtyard's wrought-iron gates. With no desire to ride out along the muddy lanes, she passed many of the short afternoons playing chess with Colin before the library fire.

Patrick spent little time at home. Even when he was physically at the supper table, Elizabeth felt he was not really there. Tense and silent, he seemed off in some world of his own.

Early in December Elizabeth had reason to believe that his other world no longer included Moira Ashley. When Rose brought in the tea one morning, she fussed elaborately over the tray she had placed across her mistress's lap, moving the cup and saucer about, and lifting the teapot's lid to look inside. Finally Elizabeth realized that these maneuvers were meant to draw attention to the ring on the girl's right hand, a ring of some silvery-looking metal with a red-glass setting.

"What a pretty ring! Where did you get it?"

My friend Molly, over to Wetherly, bought two of these from a peddler and gave me one. The young gentleman who's there so often now asked Molly to tighten some loose buttons on his coat, and she did it so nice he gave her three shillings."

The girl's face and voice were bland. Nevertheless,

206

Elizabeth realized that Rose, the recipient of a gift, was in turn bestowing one. She wanted her mistress to know that Lady Moira had taken a new lover. "What young gentleman?"

"Michael Halloran, Sir John Halloran's youngest son. Molly says he is there all the time."

Elizabeth was sure that in that case Patrick no longer visited Wetherly. He was scarcely the sort to share a mistress with another man. She said, "It's a nice ring, Rose. Will you please tell Mrs. Corcoran that I would like to see her now?"

Annoyed with herself for the leap of hope in her heart, she watched the girl leave the room. What reason did she have to think that Patrick might turn to her now? If anything, he had seemed more distant than ever these past few weeks. Again she was touched by the half-frightened thought: if he was not with Moira, what was he doing during his absences from Stanford Hall?

Over the next few days she felt a heightening of that unease, as if some disaster she could not name impended. At supper he would sit at the other end of the long table, dark face unreadable, speaking scarcely a word to her or Colin. Twice in the night she was awakened by the sound of him pacing up and down his own bedroom.

And then, as she and Colin sat at supper one evening, they heard the thunderous striking of the door knocker, followed by Clarence's hurried footsteps along the hall. Patrick appeared in the dining-room archway. Elizabeth gasped. His face, bleak-eyed and with its dark skin grayed by pallor, was like that of a man who had just heard his death sentence.

"Come into the library," he said hoarsely, "both of you."

Beside Colin, Elizabeth hurried across the hall. Patrick was already crouched beside the strongbox. "Close the doors!"

Colin obeyed. Elizabeth said, past the nameless fear crowding her throat, "What has happened?"

With both hands Patrick drew papers from the strong-box. "I must get out of Ireland, right tonight."

After a stunned moment she cried, "But why?"

Not answering, he stood up. Colin asked quietly, "You have been betrayed?"

"I have." He moved toward the fireplace. "I can only hope that not many others have been."

It was Georges Fontaine who had given him the news, less than an hour ago, there in the upstairs room of the village public house. Someone had gotten word to London about the planned uprising. Agents of the king, armed with a warrant for Patrick's arrest, were already on their way across the channel. Unless he managed to escape, he would soon be in London. He thought of himself in the hands of his Majesty's interrogators, his will no longer in control of his painracked body, his tongue babbling out the locations of all those arms secretly assembled over the past years, and the names of brave men who would have led that uprising on Christmas Eve. And if he survived the torture, there would be the cart ride through the jeering crowd to a traitor's death on the gallows.

Feeding papers into the flames, he said over his shoulder to his brother, "And don't remind me that all along you have warned that this might happen."

Colin said, in that same quiet voice, "I did not intend to remind you."

Terrified and bewildered, Elizabeth cried, "What are you talking about? What has happened?"

Patrick turned to face her. "You'll find out when the English get here, and so I might as well tell you now." He did so in swift, curt sentences.

Unable to take in the details, but now as aware as he that his remaining here would mean certain death, she fought for self-control. "But where are you going?"

He studied her with narrowed eyes. During the past terrible hour it had crossed his mind that his own wife, hating him as she did, might have been his betrayer. He was sure that Colin had told her nothing. But perhaps, during his own many prolonged absences from the hall, she had gained an inkling of his activities. He had tried to be careful. Any incriminating papers not locked in his strongbox he always had consigned to the fire. But perhaps she had found some partially burned scrap . . .

And certainly she had seen those cases of muskets in the cave near the village. According to Colin, she had assumed the cases contained tea or some other harmless sort of smuggled goods. Perhaps later, though, she'd had second thoughts . . .

But no. Not even the greatest actress alive could counterfeit the bewildered fear he read in her white face and distended gray eyes. He said, "There is a French merchant ship anchored in a cove a few miles from here. A fishing boat from the village will take me to it. If it does not run into an English patrol, the ship should be well on its way to a French-held island in the West Indies after a few days' run. There is no need for you to know which island.

"As for you yourself," he went on, "the English will arrest you when they get here, but I do not think they will hold you for long. True, I have used your money to buy arms, and they will soon find out that I have. But it was without your consent or even your knowledge. I think you will be allowed to rejoin your mother."

Speechless, she stared at him. He had used her money to arm would-be rebels against her own country. Outrage surged through her, and then subsided.

Strange that her anger should be so brief. And even stranger that it should be replaced by a thrill of admiration for this grim-faced man. Perhaps it was because she had seen with her own eyes the starving Irish scarecrows grubbing sullenly in their tiny fields. Perhaps it was because she was glad that, no matter what his treament of her, the man whose name she bore had set himself apart from the idle, ruthlessly selfish Anglo-Irish of his class.

He had brought more papers from the strongbox to toss into the flames. She said, "There is no guarantee, is there, that the English will treat me kindly?"

He shot her a haggard look. "I am afraid not. If I had thought you would be in jeopardy . . . But I had no idea we would fail. We had planned so well, and worked for so long . . ."

Unable to go on speaking, he fed the last of the papers onto the fire. Again he told himself bitterly that it must have been Henry Owen who had turned Judas. Probably he would never know for sure.

Elizabeth thought of herself in an English prison, questioned hour after hour by determined men, and perhaps not knowing whether Patrick was free or under arrest, alive or dead. She said, almost before she knew she was going to, "Take me with you."

He stared at her, dumbfounded. "To the West Indies?"

"I would be better off than in an English prison." She added evenly, "Surely you owe me that much."

Inwardly flinching at that last sentence, he forced his harassed mind to consider the idea. Certainly there was no guarantee that the English, unable to lay their hands on him, might not vent their frustration upon his wife. And the French merchant ship would have a good head start. With any luck . . .

He said curtly, "Very well, if that is your desire." He turned to his brother. "You have had no part in all this, Colin. Perhaps you can make the English believe you did not even know about it. If so, you will be able to hold onto your own lands, even though mine, of course, will be confiscated."

Colin said, in a stubbornly calm voice, "I am going with you."

Patrick cried, "Good God, man! Why? Out of some kind of brotherly loyalty? If you come with me, it will be the same as confessing that you were part of the rebellion. If we are caught, Elizabeth won't hang, no matter what else they might do to her. She's a gentlewoman, and English. But you'll dangle from a gallows as surely as I will."

"All this is true. But I would still rather take my chances aboard that ship. Besides, I know the West Indies. I might be of help to you down there in making a living."

God knows he would need help, Patrick thought. The money he had here at the hall would not keep them for more than a few months. "Do as you like."

Colin turned toward the door. "I had better write some letters for Clarence to deliver after we leave." He would write to Mr. Slattery, his overseer, and to his mother, and to Catherine Ryan, that calm-faced widow whose bed he might never share again.

When the door had closed behind Colin, Patrick said to Elizabeth, "Can you be ready in an hour? None of us can take much baggage. The fishing boat is small."

Despite her shock, her fear of what the next few hours might bring, let alone the coming days and weeks, Elizabeth forced her mind to practical matters. She would take one other woolen gown for the voyage, and fill the rest of a small hand trunk with lightweight clothing.

"Yes, I will be ready."

27

Afterward the events of that night were to Elizabeth an unreal blur. The hurried packing in her room. The leave-taking of the servants assembled in the downstairs hall, all of them with stunned faces, and Mrs. Corcoran and Rose actually in tears. They need not fear, Patrick told them, for either their lives or their freedom. Only fools—and certainly the English were not that—would believe that he had involved his household staff in his activities. "Whoever the English appoint to take charge here probably will continue to employ most of you. As for the rest, I have given Clarence a sum of money to tide you over until you find new places."

After that, there had been the swift carriage ride through the moonless night to the village, where two silent men, only shapes of deeper dark in the darkness, handed them into a small, fishy-smelling boat. Patrick guided her to a place in the stern. She sat huddled deep in her cloak against the chill December night while the fishermen rowed the boat almost soundlessly down the inlet to the sea. Here a white mist hovered above the black water. She heard a subdued rattle as the two villagers hoisted sail. Slowly, with the fishermen taking to the oars whenever the faint breeze died, the boat moved through the thickening fog.

Standing beside her, Patrick spoke only once. "I was to occupy the owner's cabin. Instead, you will have it. Colin and I will find some other place to bed down."

Her voice was cool. "Thank you."

The white smother had become so thick that she did not know they were near the French merchantman until one of the fishermen gave a cautious hail. Almost immediately it was answered from somewhere ahead in the fog. Gradually the ship took shape, a small three-master with a raised afterdeck. As nearly as she could tell, its sails were already set. But no lights were showing, not even the faint glow of a binnacle light.

Patrick and Colin climbed to the deck. Then Elizabeth, aided by one of the fishermen, stepped from the swaying boat onto the rope ladder. Hampered by her skirts, catching her heel in the hem of her heavy cloak and then pulling it free, she managed to climb a few rungs. Hands reached down and drew her the rest of the way over the bulwark to the fog-wet deck.

She found herself part of a cluster of dark figures. One of them was saying in heavily accented English, ". . . you would be alone."

"I am sorry, Captain Marquette. My wife and brother chose not to risk arrest. If you have no objection, my wife will occupy the cabin you intended to assign to me."

"Very well." The captain still sounded upset. Now she could distinguish his short, burly shape from that of the other men. "You, there," he said to one of the crewmen, "carry Lady Stanford's trunk. Lady Stanford, please come with me."

She followed the two figures to the raised afterdeck. A door opened, letting a swath of yellow light into the fog. "Please go inside quickly, Lady Stanford."

In the cabin the thin young sailor carrying her hand trunk placed it on the floor. Captain Marquette said, "Don't pull back the curtains at the portholes, Lady Stanford. Until we are clear of these waters, we must show as little light as possible."

She could see his plump face now. It was not ill-natured, only worried. She could understand that. In English waters he had three fugitives from English justice, one of them a woman, aboard his probably unarmed merchant ship. "I will be careful."

He bowed, and followed by the young sailor, left the cabin. She looked around her. Oil lamps hung in gimbals showed her the bunk bed, the washstand against the opposite bulkhead, the worn dark red carpet, and the heavy brown curtains drawn across the two portholes.

Seated on the bed, she heard running footsteps along the deck, and the clanking of the anchor chain. Slowly at first, the ship began to move. She rose again, turned back the dark red counterpane and the blankets that covered the coarse but clean sheets, and undressed. In her nightshift, she extinguished the lamps and groped her way to the bed.

Silence now except for the creak of ship's timbers and the faint seethe of water past the hull. She thought, feeling almost incredulous: Only a little more than a year ago I lived quietly in the English countryside, looking forward to my marriage to Donald and the children we would have. And now? Now I'm the penniless, childless, ignored wife of a man fleeing an English gallows. It's as if the unspeakable thing my brother did in that empty London house set a whirlwind in motion, one that soon caught me up. Now it has dropped me aboard this ship, plowing without lights through waters controlled by a country I no longer have a right to call my own.

And yet, in spite of the sorrow for all she had lost, she had this strange sense of freedom, even exhilaration. It was almost good to be moving farther away from England and that bedroom Patrick Stanford had brutally invaded. And good to be moving farther away from Ireland, where she had lost the child conceived that terrible night. No matter how uncertain the future appeared, it at least held the promise of a new beginning.

Exhausted, and lulled by the ship's gentle rolling, she fell asleep.

She woke, to see dim light filtering through the porthole curtains. Quickly she crossed the cabin and thrust the curtains aside. No fog now, and no sight of land, at least not from the ship's starboard side. Just cloudless blue sky meeting a darker blue sea flecked with whitecaps. Moving to the washstand, she poured water from a pitcher into the heavy white basin.

She had just finished washing and dressing when someone knocked. She said, past the quickened pulse in the hollow of her throat, "Come in."

But it was only the young sailor of the night before, a breakfast tray in his hands. Smiling shyly, he placed the tray on a straight chair beside the bed, let down a folding table from one bulkhead, and transferred the tray to the table.

Elizabeth asked, "Am I to take all my meals here?"

"Pardon, madame?"

Drawing upon those long-ago lessons from her father, she asked the question in halting French.

For the time being, yes, he told her. They were still in English waters. Elizabeth nodded her understanding. As long as an English frigate might hurl a cannonball across the decks, it was preferable that she remain in the comparative safety of her cabin.

She passed the morning inspecting the few garments she had brought with her. At the last moment she had remembered to thrust a sewing kit into the hand trunk. Now she used it to mend a torn lace cuff on a green summer gown, and to resew her cloak's hem where she had ripped it as she climbed the ship's ladder.

The young sailor had just taken her luncheon tray away when again someone knocked. This time it was Patrick, carrying two books bound in dark brown leather. "Did you sleep well?" His voice was formally polite.

She managed to match his tone. "Yes, thank you."

He studied her. How calm she looked, and how lovely in the plain dark blue frock she had worn the night before, her gray eyes clear, her chestnut hair brushed to a sheen. Why in hell had she chosen to come with him? If she had stayed, she would have been in little danger of more than a brief imprisonment. By telling the English of his treatment of her, surely she could have convinced them that, far from wanting to help his cause, she had a fervent desire to see him hang.

And why in hell had he allowed her to come with him? A fugitive with little money, he would have no easy time on the island of St.-Denis, even if he managed to get there. She would only add to his problems.

Yet, she looked so desirable, and so brave. But then, she had always been brave. He thought of her trying to wrest the pistol from his hand in that lonely house north of London. He thought of her, body swollen with her unborn child, hurling her defiance at him in the library at Stanford Hall.

He said, "Captain Marquette thought you might like some books. Do you read French?"

She felt wry amusement. She had been his wife for almost a year, and yet he did not know whether or not she read French. "A little."

"Then perhaps you will enjoy these." He placed the books on the chair, and with a courteous bow, left the cabin.

For a moment she stared at the closed door. Behind the polite masks they often assumed, what did they feel for each other, she and this tall man whose name she bore? So far, the only naked, unmistakable emotions that had flared between them were hatred and rage and physical lust. And of late, apparently, he had ceased even to feel lust for her. Yet, she had chosen to flee Ireland with him, he had allowed her to do so.

Could it be that in time . . .? No, better not to dwell on the possibility that someday theirs might become a real marriage, holding both physical satisfaction and mutual tenderness and respect. It would be enough if, on that island she had never seen, she could build a busy and reasonably peaceful life for herself.

Determinedly she turned her attention to the books he had left. She found that they were the memoirs of Saint Simon. For the rest of the afternoon she read the vain and gossipy French duke's account of life at the court of Louis XIV. When the light began to fade, she looked out a porthole and saw that the day was no longer fair. The last rays of the sun, low on the horizon, struggled through fog. She drew the curtains, and taking the box of flints from its metal holder affixed to the bulkhead beside the door, lit the lamps.

When the young sailor had taken her supper tray away, she turned back to her book. She was deep in the account of La Grande Mademoiselle's ludicrous pursuit of her unwilling young lieutenant when she became aware that something was happening on deck. She heard sharp, low-voiced commands, running footsteps, and the rattle of sail. Several moments later she became aware that the ship had lost most of its forward motion.

Nerves tightening, she sat rigid. Why were they stopping? And why were there no sounds at all from the deck now, as if everyone aboard except herself had died? She knew there could be only one explanation. She pictured the little merchant ship, fog-enshrouded, rocking in the black sea, pictured the silent men on deck waiting to hear an English voice call across the water, "What ship?"

Unable to remain alone any longer, she rose from her chair, extinguished the lamps, and stepped out on deck. No light anywhere, only a thick gray smother through which she could barely make out the dark figures in the mainmast rigging. Not speaking, and with only a subdued rattle of canvas now and then, they were still taking in sail.

She looked to her left. More dark figures standing against the waist-high bulwark, one of them a head taller than any of the others. She moved across the fog-wet deck. "Patrick!" she whispered. "What is it?"

She sensed rather than saw his startled frown. Arm around her waist, he drew her a few feet down the deck. "Ships," he said in a swift, low voice. "At least three of them, almost dead ahead. The lookout saw their mainmast lanterns through a rift in the fog."

She asked tautly, "What sort of ships?"

"Battle frigates, to judge by the height of their masts. If they stay on course, they should pass less than a hundred yards off our port."

"You're sure they are English?"

"In these waters? Of course."

She understood the captain's decision. If his little ship was seen, he could have no hope of outrunning men-of-war. And so he had chosen to reef sail, bringing the ship to a halt. Lights out, it lay rocking in its cocoon of fog, like a rabbit trying to hide from coursing hounds.

Through the hammer of her heartbeat she could now hear other sounds, growing more distinct by the moment. Creak of canvas; even faint, fog-distorted voices. A diffused light shone through the smother, although the ship itself was invisible. With agonizing slowness, the blurred glow passed and was lost in the fog, only to be replaced by a second ghostly spot of radiance. It too passed, but as the third ship drew close, she realized with a leap of terror that the fog was thinning. Already, below the bulwark a streak of black water widened where only moments before there had been swirling grayness. And she could see other lights on the English ship, perhaps deck lights, or the glow of confidently unshrouded portholes. She could even make out the blurred bulk of the ship itself. How soon would one of her countrymen, moving about on the deck over there, or perched as a lookout in a mast, see the shadowy shape of the French merchantman?

The warship kept its steady course. Its light and the voices of the men aboard it faded into the fog. Now she could hear no sound except her own thudding heartbeats and the gentle slap of water against the hull. With a shuddering breath she turned to the man beside her and collapsed against him.

For a moment he stood motionless. Then he made an inarticulate sound. His arms went around her, and his mouth, warm and desirous, came down on hers. The sweet shock of that kiss seemed to go through her whole body. Then it began, that warm yearning, as if something deep within her had begun to melt.

Around them the ship was coming alive. On the raised afterdeck Captain Marquette's voice issued crisp commands. Running footsteps sounded, and unfurling canvas snapped. Not speaking, arm around her waist, Patrick drew her along the deck and into the cabin. "Where is the flint box?"

"On the right side of the door." She was aware that already her voice sounded strange, heavy with desire.

Lamplight bloomed. He looked at her for a long moment and then said, in a thickened voice, "Turn around."

She felt his hands undoing the hooks at her back, felt them rush over her erect nipples and then her belly and thighs as he pushed her garments downward. Naked, shameless in her need, she stepped out of the circle of crumpled clothing and turned to face him. He held her tight against him for a moment, warm mouth covering hers, and then said in that same constricted voice, "Lie down."

Stretched upon the bed, she watched him as he undressed and lay down beside her. For a while her body stirred only languorously as his hands stroked her, as his

lips kissed her mouth and her throat and his tongue
teased her nipples. But as the hunger deep within her intensified, she heard herself whimpering with desire, found
her body arching against the leg that, bent at the knee,
had placed across her. Then his weight was upon her, and
his thrusting body was carrying her higher and higher
toward the long, exquisite, almost painful fall.

For a while afterward they lay side by side, spent and
silent. Then he propped his dark head on one hand and
looked down at her. His lips smiled, but his eyes were
somber. "Was it still only your body?"

Weighted with languor, she did not want to even think
about that question. "I don't know."

"Let me rephrase it. Do you still hate me very much?"

Reluctantly she forced herself to consider. "You have
given me every reason to."

"I know. I realize I evened the score between us well
before last night. And now you are even cut off from your
country."

She answered slowly, "Somehow that does not seem to
matter." Then, unable to bear the conflict between her
physical need of this man and the thought of all the havoc
he had wrought in her life, she cried, "Leave it be! Don't
talk."

After a moment he said, "Yes, we have better things to
do than talk," and leaned down to cover her mouth with
his own.

This time their coming together was less frenzied. To
the gentle rolling of the ship, they made long, slow love.
Afterward they lay silent for a while. Then he said, "Shall
we sleep now?"

He got out of bed and crossed the cabin toward the
lamp swaying in its gimbal. She looked at the wide shoulders, the lean waist and flat buttocks, the long-muscled
legs. Not knowing quite what the words meant, she
thought: Perhaps you are my country now.

28

To Elizabeth, standing on deck beside Patrick and Colin as the little ship neared the wharf, St.-Denis looked like an island out of a young child's dream, magical in its perfection. In its interior, jungle-clad mountains rose, appearing not green in the late-afternoon light, but a deep, velvety blue. She could made out the white thread of a waterfall descending from near the top of the loftiest peak. Not far from the falls, the gray-stone turrets of what she knew must be a fort poked above the trees. Her eye, sweeping downward toward the island's shore, found the dazzling white square of the town of St.-Denis, surrounded by pastel-colored buildings, yellow and blue and pink. From the square a road, also bordered by houses, sloped down to a palm-fringed crescent of pinkish beach. Jutting out from it was a long wharf with three ships moored beside it.

She did not know then that the buildings that bordered that sloping street were grog shops and brothels. As yet, she'd had no experience with the insects that infested tropical kitchens and the mildew that attacked carpets, furniture, and clothing. Nor had she met her future neighbors—planters and their bored wives, enjoying luxuries and status they could never have attained back in France, but always afraid of the sullen black slaves sweating in the cane fields and rum distilleries. No, to Elizabeth the island appeared like a bit of Paradise afloat on an opalescent sea that shifted in color from blue to turquoise to emerald.

She had enjoyed these past weeks. Once the ship was well out of English waters, she had moved freely along its decks. Each evening she and Patrick and Colin had dined with Captain Marquette in the master's cabin. Eagerly she had listened to her husband and brother-in-law make plans for the future. Always, Captain Marquette said, there were planters in the islands who wanted to sell their properties and go back to France. Right now there was such a man on St.-Denis, a distiller named Armand Duval.

"Duval's trouble," Captain Marquette said, "is that he likes his own product too much. Already he has stopped operating his distillery. I assume he and his family are living off what money he obtained from the sale of his slaves."

Patrick asked, "How much do you think he would want for his distillery?"

"In pounds? I should think a thousand would buy it."

Patrick looked at his brother. Colin nodded. "At that price, we should have enough left to start operations and to keep ourselves fed and housed until we began to make a profit."

"Of course," Captain Marquette said, "you'll have to buy slaves."

Elizabeth felt an inward shrinking. True, she already had had some experience with slavery. In London several women of her acquaintance had owned black "pages," small boys who were petted and pampered and dressed in satin pantaloons and ostrich-plumed turbans. As soon as they were no longer small and cuddlesome, they were banished to the scullery or, in some cases, turned out into the London streets to make their way as best they could. Repellent as such careless cruelty was to Elizabeth, it seemed less so than the thought of men and women working all their lives for nothing more than some sort of roof over their heads and enough food to keep them alive and productive.

Patrick said, "I am not going to tie up my capital in slaves. It will be cheaper to contract with some planter for workers."

Elizabeth looked at him. Was that his only reason, that it would be cheaper? Whatever his motive, she was glad of his decision. True, the planter, not the slaves themselves, would receive whatever money Patrick paid for their labor. Still, it seemed to her a less repellent arrangement than outright ownership of other human beings.

Slowly the ship had moved south, exchanging hails now and then with other merchantmen—French or American or Spanish—but sighting no more English warships. Spending most of each day on deck, Elizabeth had seen the first dolphins arching playfully beside the ship, the first flying fish, and swimming several feet down in the green water that slipped past the hull, the first tropical turtles, large and brown and grotesquely awkward.

For Elizabeth the voyage had not been without its worrisome moments. One night as she and Patrick lay in the bunk bed, her head on his shoulder, she asked hesitantly, "Will you mind it so very much, never seeing Ireland again?"

"But I will see it again! Not only see it, but fight for it. It may take me years, but I'll get back there."

She tried to keep her voice mild, unchanging. "But, Patrick, already you've given ten years of your life to the cause of—"

"And I failed. Is that what you were going to say? Elizabeth, do you know how long the Irish have been struggling against English invaders? More than six hundred years! What are ten years compared to that? I'll keep fighting, and other Irishmen will too, and someday we will win. It may not be in my lifetime, or even in my grand-son's, if I have one, but someday we will win."

She wanted to cry out against his stubborn folly. How could he dream of returning to a country where he was landless now, and where his neck would be in danger the moment he stepped ashore? But no. Best not to argue with him, lest she only strengthen his resolve. If he found success and contentment in the West Indies, eventually he might abandon the thought of returning to Ireland.

Now she said, gaze fixed on that distant waterfall, "How beautiful, more beautiful than any of the other islands we have seen." Entering the West Indian archipelago at a point north of Haiti, they had passed many islands, some little more than uninhabited dots of sand and palmettos, others with settlements visible near their shores. All of them were either unclaimed or in French hands.

Patrick, eyes fixed on the shore, merely nodded in answer to Elizabeth's remark. But Colin said, "Yes, it's beautiful. Be prepared, though, for the unpleasant things—the spring and fall rainy seasons, for instance, and the roaches all year around."

"Roaches?"

"A variety of what we call black beetles. But down here they are brown, and they fly, and they are almost the size of hummingbirds. And you should be prepared, too, for the voodoo drums." Seeing Elizabeth's puzzled expression, he added, "or perhaps it is called obeah on this island. Anyway, it is a religion the blacks brought with them from Africa. Their nighttime ceremonies involve drumming, and that gets on white people's nerves."

Patrick said, "It won't get on mine. And as far as I'm concerned, their religion probably makes as much sense as anybody's."

Behind them, crewmen swarmed through the rigging, securing the sails already wrapped around the yardarms.

In the bow, a sailor stood poised to toss a line to a dock worker standing on the wharf. Patrick said, "Have you finished your packing, Elizabeth?"

"Not quite. And I want to change my gown."

"Take your time about it. I want to talk to Captain Marquette. Perhaps he'll arrange for me to meet this Armand Duval yet today."

She did take her time about it, dressing in a green lawn gown and in the one hat she had brought with her, a wide-brimmed leghorn straw which she had placed in the hand trunk atop folded garments. Carefully she scrutinized her image in the mirror above the washstand. Since she hoped fervently that Patrick would be content to settle down here, she wanted to make a good first impression upon the townspeople.

Her husband opened the cabin door. "It is arranged. Marquette will ask Duval to call upon us at the inn this afternoon."

"Is my appearance all right?"

He looked at her face, shadowed by the leghorn hat. A wide green ribbon the same shade as her gown ran beneath her chin from one side of the wide brim to the other, holding the hat in place. "You don't need my opinion. I am sure your mirror has already told you you look lovely."

She said, still worried, "I am afraid my complexion . . . Perhaps I should have stayed on the shady side of the deck."

"I like your face when it's that sun-warmed color." He always had, from the moment he saw her.

When they emerged onto the deck, they found that the ship, now tied up at the wharf next to an American merchantman, was deserted. Captain Marquette and Colin, seated in an open public carriage, waited on the dock below. As the carriage, drawn by two aged gray horses, rattled over the wharf planking, Captain

Marquette said, "I regret, madame, that I must take you along what is called Rue du Port, or Harbor Street. Although most unsavory, it is the only approach to the town from the wharf."

Elizabeth said demurely. "Thank you for warning me. I shall keep my gaze fixed straight ahead."

She did not, of course. Her eyes, shadowed by the hat brim, shot glances right and left as the carriage moved past small blue or pink or yellow houses, most of them scabrous with peeling paint, where women of every shade from white to coal black sat invitingly at windows or in doorways. From the shadowy recesses of an open-fronted café came the wheeze of a concertina and the sound of drunken shouting. Along the sidewalk moved French soldiers from the fort and merchant seamen from those ships tied up at the wharf. Some seemed fairly sober. Others tacked wildly from one side of the sidewalk to the other, like vessels beaten by conflicting winds. She wondered if any of those men were off pirate vessels. All of the merchant ships in the harbor had flown either the French fleur-de-lis or the red-and-white-striped flag, with its white stars set in a circle on a blue field, of the rebellious American colonies. But that, of course, proved nothing. No pirate ship would enter a port flying its death's-head insignia.

Glancing to her left, Elizabeth saw someone she recognized, the shy young sailor who had brought her all her meals her first few days aboard ship. Moving down the sidewalk with a half-empty rum bottle in one hand and the other arm around a pretty mulatto girl, he did not look in the least shy now. Elizabeth said, before she could check herself, "Captain, isn't that Richard from your ship? Why, he can't be more than seventeen."

"He is not yet sixteen. Boys grow up fast at sea. But do not be alarmed, madame. The . . . er, feminine inhabitants of Harbor Street never invade the respectable part of town, nor do off-duty soldiers and merchant sailors, unless they are completely sober. To do so would bring instant arrest."

The carriage entered the limestone-paved square. Along the sidewalks, shadowed by second-floor balconies, moved a motley crowd—soldiers in groups, white men and women in European dress, and black women, graceful as Greek caryatids, balancing bundles on their white-turbaned heads. On the far side of the square the carriage stopped before a three-story pink building with tall jalousied doors on the ground floor and lacy wrought-iron balconies above. This, Captain Marquette explained, was the combined coffeehouse and inn.

"I will find Armand Duval now, and tell him you would like to see him as soon as possible."

The accommodations to which the inn's proprietor showed them—a sitting room and bedroom for Patrick and Elizabeth, and a single room across the corridor for Colin—looked clean and comfortable, although not luxurious. Carpets of woven straw covered the floors. The bedsteads and even the washstand were of white-painted iron. In the tropics, the innkeeper explained, where only constant vigilance could keep wood-boring insects at bay, it was wise to use metal wherever possible.

Elizabeth had just finished unpacking when Armand Duval arrived. He was a man of about forty-five, with a once-husky body now gone to fat, and a yellowish tinge to the whites of his eyes. He declined Patrick's offer of brandy. Obviously he feared that the weakness for liquor that had ruined his business might now interfere with his disposal of it.

Elizabeth sat silently by while the two Irishmen and the Frenchman discussed the distillery. It was not her husband but her usually self-effacing brother-in-law who took the lead.

Colin asked, "How many vats for cooking sugarcane do you have, Mr. Duval?"

"Three, and two vats for distilling rum."

"Do you employ molasses or fresh cane juice?"

"I use the fresh juice. So does every other distiller on St.-Denis."

"I see. And how many gallons of rum have you produced in your best year?"

Duval hesitated momentarily, puffy hands tightening on the knees of his fawn-colored breeches. "Oh, around six thousand."

Colin's dark brows lifted. He repeated, with a smile, "Six?"

The Frenchman's face flushed. "Forgive me. I meant to say almost five thousand."

Colin said smoothly, "Yes, that is about the maximum output I would expect for a distillery of that size."

Elizabeth felt surprised and impressed by her quiet brother-in-law's shrewd knowledgeability. It was indeed fortunate for her and Patrick, she reflected, that he had chosen to come with them. Then she saw Colin look at Patrick, as if stepping aside to allow his brother to start the bargaining.

Patrick asked, "What is your price, Mr. Duval?"

The distiller named a sum in French louis. Not even trying to translate the figure into pounds, Elizabeth looked at Colin and saw him nod. He said to his brother, "It sounds fair. Of course, we must see the distillery first, and we can't do that today."

Elizabeth understood why. The light streaming in at the jalousied windows had already taken on the reddish tint of late afternoon. And aboard ship she had learned that in these latitudes, once the sun had set, darkness descended swiftly.

"But you could see my house yet today. You will need

someplace to live." Elizabeth noticed that his hands, resting on the knees of his none-too-clean breeches, trembled visibly. "The house is sound, although a bit run-down. And you can have it very cheaply. I want to sell everything, including my carriage and pair, my saddle horse, and the pony and small gig my wife and daughters sometimes use."

Patrick said, "Elizabeth?"

She nodded. "I would like to see the house."

At the curb outside the inn, two bay horses stood between the shafts of a carriage badly in need of polishing. With Monsieur Duval handling the reins, they left the square by a road opposite the one by which they had entered it. On either side, separated from the road by low plaster walls and surrounded by luxurious tangles of palmettos and scarlet hibiscus, were houses of one or two stories. They belonged, Duval told them, to small-plantation owners and the town's shopkeepers. "The few large-plantation owners, of course, live in fine big villas in the island's interior." The resigned melancholy in his voice told Elizabeth that once, before his addiction made the dream impossible, he had hoped that one day he would live in such a villa.

Abruptly the stretch of houses gave way to jungle, with tree branches meeting above the road, so that the carriage moved through a murky twilight. Interlaced among the trees—many of them West Indian mahogany, Duval said—were vines as thick as a man's waist. Beyond the first line of trees, grotesquely beaked parrots and brightly colored smaller birds flashed through the dim light.

The stretch of jungle gave way to more dwellings. Then Duval stopped before a white one-story house. "Madame Duval will be expecting us. I told her I might bring you back with me." As they went up the flagstoned walk bordered by a tangle of dwarf palms, hibiscus bushes, and trees with large leaves as lustrous as English holly, Elizabeth noticed that the plaster facade of the house, while in need of whitewash, at least was not peeling away in patches.

Madame Duval opened the door to them. A thin, blondish woman, she had the sort of expression—martyred, and yet tinged with a certain smug moral superiority—that Elizabeth had seen before in the faces of women married to drunkards. From somewhere beyond her came the shrill voices of quarelling children.

Madame Duval showed them over the house. As her husband had said, it indeed was rundown. White plaster walls in the long hall were dingy. In the parlor, mahogany and red plush furniture, more suitable to a French middle-class house than to the tropics, looked shabby. In the dining room, where two girls of about nine and eleven stopped squabbling long enough to drop curtsies to the visitors, the blue plush rug bore food stains and the glass chimney of a wall lamp was cracked.

The two bedrooms, furnished with iron bedsteads and washstands and straw rugs, were pleasant enough, and the larger one had French doors opening onto a roofed terrace. Nevertheless, Elizabeth caught an appalled look on Patrick's face. It was not just the shabbiness that oppressed him, she felt sure, but the smallness. At Stanford Hall, almost this entire house could have fitted into the space between the massive front doors and the foot of the twin staircases. Never mind, she thought. If he could forget Ireland and that cause of his, perhaps someday they would build a spacious villa back in the hills.

They ended the inspection tour with the kitchen. Although supper's roast fowl sputtered on the fireplace spit, unwashed dishes from some previous meal still littered a bare table. "All is most difficult," Madame Duval explained, "now that one has no servants. And even when one could afford servants, they were lazy and useless. Oh, life on St.-Denis has not been easy for me, madame, what with indolent blacks, and snobbish whites looking down their noses just because my husband . . ."

She broke off, as if suddenly aware that such discouraging talk might jeopardize the sale of the distillery. "But to you, madame," she went on swiftly, "the French people here will behave charmingly. Plainly your husband does . . . does not share my husband's weakness. As for servants, surely they will work for a chatelaine of such competent appearance as yourself."

Although she was not sure she found it flattering to be told she looked "competent," Elizabeth murmured a thank you. Then she turned and looked out the kitchen's rear window. Beyond it, a garden stretched away to a stable and carriage house. The garden was just a tangle of vines and overgrown shrubbery now, but once the vegetation was trimmed, and the gravel walks raked . . .

So close that she flinched backward with a cry, a large brown insect flew past her face and landed on that littered table. "*Ma foi!*" Madame Duval said with Gallic despair. "No matter how one strives for the cleanliness, one cannot rid oneself of those *sales bêtes.*"

Elizabeth thought, grimly confident: We will see about that.

29

Three days later Patrick bought both the distillery and the house. Two days later the Duvals sailed for France, and the following day Elizabeth, aided by Jules and Jeanne Burgos,- a mulatto freedman and his wife, set about making the house livable. Each morning, Patrick and Colin, in the carriage that had belonged to the Duvals, deposited her at the house, where she stayed until they stopped for her on their way back to the inn.

After the long idle weeks aboard ship, Elizabeth delighted in using her energy and ingenuity. Walls were whitewashed, floors and windows and cupboards scrubbed. She sold the plush rugs and heavy furniture to a dealer in secondhand articles, and replaced them with inexpensive but clean straw rugs, and white wicker chairs and settees of the sort she had seen in the inn's parlor.

Exactly three weeks after its purchase, she and Patrick moved into the house. Colin was not with them. Because the house was so small, he had said from the first that he would prefer to stay on at the inn.

One morning less than a week later, she rode with Patrick and Colin along jungle-walled roads to the distillery. As they turned into the clearing in which the long, low shed stood, she exclaimed, "Why, about half the shingles on that roof look new!"

"So they are," Patrick said. "What's more, to get the task finished as quickly as possible, Colin and I helped nail them in place." He laughed. "The blacks looked dumbfounded. Apparently they had never seen white men working with their hands before."

He helped Elizabeth to the ground. Circling one end of the long, one-story building, she and the Stanford men mounted two steps to a wooden platform. On one side of it a small, clear stream ran down the gentle slope, to disappear into a wooden culvert beneath the road. On the other side, a wide doorway in the shed revealed bare-to-the-waist blacks, stirring the contents of the big copper vats above roaring charcoal fires. As she shrank back from the heat and the sickeningly sweet smell of boiling sugar, Patrick said with a smile, "Not exactly like the scent of a new-mown Irish meadow, is it? Come, we'll look into the distillery. You'll find that more pleasant, especially since it isn't in operation yet."

They moved on down the platform past a long table on which lay a number of formidable-looking cleavers. "That is the chopping table," Patrick told her, "where the cane is cut into short lengths for boiling in the vats."

Ahead of them at the platform's edge stood a slender black youth holding a long pole that ended in a stout metal hook. As they moved toward him, he deftly fished a rope-tied bundle of stalks—in appearance rather like cornstalks—and deposited it on the platform.

Elizabeth asked, "Sugarcane?"

"Yes," Patrick said. "It is floated down to us from a plantation higher in the hills."

Near the end of the platform they came to the distillery's wide doorway. Because he'd had former experience with rum manufacture, it was Colin who explained the equipment to her. "In those big vats we'll reboil the sugar from the cooking sheds. Do you see those coiled metal pipes? The distilled liquor will run through those."

"And the big hogsheads over there in the corner?"

"We'll use those to store and age the rum."

A few minutes later, leaving Colin to eat the midday meal packed for him by the cook at the inn, Elizabeth and Patrick drove back to the house and to the luncheon that, with the help of Jeanne Burgos, she had prepared that morning.

In the small ingrown community of St.-Denis, the Stanfords' arrival had caused quite a stir. Even before they moved from the inn to their house, the invitations had begun to arrive. Monsieur and Madame Raoul Gaspard begged the honor of Sir Patrick and Lady Stanford's presence at dinner. Madame Reynard requested the pleasure of Lady Stanford's company at morning coffee. Patrick and Elizabeth accepted some of the invitations. Unlike the Duval ménage, none of the households presented a slatternly appearance, but again and again Elizabeth saw expensive, plush-upholstered furniture that seemed so unsuitable in the humid heat of the tropics. And an upland villa they visited, whose owner had started out in life apprenticed to a Paris apothecary, was grand indeed, with a mirrored ballroom and gilded furniture that might have graced a French château.

That night, as they undressed in the airy bedroom of their little house, Patrick said, "I hope those people don't expect to be entertained here on the same scale. I will be damned if I will spend money on French champagne and pheasant shipped from Port-au-Prince. I need every cent for the distillery."

"Don't worry. The people here will be glad to come to your house, no matter what we serve. After all, you're a baronet."

"I am also," he said sardonically, "a fugitive, probably with a price on my head by this time."

"To these French people, that is all to your credit. You are a fugitive from their enemy."

As often happened, she felt a twinge of sadness at the thought that now she would be considered an enemy of the land of her birth. But she had made her choice that night at Stanford Hall when she had said, "Take me with you." And the sadness slipped away entirely when, in bed a few minutes later, Patrick's stroking hands and nipple-teasing lips and tongue aroused hunger deep within her. Eagerly she accepted the weight of his body and the pounding thrust of him, so pleasurable that it was almost an exquisite torment as it brought her closer and closer to the long, ecstatic, shuddering release.

But afterward, as she lay quietly beside him in the darkness, she felt a return of that melancholy. Her body and Patrick's each seemed designed to satisfy the physical passion of the other, a passion that only moments ago had fused them together so that they seemed quite literally one flesh. Yet tonight, as always, their minds, their spirits, had held aloof from one another. It had not even occurred to her to tell him of the sadness the thought of Enland brought her.

Aware that she was slipping into self-pity, she commanded herself to think of something else. Colin, for instance. Now, there was someone who had reason to pity himself, because he was alone in every sense of the word.

Colin had also been a guest at the upland villa that evening. She had observed that several unmarried young women present, and their mothers too, had bestowed encouraging smiles upon him. As the three of them, with Jules Burgos driving the carriage, rode home from the party, Elizabeth had commented upon how attractive the girls were. Colin said, in a light tone, "Don't start hoping to marry me off, Elizabeth. No woman would have me."

"That," Elizabeth had said firmly, "is so silly that it does not deserve an answer."

Seated beside her in the left-hand corner of the carriage, Patrick said, "She is right, Colin. You can have little hope of passing yourself off as a thirty-six-year-old virgin." In the darkness, Elizabeth could not see his expression, but she could hear the amusement in his voice. "Many a wench in the countryside around Stanford Hall could testify that you are not. And besides, there is Catherine Ryan." Patrick paused. "Have you thought of writing to her that you would like her to join you in St.-Denis?"

Several seconds passed before Colin answered. "It is a rare woman who will follow a man into exile, especially if she is not married to him." As if determined to change the subject, he added swiftly, "Patrick, I saw you talking to Etienne Duchamps tonight. Did you gain any idea of how much rum the Duchamps distillery produces?"

As she listened to the business talk of the two men, Elizabeth realized that Colin really had not said whether or not he had asked Catherine Ryan to join him. Perhaps, self-effacing man that he was, he had felt he had no right to do so. Or perhaps he had asked her, and the widow had been too afraid to travel to a strange land, or too loath to leave her almost grown sons.

Well, perhaps sooner or later some St.-Denis girl would snare his interest.

She became aware that Patrick's breathing had taken on the slower rhythm of slumber. Emptying her mind of thought, she too drifted toward sleep.

Less than a week later, when a ship from Calais arrived with Georges Fontaine aboard it, Patrick learned that indeed there was a price on his head. At dinner that night in the little Stanford house, with the first spring rains drumming on the roof, he told them that the English had offered a reward of fifty thousand pounds for Patrick's capture.

"Good God!" Patrick said. "That's a fortune." He added, with a short laugh, "I suppose I should be flattered."

"The English need desperately to lay their hands on you. They have found only a few arms caches, and those only by accident. And they have the names of none of the other leaders."

Patrick said, pleased but astonished, "I should have thought that by now . . ."

"Apparently whoever informed the English knew no other names, or else chose not to give them. As I told you before you left Ireland, someone had written an anonymous letter to the English government denouncing you. Agents of ours in London got wind of the letter. While the English were still making arrangements to cross the channel and arrest you, our agents dispatched a message to me by an Irish fishing boat."

Patrick sat silent, frowning. At last he said, "Then probably Henry Owen was not the informer."

"I agree," the Frenchman said.

"If Owen had been the one who turned his coat," Patrick went on, "he would have made a thorough job of it. He would have given the names of other Irish rebels he had met with."

Fontaine nodded. "And he would have given my name. I would not have been free these past few months to travel all over Ireland taking orders for wine."

Then who was it, Patrick wondered, who had written that anonymous letter? He thought of Moira screaming at him the last time he saw her. "You'll be sorry for tonight!" Could it be that during one of those many nights he had spent in her ornate bed he had said something in his sleep, something that had led her to suspect him? Or, careful as he had always tried to be, had he carried some betraying paper to Wetherly in his clothing? He had a vision of Moira in that luxurious bedroom, going through his pockets while he lay asleep.

He shot a glance at Elizabeth. Much as he wanted to ask Fontaine about Moira Ashley, it would be best to wait until later. And so instead he began to question the Frenchman about events at Stanford Hall. "When the English confiscated my house and lands, did they dismiss the servants?"

"Only some of them. I hear the housekeeper and the head footman are still there, as well as the cook and one or two of the maids. An empty house deteriorates, you know."

Patrick's nod was grim. "And of course the crown is interested in preserving its newly acquired property. Now, what has been happening to my lands?"

"Your brother's steward . . . What is his name? Sullivan?"

"Slattery."

"With Mr. Slattery acting as overseer, spring planting has begun on both your land and your brother's."

"Then Colin's land . . ."

"Confiscated along with yours, of course." The Frenchman shrugged. "If he had stayed, he might have saved
them."

Poor Colin, Elizabeth thought. Although he had taken
no part in planning the thwarted rebellion, he had lost
even more than Patrick had—not only his property, but
the companionship of the only woman who, apparently,
had ever suited him.

Less than an hour later, Fontaine kissed Elizabeth's
hand in farewell. Patrick drove their guest in the carriage
back to the inn. On the way, Patrick asked, "Do you have
any news of Lady Moira Ashley?"

"Ashley? Oh, yes, your neighbor. I did hear something.
She mortgaged most of her properties to buy stock in
some South American company, and lost her entire investment. Now she may lose her lands, too."

Well, Patrick thought, he had warned her. But despite
his suspicion that she might have been the writer of that
anonymous letter to the English, he found he could take
no satisfaction in her plight. He thought of how woebe-
gone she had looked that last night, with the tears of rage
and pain running down her face. Always, despite her
beauty and wealth and arrogance, he had sensed something pitiable in her, something maimed.

And certainly he had reason to be grateful for the
many hours he had spent with her. Driving beside the
silent Frenchman along the stretch of jungle-bordered
road, he recalled the touch of Moira's amorously skilled
lips and hands, and the suppleness of her body. His
thoughts were untinged by any sense of guilt concerning
that other woman, now probably undressing in their bedroom. He still felt guilty for his rape of her, and for the
quarrel that had led to the loss of their child, and for the
circumstances that had made her an exile in a strange
land. But sexual infidelity was another matter. Just as he

had never felt guilty for enjoying Moira in actuality, he felt no guilt in memories of pleasures in her arms.

He turned onto the town square and stopped before the inn.

30

Jeanne Burgos, the mulatto housemaid, came in for only a few hours of housework each morning. Since they were short of money, Elizabeth had insisted to Patrick that it was best not to employ a servant full time. The truth was that she wanted to keep busy. She had no intention of slipping into the languid idleness, and consequent overplumpness, of some of the women who played hostess to her and Patrick, and in turn came to dinners served by Jeanne and her husband, Jules. Too, keeping busy helped her hold at bay any tendency to brood over the past.

Even so, she found herself with leisure time. She spent it reading, or writing to her mother, or driving about in the pony-drawn gig once owned by the Duvals. Sometimes she stopped at the distillery, where Patrick and Colin, in their eagerness to keep the rum vats supplied with cane juice, often stood with their workmen at the long chopping tables, cutting the cane into sections for the huge copper kettles. After that she sometimes took the road that wound up the mountainside—through rapidly cooling air, through vegetation that changed from vine-entangled jungle growth to tall pines—and stopped at a jumble of rough-hewn stones, the remains of an ancient fort. From there her gaze could travel down to terraced cane fields carved out of the jungle, and to the pretty little town, and then out over shimmering water, emerald and turquoise and aquamarine, to the French-held island of St.-Marc and to the dark blue blur on the horizon that she knew was Haiti.

She and Patrick continued to be invited to dinner by the French planters, and to entertain them in turn. But lately she had sensed a certain coolness toward Patrick and herself at those elaborate dinners. One night they had dined at a spacious upland villa. Now that the spring rains were over, the throb of voodoo drums higher in the hills came through the jalousied windows to mingle with the sounds of polite conversation and the faint tinkle of cutlery. As the carriage, driven by Jules Burgos, took her and Patrick home through the warm darkness, Elizabeth said, "Did you notice how . . . distant everyone seemed tonight?"

"I did not." Patrick yawned. The five kinds of wine served at dinner had made him sleepy. He added, "Although I would not blame them for being annoyed about that rum contract."

"What contract?" Here on St.-Denis, Patrick of course was less reticent about his activities than he had been back in Ireland. Nevertheless, there was much she did not know about his business affairs.

"A three-year contract I signed with a rum buyer from the American colonies." He chuckled. "Colin and I did it by underpricing every distiller on the island."

"I don't think it was that which made people seem so strange tonight. I think it was something else, something to do with the drums."

"The voodoo drums? Well, of course the whites don't like hearing them. They are afraid of having the blacks assemble in large numbers for any reason, religious or otherwise. That's why voodoo has been outlawed on this island. Nevertheless, I guess we'll go on hearing the drums several nights each week all through the dry seasons."

"But did you notice how everyone looked at you when the drumming began?"

"Nonsense. The Frenchies can be annoyed with me for beating them at their own game, but they can scarcely blame me for anything the blacks do."

Less than a week later she learned that the Frenchies not only could, but did. Invited to a morning coffee at a Madame Ribeaux's, Elizabeth sensed the tension in the atmosphere as soon as she entered the elaborately furnished salon. The usually languid ladies sat bolt upright on red plush chairs and sofas, coffeecups rigidly poised, smiles fixed.

Madame Ribeaux, a brunette of forty-odd, who somehow, despite rich food and little exercise, had remained thin to the point of scrawniness, evidently had been chosen spokeswoman for the group. As soon as she had served coffee to Elizabeth, she leaned forward and said, "Lady Stanford, we all hope you can influence Sir Patrick."

Puzzled and wary, Elizabeth said, "Influence him? How?"

Madame Ribeaux's reply was indirect. "I am sure you know that the blacks still hold their illegal gatherings in the hills. Don't you realize that we all live in fear of a slave revolt?"

"A revolt? With a fort filled with soldiers on the island, and warships in the bay more often than not?"

"But once our war with England is over, the ships will be gone, and many of the soldiers too. Who will protect us then?"

"I don't know. But I cannot see what this possibly has to do with my husband."

"Lady Stanford! Everyone knows that Sir Patrick and his brother oversee operations at his distillery."

"And?"

"That alone would be bad enough," the Frenchwoman rushed on. "Other distillers and plantation owners use mulatto overseers. But it is also said that sometimes Sir Patrick and his brother work alongside the blacks, chopping the cane and carrying it to the hoppers!"

Aware of the ring of hostile faces, Elizabeth tried to speak calmly. "Sometimes a great quantity of cane is floated down from the plantation above. My husband and brother-in-law must lend a hand at the chopping tables, if operations are to continue smoothly." An indignant tremble came into her voice. "Is there a law against that?"

"There should be!" a woman on her right cried, and Madame Ribeaux said, "Exactly! Every one of us must maintain a position of superiority at all times, and in every relationship, with the slaves. Not to do so may encourage them in . . . rebellious ideas."

Elizabeth got to her feet. "If the slaves on this island ever revolt, it will not be because my husband sometimes stands at the chopping table! It will be because they feel a not unnatural disinclination to go on being slaves. Good day, ladies," she said, and walked out.

Driving home in the gig, she seethed with anger. Lazy, greedy women! French bourgeois snobs! How dare they criticize Patrick? Whatever his faults, he was vastly superior to them, just as he had been superior to the other Anglo-Irish landlords on that other island far to the north . . .

With a sense of shock, she realized the signifigance of her emotions. Why, she was not only proud of him, but defensively so. When had her bitterness slipped away, leaving her free, not just to desire him, but to feel this pride, this fierce protectiveness? She did not know. She only knew that until he came riding home from the dis-

tillery for luncheon, every minute was going to seem an
hour.

Her anger did not abate even after she reached home.
She was pacing up and down the bedroom when she
heard Patrick's footsteps along the hall. The moment he
appeared in the doorway, she flung herself into his arms.
"Oh, Patrick! Those awful, awful women!"

"Here, now! What is all this?"

"The women at Madame Ribeaux's this morning! They
. . . they acted as if you and Colin were about to get
them all murdered in their beds. I mean, just because you
two sometimes work at the chopping tables, they think
you are encouraging the slaves to revolt. Oh, they made
me so furious! I told them that if the slaves ever revolt, it
will be because they don't want to go on being slaves.
What makes them think that black people enjoy sweating
out their lives so that fat, lazy women like them can get
lazier and fatter—?"

"Here, now!" he said again. He was laughing. "Apparently you gave as good as you got. And what do we
care what the Frenchies think? They will continue to ask
us to their houses, if only in hopes of learning how well or
badly my distillery is doing." He kissed her. "What sort of
meal are we having?"

Her arms tightened around him. "Later." Her voice
sounded drowsy. "We can have it later."

"Well!" he said after a moment.

Fingers busy with the hooks at the back of her gown,
he went on, "Promise me something, Elizabeth. Take
coffee with those harpies four mornings a week. Not more
often than that. I need to save enough energy each afternoon to ride back to the distillery."

"Don't make jokes!" He often teased her at such moments, and Elizabeth, single-minded in her feverish need,
found it distracting.

"Very well. No more jokes."

As Patrick had prophesied, the French families continued to ask them to dinner. After an interval of almost three weeks, the island women again began to invite Elizabeth to morning coffees. She accepted some of the invitations. Evidently the women had given up hope that, through her, they might induce Sir Patrick to keep a proper aloofness from his workers, because they never brought up the subject again.

His rum business continued to prosper. On some nights both Patrick and Colin returned to the distillery after supper to work on the books and to answer correspondence from importers in America and Europe. Elizabeth felt a growing hope that Ireland, and the fiasco in which the long-planned-for revolt had ended, were fading from Patrick's consciousness. As for herself, she found life on St.-Denis increasingly pleasant. With the steady trade winds mitigating the tropic heat, the days were cool enough that she could work in that lush rear garden. Some evenings she and Patrick sat on a stone bench she had placed out there, enjoying the fragrance of jasmine and frangipani, and the sight of wild white orchids, ghostly in the darkness, which clung to the trunks of palmettos.

One afternoon Elizabeth lay on a wicker chaise lonuge on the terrace outside her bedroom, relaxing until it was time to start preparing supper. The eaves shadowed her face and closed eyes from the sun, but she could feel its pleasant warmth through the thin fabric of her white gown and petticoats.

Light footsteps sounded along the terrace. She realized it must be Jeanne Burgos. Even though her wages were not due until the next day, the little maid had asked if she might come by for them that afternoon.

The footsteps stopped. Someone's shadow blotted out the warm sun from Elizabeth's body. She said, not opening her eyes. "Your money is on the dining-room table."

An amused voice said, "So there is where it is. And I thought I had lost it in South America."

Elizabeth's eyes flew open. A vision in yellow silk and a black hat ornamented with a yellow ostrich plume, hands crossed on the handle of the closed yellow parasol she held planted on the terrace flagstones, Moira Ashley smiled down at her.

31

Elizabeth sprang to her feet. Shocked out of any semblance of courtesy, she cried, "What are you doing here?"

Moira's eyes widened innocently. "Why, when my knock on the door was not answered, I came around to see if there was a side entrance. Tell me, don't you keep a servant?"

"I meant, what are you doing on St.-Denis?"

"I came to make my fortune, or rather to try to recoup it." She glanced about her, as if looking for another chair. "Is there a place where we can talk?"

Aware of the pulse hammering in the hollow of her throat, Elizabeth looked at the woman in whose arms her husband had spent so many nights. After a moment she managed to answer, "Come this way."

She led her visitor through the bedroom, aware that Moira's gaze must be lingering on the bed, and then into the hall. As they moved along it, Elizabeth asked, "How did you find out . . .?"

"That Patrick was on St.-Denis? In Dublin some weeks ago I met a couple named Lestrand. Madame Lestrand was a Dubliner before her marriage. They are from your neighboring island. What is the name of it? St.-Michael?"

"St.-Marc."

"Oh, yes. The Lestrands mentioned that an Irish baronet, Sir Patrick Stanford, had taken refuge on St.-Denis."

Elizabeth led the way into the parlor, not caring how poor the wicker furniture and straw rug might appear in Lady Moira's eyes, and waved her to a chair. Then she asked, "May I serve you something? Wine? Tea?"

"No, thank you. I can stay only a few minutes. I must not keep Lieutenant Serraut waiting. We were introduced at the inn, and he asked to escort me here."

Elizabeth looked through the window. One of St. Denis's three carriages for hire stood out in the road. Seated in it was a young man with reddish sideburns and a surpassingly handsome profile showing beneath his tall officer's hat. The sight brought Elizabeth small comfort. It would be foolish to hope that Moira, after following Patrick these thousands of miles, would be distracted by a lieutenant, however handsome.

She sat down opposite her visitor. "You said you came here . . ."

"To try to mend my fortune. Surely Patrick can help me. He always has given me good financial advice, which unfortunately I haven't always followed." She paused. "He is not at home now?"

"No, he's at the distillery."

"Ah, yes, the distillery. I heard about it from the Lestrands and also from the innkeeper here. You see, I intend to invest what money I have left either in a sugar plantation or in the manufacture of rum. Perhaps Patrick can guide me in the purchase of a plantation or distillery."

"As far as I know," Elizabeth said coldly, "there are no such properties for sale on St.-Denis."

"Unfortunate. Perhaps on one of the other islands. . . ." She got to her feet. "It has been pleasant to see you again, Lady Stanford."

Elizabeth wanted to make the conventional response, but the words stuck in her throat. Moira's smile seemed to say she knew that. "Well, good day, Lady Stanford."

"Good day, Lady Moira."

Four hours later, Elizabeth, white-faced and saying little, sat opposite Patrick at dinner. She knew Moira must have sent a message to the distillery, or perhaps even gone there, and yet Patrick had said nothing about it. He would have to be the first one to speak of the Irishwoman. Certainly she would not.

A night-flying insect struck the jalousied window. At the sound, Elizabeth's overstrained nerves snapped. She blurted out, "Moira Ashley is here."

His eyes, half-hooded, met hers through the candlelight. "I know. She sent a message to the distillery."

"A message?"

"She wants to see me at the inn at nine tonight."

"Why?"

"Her note said that she needed my advice about financial matters. I gather her South American investment did not turn out well."

"She told me it did not." In answer to his startled look, she went on, "Yes, she was here today, looking for you. But I don't think she has come all this way just for your advice."

Patrick remained silent. He had his own suspicion about why Moira Ashley had come to St.-Denis.

"Are you going to see her?"

"Of course. No matter why she is here, she is an old friend and neighbor, many miles from home."

Elizabeth cried, "I forbid you!"

Patrick's right eyebrow arched. "Forbid?"

"Yes! As your wife, I forbid you!"

He laid down his fork. "As my wife, you have certain rights. Those do not include dictating whom I shall see or not see."

Certain rights, she thought bitterly. She had a legal right to his support, and if he had no male heir, to inherit his property. But she had no right to keep him out of Moira Ashley's bed, or any other woman's.

She had a heart-wrenching vision of what her life, if her path had not crossed that of the saturnine-faced man opposite her, could have been by now. A quietly happy life with a faithful husband in that vicarage at Hadley. A living child, and perhaps another on the way. But as it was, she had no child. And even though she had accompanied this man into exile, thus making herself an enemy of her native land, even though she had striven to make this once slovenly house pleasant, even though she had brought to their bed a passion that matched his own, he still felt free to flaunt that titled strumpet in her face.

Head held high, mouth set in a bitter line, she pushed back her chair and walked out of the room.

A few minutes after nine that night, wearing an almost transparent champagne-colored peignoir of which Patrick had pleasant memories, Moira Ashley admitted him to her room at the inn. He had speculated as to what she might look like now. Tense and anxious, as befitted a woman who had lost a fortune? Outwardly smiling, but with eyes holding a trace of the bitter fury he had seen there at their last meeting? Instead, he saw a woman of undiminished beauty, smiling the serenely seductive smile with which she had greeted him so often at Wetherly.

She said, "Well, Patrick how long has it been? Seven months?"

"Nearer eight."

When they were seated together on a wicker settee, glasses of the white wine she had poured resting on a nearby table, he said, "I gather that your diamond venture was a disaster."

She wrinkled her lovely nose at him. "Don't scold, Patrick darling. I didn't come all this way to be scolded."

"For what reason did you come?"

She picked up her glass and looked at him over its rim. "At least two reasons. I still have a little money. I hope to make more of it, perhaps enough to buy Wetherly back. I hope you can guide me to making an investment in St.-Denis sugar or rum."

"At the moment, there are no such investment opportunities on St.-Denis."

"Not even in your distillery? Wouldn't you welcome someone with five thousand pounds to invest?"

"No. My enterprise is still too small to return a reasonable profit to even my brother and myself, let alone a third person."

"Then I might consider another island, such as St.-Gertrude. It's less than a hundred miles away, and I have heard there are properties for sale there. Perhaps you would be kind enough to make the journey with me. As I understand it, no large ships call there, but we could take passage on one of the interisland trading boats."

He had been expecting her to make some such proposal. It would be at least a twenty-four-hour sail to St.-Gertrude, in a boat manned by only one or two natives. He pictured an English frigate, suddenly appearing out of the darkness . . .

"Tell me, Moira, how much did you lose in that South American venture?"

"Almost sixty thousand pounds."

"Then with fifty thousand pounds you would be nearly as well off as before."

She appeared puzzled. "Fifty thousand pounds?"

"The amount you would receive if you could manage to

lure me off this island, so that the English could get their hands on me."

"Patrick!"

The hurt shock in her face appeared genuine. But then, she must have known when she first thought of the St.-Gertrude proposal that he might suspect her of a trick. Knowing that, she'd had ample time to rehearse a response to his accusation.

"Do you believe that I would betray you to the English for any amount of money in the world?"

"Perhaps not." But if she had done it once for revenge, he told himself silently, she might well do it again for money. He went on aloud, "Nevertheless, I intend to stay safely on St.-Denis. I am sure you will find no lack of male escort if you decide to make the trip to St.-Gertrude."

He thought of the stir this beautiful and frankly amorous woman would make in St.-Denis. Every unmarried planter or army officer, and many of the married ones, would be panting after her. He felt a twinge of jealousy at the prospect. True, she had ceased to be his mistress even before he left Ireland. And true, under his tutelage his wife's slender body had become as eager for physical love—and almost as skilled—as Moira's voluptuous one. Just the same, the displeasure he felt at the thought of St.-Denis men trying to take her to bed made him realize that he still felt a male possessiveness toward her.

Almost as if she had read his thoughts, she leaned closer to him, full breasts swelling above the peignoir's low décolletage. "Very well. Perhaps it would be best if you did not venture off this island. But you have not asked me my second reason for coming here."

Patrick said nothing.

"I thought I hated you when you walked away from me that last time. But when I heard that you'd had to flee Ireland, leaving everything behind you, I knew that I loved you as much as I ever had. As soon as I learned where you were, I started making plans to come to you."

Gaze traveling from that proffered bosom up to her smiling face, he still said nothing. After a moment she asked, striving for a light tone, "Are you still besotted with that wife of yours?"

For a few disquieting moments that afternoon, Moira had wondered if Elizabeth was as cold and unresponsive to Patrick as she had always judged her to be. But other factors could have accounted for the Englishwoman's obvious agitation today. No woman, however cold, relishes the pity and ridicule that is the lot of an unfaithful husband's wife.

Besides, it did not matter what Elizabeth thought or felt. Only Patrick mattered. And Moira knew that she attracted him as much as ever. The very air between them seemed charged with his physical awareness of her.

He said, "I never told you details about my relationship with Elizabeth. Nor do I want to discuss her any more than I ever have."

"Very well. But what of me? Do you find that I have so fallen off in looks that—"

"You know you haven't," he said, almost harshly. He stood up. "But I am a fugitive now, and a relatively poor man, straining every nerve to build up a profitable enterprise. You are a distraction I cannot afford."

Nor did he trust her. But she knew that. There was no point in telling her so again.

Smiling, she too rose. "Nevertheless, I shall stay here for a while. Thank you for responding to my message."

Lying in the darkened bedroom, Elizabeth heard Patrick come down the hall and into the room. She had resolved to pretend to be asleep, but as she saw him, in the dim light filtering through the blinds, begin to take off his coat, she asked, "Did you see her?"

"Yes."

She had also resolved that for pride's sake she would not allow herself to appear jealous, and yet she heard herself burst out, "Did you make love to her?"

"No." But he knew that he might, if not at their next meeting, then at the one after that.

Moira Ashley was dangerous, perhaps to his neck, and certainly to much he had come to enjoy these past months. Although Ireland frequently was in his thoughts, he had achieved a certain amount of contentment here in his prospering enterprise, and in the companionship and warm physical response of the gray-eyed woman whom, no matter how reluctantly, he had married.

Moira's presence threatened all that. And yet tonight he had felt as strongly attracted to her as he had that day nearly a decade ago when she had walked out onto the terrace where he stood talking with her elderly husband. Damn her! Damn that beautiful—and probably treacherous—Irishwoman to hell and back. Why hadn't she stayed where she belonged? If she had, he would have recalled less and less often, as time passed, that wanton, teasing laugh of hers, and that pliant body with its slender waist and flaring hips and bosom. But now she would be right here on this tropical island, where even the warm, flower-perfumed air held a disturbing sensuality. And those indigo eyes of hers always would be challenging him to reach out for her. . . .

He shrugged back into his coat. "Go to sleep, Elizabeth." His inner conflict made his voice harsher than he had intended it to be. "I am going to take a few turns in the garden."

32

In the weeks that followed, Elizabeth and Patrick by
unspoken agreement did not mention Moira's name to
each other. And yet Elizabeth never lost her awareness of
the woman's presence on the island.

At least two and sometimes more evenings each week,
Patrick would rise from the supper table with the an-
nouncement that he and Colin were riding up to the distillery to work on accounts and correspondence. Whether
or not he saw Moira Ashley some of those evenings, Elizabeth didn't know. She rather thought not. Otherwise the
women at the morning coffees she attended would have
contrived to let her know about it.

In mid-August she had become almost certain that
even if Patrick had briefly resumed his relations with
Moira, he had broken them off. The Lady Moira, Elizabeth learned from over-the-coffeecups gossip, had rented
a secluded house about a mile from the Stanfords'. Victor
Serraut, the handsome young lieutenant, was not only a
frequent visitor. He also, it was rumored, helped support
the establishment.

Nearly every hostess in St.-Denis had been plunged into
conflict by Moira's presence. On the one hand, they
longed for a closer acquaintanceship with a woman who
was a peeress, and therefore of more exalted rank than
the Stanfords. On the other hand, they feared this beautiful and unabashedly seductive woman. In most cases, social ambition won out over fear. Moira attended none of
the exclusively feminine gatherings, but soon she, escorted

253

by Lieutenant Serraut, was the center of attention at many evening parties. Elizabeth saw that Patrick's gaze, like that of every man present, tended to follow the Irishwoman about the room.

Elizabeth continued to keep busy with books, and letters to her mother, and helping Jeanne keep the small house clean and sparkling. But she felt little of the contentment, the joy in the island's beauty, that she had known for several weeks before Moira's shadow fell across her there on the sun-flooded side terrace.

At night in Patrick's arms she sometimes, in spite of herself, was swept up to the heights. Other times—when she had caught a glimpse of Moira in the town square that day, or seen Patrick's eyes following the woman at an evening party—she remained cold, inert.

On one such night he spent several minutes trying to woo her, holding the length of her body close to him, so that she could feel the hard warmth of his arousal, stroking her hips, kissing her mouth and closed eyelids and then her throat and breasts. She lay passive in his arms, silently enduring his caresses.

At last he moved away from her. Staring into the darkness, he asked, "What is the matter with you?"

She burst out, "Moira Ashley is the matter!"

"What has she to do with us? She has that Lieutenant What's-his-name now. Victor Serraut."

"But you still find her desirable!"

He answered, after a moment. "Any man would. She's an extremely attractive woman."

She cried, "And Victor Serraut is an attractive man! So is Colin. So are half a dozen men on this island that I could name. But I don't go panting after them in my imagination."

Enough light came through the blinds that she could see him shrug. "All that proves is that men are different."

She wanted to say: That's not true! You would not be

different, as you phrase it, if you loved me. But she knew that if she said that, he might reply, calmly and truthfully: I have never told you that I loved you.

The autumn rains came, heavier than those of the previous spring, rattling like gunfire of the stiff palm fronds, drumming on roofs, and stilling for several weeks that other drumming in the hills. Parties in the houses near town, and the larger ones in the hills, became more numerous and livelier. The inhabitants of St.-Denis had much to celebrate. A French fleet of twenty-five vessels, assembling at Haiti in early August, had sailed across the Atlantic to Chesapeake Bay and there defeated nineteen English ships of the line. Then, in mid-October, England's General Cornwallis had surrendered his sword to the colonists' General Washington at Yorktown. Although English troops still held out in New York, it was obvious that they had lost the war.

Seeing the exultant faces at those parties, hearing the triumphant toasts, Elizabeth felt mixed emotions, relief that the war soon would be over, and yet sorrow at her homeland's humiliation. And she felt something else— fear. The grim exultation in Patrick's face convinced her that in his heart he had never surrendered the cause for whose sake he had been forced into exile. Even now, she was sure, he was speculating as to how England's defeat might be translated into Ireland's freedom.

The wet season, with rain clouds boiling up almost every day to drench the island, gave way to clear skies and balmy trade winds, almost as steady and gentle as the wash of waves on the island's pink beaches. Then, one January afternoon, something happened that for a time drove the war and even Moira Ashley from her thoughts.

She came out of the mercer's shop onto the square's sidewalk that day, a package containing fifteen yards of yellow muslin in her arms. She placed the bulky package in the gig. About to climb into the driver's seat, she glanced to her left. A slender young man was coming toward her along the sidewalk, a portmanteau in his hand, shoulder-length ringlets pale and shining in the sunlight.

After a stunned moment she felt a rush of gladness, and then terrified dismay. It couldn't be Christopher, not here on St.-Denis.

He stopped short, and then broke into a run. "Liza! Darling Liza!"

Stiff with shock, she allowed him to draw her into his arms and rain kisses on her face. "Oh, Liza! I was just about to start asking people where to find you."

She regained her power of speech. "In God's name, Christopher, why have you come here? If Patrick finds out—"

"Is that your gig?" he rushed on, as if she hadn't spoken. "Oh, Liza, do take me home with you, so that we can talk."

She said, very pale, "Perhaps there is some ship sailing today . . ."

"There is not. Except for a French battle frigate, the Netherlands ship I came on is the only one in the harbor, and it will be here for a week. Oh, Liza! Don't look like that. Everything will be all right. Now, let's go to your house."

Still dazed, she let him help her into the gig. He got onto the seat beside her. As she drove along one side of the square, she said, "I suppose Mother told you where I was."

"Yes, the letters Mama sent to me in Paris told me all about how you and Patrick had had to leave Ireland. Oh, my poor Liza! You must have had such dreadful times!"

She said grimly, turning from the square onto the road, "Never mind about me." Now that he sat beside her, she saw that his face had changed. Although still strikingly handsome, it had a slightly puffed look, which made her think that perhaps her young brother had become overly fond of the bottle. "Why did you leave Paris?"

"Oh, Liza! Cordot's Emporium failed. I lost my employment."

The only failure had been Christopher's—a failure to manage his bookkeeping adroitly enough to cover up his small but frequent embezzlements. Informed by her manager that her accountant and bedmate had been stealing from her, Yvette Cordot had gone to the police. Fortunately for Christopher, the outraged manager first had told the culprit of his intention to inform Madame Cordot. Thus Christopher had been able to slip aboard an Amsterdam-bound vessel before the police could lay their hands on him. In Amsterdam he had waited, in the cheapest lodgings available, until he could board a ship for the West Indies.

"Liza, I did not want to go back to England, not after . . . what had happened there. I tried to find other employment in Paris, but could not. And now I have no money."

That last was true. For perhaps the hundredth time, he cursed himself for not having saved the money he took from the emporium. But each time the sum was small, and each time there had been something he wanted to spend it on—some pretty harlot, or a fling at the gaming tables, or wine of a quality that that tight-fisted Yvette would not buy for her own table. And so by the time he fled Paris he had scarcely enough money to get to Amsterdam, keep himself there for several weeks, and then buy passage to St.-Denis.

Elizabeth said desperately, "We'll have to find a place where you can stay until you leave here. There is a small settlement on the other side of the island . . ."

"Liza, Liza! Surely by now you have been able to convince Sir Patrick that I had nothing to do with his ward's death."

"I have tried to convince him of nothing." And besides, she wanted to cry out to the youth sitting beside her, his hair gleaming palely as they traversed the stretch of jungle-walled road, you and those other degenerates did ravage that poor young girl and send her plunging to her death.

But even in her frightened dismay over his arrival, and her loathing of what she was sure he had done, she still was conscious of the irresistible child he once had been. Whatever else he was, he was her young brother, and the adored son of that frail woman back in England.

"But, Liza! Even if he still has doubts about me, surely he loves you enough that for your sake alone he would re-strain himself. How could he help but love you, as beauti-ful and good as you are. And happy people are not bitter and vengeful. Surely he must be a happy man now, even if he has lost his Irish properties. He has you. And Mama wrote me that in your letters you said the distillery was doing very well." He paused. "It is doing well, isn't it?"

She said distractedly, "Yes." Perhaps she could per-suade Patrick to give her a sum of money, enough to pay Christopher's passage back to Paris. No, that was un-likely. Straining every nerve to make a success of his en-terprise, Patrick would not pay for anyone's voyage of several thousand miles, especially Christopher Montlow's.

"Liza, don't you see that if I had done . . . what he thought I had, this island would be the last place in the world I would come to? Can't you see that *he* will realize that?"

She looked at him, her belief in his guilt momentarily shaken. Then she reflected that his coming here proved nothing. Perhaps he had counted upon them considering his arrival as evidence of his innocence.

She said, unable to think of any other solution, "All right, Christopher. Even if you went to the other side of St.-Denis, or to another island—"

"I can't!" he cried. "I told you! I don't have money for a half-dozen decent meals, let alone passage to—"

"I was going to say, Christopher, that even if you went

to another island, he would soon hear about you. You are not an inconspicuous person, you know. So I will plead your case with Patrick. Until then, stay out of his sight."

When they reached the house, Elizabeth drove back to the stable. Christopher helped her unhitch the pony and then followed her through the kitchen and along the hall to the parlor. He said, looking at the wicker furniture, the straw rug, the bouquet of scarlet hibiscus on a stand set against the white wall. "How charming you have made this room, Liza!" Obviously, he was thinking. Patrick Stanford must be plowing what profits he made back into his business. Certainly he had not spent much on this pokey little house.

He said, "The walk up from the hill made me thirsty. Do you have wine, or perhaps a little brandy?"

"I have both," his sister answered grimly, "but you will have none of it, not now. When you talk to Patrick, you will need all your wits about you."

She was watching from the kitchen window when Patrick rode his roan gelding back to the stable. He emerged almost immediately, which meant he had left the horse saddled. Obviously he intended to return to the distillery after supper. She opened the door and hurried down the walk to meet him.

He looked at her through the rapidly fading light. "What is it?"

"It's . . . it's Christopher," she said past the fear tightening her throat. "He lost his situation in Paris. He had only enough money to pay his passage to St.-Denis, and so . . ."

Terror made her stop speaking. Patrick's face had taken on the murderous look she had seen there one February afternoon when he had stared through Old Bailey's murky lamplight at Christopher standing in the dock.

"You mean he's here?" His voice was thick. "In my house?"

He moved past her. Whirling around, Elizabeth clutched his arm with both her hands. "Patrick! Don't you see? If he were guilty of that girl's death, do you think he would have come here?"

"I think that is what he counted upon my thinking."

She said desperately, "Don't harm him. For my sake, don't harm him."

Enraged heartbeats gradually slowing, he looked down at her upturned face, pale as death in the gathering dark. Once she had relinquished a chance for vengeance. She could have remained at Stanford Hall, fairly confident that the English would treat her gently. She might even have been awarded some share of his confiscated lands. Instead, she had chosen to go with him into exile.

He owed her a debt, and he always paid his debts. He would have to forgo what he had longed for these past two years—the feel of his two hands around Christopher Montlow's white neck, squeezing until he felt the windpipe collapse.

Dizzy with relief, she sensed that at least momentarily he had checked his desire to kill. She said, "I know that paying his way back to France is too much to ask. But if you could send him to another island—"

"And have him turn up back here as soon as he runs out of money or has to flee the authorities? Better that he stay here, where I can keep an eye on him. All right." he added abruptly, "where is he?"

When Patrick and Elizabeth entered the parlor, Christopher was standing in the middle of the room, shoulders drooping, face humble and defenseless. Even though Elizabeth's quick smile told him that he was in no immediate danger, it was only with an effort that he met Sir Patrick's gaze. What terrible eyes the Irishman had, cold eyes that seemed to look straight into your thoughts.

Wisely, Christopher remained silent. After a moment

Patrick said, "Elizabeth has told me that you are without funds."

"That is the case, Sir Patrick. But if you will allow me to remain here—"

"Not under my roof, " Patrick said harshly. "You will stay at the inn."

Christopher bowed his head. "Very well." As if he wanted to stay here! While his sister had watched for her husband from the kitchen window, he had made a soft-footed inspection of the house, including the small second bedroom. Surely he would be more comfortable at the inn, as well as freer.

He went on, "As for my employment, sir, if you could recommend me to some merchant in the town . . ."

"There is no merchant," Patrick said dryly, "whom I dislike to that extent. You will work at the distillery."

Eyes widening, Christopher recoiled from a vision of himself in a cooking shed, standing in one hundred and twenty degrees' temperature over one of those huge vats he had heard about.

Patrick gave a short laugh. "No, you won't get your hands dirty. You can help with the accounts. But keep in mind that my brother, who has a sharp eye indeed, will inspect all your figures."

33

The matrons of St.-Denis found Christopher Montlow a welcome addition to local society. Now, while their husbands clustered around Lady Moira, they had a handsome young bachelor to dance with them, admire their gowns, and murmur compliments to even the plainest of them.

None of these women, though, would have welcomed Christopher as a suitor for a marriageable daughter. There was a rumor, perhaps started by Lady Moira, that he had been involved in some dreadful scrape in London, something that had resulted in the death of a seventeen-year-old girl. Some even maintained that the girl had been Sir Patrick Stanford's ward. That part, of course, could not be true. Otherwise, Christopher would not even be on St.-Denis, let alone keeping the accounts at Sir Patrick's distillery. In fact, when Christopher looked at them from those gentle, candid blue eyes, they could not believe that any of it was true. Nevertheless, they were glad that at parties and balls he treated their daughters with distant politeness, not even seeking them as partners for the gavottes and polkas.

What they did not know was that Patrick had issued him a stern warning. "Stay away from respectable young girls. If you want a girl, there are plenty of them on Harbor Street."

With amusement Christopher recalled those words one night, about a month after his arrival in St.-Denis, as he lay beside Moira Ashley in a bedroom of her secluded house. He smiled, head resting on his elbow-propped hand, face and naked torso illumined by a swath of moonlight.

She asked, "Of what are you thinking?"

"My esteemed brother-in-law. He warned me away from the maidens of St.-Denis. I was to confine my attentions, he told me, to the Harbor Street whores."

"I hear you are not unacquainted with the establishments along that street."

"I have gone there solely as a sightseer," he said blandly. "But the point is this. When he issued that warning, I wonder if it occurred to him that you and I might—"

"I am sure it did not," she interrupted coolly. "And in fact, I am really rather surprised at myself. You are a beautiful boy, Christopher, but compared to Patrick, or even Victor Serraut, you are an inadequate lover."

"He said, "Inadequate? I should think that thrice in one evening . . ."

"It is quality, rather than quantity, which counts."

"Perhaps, although other women have not found me inadequate in either respect. But then, most of them were less experienced than you." He had not really expected her to take offense, and her shrug told him that she had not. He went on, "Besides, having me in your bed brings you another satisfaction, perverse though it may be."

"What satisfaction?"

"Revenge. I'm the brother of the woman you hate. You hate her because she is Patrick's wife, and you hate him for the same reason. Oh, yes, Moira, I have seen you looking at them, and I know you hate them both. You've probably been obsessed with loving him, and hating him, for a long time. What better revenge than pleasuring yourself with me, a man he'd like to kill?"

That word again. She lay motionless, too angry to speak.

"Perhaps even before this you enjoyed another kind of revenge. Who was it, I wonder, who told the English that your neighbor Sir Patrick Stanford plotted treason?"

"You prate of things you know nothing about," she said coldly. "You must swear not to talk of such matters again, not if you want to continue coming here."

He said swiftly, "I swear." Moira was not only beautiful. The wines and Port-au-Prince pheasants, brought by Lieutenant Serraut from the fort to his mistress's house, were excellent indeed.

"And now you had best leave. It must be getting on toward dawn."

" 'Oh, no,' " he said, fingers playing with a lock of her

silky dark hair, " 'it was the nightingale, and not the lark.' "

"What nightingale? What nonsense are you talking?"

He leaned over and kissed her. "Sometimes your beauty makes me forget you are not an educated woman. I quoted Shakespeare. *Romeo and Juliet*, act three, scene five."

"I may not know Shakespeare, but I do know Victor Serraut. If he ever learns that you have been coming here, he will kill you. Now, go."

34

For the first time since her arrival on the island, Elizabeth found that the very perfection of the weather in the dry season had begun to fray her nerves. Each day the sun shone from a cloudless sky, and the placid sea shimmered, and the lush vegetation around the little white house rustled in the faint breeze that blew ceaselessly from the west. She began to long for the sight of leafless elms and beeches against a gray English sky, and muddy roads with crusts of ice in the ruts.

But she knew it was really not the monotonous perfection of the weather that oppressed her. It was the presence of both her brother and Moira Ashley. True, she was almost certain that Patrick did not visit Moira Ashley's house. True, she knew that her brother, under Colin's alert supervision, was performing his work satisfactorily. And yet she had a sense of impending disaster, almost as if she could hear rumblings from inside the long-extinct volcano that formed the island's central peak.

When disaster came, it came swiftly, and on a morning as bright as any that had preceded it. Trimming back the ilex and hibiscus bushes that always threatened to engulf the garden paths, she heard the swift beat of horse's hooves along the drive. She straightened, Patrick reined in beside the stable entrance, his face dark with rage.

The garden shears dropped from her hand. She said, hurrying toward him. "What is it?"

"Your brother." His voice was thick. "He's disappeared. So has almost six thousand dollars in gold coins. He broke open the strongbox at the distillery sometime during the night."

She whispered. "Oh, no!" Then: "Are you sure? Perhaps some of the blacks—"

"Don't be absurd, Elizabeth. It's your brother who has disappeared."

She said, still dazed. "Six thousand dollars. So very much money . . ."

"Yes! A lot of money, full payment for the last two shipments of rum. Enough money that if I can't recover it we will be about as poor as when we arrived here. The American agent came up to the distillery after dark yesterday. Only Colin and I were there. We decided to leave the money in the strongbox overnight."

"But how did Christopher . . .?"

"He must have passed the agent on the road, and guessed he was carrying money. Colin's gone over to the cove to see if he can find a trace of him." Elizabeth knew what cove he meant, a shallow one on the southern shore of the island from which small boats in the interisland trade sailed. "I am going down to the waterfront to learn if he managed to sneak aboard some ship in the harbor."

As he whirled his mount, the skirt of his coat fell back, and she saw the pistol he had thrust into the waistband of his breeches. She watched until he disappeared around the corner of the house. Feeling numb, she walked to the kitchen door.

The brief tropic twilight had fallen by the time Patrick returned. From the parlor window she watched him tether his horse to the gatepost. She could not make out his facial expression, but frustrated rage was evident in his very stride as he came up the walk.

She met him just inside the front door. "What—?"

"Has he come sneaking back here?"

"No." All day she had feared that he might. All day she had wondered what she would do if her handsome, monstrous young brother came slipping into the house, pleading for her protection.

Patrick's dark gaze searched her face. Apparently satisfied that she told the truth, he said, "There's no trace of him. We've searched everywhere on this side of the island. The police *commissaire* and I even went aboard that Portuguese ship in the harbor and those two American merchantmen, and searched them from stem to stern."

"Did Colin, over at the cove . . .?"

"He talked to freedmen who live in the shacks there. They said that only one trading vessel had sailed from the cove since yesterday afternoon, and that there had been no one of Christopher's description aboard it."

"And the people at the inn?"

"They have not seen him since yesterday morning, although he must have been there sometime last night. He left that hired mare of his at the inn stable and then just . . . disappeared."

Because she could think of nothing else to say, she asked, "Have you had food? I have made some—"

"I want no food," he said, and turned toward the door.

She cried, "Where are you going?"

"I don't know. Perhaps to St. Amalie." That was the settlement on the Atlantic side of the island. "Although how he could have gotten there on foot, through fifteen

miles of jungle . . ." Not completing the sentence, he
went out the door and closed it behind him.

Unable to eat the supper she had prepared, unable to
do anything except sit in the parlor, hands clasped in her
lap, she waited until almost midnight for his return. Then
she went to bed and stared, wide-awake, into the
darkness.

Christopher lay on the sagging bed in the tiny top-floor
room, hands crossed behind his head, and watched the
girl. She sat with his coat across her lap, fingers stitching
still another tiny pocket in its lining. Light from the oil
lamp on the rickety table beside her gleamed on the gold
coins stacked around the lamp's base, and on her bent
dark head and the needle she plied so awkwardly.

Her name was Solange. Her mother was a quadroon,
and so she knew she had at least some African blood, but
as to the nationality of her various white ancestors, she
had no idea. She looked fourteen, was actually sixteen,
and had been a prostitute for more than a year. Christopher liked her, not only because she was pretty but also
because of the childlike awe in her face whenever she
looked at him.

For almost fifteen hours now, ever since he had left his
horse at the inn stable in the predawn darkness, crossed
the deserted square, and walked down the alley to the
rear door of this brothel, Solange had been sewing those
pockets into his coat lining. There had been interruptions,
of course. Several times she had slipped downstairs to
fetch him food or brandy. Once the brothel-keeper, a
stout man with a cast in one eye, had looked in and said
apologetically that Solange must come down to a room on
the floor below. Otherwise, a favored customer would
make trouble. And less than an hour ago Christopher
himself had slipped out into the alley, made his way onto

the beach and then the wharf, and struck his bargain with
the master of the Portuguese ship.

He looked at the stacks of gleaming coins. They num-
bered a few less than when he had taken them, in their
stout leather bag, from the distillery strongbox. He had
given two coins to the brothel-keeper. Even though he
knew it was not necessary, he had given one to Solange,
who had stared down at it with her usual awed expression, either not understanding or not believing him
when he told her that it was more than she could hope to
earn in several months. And he had given three gold
pieces to the Portuguese captain. Just before the ship
sailed with the predawn tide, he would slip aboard.

Uneasily, he frowned. He did not entirely trust that
captain. There was at least a chance that once the ship
was well out to sea the Portuguese colors would come
down and the death's-head flag go up. But Christopher
thought not. What cargo he had seen, sugarcane and West
Indian mahogany, was that of an honest merchant ship.
And even if the captain did demand an additional bribe,
Christopher would still reach Lisbon, and eventually
Paris, with enough that he would need no Yvette Cordot
this time, and no employment. He would be able to live
comfortably for five years, or, if he chose, luxuriously for
half that long.

Solange bit off a thread with her sharp little teeth.
Christopher rose, took his coat from her hands, and
spread it, lining up, on the bed. Swiftly his eyes swept
over the rows of awkwardly stitched little pockets.

"All right, Solange. I'll put the coins in, a few at a
time, and you will sew up the pockets."

Elizabeth came groggily awake in the dawn light, aware
that she could not have been asleep for more than an
hour. Patrick was in the room, taking off his coat. She
said, memory rushing over her, "Patrick . . ."

"No trace of him." His voice was harsh. "I want to get some rest if I can. Now, go back to sleep."

She lay back down. Dimly she was aware of Patrick getting into bed beside her. Then exhaustion overwhelmed her, and she slept.

She awoke to early sunlight. The clock on the bedside stand pointed to a little past six. Patrick could not have rested for long. He was gone from the bed, and as she discovered a few minutes later, from the house as well. Had he gone to the distillery, she wondered dully, or had he set out on another search for Christopher?

She forced herself to dress, brew tea in the kitchen, carry her cup and saucer back to the parlor. She had taken one sip and was just sitting there, staring down into the cup, when she heard a vehicle stop out in the road. She went to the window. The Burgoses' wooden cart, drawn by a spavined gray horse, stood just outside the gate. Jules held the reins. Jeanne was running up the walk. Elizabeth felt bewilderment. Never before had either of the part-time servants come to the front entrance.

She hurried into the hall just as Jeanne began to knock, and opened the front door. The maid's café-au-lait face beneath her white turban held frightened distress.

"Oh, milady! Monsieur Montlow . . ."

She broke off. Elizabeth said, her stomach knotting with fear, "What has happened to him?"

Apparently Jeanne could not bring herself to say. "Oh, milady! Come with us."

Elizabeth hurried down the walk. As she climbed to the wooden-plank seat, it did not occur to her to think of how anyone abroad at that early hour might react to the sight of her riding between her two servants in their cart. The vehicle lumbered down the road, across the empty square, down the slope past the shuttered grog shops and brothels. Now she could see, not far from the foot of the wharf, a group of people gathered around something on the crescent beach. They appeared to be blacks, mainly, barefoot men in white cotton breeches and shirts, barefoot women in brightly colored dresses and white turbans. Elizabeth found herself out of the cart and running awkwardly over the sand.

The knot of people parted at her approach. She stared down at the sprawled figure—the soaked breeches and coat, the waxen face with its pale-lipped wound, no longer bleeding, along the left temple, the fair hair matted with sand. She had no doubt that he was dead. And yet, as she dropped to her knees beside him, her first emotion was not grief for Christopher, but anguish for her mother and his, that frail woman who felt, not just love for her son, but blind adoration.

35

A hand touched her shoulder. Someone said, "I am sorry, madame."

She looked up. It took her several seconds to recognize the thin, middle-aged white man standing beside her. Armand Montreux, one of the two deputies of the island's police commissioner. She asked, even though she already knew the answer, "He is dead?"

Montreux hesitated, and then answered, "I fear it is of a certainty, madame, although it is the duty of the *commissaire* and the surgeon to pronounce him so. Someone has gone to fetch them."

"How . . . ?"

"Bertrand here found him." The deputy looked at a tall

young black man, who ducked his head shyly. "He came down at dawn to fish, and saw Monsieur Montlow's body being washed ashore."

"How did it . . . ? What do you think . . . ?"

The deputy said, after a moment, "Perhaps he was not quite himself last night, and fell from the wharf."

Not quite himself. Her numbed mind made the translation. Stupefied with drink.

"Perhaps," Montreux went on, "he received that head wound when a wave washed him against a piling, either before or after he drowned."

It was the kindest explanation. No doubt that was why Montreux had made it. But it could not be the true one. If Christopher had washed against a barnacle-encrusted piling, there would be more lacerations on his waxen face. Instead, there was just that one straight-edged gash.

Almost as if she had been there, she saw the two shadowy figures on the dark wharf, saw a raised hand bring the pistol barrel down on Christopher's temple, saw him fall—already dead, or at least too stunned to save himself—into the black water below.

She said, "His coat . . ." One side of its skirt had fallen away from his body, so that she could see the lining. Gray muslin patches, awkwardly stitched, almost hid the dark blue satin. Her hand reached out.

"Best not to touch him," Montreux said, "until the *commissaire* arrives." He added, embarrassment in his voice, "One would say, madame, that there is money sewn into his coat."

Patrick's money.

She felt hands under her armpits. "Please, milady," Jeanne Burgos said. "Please let us take you home."

Elizabeth allowed herself to be drawn to her feet.

Around eight that night she sat in the parlor, hands clasped rigidly in her lap, face almost as white as her dead brother's had been. She heard the muffled clop of hooves on the road and then along the drive beside the house.

Before noon, a note from the commissioner had arrived, expressing his sympathies and telling her that Monsieur Montlow's body was at the hospital, which also served as the small community's morgue. She could claim the body tomorrow after "certain official matters" had been attended to.

Aside from reading that note, she did not know what she had done that day except wait for Patrick. Patrick, who had murdered her brother, come back to the house, and actually lain down beside her in their bed.

The rear door opened. Footsteps in the hall. "Elizabeth?"

She got to her feet and said in a voice she would not have recognized as her own, "I'm in here."

He appeared in the doorway, his dark face looking bleak but controlled. She said, "Did you get your money?"

She could tell, by the widening and then the narrowing of his eyes, that he had not expected her to greet him with that question. "The commissioner will release it to me when I call at his office."

She said, in a thick voice, "I have always known there was hatred and violence in you. Who could know that better than I? But until now I did not know that you were also a coward."

He said slowly, "What in God's name are you talking about?"

"You could have shot him, and then surrendered to the commissioner. Nothing much would have been done to you. After all, he had stolen your money. But you did not want to take the responsibility for his murder. And so you struck him down, and then pushed him—"

"Stop that! I was on the other side of the island looking

for him last night. And today I went down to the cove to see if—"

"Liar," she said quietly. "Liar and murderer."

"Elizabeth, for God's sake! If I had done what you think I did, wouldn't I have recovered my money before I pushed him into the sea?"

Because she had known he would say that, she had had all day to think of her answer. "Perhaps you did not know it was sewn into his coat. Or perhaps you did know, and left it there so you could say to everyone what you have just said to me. Your money was still in his coat, and so you could not have been the one who killed him.

"Or perhaps," she went on, her voice thickening, "you hated him so much that for the moment you forgot about your money. All you wanted was to kill him. And you did, and then you came back here and got into bed beside me—"

"Elizabeth!"

He took a step toward her. She shrank back. "Don't touch me. How can you think I would ever let you touch me?"

He looked at her bleakly for a long moment. This was how he had thought it might be. From now on the body of that unspeakable degenerate would lie between them, an uncrossable barrier.

"Very well. If that is what you prefer. I will never touch you again."

His footsteps went back along the hall. She stood rigid until she heard him ride down the drive and turn toward the town. Then she slumped into a chair and sat huddled against the backrest, hands covering her face.

Something had happened to her time sense during the past dreadful hours. Now she did not know whether fifteen minutes had passed, or twice that, before she became aware of the hot, heavy silence in the room, broken only when some insect struck against the jalousies. Nor did she

know how long it was after that that she became conscious of her terrible aloneness.

Suddenly the pendulum of her emotions swung. What if
Patrick had told the truth? Without her knowing it, Christopher could have made other enemies since coming to
this island. Or, if he had been last night in one of those
grog shops or brothels on Harbor Street, he could have
become embroiled in a drunken argument with some sol-
dier or merchant sailor, someone who had followed him
out into the night . . .

Patrick had said, "I will never touch you again." Had
he also meant that he would never see her again?

As Jeanne and Jules led her back to the cart that
morning, she had been vaguely aware that, next to a vacant anchorage where for the past week a Portuguese
merchantman had lain, men were loading rum barrels
aboard an American ship. What if it was due to sail with
the next tide? And what if Patrick, after obtaining his
money from the commissioner, had gone aboard it?

She tried to reason the thought away, but then panic
overcame her, and she stopped even trying to reason. She
knew only that she must try to find him. She ran down
the hall and snatched a lantern from its hook beside the
kitchen door. Hands shaking, she struck a flint. Then the
lantern cast a swinging swath of light over the graveled
path as she ran back to the stable.

Only minutes later she drove the gig across the town
square. Light shone from the inn's open double doors,
and farther along the street, from the windows of the
commissioner's office. Was Patrick in there? She dared
not take the time to find out. Perhaps even now that
American merchantman was lifting anchor.

She started down that sloping street where no respectable woman ever ventured except to or from some ship,
and only then with an escort. She was halfway down the
street when she reined in. There in front of a grog shop,

tethered to a hitching post, was Patrick's bay gelding with the white forehead blaze.

As she got out of the gig and crossed to the grog shop's open door, she did not even see the men and women on the sidewalk, staring at her in astonishment. Just inside the doorway, she halted, dimly aware of yellow lamplight, of the smell of rum and tobacco smoke and cheap scent, of the raucous sounds—loud male voices, shrieking feminine laughter—which gradually died as person after person in the low-ceilinged room caught sight of her.

As yet, Patrick had not done so. He sat at a table, laden with a half-filled bottle and three glasses, against one smoke-blackened wall. Two women sat with him, a thin brunette of about thirty-five, and a much younger and quite pretty blond. Although Patrick, somber gaze fixed on his almost empty glass, seemed unaware of it, the blond had her arms wrapped around his neck and was whispering in his ear.

For a moment Elizabeth felt dizzy with relief. Then she experienced something else, a surge of irrational anger at the blond woman. Aware that she trembled, she walked toward the table.

Patrick looked up. An almost ludicrous expression of shock came into his face. He got to his feet so abruptly that the clinging girl lost her balance and nearly fell from her chair.

"Elizabeth! What in God's name . . ."

He came around the table, seized her arm, hustled her out into the night. On the sidewalk, he tossed a coin to a bystander, a wizened little man with graying dark hair. "Take my horse to the livery stable." Then he was in the driver's seat of the gig, with Elizabeth beside him. He wheeled the vehicle around, and with a lash from the whip, sent the pony trotting up the slope.

He did not speak as they rattled across the square and passed the stretch of houses beyond. Then, as they moved between the two walls of black jungle, he demanded, "What did you plan to do? Denounce me to the assembled riffraff as a murderer?"

She began to weep. "I was afraid you were gone. I was afraid I would never see you again."

It took him a moment or two to realize the significance of her words. Abruptly he reined in. He caught her to him, kissed her mouth that tasted of tears, and her throat. As she clung to him, fingertips digging into his wide shoulders, she felt all her emotions of the past few hours—the fear and the bitterness and the hatred—give way to her need for this man's lovemaking.

He said, in a thickened voice, "We'll go home now."

36

Afterward Elizabeth often wondered if their child had been conceived that night. Certainly, never before had she been so abandoned in her response, so open to him. Afterward, too, she felt shocked at the realization that their frenzied lovemaking followed only hours after Christopher's death. It was as if the very ending of his sorry existence had made her poignantly aware of her own living body, and of its need for the man who held her.

When at last they lay quiet, he said, staring into the darkness, "You know, don't you, that perhaps I can never prove to you that I told you the truth earlier this evening?"

"Yes." In the absence of any sure knowledge about Christopher's last moments on earth, there would always be that dark question in her heart. Then she said, "But I will believe you without proof. I will believe you because I *must* believe you."

He drew her head onto his shoulder and stroked her hair. "Then that will suffice."

In those latitudes, funerals could not be delayed. The next afternoon, Christopher was buried in the little public graveyard, two miles from the center of town, where those not of the Catholic faith were laid to rest. No clergyman was present, but Colin had persuaded a gaunt-faced man from Boston, a ship's carpenter and an elder of the Plymouth church, to read the Twenty-third Psalm beside the grave. When she and Patrick had deposited Colin at the inn and then returned to their own home, Elizabeth sat down and wrote to Donald Weymouth, telling him that Christopher had died "by drowning," and asking him to tell her mother.

Two weeks later, unable to find anyone who would admit even to seeing Christopher the night he died, the police commissioner and the town surgeon, who was also the coroner, gave as their verdict that Christopher Montlow had met "death by misadventure."

As the weeks passed, bringing a return of the rains that drenched the island for a few hours almost every day, and bringing a quickened tempo to the island's social life, Elizabeth felt relieved that the etiquette of bereavement forbade her and Patrick taking part. She did not relish the thought of idle chatter at the morning coffees and endless talk of war at the evening parties. It was chiefly a naval war now. The English, resigned to the eventual loss of the colonies, now used their battle frigates to harry the French along the North African coast and in the Caribbean. As yet, no English men-of-war had appeared in their particular part of the far-flung West Indian archipelago. But she could imagine the talk at those parties, the women expressing their fears, the men gallantly reas-

suring them that they need not trouble their lovely heads,
because the French fleet, although usually invisible beyond the horizon, patrolled ceaselessly to protect Haiti
and its neighboring islands. No, just as well to be away
from such talk. Just as well to live quietly with Patrick,
and wait with what patience she could muster for a letter
from Donald or her mother.

No letter came from either of them. But on one of the
rare sunny afternoons that April, as she was about to
hang freshly laundered curtains at the dining-room windows, she looked out and saw Donald Weymouth walking
down the road. The curtains dropped from her hands, and
she stood motionless, unable to believe that he was on
this tropical island thousands of miles from the vicarage
at Hadley. He turned in at the gate.

Then, as she realized the undoubted reason for his
presence, grief twisted her heart. The shock was not as
great as it might have been. These past weeks, even as
she had felt an increasing hope that she carried new life
within her, she had sensed that her mother no longer
lived.

She moved to the door, opened it. Donald said, with
that grave, gentle smile she once had loved so much,
"Hello, Elizabeth."

For a moment, overwhelmed by memories of her
mother, and of home, and of this man she had once
planned to spend her life with, she could not speak. Then
she said, "Come in, Donald."

When she had led him into the parlor, she turned to
face him. "My mother is dead, isn't she?" Then, as he
hesitated: "You can tell me. Somehow I have known it."

He reached out and took her two hands in his own.
"Yes, but it did not happen as you might think. I never
told her of your letter. She was very ill when I received it.
I did not know what to do, except pray for guidance."
Wryness touched his voice. "The guidance never came.

While I was still undecided, your mother died one afternoon in Mary Hawkins' arms."

Elizabeth withdrew her hands. She said, from a tight throat, "I think you did receive guidance. I am glad she never knew what was in my letter. And now you have come all this way . . ."

She broke off, and then said distractedly, "Forgive me, Donald. Please sit down. I will make us some tea."

He did not move. His gaze, fixed on her face, held such a strange, searching expression that for a moment she thought he had not heard her. Then he said, "Thank you, Elizabeth, but please don't make tea. There may not be time for it."

She said, bewildered, "Not time for . . ."

"The Netherlands ship I came on will sail for Haiti in a few hours. It stopped here only to discharge me and one other passenger. Perhaps I will sail with it. It depends upon you."

She waited, a silent question in her eyes. He said, "I did not want you to be alone when you learned of your mother's death. But I had still another reason for coming here. You see, there is a young woman, the daughter of a family who moved into my parish six months ago. I have found myself becoming fond of her. But first I had to learn if there was any hope that you would come back to England with me, now that Christopher and your mother . . ."

Breaking off, he again searched her face with his eyes. "Your feelings for me have changed, haven't they, Elizabeth?"

She remembered herself standing in the muddy Irish road in Donald's arms, remembered saying, "I will always love you." It seemed to her that it was another woman in another world who had spoken those words. She shrank from answering his question, but she knew that the very least she owed him was honesty, complete and immediate.

"Yes, Donald, my feelings have changed."

Again that searching gaze. "But you do love someone, don't you? You have . . . a fulfilled look now, not that lost one you had in Ireland." He paused. "You love your husband?"

"Yes."

"And he loves you?"

"I don't know," she said painfully. "Perhaps as much as he could love any woman. Perhaps not. I just know that I cannot leave him." She added, "Oh, Donald! Forgive me!"

He had paled slightly, and his smile was a bit uneven, but still it was a smile. "For something you cannot help? I think I knew as soon as you opened the door to me. But I had to come here. I had to know whether you were entirely lost to me, before . . ."

He broke off. She said, "Oh, Donald! That young woman. I hope she knows how fortunate she is."

His smile was quite steady now. "If she refuses me, perhaps you will write her a letter extolling my many virtues."

"There will be no need for such a letter! And, oh, Donald! Be happy."

"I shall try. As you must know, my poor Elizabeth, from the many times I quoted him to you, Samuel Johnson is my favorite sage. The good doctor says that it is the duty of the wise man to be happy. I shall try to be wise." He reached out and touched her cheek. "I had best get back to the ship now. Good-bye, Elizabeth."

That night in bed, with Patrick holding her close, she wept out her grief for her mother. When at last she lay quiet in his arms, she expected him to ask the question he had not asked when, earlier that evening, she had told him the news Donald had brought.

Instead he said, after a while, "Weymouth must have

sailed with that ship, all right. I heard that some Englishman came ashore for an hour or so and then went back
aboard."

Again she waited. But he just stared up at the darkened
ceiling, one arm around her, the other crooked behind his
head. Was he afraid to ask what emotions that brief reunion with Donald had brought her, or was he so confident of her that he did not need to ask? Or did he, quite
simply, regard the question as of no importance?

She wondered if she would ever really know him, and
what went on inside his dark head. Perhaps not. But it
was best to resign herself to ignorance. She had learned
how completely her emotions bound her to him. Now
there was a new bond. These past few days, she had become certain that again she was pregnant. And pray God
that this time the child would live.

On a night a few weeks later, Patrick stood in the distillery's cooking shed, uncrating two iron rollers that, once
installed, would be used to extract juice from the sugarcane fed into them. Shipped from France, and then carried by mule back up to this low-ceilinged shed, they
would replace ancient stone rollers that, cracked and
eroded by a half-century of use, were no longer efficient.

Through the open doorway of the adjoining room that
housed the huge rum caldrons, he could see Colin seated
at the littered desk in one corner. He was bent over a
ledger, oblivious of the sound of Patrick's chisel and to
the throb of drums higher in the hills. It was definitely the
dry season now. For three days no rain had fallen. And
so the blacks, obeying the call blown on a conch shell—
an eerie, drawn-out sound that had echoed two hours ago
through the early darkness—had slipped out of their ram-
shackle quarters and made their way through wind-stirred
cane fields and along all-but-invisible forest trails to the
meeting place.

Suddenly through the drum throb Patrick heard something else, a deep, rolling sound like distant thunder. For a moment he stood motionless, realizing what the sound must mean, and thinking bleakly: So perhaps we'll have to run again. Then he dropped the chisel, left the shed, and crossed the narrow dirt road carved out of the hillside. From there he could look down the tree-covered slope to the coastal plain and the lights of the little town, and then out over the black water. Out to where ships' cannon flashed, raining iron on the island of St.-Marc. Evidently the fortress on St.-Marc had been caught unprepared, because there was only occasional answering fire.

So English men-of-war had managed to slip through the French Caribbean patrol to attack the small island. And there were many ships. Cannon fire flashed from all along a rough semicircle that appeared to be about a mile in length. It would not take such a force long to subdue St.-Marc. Probably English longboats, under cover of cannon fire, were already putting men ashore. And once they held St.-Marc, it would be St.-Denis's turn. He thought of cannon pounding the fort to rubble, and of the pinkish beaches reddened with blood as the invaders fought the fort's outnumbered survivors with musket and sword. He thought of himself and Elizabeth and Colin sailing under guard back to England, where he and Colin would receive a speedy trial and an even speedier strangling by the hangman's rope.

Stomach tightened into a knot, he realized that the English, in their present mood, might not be too gentle even with his pregnant wife. After all, she had not only come here with him but also stayed with him, a rebel with a price on his head.

Until Colin spoke, Patrick was unaware that his brother had limped across the road to stand beside him.

"There are four American merchant ships tied up at the wharf."

As Patrick turned to look at him, Colin added, "Since they won't want to fall into English hands, they must be hurrying preparations to sail now. If we could sail with them . . ."

Instantly Patrick realized that one of those American ships could offer the best solution, perhaps the only solution. But the captain might ask a stiff price for taking three passengers aboard at the last minute.

He asked swiftly, "Colin, how much money do you have?"

"Damn little. A few louis in my pocket, and perhaps two hundred dollars American back at the inn."

And the only other money they had between them, Patrick realized grimly, was in the distillery strongbox. "Come on."

They hurried back to the long shed. Kneeling at the strongbox beside the desk, Patrick opened it and took out a leather bag containing coins—English sovereigns and French louis and American dollars. The bag had been much heavier before Patrick took delivery of those iron rollers that afternoon. The rollers were useless to them now, just as the whole distillery was useless, and the little house Elizabeth had refurbished, and everything else they owned except money.

He handed the bag to Colin. "I'll leave the bargaining at the wharf to you. I'm going straight to the house. For God's sake, don't pay a cent more than you have to."

Colin gave a short laugh. "Don't worry. I have no more desire to starve in the American wilderness than you do." He left the shed.

As Patrick slammed the door of the empty strongbox and extinguished the oil lamps, he heard the sound of Colin's horse dwindle away down the road. Patrick stepped out into the darkness and untethered his own horse from a tree. The drumming high in the hills, swifter now, seemed to hold an elated note. Poor devils, he thought. Did they hope that they would fare better with English masters? Probably not. More likely they celebrated the fact that soon this island would be filled with the din and smoke and cries of white men fighting white men. He swung into the saddle and turned his mount's head toward the road.

When he strode up the walk behind the little white house, Elizabeth opened the kitchen door to him. He said, "We have to get off this island. You had better start packing. Take as little as possible."

She nodded. "Jeanne and Jules were here half an hour ago. They told me what is happening. I have already started to pack."

He looked at her appreciatively. What a woman she was. Aside from her pallor, she seemed quite calm.

"I had best see what sort of bargain Colin has made." He turned and went back down the walk to his tethered horse.

When he had ridden down the drive to the road, he reined in for a moment. Colin could be trusted to make the best bargain possible. And none of those American ships could sail for another two or three hours. They would have to remove loading gear from their decks, batten down hatches, hoist sail. And ships' officers would have to round up crewmen from Harbor Street grog shops and brothels, rousting out the ones too drunk to be even aware of the bombardment a few miles away.

Yes, he would have time. Turning in the opposite direction from the harbor he rode at a gallop for almost a mile and then turned in at a graveled drive.

37

The two-story house ahead looked white in the darkness, although he knew, from the many times he had looked up this drive as he passed along the road, that it was actually pale blue. Light shone from a ground-floor window.

He dismounted, knocked on the door. After a moment Moira opened it. She wore a gown he remembered, a pale green silk one. And she was more than a little drunk.

The leap of mingled pleasure and pain in her face gave way to a sardonic look. "Sir Patrick, after all these months! Enter, Sir Patrick. Enter without fear, for I am alone." Turning, she moved rather unsteadily toward an archway. Over her shoulder she added, "But then, you must have realized that my lieutenant would be at the fort."

He followed her into a room large enough to be called a salon rather than a parlor. He gained a swift impression of thick rugs and gilt furniture, perhaps shipped from Port-au-Prince or even France, and a few small objects—a clock ornamented with gilt cupids, an ivory-framed mirror—that he remembered from Wetherly. She stood at a small rosewood table, the bottle in her hand poised over a glass.

"Wine, Sir Patrick?"

"No," he said harshly, "and you had best not take any more. Did you know that the English will soon invade this island?"

She filled the glass, sipped from it. "Of course. Why else

should Victor leave me so abruptly to return to the fort?"

"My wife, brother, and I are sailing for America tonight."

He saw fleeting pain in her almost indigo eyes, but when she spoke, her tone was light. "Right through the English fleet?"

"Of course not." He knew that the American ships would slip around to the Atlantic side of the island, and then under full sail make a run straight north through the darkness. They would not turn west until they were at least a hundred miles from St.-Denis.

"There may be hard fighting here. I thought you might want to come with us."

Again she drank. "Why should I care? No one will fight *me*. And what is it to me if the English take this island? I have always been a loyal subject of King George."

Hearing her slight emphasis on the word "loyal," he wondered again if it was she who had denounced him to the English. Well, now he would have less chance than ever of finding out.

"Besides," she went on. "I have heard that Admiral Jameson is with the Caribbean fleet. I met him in London five years ago. He is rich, handsome, and a widower. And he liked me. Who knows? St.-Denis's bad fortune may be the making of mine."

"Very well. But I felt that I . . ." He broke off.

"That you owed me a chance to escape? Owed it to me for all those nights, not to mention mornings and afternoons?"

"If you care to phrase it that way." How beautiful she still was, even with that faintly blurred look intoxication had brought to her face.

"I wonder if once I might have gone with you. I know your wife believes . . ."

She stopped, eyes brooding over some memory. Then her face cleared. "But perhaps I am no longer what she said I was. Or perhaps it is the red Indians. I'll concede that I might go with you—yes, with the three of you—if that ship were sailing for Europe. But not even for you will I go to a wilderness and get scalped by savages. So bon voyage, Patrick. You owe me nothing."

More than an hour later Elizabeth and Patrick set out for the ship, where Colin already awaited them. In the gig, with their baggage piled behind them, they drove down the dark road and into the square, where men and women had gathered on the sidewalks in excited little groups. On the long slope of Harbor Street they saw only women. Their customers were back at the fort now, or aboard ships in the harbor.

As the gig's wheels rattled over the wharf, Elizabeth said, "You went to see Moira Ashley, didn't you? Did you offer to take her with us?"

He threw her a startled look. How the devil had she guessed he might do that ?"Yes. She refused. But I had to make the offer. She's a countrywoman, and for years she was my friend and neighbor."

Had those been his only reasons? Elizabeth did not know. But what mattered was that however wild or dangerous their destination might prove to be, at least Moira Ashley was unlikely to appear there.

38

From where she stood at one of the inn's third-floor windows, Elizabeth looked down into the wide Philadelphia street. During the week she had been here she had never tired of looking out the window. She loved the street-corner orators, standing on wooden crates as they quoted Paine and Rousseau and Franklin to knots of cheering listeners. She loved the often ragged-looking American soldiers who still drilled up and down the cobblestoned street behind their drummer boys, because no one knew but what their services still might be needed, what with the English hanging on in New York. She loved the red brick row houses opposite, with their scrubbed white steps. They reminded her of houses in parts of London. And she loved the voices that floated up to her, voices that spoke English, and yet, already with an accent she had never heard in the land of her birth.

In short, she loved the vitality and excitement of this new young nation. She wished that she could stay here in this city where it all began, a city where men had penned bold words—about the rights of all men, about governments having no just rights without "the consent of the governed"—that must have sent a wave of alarm through every court in Europe.

But they could not stay here. There were no distilleries for sale in Philadelphia, even if Patrick and Colin had had the price. And the Stanford brothers had no profession, nor even sufficient manual skills to offer an employer. The solution, one that Patrick was determined upon, was to acquire land. But already the prices of land around Philadelphia were soaring. Each day he and Colin had ridden out, on hired mounts, to inspect farmland, and each day they had found the price beyond them. Well, they would just have to keep looking.

Suddenly she smiled and leaned a little farther out the window. Two men in stocking caps, arms about each other's shoulders, reeled down the opposite sidewalk, bawling out a sea chantey about a fair young mermaid. Behind them, imitating their unsteady gait, trouped a number of small boys. Elizabeth knew the men must be sailors from some ship in the harbor. They reminded her of the boatswain who, on the long voyage from St.-Denis, had helped relieve the monotony for crew and passengers by singing chanteys, most of them severely expurgated to make them suitable for Elizabeth's ears.

On the whole, the voyage had not been too unpleasant. True, the first forty-eight hours while they sailed northward, with no lights showing at night, lest they encounter an English ship, had been tense. But after that, the voyage had been uneventful. The captain, evidently well pleased with the money Colin had paid him, had turned over his cabin to Patrick and Elizabeth and moved in with the first mate. Colin had shared the second mate's cabin. Several times Elizabeth had felt seasick, but remembering her first pregnancy, she realized she might have experienced nausea even on dry land.

Now, hearing familiar footsteps along the hall, she turned away from the window. Patrick came in, his dark face triumphant. "We have it. A hundred acres for us, and a hundred for Colin."

"Where?"

He looked uncomfortable. "I bought up some scrip." At her puzzled look, he added, "Perhaps you haven't heard. The new government here has paid off some of its soldiers in scrip redeemable for land."

"I see. But where is this land you've bought?"

"A little more than two hundred miles from here, on the other side of the Alleghenies."

Dismay held Elizabeth silent. Western Pennsylvania was still a wilderness, chiefly because the English government, afraid that it could not protect its colonial subjects against the French and their Indian allies, had forbidden anyone to settle "beyond the mountains." In fact, the Americans' desire to expand westward had been one of the reasons for their rebellion.

He said, "Where we are going is not as wild as you

might think. There is already a road, not just a trail, across the mountains to New Canterbury and beyond. New Canterbury is the name of the settlement where we are going."

Elizabeth found her voice. "But the child . . ."

"I will bring you back to Philadelphia in ample time for your lying-in. Now, I've already bought two horses," he went on swiftly, "and a wagon. It has a sailcloth top, like the gypsy caravans back in Ireland. I've also bought axes and a plow and seed. But you must select what you will need to set up housekeeping—bedding and cooking utensils and so on. Buy only what is necessary. The horses will have trouble, as it is, drawing us over the mountains."

As she listened, Elizabeth had a feeling that had become familiar to her since her path had first crossed Patrick Stanford's, a sense of being in the grip of a whirlwind that might set her down anyplace, and then snatch her up again. And yet, beneath her apprehension, she was aware of that same stirring of the blood, that same eager curiosity about the future, which she had felt as the French merchantman slipped through the black water toward the West Indies.

She lay on her pallet in the heavily laden wagon, listening to the sounds of the forest night. The sough of wind through pine branches, the melancholy hoot of an owl, the liquid voice of the brook in which, three hours before, she had washed the cooking pot and the pewter plates she and the Stanford men had used for their supper of hare boiled with onions and carrots.

On the ground beside the wagon, Colin muttered something in his sleep. Ever since, ten days ago, they had left the last of the towns near Philadelphia behind them, the men had slept on the ground—beside the wagon on clear nights, beneath it on rainy ones—lest some marauding Indian or French trapper steal the horses.

Not that they had encountered hostile men of any race or nationality during their journey. Twice they had been welcome overnight guests at settlements along the way. Their hosts, some of English descent, some of Scotch-Irish, had used their arrival as an excuse for outdoor suppers, with food spread on rough-hewn tables, and two campfires blazing in the cool June twilight.

At both settlements, French trappers and Algonquian Indians were also among the guests. The trappers were deeply sunburned, wiry men, wearing fur hats and buckskin shirts and trousers. Used to slipping silently through forests and along riverbanks in search of game, they moved quietly and spoke softly even here in these outposts of civilization. Elizabeth found it almost incredible that they were of the same stock as the mincing French aristocrats she had sometimes met in London ballrooms, or the snobbish French bourgeoisie of St.-Denis. But then, these Frenchmen seemed to feel that little except their language bound them to their mother country. King Louis's quarrels with the English, obviously, were not their quarrels. Even before the colonies had revolted, the French *voyageurs* had brought their furs to such outposts as these and traded for salt, whiskey, tobacco, and other supplies.

The Algonquians, too, although they never smiled, seemed friendly enough. Perhaps it was because they felt a lingering goodwill from the days of William Penn, one colonial founder who had treated the Indians within his borders fairly. Elizabeth saw that these naked-to-the-waist savages, with their deerskin trousers and braided, feather-trimmed hair, seemed to feel an instant rapport with Patrick, even though it was manifested only as a fleeting expression across their bronze faces. One night as she looked across at the other campfire, and saw her husband sitting between Colin and a silent, pipe-smoking brave, she thought: He looks like an Indian himself!

The owl had stopped hooting. The wind had died. Nothing but silence. Silence, and her own sense of a vast wilderness stretching westward to a broad river called the Mississippi. Someday Americans might build settlements that far west. Not beyond it, of course. The regions beyond the Mississippi, stretching to a fabled land called California, belonged to the French and Spanish. Still, she felt almost dizzy with awe at the thought of the huge landmass stretching from ocean to ocean.

She must sleep. There was still hilly land ahead, the western foothills of the Alleghenies. Perhaps tomorrow, as they had several times before in their journey across the mountains, she and the two men would have to go forward on foot, so that the struggling horses could draw the wagon up a steep ascent.

But no matter. Tonight at supper Patrick had said that New Canterbury lay not more than five days' travel ahead. She turned over on the narrow pallet and drifted off to sleep.

39

Late in the afternoon five days later, Patrick reined in the horses on the crest of a low line of hills. Below them lay a gentle valley, heavily wooded, with the silver gleam of a river showing here and there among the pines and broad-leaved trees. In a clearing not far from the river stood a cluster of log houses, the smoke from their chimneys rising straight up in the still air.

Elizabeth, seated between the two men on the wagon's

plank seat, felt her heart quicken with mingled hope and trepidation. She said, "New Canterbury?"

Patrick answered, "It has to be."

"But it is so small!" She could see only four houses and their outbuildings scattered along three sides of the clearing.

"It will grow," Patrick said confidently.

"Bound to," Colin agreed, and Elizabeth noted with amusement that his speech had already acquired a few Americanisms, just as hers and Patrick's had. He went on, "That is all bottomland down there, fine for farming."

With the whip handle, Patrick pointed down the valley to where broad fields—some still bare, others already green with growing crops—had been carved out of the woodland. "Our farmland must be down there someplace." He slapped the reins across the horses' backs.

Trotting briskly now, the horses drew the wagon down the rutted road and into the clearing. A half-dozen young children broke off a game of tag to stare solemnly at the newcomers for a few seconds, and then, with excited shouts, race toward the houses to tell the grown-ups. Sunset light lay over everything, the hard-packed earth, the house fronts of unpeeled pine logs, and the faces of the men and women who came out to surround the wagon.

Colin got down, and then Patrick. He turned to help Elizabeth from the high seat. Already the settlers, faces beaming a welcome, were introducing themselves. Tired after the long day in the creaking wagon, Elizabeth absorbed only one of the names, Thompson. A middle-aged couple, the Thompsons appeared to be the eldest in the tiny community. The husband, a gaunt, craggy-faced man, told Colin and Patrick that their horses could be stabled in his shed. Mrs. Thompson, plump and motherly-looking, with gray-streaked brown hair, kissed Elizabeth.

"It's so good to have new neighbors. You see, Joe and I were the first to come here, more than six years ago. We named the place after Canterbury, because we were both born there."

Elizabeth had guessed that. Their voices still held the accents of southeastern England.

Smiling, Mrs. Thompson glanced down Elizabeth's figure. "You'll be glad to know that I'm a midwife. I delivered all but the three oldest of that lot over there." She nodded toward the group of children, who stood silent now, drinking in every word. "And five months ago I delivered Sally Jessup's baby here."

Again she nodded, this time toward a blond girl of about nineteen who held a fat infant on her hip. Sally smiled shyly and ducked her head.

The children looked in robust health. So did Sally Jessup's baby. Elizabeth felt relief. So there would be no need for her to go back to Philadelphia for her lying-in. All the way here over the rough road, she had dreaded the return journey.

Mrs. Thompson put her arm around Elizabeth. "Come, dearie. You'll stay with us until your own place is built."

That night the entire settlement gathered at the Thompson's for a feast of welcome. Men carried an extra table, roughly constructed of pine, into the big room that, together with a lean-to and a sleeping loft, comprised the entire house. Soon both tables were laden, not only with the Thompsons' roast venison but also with contributions from the other households. Warm cornmeal bread from young Sally Jessup and her almost equally shy young husband, John. Snap beans and creamed onions from the Wentworths, a couple in their mid-thirties who, like the Jessups, were native-born Americans from Providence, Rhode Island. Elizabeth learned that the four youngest of the children, gathered in a noisy group at one end of the joined-together tables, belonged to the Wentworths. The remaining couple, who had contributed two apple pies to the feast, were named MacPherson. About the Wentworths' age, they were both from Scotland, and both red-haired. So were their eleven-year-old twin sons, the eldest and noisiest of the group of children.

As she sat on the women's side of the table, Elizabeth was aware of the roughness of her surroundings. The stone fireplace with its hooks to hold pots suspended over the coals. The built-in double bed on one side of the fireplace, and Mrs. Thompson's homemade loom on the other side. The wooden ladder leading up to the loft's trapdoor.

Every now and then she looked across at Patrick and Colin, seated on either side of red-haired Duncan MacPherson. Sir Patrick Stanford, fourth baronet. But no one here knew he was that. He and Colin and Elizabeth had agreed that in the raw frontier toward which they were heading, any mention of former titles would handicap them. To the women, he, like Colin, was plain Mr. Stanford. To their middle-aged host, Joe Thompson, he was already Patrick.

Colin slept that night in the loft. Elizabeth and Patrick occupied the homemade bed in the lean-to. ("It used to be our son's bed," Mrs. Thompson said sadly. "But last summer he married a girl in a settlement twenty miles to the north, and went there to live.") As they lay there in the darkness, Patrick said, "We can't start work on the house tomorrow."

"I should think not. After that long journey, you and Colin must be very tired indeed."

"It is not that. Tomorrow is Sunday. Joe Thompson told me that even though there is no church here yet, New Canterbury observes the Sabbath strictly. The men stay home from the fields, and in the evening everyone goes to the Wentworths' for some kind of meeting."

"They call it a Bible-reading. Sally Jessup mentioned it, I remember now. And, Patrick! No matter how you feel about religion, I think we also had best go to the Went-

worths'. Our neighbors are far too few for us to antago-
nize any of them."

"Don't you think I realize that? I'll sit there and listen
to whatever sort of mumbo-jumbo they fancy. But on
Monday," he said, his voice quickening, "we'll start building our house. It will be like this one, only a shelter until
our land is cleared and making money. But someday we
will have a fine house on our own acres."

"With twin staircases?"

Instantly she regretted her words. She did not want to
remind him of his lost property in Ireland. She wanted
even less to remind him of the cause that had ended in
disaster and that, she feared, still often occupied his
thoughts.

But when he spoke, his voice was calm enough. "Why
not twin staircases? I hear that many houses in this country are almost as fine as any in Ireland or England. Why
shouldn't ours be?"

40

With Patrick and Colin working from dawn to dusk,
and the other men helping after they returned from their
fields, the Stanford house took shape with what seemed to
Elizabeth unbelievable rapidity. Within a week the well
had been sunk, the cellar dug, the floor beams laid.
Within a month there it stood, a log house almost a duplicate of the others in the clearing, with a lean-to shed
housing the well pump, and a lean-to stable for the horses
and wagon.

Colin did not move into the house with them. Instead, he chose to stay with the Thompsons, waiting until the fall to build a small shelter for himself. Often Elizabeth found herself wondering about her brother-in-law. Was he lonely, living as a boarder beneath another man's roof? It was impossible for her to tell. He seemed much the same quiet, hardworking, practical-minded man that he had appeared to be on the island of St.-Denis. But, just as she had on that tropical island, Elizabeth felt that there was an abiding sadness in him that he allowed no one to see.

With the house completed, Patrick and Colin started clearing their lands, the northern boundary of which lay less than a mile from the settlement. Working twelve and sometimes fourteen hours during the long summer days, they felled pines and oaks and maples and beeches, and used the horses to pull the stumps from the rich dark earth. It was too late in the season now to plant anything except field corn to serve as fodder for the horses. But next year, Patrick said confidently, they would be able to grow enough food for their own needs. And within a few years their land would include many acres of pasturage upon which to graze cattle. Surely the fast-growing settlements between New Canterbury and Philadelphia would provide a ready market for milk cows and beef cattle.

While Patrick worked on the land, the women of the tiny community taught Elizabeth the skills of a frontier housewife. She learned to weave on the heavy loom that Patrick, aided by Joe Thompson, had built for her. Using molds lent to her by Mrs. MacPherson and Mrs. Wentworth, she learned how to make tallow candles. Gathering with the other women at the Thompsons' house, she helped salt down partridges and wild turkey and venison the men had shot, and trout and bass they had taken from the river. In return for her labor, she received a barrel of salted fish and a haunch of venison to store in her own cellar.

Late in October, work on Colin's house began. Situated on the opposite side of the clearing near the young Jessups', it was to be a small house, little more than a hut—a house suitable for a man who did not intend to marry. With the deerskin flap unhooked from the window on this mild afternoon, Elizabeth watched Patrick and his brother stake out an area not more than twenty feet square. To her, aware of the new life within her swollen body, it seemed sad that Colin apparently intended to live out his days as a bachelor. True, there were no unmarried young women in this little settlement, but that situation could change as new families arrived. And there were marriageable girls only a few days' journey away, in the second of the settlements where they had stopped on their way to New Canterbury. But in all these weeks, Colin had made no move to return there.

On a gray afternoon in early December, her daughter was born, after a brief and far from difficult labor. She awoke two hours later to candlelight. Mrs. Thompson sat beside the fireplace, stirring stewed chicken in a pot that hung over the coals. Near the bed, Patrick was looking down into the cradle he himself had built. Elizabeth must have made some sound, because his dark face turned toward her. Then he came and stood beside the bed.

He said, holding her upstretched hand in both of his, "How are you, Elizabeth?"

"A little tired." She hesitated. "Are you disappointed?" It was a question she hated to ask, because she knew it would conjure up for him, as it did for her, that bitter day at Stanford Hall when she had lost their son.

He said frankly, "When I first heard the child was a girl I was not certain as to how I felt." He had spent the hours of waiting at the MacPhersons'. "But now that I have seen her, I wouldn't want her to be anyone else."

Elizabeth felt relief, and a happiness so deep she could not express it. And so she said, "What hair she has is yellow. But her eyes are a deep brown, like yours. Did you notice?"

"I did."

"What shall we name her?"

"I have been thinking about that. Unless your heart is set upon some other name, I would like her to be called Caroline, after my mother."

She said the name over to herself. Caroline Stanford. "I like that. She will be Caroline."

41

Winter was mild that year, so mild that the men of the settlement often were able to fish from the riverbank, rather than, as in seasons past, through holes carved in the ice. With no heavy snow to impede them, Patrick and Colin continued to clear land. And like the other men, they took advantage of the mild weather to hunt, so that they could supplement with fresh meat the provisions salted down months earlier.

Busy with household tasks, and with caring for an infant daughter who seemed to grow rosier and more enchanting almost by the hour, Elizabeth did not mind the short winter days. To conserve firewood, she and Patrick went to bed soon after supper each night. Sometimes, tired out, they fell asleep almost immediately. Other times, while the banked fire still sent a faint glow over the big room, they made love. One night, as she looked up through half-lidded eyes and saw the brooding look that desire always brought to his face, she suddenly remembered words from the marriage service. "With my body I thee worship."

Was it only with his body, and only at times like this, that he could be said to love her? Right at this moment, were his feelings any different from those he used to experience when he held Moira Ashley in his arms? Perhaps actually that beautiful and high-spirited Irishwoman had aroused more protectiveness and tenderness in him than she herself did. Elizabeth had a painful memory of a candlelit room in that Dublin inn, and Moira saying, with the complacent laugh of a truly cherished woman, that Patrick would scold her for not following his financial advice. . . .

Elizabeth felt Patrick's lips warm on her mouth, and his hand cupping her breast, arousing the first tremors of desire deep within her. Soon all thought of Moira Ashley was swept from her mind.

An early spring brought a quickened tempo to the whole community. On the first warm day in March, a big iron caldron was set over a fire in the center of the clearing, and Elizabeth and the other women took turns stirring the bubbling mixture of tallow and lye that eventually would solidify into soap. When the ground grew sufficiently soft, Patrick used the hand plow he had brought from Philadelphia to prepare ground behind the house for a kitchen garden. Using seeds they had bought in Philadelphia, as well as ones donated by their neighbors, she planted peas and spinach and green onions. Several times during the late spring and early summer, leaving Caroline with Mrs. Thompson, she took the trail through the woods to where Patrick and Colin planted potatoes, sweet corn, and squash, and, on newly cleared ground beyond, timothy and red clover, which perhaps next year would provide pasturage for cattle.

No new settlers arrived. But the long summer days did

bring visitors, families on their way to take up land farther west, and French trappers, some bound for Philadelphia, others for the rivers and dense forests of Ohio and
beyond. The ones traveling toward the Ohio and Mississippi rivers carried money, with which they bought cornmeal and dried meat to sell in the little French settlements
along the river route to New Orleans. Late in August,
Patrick hauled up from the cellar most of the venison and
dried fish stored there and sold it to two black-bearded
voyageurs. When Elizabeth protested that they themselves
might need that food, he said confidently, "We won't. As
soon as the harvest is in, Colin and I will hunt, just as we
did last fall and winter. What we do need is money, if
we're to start buying cattle next spring."

By September Caroline was able to stand alone in her
crib, gazing with eager brown eyes at the big world beyond its bars, and gurgling comments that, Elizabeth was
convinced, would make perfect sense to her and Patrick if
they had the wit to understand them. Looking at the
brown-eyed little face in its halo of blond curls, Elizabeth
found it amazing to recall that before Caroline's birth she
had hoped for a son. Oh, she and Patrick would have
sons. Any frontier family needed several sons. But she
hoped that for a while Caroline would remain their only
child. She wanted to give her undivided attention to this
enchanting creature, wanted to enjoy to the fullest the
sight of one-year-old Caroline taking her first steps, and
two-year-old Caroline running about the clearing.

One afternoon in late September as she knelt in the
kitchen garden weeding between the rows of bush beans,
she suddenly thought: Why I'm happy! Not just reasonably content. Happy.

She knew that many would say she had little reason to
be. She and Patrick were poor now. He worked as hard as
any half-starved peasant in Ireland, or slave on St.-Denis.
The harsh lye soap she used for household tasks had

reddened her own hands, and the dark blue gown she wore was of homespun, inexpertly woven by herself. What was more, she still did not know whether or not her husband felt anything more for her than a sense of legal responsibility, plus the physical desire he might feel for any attractive woman. And yet she was happy.

Perhaps the reason was that she felt she had finally escaped the past. She had lost all fear that Moira Ashley might follow them to this wilderness. And although she sometimes woke with vague memories of a dream in which two dark figures struggled on a wharf jutting out into a black tropic sea, she had long since ceased to speculate in waking hours about the mystery of Christopher's death. No, the past was past. For her, America indeed had proved to be a new world. Smiling, she rose, shook the damp earth from her skirts, and went into the house to start supper.

Because her sense of having escaped into a new life was so strong, she felt doubly shattered when, three weeks later, the past came crashing in upon her.

On that Sabbath afternoon, a hush lay over the settlement. The children who on weekdays raced noisily from doorstep to doorstep were in their separate houses. But even so, Elizabeth was aware, as she tended a pot of venison stew, that the clearing was not empty. Half an hour ago a cart bearing two westbound trappers had stopped out there, and the men of the community had gathered around it. Soon Patrick would come in to tell her whatever news the Frenchmen had brought—news of progress on the peace treaty that the Americans were still negotiating with the English, or perhaps word of new settlers in the communities to the east.

She heard the door open. Turning from the fireplace, she saw him standing there, a kind of grim exultation in his face. Even before she knew the cause of that look, she felt a chilly premonition.

"What is it, Patrick?"

For answer he reached into the pocket of his buckskin shirt, walked past the crib where Caroline lay sleeping, and held out a folded sheet of paper. Fingers unsteady, she unfolded it.

It was crudely printed broadside of the sort she had seen handed out on the London streets to advertise some public event, such as a hanging. It read:

Irish-born Americans! America is free, but the land of your birth still groans under the English yoke. Help free Ireland also! Meet with the American Sons of Ireland in Hagerstown, Maryland, October 27.

Her voice sounded thin. "Where did this. . . ?"

"Men were handing them out on the streets in Philadelphia. Those trappers agreed to distribute them in the settlements they passed through."

He moved to the foot of the bed and opened the wooden chest that stood there. In it they kept the clothes they never wore in New Canterbury, his cambric shirts and broadcloth coats and breeches, and the few gowns she had managed to pack before their hasty flight from St.-Denis. It also held a metal box containing money.

"Patrick! What are you doing?"

"I'm going to Hagerstown, of course. I'll leave before daybreak tomorrow."

"Patrick!"

"I'll go on foot. Colin will need the horses, if he's to go on clearing land. Undoubtedly I will get a ride in a cart or wagon now and then. Anyway, I should be there by the twenty-seventh."

She cried violently, "But why? You are an American now. Why should you concern yourself. . . "

He straightened up and faced her, the metal box in his hands. "Yes, I am an American. And now that I have seen what free men can do, I am more determined than ever that Ireland shall be free." His voice grew harsh.

"Did you think that a hundred acres of American soil would make me forget all I planned for, worked for, for a dozen years? Did you think me that shallow?"

"I hoped you were that sensible," she said bitterly. "What do you plan to do, abandon Caroline and me so that you can go back and fight for your precious cause?"

"Don't be absurd." He placed the box on the bed. "I will be back in three weeks, a month at most. You will be safe enough. And Colin is a good shot. He will keep you supplied with game in case the food in the cellar runs low."

"But if you don't plan to go back to Ireland, then why go to this meeting?"

"Because I can give highly valuable information to those who will be going. Do you remember how back in St.-Denis, Fontaine told us that the English had discovered only a few of those caches of arms? Perhaps at least some of them are still undiscovered. Before we left Ireland, I burned all my papers, but I still carry the list of those locations in my head."

She cried, out of some black foreknowledge of disaster, "Your duty is here! I forbid you to go!"

His eyes narrowed. "Forbid? I have told you before, Elizabeth, that you cannot forbid me to do anything. Nor do I need you to tell me where my duty lies."

She heard a whimper, then a frightened cry. Their raised voices had awakened Caroline. Elizabeth turned, reached into the crib, and lifted the baby out. With the warm little body against her shoulder, she turned back to Patrick. He sat on the bed, opening the metal box. He took out a leather bag and upended it on the counterpane. Money spilled out, large silver dollars and small five-dollar gold pieces—what money remained to him after the long journey from the West Indies to New Canterbury, plus the sum the French trappers had paid him for supplies to take downriver. Bitter-eyed, she watched him stack the coins into piles.

"Are you taking that money with you?" Lest she set Caroline to crying again, she tried to keep her voice quiet and matter-of-fact.

"Yes."

"Why?"

For the first time since coming into the house, he seemed hesitant. "I may find I can make an advantageous bargain for cattle. Even though I won't be able to take delivery until next spring, I can seal the bargain now if I have money with me."

Did he believe, at least at the moment, that he might buy cattle? Perhaps. But she was sure that the money would be used either for his passage to Ireland or for that of some other diehard fanatic. One way or another, that money, like her dowry, would be swallowed up by this cause of his, the cause that seemed so much more precious to him than any one human being, even his wife or his child.

That night in bed he drew her into his arms and tried to arouse her with kisses and caresses. She lay silent and unresponsive. He did not react with the resentment she had expected. Instead he said quietly, "Very well, Elizabeth. Just let me hold you." She wished that she had the moral strength to free herself from his arms and move to the far side of the bed. But beneath her rage, her bitterness, there was an anguished premonition that this might be the last night he would spend with his long, lean body stretched out beside hers. And so she lay with her head on his shoulder, eyes staring blankly into the dark, until long after she knew by the sound of his breathing that he slept.

42

At the last moment, just before he stepped out into the predawn darkness the next day, she was able to overcome her bitterness sufficiently to go into his arms and return his kiss warmly and tenderly. Then he held her close, his cheek against her hair. "I'll return very soon, Elizabeth. I promise you."

She moved back in the circle of his arms and looked up into his face, grave in the candlelight. Did he mean that promise? Probably, at least at this moment. But she still had that terrible sense that she might never again look up into that thin dark face.

"And it is not as if I am really leaving you alone," he went on. "Colin will be here to watch out for you and Caroline."

He kissed her again and then gently put her away from him. "I must get started. Good-bye, Elizabeth."

She managed to smile. "Good-bye Patrick."

In the days that followed, she became glad that she had been able to send him off, not with bitter reproaches, but a kiss and a smile. Because almost as soon as he had stepped through the doorway into the darkness, all her anger was lost in her longing for him. Let him give away their money to his fellow diehards, if he felt he must. Let him do anything, as long as he came back.

The days, with plenty of work to do in the house, and outside autumn sunlight warm upon pines and golden maples and scarlet oaks, were not too unpleasant. It was the nights that were hard to get through. When with Caroline on her lap she sat at the table, eating her own supper and spooning food into the little girl's pink mouth, her awareness of that vacant chair opposite was like a weight upon her.

True, all her neighbors had invited her to have supper with them "whenever you like." But she could not impose upon them every night. Better to get used to loneliness. Many nights, though, she thought of Colin, cooking and eating his own solitary meal in his little house. It seemed sad that they could not take supper together, as they had on so many otherwise lonely nights at Stanford Hall. But no. It would not do to arouse even a shadow of suspicion in the minds of their kind but sternly moralistic neighbors.

Apparently Colin also realized that. The first evening after Patrick's departure, Elizabeth heard her brother-in-law stabling the horses in the lean-to behind the house. Then he came around to the front door and knocked.

When she had opened the door, he asked, "Is there anything I can do for you?"

"No, Colin." She looked into the face that was so like that other, beloved face, and yet so unlike it—the planes of jaw and cheekbones less pronounced, and the dark eyes softer, with that hint of sadness in their depths. "But thank you very much."

"Whenever you do need anything, tell me. Good night, Elizabeth." Quickly he turned and limped toward his own little house.

Each evening from then on, once he had stabled the horses, he came to the front door to learn how she and the baby were faring. But he never stepped across the threshold, let alone hinted for a supper invitation.

Patrick had been gone almost three weeks, when, one afternoon, Caroline caught hold of a chair's edge to pull herself up from the floor, stood there for a moment, and then took three tottering steps to catch hold of Elizabeth's outstretched hands. As she lifted her triumphantly gurgling offspring into her arms, Elizabeth wished that Patrick had been there to see his daughter's first steps. But no matter. He would be back in a week at most. And how surprised he would be to find the infant-in-arms he had left toddling about with that look of proud glee on her little face.

But Patrick did not return the next week, or the next. Then, on a morning in late November, a French trapper knocked at her door. He told her he had a message from her husband. It had been given to him by another trapper, who in return had received it from still another. Heart pounding, she unfolded the creased, soiled piece of paper the Frenchman handed to her.

Not all the men he wished to meet had yet arrived, Patrick had written in his tall, distinctive hand, and so he might not start his return journey for another week. "But even so, I will surely be there by the twentieth of November."

The twentieth had been two days before.

Bitterness in her heart, she thanked the trapper and closed the door. She wished that she could rip Patrick's note to pieces and toss it onto the fire. Instead, after a moment, she thrust the folded piece of paper down the bosom of her dress.

Less than a week later, the unseasonably warm weather broke. On a day that began as brightly as any that preceded it, clouds blotted out the sun around noontime, and a chill wind began to strip the trees of the last of their colorful autumn foliage. By two o'clock, heavy rain mixed with hail began to fall. Unhooking the deerskin covering at a window to look out at the clearing, muddy now and strewn with hailstones, Elizabeth felt a new fear clutch at her heart. Like the other men, Colin had wanted to clear as much more land as possible before the onset of bad weather. Consequently, he had not shot any game.

And thanks to the sales of salted meat and fish that Patrick had made to those trappers, the supplies in the cellar were running low.

Colin must have realized that she would be anxious. At dusk, with the cold rain still falling, he knocked at her door. Standing there in the inadequate shelter of the little roof above the step, he smiled at her and asked, "How is your food holding out?"

"I have plenty cornmeal and potatoes and dry onions. But there is only a third of a barrel of dried fish left, and a little venison."

"Don't worry. I'll spend one more day clearing. Then I'll go after partridge for you. Perhaps I'll even get a deer."

Again he smiled at her. He looked so much like Patrick at that moment—a gentler, kinder Patrick—that it was almost all she could do to keep from saying: Come in, Colin. Don't leave me.

"Well, good night, Elizabeth." He started to turn away.

"Colin!"

He turned back to her. She wanted to say: Do you think Patrick has sailed for Ireland? In spite of that price on his head, in spite of his promise to me? But she could not, even to Colin, voice the growing fear to which she awoke each morning.

And so instead she asked, "Why do you think it is that Patrick has not come home?"

His smile died. Anger leaped into his dark eyes. After a disconcerted moment she realized that the anger was not for her, but for his brother. Then he said, once more smiling, "Perhaps the meeting lasted overlong. Anyway, I would not worry about something bad happening to him. My brother is like a cat. He always lands on his feet. Good night," he added, and again turned away.

The rain stopped a few hours later, but the temperature plunged so steeply that, for the sake of warmth, Elizabeth took Caroline into the big bed that night. In the morning, the skies were leaden gray, and in low spots the clearing was covered with crusts of ice, milky white against the dark frozen ground.

Late that afternoon, while she was peeling potatoes for a fish stew, she heard voices in the clearing, men's voices, and the high, excited voices of children. Heart swelling with hope, she went to the door and looked out.

But Patrick had not arrived. Instead, young Jessup and the red-haired Duncan MacPherson, followed by Thompson and Wentworth and by the children who had been playing in the subfreezing temperature, carried a litter of lashed pine boughs toward the Thompson house. Colin lay on the litter, and his blood was dripping from it onto the dark earth and the patches of gray ice.

Cold with alarm, she lifted Caroline into her homemade high chair, lest in her absence the child venture too close to the fire. Then she snatched her red knitted shawl from its hook beside the door, flung it over her head, and as rapidly as she could over that treacherous ground, crossed to the Thompson house.

Mrs. Thompson opened the door for her. "He's hurt his foot badly. They've put him in the lean-to."

"How. . . ?"

"He was chopping down a tree. He slipped on the ice, and the ax blade came down on his left foot."

His left foot, the sound one. Colin was crippled indeed now.

"Just how bad is it?"

"I'm not sure. My husband is getting his shoe off now. You'd better sit down. You're white as a ghost."

Elizabeth sat there, aware that Mrs. Thompson had gone into the lean-to, and that her husband had come into the big room to take a sheet from the linen press against one wall. At last Mrs. Thompson stood before her. "I've bandaged his foot. You can see him now."

"Is it. . . ?"

"It's quite bad. It may be many weeks before he walks again."

Elizabeth rose, moved into the lean-to. Colin, covered with blankets, eyes closed in a face grayed with pallor, lay on the bed where she and Patrick had slept during their first weeks in New Canterbury.

His eyes opened. "I'm sorry, Elizabeth."

She dropped to her knees beside him. "Sorry! What are you talking about?"

"You and the little one need me. And now I—"

"Colin, don't think about it. Just get well as fast as you can."

She went back into the main room. "Mrs. Thompson, when can he be moved to my house? It isn't fair that you should have the care of him."

"No, child." Her voice held a trace of sternness. "It would not be fitting, you a young woman, and your man not there. Besides, I have more experience in these matters. You had best get back to Caroline now."

Elizabeth went out in the gathering dark. A more selfish fear than her concern for Colin clutched at her now. As soon as she reached her house, she lifted the trapdoor and went down into the cellar. With the lamp held high in her hand, she inspected her dwindling supplies of meat, fish, and winter vegetables.

Well, despite Colin's accident, everything would be all right if Patrick returned within a few days. Even if he did not, her neighbors could supply her with food—that is, if they could spare it from their own families' needs. But all of them, made optimistic by last winter's good hunting, had sold food to those Mississippi-bound trappers, although not as recklessly as Patrick had. And if heavy snow fell, or if the deer and rabbits and game birds had become too few after last year's heavy hunting . . .

Don't think about it, she commanded herself, and climbed the ladder.

When she awoke in the morning, the air was ice-cold. Caroline lay huddled against her back. By a certain glimmer of the light that filtered through the semitransparent window coverings, Elizabeth knew that snow had fallen. Careful not to disturb the sleeping child, she got out of bed and dressed, shivering with cold, not taking off her nightshift until she had drawn on her stockings and petticoat beneath it. When she had put on her gown, she opened the door a crack and looked out. Yes, at least two inches of snow lay in the clearing, and an iron-gray sky promised that more would fall.

She had a fire going when someone knocked. It was her nearest neighbor, Duncan MacPherson, a coonskin cap covering his red hair. "I've been over to the Thompsons'. Colin seems to be doing all right. He's pretty weak from loss of blood, but there's no fever, and that means no blood poisoning."

Elizabeth thanked him. He said, "We're all taking to the woods today. We ought to be able to bring back some game, if the snow holds off."

Well before noon, Elizabeth opened the door a crack and saw the first big white flakes spiraling down. When she again looked out, about an hour later, snow was falling so thickly that she could scarcely make out the MacPherson house. By that time she was hearing, now and then, gunfire in the woods. She imagined the men on snowshoes out there, trying to aim at dim animal shapes through the thick smother, and then, with half-frozen fingers, ramming powder and shot into their flintlock barrels for another attempt.

She walked back to the fire, a thriftily small one. The stack of firewood in the lean-to that sheltered the horses and wagon was still high, but she had decided it was best not to burn it recklessly. Caroline sat on a pallet close to the hearth, shaking the rattle, a gourd filled with dry peas, which occasionally interested her, even though she was a year old now. Standing beside the child, Elizabeth stared into the fire and thought of a grim story she had heard at the first of the settlements at which she and the Stanford men had stopped on their way here. A dozen years earlier, a woman told her, other families had occupied those log houses. But they had suffered a bad harvest, followed by a winter of snows so high that the houses were cut off from one another. In the spring, French trappers had found them all dead of starvation and cold, each family in its separate house.

She shivered, wrapped her arms around her, and looked down at her child. The small face, rosier than ever in the firelight, wore an absurd look of concentration as she wielded the rattle. If, because of Patrick's prolonged absence, something happened to Caroline . . .

Stop that, she commanded herself.

Again she went to the door. The snow had slackened, at least enough that she could see the MacPhersons' house and the dark, wind-flattened streamer of smoke from its chimney. Best to start clearing the short path between the house and the privy before it became impassable. She went out to the combination stable and woodshed and grasped the long-handled wooden shovel.

Shortly before dark, someone knocked. It was Duncan MacPherson again, his fur cap white with the still-falling snow. From thongs he held dangled two rabbits and two squirrels.

"We've divided up what we shot today." Despite his smile, she could see the anxiety in his face. "We didn't have very good luck. Not much game about, and with the snow falling . . . Anyway, here is your share."

She looked at the small creatures. She thought of the MacPhersons, with two children to feed, and the Wentworths, with four. She thought of the young Jessups, already with one child, and Sally Jessup pregnant again. She thought of the Thompsons and of Colin. A man weakened by loss of blood would need good nourishment to get through the winter.

"Just give me the rabbits. I don't need much food, and Caroline even less. Besides, our supplies are holding up."

"You are sure?" She could see the relief in his face.

"I'm sure." She took the thong upon which the rabbits were strung, thanked him, and closed the door quickly, lest more heat escape.

Almost three more inches of snow fell during the night, although by the time she awoke it had slackened to an occasional flurry. Dressed in the greatcoat Patrick had not taken with him, head wrapped in her shawl, she took the shovel and again cleared a path to the privy. Despite the icy temperature, by the time she came back into the house, she was sweating.

Out in the clearing, other shovels scraped. She opened the door a crack. Except for Colin, all the men were out there, shoveling paths between the houses.

About an hour later she became aware that the shoveling sounds had ceased. When she went to the door, she saw why. Snow was again falling, faster than anyone could hope to shovel away. To the distance of about a foot, she could see the individual flakes falling straight downward. Beyond that, the snow was a gray-white wall.

If snow kept piling up, Patrick would not be able to return, even if he wanted to.

With a sense of helpless terror, she closed the door.

43

A mourning dove had landed on the windowsill. Huddled in Patrick's greatcoat beside the unlighted fireplace, Elizabeth could see the bird's shadow, cast by the bright, subzero sunlight on the deerskin window covering. She looked at it listlessly.

As she sat there, she had been trying to figure out what the date was. Around the end of February, she had decided. That meant that four months had passed since Patrick had left her, and about two months since Duncan MacPherson had handed her the two rabbits. A few times after that she had seen the men trying to clear paths between the houses, only to retreat indoors as more snow fell. Now about four feet of it blocked her door and those of all the other houses. For a while Mr. and Mrs. MacPherson had called out a window once every day, asking her how she was, and relaying the news that Colin was "getting better." But for more than two weeks she had not had even that small contact with her neighbors. She knew, though, that they were still alive. Opening the door a crack each morning, she had seen smoke rising from the chimneys of the other houses. Perhaps her neighbors, like her, had been reduced to using firewood only for cooking. If so, they would not want to open their windows to the icy air just for conversation's sake.

She found herself thinking of the Jessups. Sally must have given birth by now. Had she remained sufficiently well nourished so that there was enough milk for her baby?

The thought reminded her of her own child. She turned and looked at Caroline, asleep beneath the heavy layer of blankets on the bed. So that she would be warmer, Elizabeth kept the child in bed as much as possible. At first Caroline had protested. But for the past week she had been docile, frighteningly docile, as if she had no energy to expend in rebellion, or even in staying awake for more than a few hours at a time.

And no wonder, Elizabeth thought. For nearly three weeks now they had subsisted on cornmeal plus a meatless soup made of onions and the potatoes she dug from where they were stored under a pile of earth in one corner of the cellar. How could a young, fast-growing child stay well on such a diet? With fear crowding her throat, she looked at the pale little face with its faint shadows under the closed eyes.

A cooing noise made her turn her head. The dove was still on the windowsill. Her heart leaped with sudden hope. Hunger and cold must have rendered her stupid, she realized now, because right there outside the window, if she were quick and clever enough, was a means of bringing a little color back into Caroline's face.

She got up and went into the lean-to, where the horses, breath steaming in the frigid air, stood in their stalls. With a familiar bitterness she reflected that it was lucky for those animals that the *voyageurs* hadn't offered Patrick money for field corn. Otherwise the horses might have starved by now. Then she reflected grimly that one of them might soon be dead anyway. Important as they were to a family trying to carve a living out of the wilderness, she would not hesitate, if driven to it, to feed horse-meat broth to her child.

She took a small handful of corn from the dwindling supply in the barrel. Back in the house, she dropped the corn on the table, and then with a string she found in a drawer of the homemade pine cupboard she fashioned a small noose with a slip knot. As she approached the window, the dove's shadow lifted with a whir of wings and disappeared. But the poor thing would be back, she was sure, as soon as it spied the corn.

She unhooked the deerskin. The air that swept in was only a bit colder than that already in the house. She scattered corn on the icy layer of snow, laid the snare. One hand holding the end of the string, she flattened herself against the wall at one side of the window and waited, heart pounding.

After several minutes the pretty creature landed on the far corner of the sill. For a few seconds, with the iridescent feathers on its neck changing from green to purple and then back again, it turned its head from side to side, looking at her from round brown eyes. Apparently it decided that she, standing motionless and with held breath, was no threat. Or perhaps hunger had made the bird reckless. Anyway, it began to peck at the corn, moving along the icy surface on coral feet.

Tensely, Elizabeth waited. The dove was approaching the snare. It skirted the far side of the string's loop, swallowed two more grains of corn. Then it turned back and began to search for any grains it had missed. . . .

Now! She jerked the string, closing the snare around one fragile leg, and drew the wildly fluttering bird into the room. Except for verminous insects, she had never killed a living thing. For a moment, as she looked down at the struggling creature, she thought that she could not go through with it. Then she seized the bird, first with her left hand and then her right, and wrung the slender neck.

As she dropped the bird to the floor, she realized that for an instant she had wished it was Patrick's neck she held between her hands.

When the broth was ready, she awoke Caroline, and

then carried a steaming bowl over to the bed. "Just see what Mama has for you!"

The child stared dull-eyed at the broth, the very smell of which made Elizabeth's mouth water. Caroline took a sip from the spoon her mother held for her and then turned her head away. "No!"

Fear squeezed Elizabeth's heart. Why should a half-starved child not want to eat? She spoke coaxingly, but still Caroline, shaking her head, kept her pale mouth closed. "Then go back to sleep, darling," Elizabeth said cheerfully. "I'm sure you'll want this later." Too frightened now to feel hungry herself, she poured the broth back into the kettle.

After darkness fell, Caroline did take a few teaspoons of broth. Less worried now, Elizabeth too consumed a little of the precious liquid. In the morning, she would add more water to the broth and the fragments of dove meat at the bottom of the pot. Combined with onions and potatoes, it would make a nourishing stew that might suffice them for at least two more days. She sat beside the small cooking fire until it died, and then went to bed.

Sometime in the night, a soft plopping sound awoke her. Rain? No, it was too intermittent for that. Then, becoming aware that the air in the room was much warmer, she realized the significance of the sound. Thaw! Icicles that hung from the eaves were dripping onto the snow.

Caroline, huddled against her mother's back, gave a dry little cough. So that was it, Elizabeth thought. She's coming down with a cold. Cautiously, so as not to waken the child, Elizabeth turned in the bed and lightly touched her daughter's face. No fever. Her cold must be a slight one. She would be all right, especially if the warmer weather held. Elizabeth went back to sleep.

In the morning she awoke to a dripping world. When she incautiously opened the front door, several inches of slush flooded in. She slammed the door shut, went to the window that faced the clearing, and unhooked the deer-skin. Bright sunlight, beating down on the whiteness, dazzled her eyes. The snow in the clearing was melting. It was no longer a solid sheet of white, but marked by darker little rivulets of water, all hurrying toward the snowy woods and the river beyond. Already she could see a dark stain about a quarter of a foot high, marking where the snow had melted, on the Jessups' door opposite, and on the door of Colin's little house.

The deerskin covering on one of the MacPhersons' windows gave way to Duncan MacPherson's red head. "You all right over there?"

"Yes, except that I think Caroline has a cold."

"So have both the twins. But we'll all be fine, now that it's getting toward spring."

Spring. Last night spring had seemed centuries away. "I lost track. What is the date?"

"March eighth. Hold on, Mrs. Stanford. If this weather keeps up, we'll start shoveling paths a couple of days from now."

His head withdrew. As Elizabeth refastened her own window covering, she heard Caroline cough twice. She pushed back the fear the sound brought her. Caroline would be all right. Even though Patrick had left them to withstand this terrible winter alone, they would survive, now that it was March, now that spring was almost here.

The warm weather held, weather that seemed almost tropical compared to what had gone before. By nightfall no icicles dangled from the eaves. The next day dawned even warmer. Elizabeth knew that soon her long isolation would be ended. But by then she could take little joy in the warm sunlight beating down, because Caroline was worse, much worse. The small face was no longer pale, but un-healthily flushed and hot to the touch. She did not turn aside from the spoonful of broth held to her lips, but merely stared at it, eyes dull, mouth closed.

That night, unable to sleep, Elizabeth sat at the bedside, listening with terror to Caroline's coughs, and to her breathing which had taken on a raspy sound. It was not until exhaustion overcame her that she undressed and got into bed beside the fevered child.

The welcome sound of scraping shovels awoke her in the dim morning light. She looked at Caroline. The small face was still flushed, and the rasp in her breathing seemed more pronounced. Elizabeth got out of bed, moved swiftly to the front window, unhooked the deerskin. Duncan MacPherson was out there, shoveling aside the few feet of slushy snow that remained between his house and her own. Beyond him she could see Joe Thompson, clearing a last stretch of path between his house and the MacPhersons'.

As soon as she was dressed, she snatched her shawl down from its hook, flung it over her head, and stepped out into the icy slush. "Caroline is sick," she said as she hurried past the Scot. "I've got to see Mrs. Thompson. . . ."

It was Colin who opened the Thompsons' door to her knock. He stood there smiling, his face pale after so many weeks indoors, his left hand resting on the crook of an ancient-looking blackthorn cane. "Elizabeth! I was going to come to your house the moment the path was clear."

She managed to return his smile. "It's good to see you standing. Is your foot. . . ?"

"It's almost entirely healed. In a couple of weeks I should be able to take to the fields again."

Mrs. Thompson came hurrying toward them, drying her hands on her apron. Her gaze searched Elizabeth's face. "Child! What is it?"

"It's Caroline." Terror tightened her throat. "She . . . she . . ."

"I'll see her," the older woman said, and reached for her shawl.

Moments later, seated beside the flushed child, Mrs. Thompson said, "It's a lung congestion."

"What will. . . ?" Elizabeth could not finish the sentence.

"I'll do my best for her. First we must get her back into the crib. We'll put a sheet over it to form a tent, and then have her breathe in steam from a croup kettle. And we will get some food down her, if we can. She must be terribly undernourished."

Undernourished, Elizabeth thought bitterly. Her child was not just undernourished, but three-quarters starved. And all because a fanatical man cared more for his fellow fanatics than for his wife, or even his own child.

44

A shrill chorus of tiny voices rose from a pond somewhere in the dark woods, a nighttime chorus that swelled and faded, swelled and faded, like the beating of a gigantic pulse. Elizabeth, seated at one side of Caroline's crib, was only vaguely aware of the spring peepers, those small heralds of a new season's burgeoning life. It was death that held all her attention, the death hovering in this silent room.

Mrs. Thompson, seated on the other side of the crib, had said more than an hour ago, "I think the crisis is near. If she lives through the night . . ."

Elizabeth did not remember whether she or the other woman had spoken since then. During this past week—a week of little sleep, of days and nights blurring together, of endless hours spent hanging over Caroline's crib—her memory had grown vague, so that she could not recall whether three or four days had passed since Caroline had not only taken a little beef broth but also, with a spark of recognition in her glazed brown eyes, had said, "Mommy?"

Now it seemed hard to believe that the suffering scrap of humanity there in the crib so recently had been strong enough to speak. Elizabeth's gaze kept moving from the small reddened face, with the whites of rolled-back eyes showing between barely opened lids, to the laboring little chest. For about forty-eight hours—or was it longer than that?—she'd had the feeling that it was only her own will that kept her child's tiny chest rising and falling.

Someone knocked. Elizabeth knew it must be one of the women settlers calling to ask about Caroline, and to hand in a bowl of soup or other food. Feeling stiff, almost old, she crossed the room and opened the door.

Patrick stood there, a gaunt-looking Patrick, his face covered with several days' growth of beard. She stared at him, not sure but what he was a phantom conjured up by her tormented mind.

After a moment he smiled and said, "Well, Elizabeth, aren't you going to let me in?"

At the sound of his voice, she knew that he was real. And she knew how much she hated him.

Oh, before this she had felt what she thought was hatred. The night he left her violated and bleeding in that lonely house north of London. The morning she had looked down at her brother's murdered body sprawled on the beach. But this was really hatred, this blackness boiling up inside her until she could taste it in her mouth.

She put her hand against the door frame, barring his way with her arm. She felt her lips stretch into the parody of a smile.

"Tell me, Patrick, did you let your friends know where to find all those arms?"

He said, his eyes puzzled, "It was too late. The English had found the last of them almost a year ago. In god's name, Elizabeth, why are you—?"

"Well, Patrick, don't feel too bad about being too late. At least you're not too late here. You're in time to watch your child die."

He seemed to turn to stone for a moment, face expressionless except for the stunned horror in his dark eyes. Then he lunged forward, breaking her grasp on the door frame, and moved past her into the room. She seized his arm with both her hands. "Yes, she's dying." Her voice was soft and thick now. "You killed her. You left us alone, without enough food, enough firewood . . ."

He broke free of her grasp and strode over to the crib. Still seated beside it, Mrs. Thompson neither moved nor spoke, but just kept her gaze on the tall man's face. After a moment, Elizabeth went over to stand beside her husband.

The only sound now was the child's labored breath, oddly mingled with the tiny frog's pulsating hymn to spring and new life. As the three adults stared down into the crib, the small chest became motionless for two seconds, three, four . . .

My baby's dead, Elizabeth thought, and felt a silent scream of agony well up inside her.

The small chest lifted, drawing air into itself. Patrick made a hoarse, strangled sound. Then he strode across the room and went out into the night.

Elizabeth stayed there, hands gripping the crib's railing, gaze fixed on Caroline's face. Then, unable to bear her torment standing still, she began to pace up and down. After a while Mrs. Thompson said quietly, "He probably went to his brother's."

Only half-comprehending, Elizabeth paused and looked

at the older woman. "He must have tried to get back, and found the road and all the trails blocked with snow," Mrs. Thompson went on in that quiet voice. "Anyway, no matter how thoughtless and selfish he was, he is your man. He will still be, no matter what happens to . . ."

She broke off, and then added, "Go to him. You are doing neither yourself nor the child any good, pacing up and down like that, and you are upsetting me. Now, go. Go on!"

Dully obedient, Elizabeth took down her shawl, flung it around her shoulders, and stepped out into the cool spring dark. There was no moon, but starlight shone on the leafless trees walling in the south side of the clearing. Except for a lamp's glow showing through one of Colin's deerskin-covered windows, every house was dark.

She started toward Colin's house and then stopped, arrested by a sound, harsh and painful, off among the trees to her left. With an odd, lurching sensation within her breast, she recognized it. It was one of the most terrible of all sounds, that of a strong man weeping.

Footsteps noiseless over the ground, she moved to the wood's edge. A few yards ahead, a patch of lingering snow glimmered. Beyond it, back turned to her, wide shoulders heaving, Patrick knelt on the damp ground. His sobs seemed wrenched from him, like something torn out by the roots.

She heard a whimpering sound, like an echo of his pain, and knew after a moment that it came from her own throat. She took a step forward. Then she halted, because he had begun to speak.

"Let the child live," he said. "I don't ask it for myself. How could I? You know what I have always been. But if You really exist, let our little girl live. I'm not even asking it mainly for the child's sake, God. I'm asking it for Elizabeth, my Elizabeth. Yes, I know I have no right to call her mine . . ."

His voice broke. For a moment there was no sound except those raw, tortured sobs. Then words again poured out of him. "And I know I have no right to feel this love for her, or expect her to feel anything but hatred for me. What sort of treatment has she known at my hands? At best, I've been blindly selfish, as when I scoffed at her fears and left her alone here. And at worst, such as the night when I broke into her bedroom in that house north of London. . . . Oh, God! If I could only roll back the years, and meet her for the first time, and woo her gently, lovingly. But I cannot. All I can do is to plead with You to spare her this suffering now. Please, please let the child live." Again his words gave way to hoarse sobbing.

Standing at the wood's edge, Elizabeth felt the ache of tears in her throat. Tenderness for him seemed to swell her heart, so that it was hard to breathe. Afraid that in another moment he would become aware of her presence, she turned and moved back across the starlit clearing to her house. She mounted the front steps and stood there weeping quietly, forehead leaning on the arms she had crossed against one side of the door frame.

After a while she wiped her face with one corner of her shawl and went into the house. Mrs. Thompson rose from beside the crib. "I was about to go to the door to look for you. I think she has passed the crisis."

Elizabeth crossed the room swiftly, and half afraid to believe the evidence of her eyes, looked down at Caroline. The child's face was less flushed now, and her breaths, more normally spaced, had lost some of that terrible rasp. Relief washed over Elizabeth, relief so profound that it left her faint. She gripped the crib's rail to keep from falling.

Mrs. Thompson said, "I'll sit up with her. You'd best go to bed, just as soon as you have told your husband. Or shall I tell him? Where is he? At his brother's?"

No one must disturb Patrick, not when he might still be

talking to that God he did not believe in. "Yes, he is with Colin. But you needn't call him. He will be here soon."

Relief and fatigue and joy combined to make her feel half-drunk. She moved to the bed, sat down, and took off her shoes. "I won't undress." She stretched out on the bed. "I will just wait here until Patrick comes in," she said—and knew nothing more until morning light and the sound of Mrs. Thompson's quiet movements awoke her.

45

Swiftly Elizabeth sat up. "Is Caroline. . . ?"

Mrs. Thompson, bending before the fireplace, turned to Elizabeth with a smile. "She's much better. I fed her broth about an hour ago. Now I'm heating water for tea."

Elizabeth swung out of bed and crossed to the crib. With a flood of thanksgiving she saw that the child's breathing seemed almost normal. True, the sleeping face, in its frame of matted curls, looked shockingly bony and white, and yet it seemed to Elizabeth that a shadow—an almost visible one that had lain over her little girl's face for a week—was gone now.

Patrick! She must tell Patrick! "Did my husband come back here last night?"

"No, he did not." If Mrs. Thompson felt curiosity about Patrick's failure to return, she was careful to keep it out of her voice. "He must have stayed with his brother."

Swiftly Elizabeth moved back to the bed, sat down, and slipped on her shoes. Then remorseful realization struck her. "You shouldn't have let me sleep! Why, you've been here all night."

"I slept. I pulled my chair up to the table and rested my head on my arms and slept real well. Now, go make yourself pretty for your husband."

Elizabeth hurried through the door into the pump house, where on one rough wall a small mirror hung above a shelf holding a white china basin, a matching pitcher, and comb and brush. A few minutes later she crossed through early-morning sunlight to Colin's little house. Smoke rose from its chimney. He must be preparing breakfast. She wondered if Patrick sat at the rough table. Or was he still asleep? He had looked so tired the night before, so thin and sunken-eyed.

She knocked. Almost immediately she heard limping footsteps. When Colin opened the door, she looked eagerly past him. No one sitting at the table or lying on the built-in bed against the far wall. She asked, "Where's Patrick?" Fleetingly, in one part of her mind not wholly taken up with her husband, she realized that Colin no longer leaned upon a cane.

He said, frowning, "Patrick! What do you mean?"

"Didn't he sleep in your house last night?"

"You mean he was here?"

"Of course he was here!" she cried. "I talked to him."

After a long moment he said, "Then he must have gone away afterward, because I did not see him at all."

She stood rigid. Last night she had told him that he had killed his own child. She had hurled her hatred at him. And so, after he had made that tormented prayer, he had simply walked away into the night.

The ground seemed to tilt beneath her feet.

Swiftly Colin was beside her, his arm around her waist. "Elizabeth! Are you all right?" When she did not answer, he said, "I had best get you back to your house."

Faint and nauseated, she allowed him to draw her

across the clearing. As they neared the door, he said, "You lie down. I will go the the other houses to see if Patrick is there."

She nodded an agreement. But she knew he would not find his brother at any of the other houses. Patrick had gone, whether back toward Philadelphia, or westward toward Ohio, or along one of the trapper trails that led north and south, she had no way of knowing. All she could hope for was that somehow he would learn that their child still lived, and come back to her.

The days lengthened. Amid the rapidly disappearing patches of snow in the woods, blue-flowered hepatica appeared, followed by Dutchman's breeches, with rows of pink blossoms, shaped like miniature pantaloons, hanging from their stalks. The first returning swallows, blue-backed and tawny-breasted, soared and dived through the air above the clearing, and finally selected the leaves of the Jessups' lean-to as a nesting site. After supper, adults sat before their houses in what remained of the twilight and watched the older children play run-sheep-run.

To Elizabeth the beauty of that spring was like a knife to the heart. So, sometimes, was the sight of Caroline, fully restored to health now, toddling after the older children. Patrick should be there to see his daughter, sturdy legs pumping, golden hair bright, as she ran across the clearing. And Patrick should be there with *her*. It was torment to lie alone in the warm spring dark, aching to be held in his arms.

Four evenings after Patrick's disappearance, Colin had urged her to leave New Canterbury. As she sat on the front step after supper, door open behind her so that she could hear the slightest whimper from Caroline's crib, Colin limped across the clearing. He looked down at her through the fading light. "Do you have any plans, Elizabeth?"

She felt bewilderment. "What sort of plan would I have, except to wait until Patrick comes home?"

The light was too faint for her to see his face clearly. Thus she sensed, rather than saw, the angry scorn in his dark eyes. "How can you be sure he'll come back? After all, a man who deserts his wife, deserts his child, even though he knows she may be dying—"

"You don't understand! I said terrible things to him! He must have felt that . . . that the best thing he could do for me was to go away."

"And leave you without money, without a husband to protect you and provide for you? Elizabeth, this is no place for you now. Let me take you and Caroline to Philadelphia."

She shook her head. "No, Colin. I want to be here when Patrick comes back. And he will come back."

"Very well," he said finally. Then, after a long moment: "I'll start spring planting by the end of the week."

Several more times as the spring advanced, as the graceful catbirds and flame-bright tanagers arrived, and swamp marigolds in the woods gave way to blue flags, Colin urged that she and Caroline retreat to the safety and comfort of Philadelphia. Did she want to risk another such winter for the child and herself in this frontier settlement?

Each time, Elizabeth thrust his arguments aside. She knew that any day now, any hour, she might look out and see Patrick's tall, lean figure moving toward the house.

But days stretched into weeks, and still she was alone. And then, one late May night as she sat on the front step in the gathering dark after supper, achingly aware of the beauty of dogwood blossoms like falling snow among the pines at the clearing's edge, she heard Colin lead the horses into the lean-to stable. Strange that he was coming back from the fields so late. The other men had returned almost an hour before.

A few minutes later, he walked around the corner of the house. Even before he spoke, something in his manner caused her nerves to tighten. He said, "I think we had better go into the house."

Too frightened now even to speak, she got up and moved ahead of him into the dark room. When her fumbling fingers found the box of flints on the fireplace mantel, he took it from her. A moment later, lamplight filled the room.

She said, from a dry throat, "What is it?"

His gaze went from her face to the crib in which her sleeping daughter lay, and then back to her face. He said, in a voice that sounded heavy with reluctance, "A French trapper came through the fields today. He said he had a message for a Mrs. Stanford. When I told him I was your brother-in-law, he gave it to me. I guess he was glad not to have to . . ."

Abruptly he broke off. She managed to move her lips. "What message?"

He reached into the pocket of his gray homespun shirt and held out a folded piece of paper. Like the note Patrick had sent her the previous fall, it was soiled and worn-looking, as if it had passed through many hands. But when her cold fingers unfolded it, she did not see Patrick's bold handwriting, but the labored, semiliterate script of someone who had signed himself "Wm. Carney."

The note was dated Hagerstown, Maryland, May 2, 1783. The first sentence told her that William Carney was "sorry" to tell her that her husband, Patrick Stanford, had drowned with two other men in Chesapeake Bay.

There were more words, something about a small boat overturning in a wind squall, something about none of the bodies being recovered. But by then a mist was closing in around her, blurring the written lines. She felt Colin's hands grasping her shoulders. Then, for an interval, she knew nothing.

Someone was chafing her hands. Lifting weighted eyelids, she found that she was lying on the bed, and that Mrs. Thompson sat on a chair beside her. Colin stood at the woman's elbow, anxiety in his dark eyes.

Mrs. Thompson said, "That's better." She turned to Colin. "I have some blackberry brandy at my house. Please ask my husband to give it to you."

Elizabeth's dull gaze followed him as he limped across the room. She would let him take her and Caroline to Philadelphia now. As soon as possible, she wanted to be away from this house, where she had once known happiness as clear and sparkling as spring water, away from this bed, where she had known the ecstasy of love. Because the man who had brought her that happiness, who had awakened her to love and physical joy, had been dead for weeks now, his fine long body buried by fathoms of water.

46

More than a week passed before they were able to leave New Canterbury. Elizabeth certainly never wanted to come back to the place, and Colin seemed equally willing to leave it forever, something that Elizabeth could well understand. No matter how much Colin had disapproved of Patrick at times, he had loved him too, loved him enough to forsake his comfortable life in Ireland and share his brother's exile.

Consequently, they needed to make arrangements for the disposal of Colin's hundred acres and of the hundred

that Elizabeth, as Patrick's widow, now owned. None of
the settlers were able to buy them out. But Jim Wentworth had heard from a cousin back in Providence who
wanted to bring his family to western Pennsylvania. The
cousin would be more than happy to buy a weatherproof
house plus two hundred acres of land, much of it already
under cultivation. Elizabeth and Colin gave Wentworth
the deeds to their property, plus a statement authorizing
him to act as agent for its sale.

As for the wagon and team of horses, they eventually
would be driven to a settlement twenty miles to the north,
and there become property of the Thompsons' young son
and his wife. In the meantime, the wagon would carry the
elder Thompsons as well as Colin and Elizabeth and Caroline to Philadelphia. The knuckles of Mr. Thompson's
hands had become increasingly swollen of late. The interval between spring planting and fall harvest seemed a
good time to learn if a Philadelphia doctor could help
him.

With such matters settled, it remained only for Elizabeth to pack the few things she wanted to take with her.
They included clothing for herself and her child, and a
few precious articles—her grandmother's gold pillbox and
ivory fan, her mother's miniature framed in seed
pearls—that she had managed to keep with her through
the wanderings of the past years.

At last the wagon lumbered eastward across a land-
scape washed by summer at full tide. Leaves of oaks and
maples and beeches that mingled with the pines were dark
green now. American birds whose names Elizabeth had
come to know—goldfinches and pine siskins and noisy
bluejays—flitted through the trees. Although she tried to
hide the fact from Colin and the Thompsons and most of
all from her little girl, the beauty through which they
moved only intensified her grief.

They spent the fourth night at a settlement. There Elizabeth found a poignant reminder of Patrick in the form of a Philadelphia newspaper some *voyageur* had left with the settlers two days earlier. It told how the English Parliament had adopted an Act of Irish Settlement, by terms of which strictures against Catholics were removed, and confiscated lands would be restored to exiles willing to take a new oath of allegiance. Would her stiff-necked husband have been willing to take the oath? Perhaps. If he had lived, perhaps they would have been on their way to Stanford Hall by now.

Two nights later, after they had made camp at the roadside, Colin and Elizabeth moved away through the trees to get water from a noisy little stream. There in the fern-smelling coolness, Colin filled three buckets and set them on the grassy bank. Then he turned to face her. "Elizabeth, I hope it is not too soon to ask you this. Have you any long-range plans?"

Although the sun had not set, evening shadows were thick here among the trees. She looked at his face, earnest and troubled there in that dim light. "Not really. But I will have some money. The Thompsons have already paid me for the horse and wagon. And later on there will be money from the house and land. Perhaps I can buy an interest in some sort of small shop, a confectioner's, say."

"On the other hand," he said quietly, "you could marry me, and we could go the West Indies together. Oh, not back to St.-Denis. I don't think either of us would want that. But there are other islands where I could earn a living for the three of us. I'll have enough money to invest in a distillery."

She said, a bit dazedly, "Colin, I . . ."

"Don't tell me that this comes as any great surprise to you. You must have known that I have been . . . fond of you from the very first."

"Yes, I've known." And his quiet sympathy had sustained her, too, at times when Patrick's behavior had been particularly outrageous. "But right now . . ."

"I realize it was much, much too soon for me to say this. But I couldn't stand the thought of your worrying about what is to happen to you and Caroline. I wanted you to know that you can turn to me."

"Oh, Colin! Dear Colin!" She stretched out her hands, and he grasped them. "I do thank you. But as you say, it is far too soon."

His hands still held hers firmly. She sensed his desire to pull her close to him, and the restraint that kept him from doing so. "Just remember that I'll always be here," he said, and released her hands.

He picked up two of the buckets. As she lifted the third one, she realized that it was only a matter of time before she became Colin's wife. True, she did not love him, but then, after Patrick, she had little hope of loving any man. As for Colin, "fond" of her as he might be, she was sure that he had never felt for her a shadow of what he had felt for Catherine Ryan.

Nevertheless, it could be a sound marriage. Reliable and gentle, Colin would be a good husband to her and a good father to Caroline. And she would be a good wife to Colin, quiet and competent and affectionate. And if, in his arms, she often found herself tormented by memories of the lover she had lost . . . well, pray God that she could hide it from Colin.

As they climbed through the growing dark toward the roadside campfire flickering through the trees, another thought struck her. She asked apprehensively, "Have you any idea of returning to Ireland? Perhaps, now that Parliament has passed that new act, you could have your lands back."

"I don't trust the Settlement Act. What's to keep the English from changing their minds? No, I will never go back to Ireland."

She felt relief. Married to Colin, she would not want to live anyplace where she had lived with Patrick. Better, far better, some West Indian island she had never seen before.

47

Early in the afternoon, more than two weeks later, Elizabeth again stood at the window of a Philadelphia inn. It was not the inn where she and Patrick had stayed more than two years before, but a newly built one, only a few yards from Independence Hall. It was far from being the only new structure. Obviously Philadelphia was prospering. The sound of hammers was everywhere. Fine carriages whirled along the wide streets, and women in what Elizabeth knew must be the latest fashions from Paris looked into shop windows filled with French china, Brussels lace, and Hepplewhite furniture.

She looked down at her own gown, the same brown merino she had worn when she and Patrick had landed in Philadelphia two years before. Her gown should have been black, of course. But she did not want to use any of her small store of money to buy mourning garments. Besides, now that the Thompsons had gone back to New Canterbury, no one here knew that her husband had been dead for only about two months.

Since their arrival in Philadelphia, Colin had made no further mention of marriage. From the look in his dark eyes, and the tone of his voice when he spoke to her, she knew it was not that he had changed his mind. He just

wanted her to have time to grow accustomed to the idea.
She also knew, from a bit of conversation she had over-
heard in the inn parlor between Colin and another man,
that already he was interviewing Philadelphia sugar importers about the possibility of buying a cane plantation
or distillery in the West Indies.

A gong sounded somewhere on the floor below. In a
few minutes, one-o'clock dinner would be served. She
crossed the sitting room to the bedroom, where Caroline
sat on a footstool cradling the rag doll that had been Mrs.
Thompson's parting gift to her. "Come, darling." With
her daughter's hand in hers, she went out into the hall,
passed the door of the single room almost opposite, which
Colin occupied, and descended the stairs. After leaving
Caroline in the small room where younger children,
served by two harassed-looking maids, ate their meals,
she went into the main dining room and took her place at
the long table. A glance across it and toward the right
showed her that Colin was absent. But there were several
diners she had not seen before, including a big man with
graying blond hair who sat directly opposite her.

As soon as she sat down, her right-hand neighbor, a
Mrs. Yarborough, began to talk of a letter she had received that morning from her daughter in Boston. Mrs.
Yarborough had five daughters, all of them great letter-
writers. She also had fourteen grandchildren, some of
whom had reached letter-writing age. Mrs. Yarborough
appeared to have no doubt that line-by-line accounts of
these missives, several of which seemed to arrive each
day, would enthrall any listener. At first Elizabeth had felt
oppressed by that flow of talk, which ceased only long
enough for Mrs. Yarborough to chew and swallow an occasional bit of food. But after a week, Elizabeth had
learned how to give the appearance of listening, smiling
and nodding now and then, while continuing with her own
thoughts.

"Excuse me, Mrs. Stanford."

With a start, Elizabeth realized that it was another voice, that of the big man across the table from her. She gave him an inquiring look.

"Excuse me," he said again. "When you said good afternoon to that lady at your right, I could tell you were English, and not long in this country, either. Then, just now I heard the other lady call you Mrs. Stanford, and I got to wondering if you were any relation to this Englishman named Stanford I met in Maryland. I mean, he talked like an Englishman, even though he said he was from Ireland."

Dimly Elizabeth was aware that Mrs. Yarborough, intrigued into silence, was staring at her. She said, past the quickened pulse in her throat, "What was his name?"

"I told you. Stanford. Oh, I see. You mean his first name. It was Patrick."

"When . . . when did you see him?"

"Day before yesterday. He's the new overseer at a horse farm down there. That's how we met. I'm a horse dealer. In fact, when I ride back to Maryland tomorrow, I'll be leading two mares for this Patrick Stanford's employer."

The disappointment she felt was like a physical blow. "For a moment I thought . . . But it could not have been my husband you met. He . . . he was drowned more than two months ago." How much she had hoped that this stranger had known Patrick, however briefly, and could give her some bit of information, however small, about what his life had been after that night he disappeared from New Canterbury.

"I'm sorry for your loss, ma'am." Elizabeth nodded an acknowledgment. "I guess the name Stanford really isn't uncommon," he went on, "and certainly Patrick isn't. But I thought there might be some connection, especially since he mentioned Philadelphia. He said he started out from here two years ago to take up land in western Pennsylvania."

Her heart was beating suffocatingly hard. "What does he look like?"

"Tall, thin, dark-haired." The man laughed. "In fact, if he hadn't talked like somebody just over from the other side, I'd have said he had Indian blood."

After a moment she was able to push back her chair and get to her feet. "Mr. . . . I'm sorry. I don't know your name."

"Haverhill, ma'am. Samuel Haverhill."

"I'm going into the parlor now, Mr. Haverhill. Would you please join me in there as soon as you've finished?"

He said, curious gaze fixed on her face. "I'm finished now, ma'am," and dropped his napkin beside his plate.

In the otherwise deserted parlor, as she turned to Samuel Haverhill, she caught a glimpse of her reflection in a small mirror on the wall. Her face was white, even her lips, and her gray eyes were enormous. She said, "I think you talked to my husband the day before yesterday."

"But, Mrs. Stanford!" He looked both pitying and embarrassed. "You just told me that your husband drowned. . . ."

"I thought he had. There was this note from a William Carney . . . But now I'm sure the note was delivered to me by mistake. As you said, Patrick Stanford is not a really uncommon name. It must have been some other man who . . . who . . ."

She broke off. After a moment, Samuel Haverhill said, "For your sake, ma'am, I hope it was a mistake, and that you're right this time."

No one could hope it as she did. What would become of her if Patrick actually was dead, if there was no reason for this joy flooding through her? To suffer that first raw grief just once had been terrible enough. To suffer it twice would be more than she could bear.

She said, "I am going to my room now, and write a message to my husband. Will you deliver it to him?"

"Of course. Tell me where your rooms are, and I'll come up in about half an hour and get your note."

Around four that afternoon she sat in a straight chair near the door of her room. Long since she had given up trying to read, or even embroider. Now she just sat there with her hands clasped tightly in her lap, and her ears straining for the sound of Colin's uneven step in the hall.

She had no doubt that when Colin heard that Patrick was alive, his joy would match her own. True, she knew that he had been sincere in his offer of marriage. But his feeling for her, surely, was a tepid one, made up of affection and sympathy and respect rather than passion. Only a small regret would shadow his thankfulness that Patrick had been restored to them both.

Her thoughts turned again to the message she had entrusted to Samuel Haverhill two hours earlier. In it she had poured out her heart to Patrick, begging him to return to her and their child, telling him of her love and longing and passionate need. She pictured him twenty-four hours or so from now, perhaps standing in a meadow in that lush Maryland countryside she had heard about but never seen, his dark gaze moving swiftly over the lines she had written. Surely he would forgive her for having called him the murderer of his own daughter. Surely, as soon as he had read that note, he would start north. . . .

Swiftly she rose, opened the door. Hand on the knob of his own door, Colin turned around. She said, "Oh, Colin! Come here!"

When he was inside the sitting room, she closed the door behind him. She said, trying to keep her voice low, lest she wake her child, "Oh, Colin! He's alive. Patrick's alive! I'm almost certain of it."

Scarcely aware of what she was doing, she threw her

arms around his neck. Weeping with joy, cheek resting against his chest, she told him about Samuel Haverhill and the message he would carry to Patrick. . . .

Something was wrong. Colin's arms had not gone around her in a joyful embrace. Instead, he stood there stiffly, saying nothing, arms at his sides.

Bewildered and a little frightened, she stepped back from him. Her eyes searched his face. It was very white, the eyes somber, the lips set. "Colin! What is it? Don't you believe me?" Terror tightened her throat. "Or is it that you know he's dead?"

Instead of replying, he said in a strange, flat voice, "So you still love him that much."

"Of course I do! Colin what on. . . ?"

"I thought you were changing," he said, in that same flat voice. "After all, you seemed disposed to marry me."

"But Colin! That was only because . . . Please, please, Colin! If you know anything about him . . . I mean, anything besides what was in that note that trapper brought . .

Her pleading voice trailed off. After a moment he said, "I know nothing, not even as much as was in the note."

She stared up at him, bewildered. His dark, bitter eyes stared back at her for a long moment. Then he said, his voice suddenly harsh, "You had best sit down, Elizabeth. I have quite a lot to tell you."

Dazedly, she obeyed. He said, bleak gaze fixed on her face, "Whether the bastard's dead or not, I have no way of knowing. I hope he is. But from what you've heard to-day, I would assume he is alive."

After a stunned moment she whispered, "You hate him, don't you? And I always thought . . ."

"That I loved him? I did, until a few years ago. But even then there was hate mixed up in it. How could there help but be? I was the firstborn, but because I was illegitimate, Patrick was heir to the title and most of the land. And if that wasn't enough, he taunted me into attempting a jump I knew my mount could not make, with the result that I was crippled for life. . . ."

He broke off. Struck dumb, she sat motionless. After a few seconds he went on, "Nevertheless, on the whole, I admired and loved him, until he brought you to Stanford Hall. You see, I already knew how brutally he had treated you. But I didn't know what you yourself were like. It wasn't until I met you—until I heard your voice and held your hand and looked down into your face—that I realized just how despicable his act had been."

His bitter voice went on, describing how hard it had been to conceal his own love for her, how hard to stand by while Patrick neglected her and flaunted his adultery with Moira Ashley. "And then, one day I heard him raging at you over that Englishman. You started running up the stairs . . . It was when you lost your child that I decided I had to do something. Two weeks later, I sent an anonymous letter to Whitehall, denouncing Patrick Stanford as a traitor."

She said incredulously, "You? But you couldn't have been the one who betrayed him! If you had been, you would have stayed in Ireland and kept your land, and even collected some sort of reward from the English. You wouldn't have . . ."

"Gone into exile with Patrick and you? You still don't understand. I thought he would be arrested. Instead, he was warned in time to make his escape. And you didn't welcome the chance to be rid of him, as I expected you to. Instead, you chose to go with him. And so I went too. That way, I could at least stay near you."

In St.-Denis, he told her, he'd almost given up hope of anything more than that. "You seemed increasingly in love with him. I knew you would suspect him of your brother's murder, and yet, not even that . . ."

He broke off. After a moment she asked slowly, "You

mean that Christopher's death. . . ? You mean that you. . . ?"

She was unable to go on. After a moment, he shrugged and said in that flat, weary voice, "There's no reason now that you shouldn't know."

He told her how that night—or rather, early morning—he had emerged from one of the brothels near the foot of Harbor Street. Looking to his right, he had seen Christopher Montlow, pale hair gleaming beneath his hat, move away along the dock.

"Because I, like Patrick, had been looking for Christopher, I was armed. I moved after him as fast as I could, and called his name. He whirled around. Evidently he realized I might shoot if he ran, because he waited until I came up to him with the pistol in my hand."

Elizabeth pictured them there in the humid tropic darkness, her angelically handsome, unspeakable brother and this crippled man twice his age. "He readily admitted that he had robbed the distillery strongbox, and was carrying the gold pieces sewn in his coat. He started to open his coat, as if to show me the lining, but that was only a ruse. Apparently thinking he'd thrown me off guard, he reached for the pistol."

Colin had wrestled the weapon free and tried to pull the trigger. The pistol had not fired. Somehow, though—for all that Christopher was younger and stronger—Colin had managed to bring the pistol barrel down on one side of the pale yellow head.

"He staggered back and fell into the sea. I moved to the wharf's edge. Even though he was invisible beneath the water, I knew that if I dived in I could probably save him. But I knew that the world would be better off without him. He not only had been responsible for poor little Anne Reardon's death. He had also delivered you into my brother's far-from-tender hands. I mean, if you hadn't

spirited Christopher out of London, Patrick would not
have invaded your house that night . . ."

Again his voice trailed off. Elizabeth looked at him,
stunned and repelled, and yet feeling too much pity to be
able to hate him. She said, "And besides, you hoped that
I would become convinced that my husband had killed
Christopher."

For the first time, his dark gaze slid away from hers.
"Yes."

And until now, Elizabeth reflected, she never had been
able to shake all suspicion that Patrick had killed her
brother. But that suspicion had not been enough to out-
weigh her love for her husband, her need for him.

Colin said, as if his thoughts had followed her own, "It
wasn't until he left you and Caroline alone in New Canterbury all that terrible winter that I again began to hope
that I could take you away from him. And the night he
came back . . . well, I saw a way to try to make sure of
it."

It must have been only a little while after Elizabeth had
seen him praying there in the woods that Patrick had
gone to Colin's house. "He told me his little girl was dying. He told me that you hated him. He asked me to do
the best I could for you, and even see that you got safely
back to England, if that was what you wanted. He gave
me what money he had—it amounted to about two
hundred dollars—and then he sat down at the table and
wrote a note for me to give to you in the morning."

Elizabeth's lips felt wooden. "A note?"

"In it he gave you the name of someone in Hagerstown, Maryland, someone you could write to if you ever
wanted to see him again. And then he left."

"His note. What did. . . ?"

"I burned it."

He had burned it. And so, for weeks she had waited
and wept, not knowing where Patrick had gone. And all

that time, Patrick, down in Maryland, with her last bitter words ringing in his ears, must have been hoping even so to receive a message from her, saying that their child still lived, and asking him to return.

Now loathing began to stir beneath her sense of shock and pity. "And that other note, the one saying that he had drowned?"

"I wrote it."

He moved to the door. With his hand on the knob, he looked back at her. "It is strange. I used to think that I was one of those destined to go through life quietly, not asking much of anything or anyone, content with the affection of a calm, good-natured woman. And then Patrick brought you home . . ."

He stopped. After a moment he added, "About your brother's death. As long as I had hopes of freeing you from Patrick, I felt I was more than justified in letting him drown. Now I see how little you could ever want to be free. And that makes me a common murderer, doesn't it?"

He went out, closing the door quietly behind him. She heard the opening and closing of his own door across the hall. Still she sat there, pulled this way and that by conflicting emotions. Pity for Colin Stanford, bastard and cripple, who'd had to keep his love hidden. Hatred of him for the suffering he had brought her these past weeks. And yet gratitude that, at long last, she would never again wonder if Patrick had taken Christopher s life.

From across the hall came the sound of a pistol shot.

She sat motionless. Even after she heard the sound of opening doors, and a babble of voices in the hall, it did not occur to her to rise from her chair and find out what had happened. She did not have to. She already knew.

48

Firelight flickered over the well-remembered room. Over the rosewood table, which still held the bowl of fruit Clarence had brought in at the end of this dinner for two beside the hearth. Over the graceful little desk where, those first months at Stanford Hall, she often had sat writing to her mother. And firelight shone on the bed where one night an angry and somewhat drunken Patrick had taught her body the joys of physical love.

The gown she wore now, a ruby-colored velvet with deep cuffs of cream-colored lace, was associated with that long-ago night, even though she had never seen it until today. Only hours ago Mrs. Corcoran—grayer now, but still plump and cheerful—had brought the gown up to this room, and told how, weeks after "your ladyship and Sir Patrick" had fled Stanford Hall, she had found the bundled-up gown in a little-used storeroom. When the housekeeper had left them, Patrick had confessed, with a sheepish smile that made his dark face look years younger, that he had carried the gown from Dublin in his saddlebags, and then, in his fury with her, had tossed the bundle to the rear of a storeroom.

Now she looked at the vacant chair on the opposite side of the table. Ten minutes ago, when Clarence had reported that he could not find a certain bottle of well-aged port, Patrick himself had left to search the cellars. Waiting for him now reminded her of another period of waiting—those two long, tormented days that, after Colin's suicide, she had spent at that Philadelphia inn, days in which she alternated between a certainty that Patrick would come to her and a terror that, after all, he was dead or, if alive, had learned how to get along without her.

On the afternoon of the second day, aware that her tense anxiety, her frequent nervous pacing of the room, was badly upsetting Caroline, she took the child downstairs and left her with one of the maids who waited table each day in the children's dining room. Then she returned to her own rooms for more tormented waiting.

It was just past four o'clock when she heard swift, familiar footsteps along the hall. She flew to the door and opened it before he had time to knock. Then she was in his arms. Wordlessly, with tears streaming down both their faces, they kissed, and then kissed again, trying to make up in those first moments for all the pain they had dealt each other.

At last he said, still holding her close, "Then you forgive me for all—?"

"Oh, Patrick! It is I who should ask forgiveness. The cruel, terrible things I said—"

He stopped her words with a kiss. "We need never talk of that night, my darling."

And then, even though it was broad daylight, and even though they both should have been tired—he from the journey at breakneck pace up from Maryland, she from the last almost sleepless forty-eight hours—they went into the bedroom and made love. For Elizabeth the ecstasy of their physical union was greater than ever before, because now she knew that he loved her, not just with his splended long body, but with tenderness. Perhaps it was a tenderness that not even he had known was in his heart until the night when he had finally made his way back over still-snowy trails to New Canterbury.

Joyful as their reunion was in that Philadelphia inn, they had still felt the shadow cast by Colin's death. As a suicide, he could not be buried in consecrated ground. And so, the morning after Patrick's arrival in Philadelphia, he and Elizabeth in a hired carriage followed his brother's coffin, borne by a wagon, out to a potter's field at the city's edge. They had stood beside the grave while all that remained of Colin Stanford, lonely and isolated in death as in life, was lowered into the ground.

It was on their way back from potter's field that Patrick first mentioned returning to Ireland. "Parliament has passed this Act of Settlement . . ."

"I know about it. In fact, I asked Colin if he might return to Ireland because of it. He seemed determined upon going to the West Indies."

"No wonder," Patrick answered dryly. "He was afraid I might turn up in Ireland."

"And do you want to go back there?"

"I think so if you do, my darling. Oh, not that this Settlement Act means that Ireland is free. It may take centuries for Ireland to become free and united, if it ever does. But the English have made concessions, enough of them that I can take their oath in good conscience."

"And the house and land in New Canterbury?"

"I'll write to Wentworth and tell him that after he has sold the property to his cousin, he can send the money to Stanford Hall. I don't imagine," he said wryly, "that you want to see New Canterbury again."

"No," she said, although now that he was beside her, his big warm hand clasping hers, it was hard for her to remember the suffering and fear of the past winter.

Their passage across a smooth midsummer sea had been without incident. Three days ago their ship had docked at Dublin. And late this morning they had arrived at Stanford Hall, where those who were left of the former staff—Mrs. Corcoran, Gertrude, Rose, Clarence, and

Joseph—had greeted them with embraces and tears. Young Rose and Caroline had taken to each other immediately, so much so that Elizabeth had not hesitated to place her child in the little maid's charge.

What matter that during Elizabeth's long absence the huge crystal chandelier in the entrance hall had grown grimy and dull, and gilt picture frames had tarnished, and drapery hems unraveled? She was back now, in the house that would be home to her for the rest of her life.

Patrick came in carrying a bottle filled with wine of almost the same shade as her gown. He sat down, filled two tiny glasses of etched crystal, and handed her one. She took an appreciative sip and then reached over to brush a bit of cobweb from his coat sleeve. "It is delicious, Patrick. But all that poking around in the cellar, just for a bottle of wine . . ."

"I wanted you to have the best tonight. Nothing less would do." His gaze went over her serene face, her slim shoulders, the swell of her small, high breasts above the red velvet. "Oh, Elizabeth, you're so beautiful!" His voice roughened. "And what suffering I've brought you, when always you should have had nothing but the best, when always you should have looked as you do now."

Not answering, she smiled at him. Yes, it was good to be warm, and safe, and richly gowned. But what he did not know, and never would, was that she had never felt greater tenderness for him than when she stood cold and half-starved and shabbily dressed at the wood's edge, and heard his harsh voice pouring out his anguish and his and his love for her.